Berkley Books by Mary Balogh

HEARTLESS
TRULY

TRULY

MARY BALOGH

BERKLEY BOOKS, NEW YORK

TRULY

A Berkley Book / published by arrangement with
the author

PRINTING HISTORY
Berkley edition / May 1996

The Putnam Berkley World Wide Web site address is
http://www.berkley.com

ISBN: 0-425-15329-0

BERKLEY®
Berkley Books are published by The Berkley Publishing Group,
200 Madison Avenue, New York, New York 10016.
BERKLEY and the "B" design
are trademarks belonging to Berkley Publishing Corporation.

PRINTED IN THE UNITED STATES OF AMERICA

10 9 8 7 6 5 4 3 2 1

Chapter 1

He had miscalculated the distance. He had not expected still to be riding this long after nightfall. And it was rather a dark night too, so that he was unable to cover the last few miles at any speed. But he had hated the thought of putting up at another inn and had pressed onward to his destination. Tegfan. Home.

Was Tegfan home?

It belonged to him certainly, had done since the death of his grandfather two years before. But was it home? He had not been there for ten years, and even that had been a short visit. He had deliberately avoided going there since. He was not sure he wanted to be there now. He was not even quite sure why he had come.

It had been a whim, a spur-of-the-moment thing. He had overheard a snippet of conversation on the street between two passersby he had never seen before and would never see again. Men who did not belong in London. Drovers, probably, he had guessed, men who had driven a herd of cattle to market and who had not yet returned home.

"—so much to do here all the time."

"But I miss the hills and—"

It was all he had heard. Words that had no real significance. Except that they had been spoken in Welsh and he had not even realized it or the more surprising fact that he had understood the words until he had felt a stabbing of unidentified longing so powerful that he had stopped walking for the moment and stood on the pavement, frowning, his eyes closed.

But I miss the hills—

And the words themselves had taken meaning in his mind. No, not his mind—his heart. They had become a nameless yearning, something he had been unable to shake off.

The hills had beckoned to him. And he had been unable to resist their call.

And so here he was, without any warning, without any reason, in Wales, in Carmarthenshire, one of its western counties, very close to Tegfan. And wondering even now if he should turn back. That chapter in his life—really a very brief chapter—was best left closed.

Except that deep down he had always known that one day he would come back.

He was riding through open, hilly country, as bare and as bleak as he remembered it. And chilly, of course, as one could expect of early spring in any part of the country. But more than chilly. Almost damp, though there had been no rain. And gusty, though there was no steady wind. Although he had not lived in Wales for sixteen years, and then he had been a mere boy of twelve, he felt the familiarity.

The road was bad. He huddled inside his cloak and slowed his horse's pace even further. Although he had passed through tollgates every few miles of his journey today, and although he knew that there were turnpike trusts set up everywhere, there was little evidence that the money extracted from travelers was being spent to make their journeys safer or more comfortable.

He was glad he had left his carriage to travel after him

with his baggage and his valet. Traveling this road in a carriage would be a severe trial.

But suddenly the night was not so dark—and yet darker too, in a way. The line of distant hills to his right was lit from behind, almost as if he had ridden the night through and the sun was about to rise. Except that the direction was more northerly than easterly and the light flickered and danced against the sky instead of remaining steady. And the time could surely be no later than midnight, if that.

There was a fire burning. He could not see the flames or smell the smoke or hear any sounds of human alarm. It was too far away to investigate and in too different a direction from Tegfan to cause him any personal alarm. But he shivered with a little more than just the chill of the air. Fires at night had no logical explanation. He had passed the industrial valleys of South Wales, in which iron furnaces might be kept alive night and day. Besides, this fire had sprung suddenly to life.

It was not his concern. He rode onward until a bend in the road and the changing contours of the hills brought darkness again. There was only a faint glow of light about the far hills when he looked deliberately back at them. He surely could not be far from Tegfan now. And yet there was another tollgate ahead. He sighed and considered riding out into the dark field to one side of the road and skirting the gate so as to avoid the delay of waking the gatekeeper. Gatekeepers seemed invariably to be sound sleepers.

And yet this one was not. The door of the small cottage beside the gate opened slowly even as he approached and a head appeared around it. Then the door opened wider and a thin, stooped figure stepped outside, clutching what appeared to be a giant club.

"What do you want?" the gatekeeper demanded gruffly in the voice of an elderly woman.

"I want to take my horse from this side of the gate to the other side," he said with weary hauteur. The woman was carrying no light. But she was still clutching her club with both hands. He also realized that she had spoken in Welsh.

He had heard it spoken all about him for the past few days of his journey. What surprised him now was the fact that without thinking he had answered the woman in her own language.

"Who are you?" she asked. But she did not wait for his answer. She was peering beyond him into the darkness. "Who else is with you?"

He was impatient to be moving on. But he realized that the woman was frightened. He did not blame her. It was a lonely stretch of road. He spoke more gently than he might have done.

"I am Wyvern," he said. "And I travel alone, Mother. I would have you open the gate if you will."

"Wyvern?" She took a step forward and looked intently and suspiciously up at him. "The *Earl* of Wyvern?" She bobbed a sudden and awkward curtsy, still clutching her club. "Oh, *Duw,* what are you doing out on the road alone at this time of the night, then? I thought you were Rebecca."

Well. To be mistaken for a woman, even in the darkness. "Rebecca?" he said, his tone more frosty.

"Come to break down the gate with her daughters and all the rest of them," she said. "I couldn't have stopped them, mind, but they wouldn't have got away without some bruised knuckles and knees." She moved her club back and forth in front of her as if to prove her point.

Was this not Tegfan land or very close to it? He leaned down from his horse's back and frowned. "Some woman and her daughters are terrorizing you?" he asked. "And threatening to damage property that belongs to a trust? I hope you have reported this matter."

"Oh, *Duw* love you, your lordship," she said. "Rebecca is not a woman and neither are her daughters. And there would be no point in reporting them. No one could catch them."

Ah. He had heard it said that the keepers of tollgates were strange people. They lived lonely lives and were not on the whole very popular in their neighborhoods. This woman was clearly mad. It was time he rode on.

"Not that they have been around here since over three

years ago, mind, in 1839," the woman said. "But they will. Did you see that?" She held the club in one hand, resting it on the ground like a staff, while she jabbed out her free arm in the direction of the hills behind which the fire had been burning earlier. "It is not a gate or a gatehouse yet. The fire was too big. Hayricks, if my guess is right. But it is a start, mark my words. Soon it will be gates and Rebecca will be back."

"No one has seen her—*him* for longer than three years? But burning hayricks and tollgates was the sort of thing she did?" he asked. The woman might be mad, but the fire had been very real. "Doubtless after tonight's work, if you are correct, she will be caught and punished."

"Oh, *Duw, Duw*," she said, "you will be trying to catch her yourself if she comes up this way, your lordship, but you never will. All the other gentlemen tried last time and the constables too. There were even soldiers looking to catch Rebecca and her daughters. But no one else was trying, do you see? Everyone else cheered them along and even went with them to smash the gates. And will again. Word has it that it is all starting again."

Ah. A local rebellion against the turnpike trusts. Led by a man disguised as a woman. It was a wild idea, not without a certain romantic appeal, he supposed. A man fighting apparent oppression. Yes, he could understand why such a man would not be easy to catch. He would have far more protectors than hunters. And yet he fought a doomed cause—if indeed he was coming back to life after more than three years. One could not fight the whole force of law and society and hope to win.

"If they have not started yet," he said, "perhaps they will not. Mrs.—?"

"Phillips," she said, bobbing another awkward curtsy. "Dilys Phillips, your lordship. But there have been a few other fires like tonight's, mind. It will be gates next."

"I will be living at Tegfan for a while, Mrs. Phillips," he told her. "I will see to it that you are not harassed. You will be safe here. My word on it."

"Oh, *Duw,* there is kind you are," she said, "and you the earl from Tegfan. But I will keep my big stick by me anyway." She laughed merrily and moved out into the road to unlock and open the gate. She appeared elderly and rather frail for such a job, the Earl of Wyvern thought. But she was able enough to perform her duties, he supposed, though it was a lonely life for an old woman. And what was the alternative? he wondered. The workhouse?

He rode forward and held out a coin. But she shook her head and took a step back. "It is free passage for the gentry," she said. "Good night to you, your lordship, and watch where your horse do set his feet. The road is rough and the night is dark."

He did not withdraw his hand though he knew that the gentry, who could afford the tolls, often rode free while the poor, who could not, were forced to pay or stay at home.

"Take it anyway," he said. "I dragged you from your bed and alarmed you by coming through so late."

She took the coin and curtsied once more.

He rode onward, hearing the sounds of the gate closing behind him. He wondered if Mrs. Dilys Phillips had noticed that the whole conversation had been conducted in Welsh. His grandfather had not spoken a word of the language. And he himself had not spoken it for the last sixteen years except sometimes during the early years in the whispered privacy of his own room—when he had had a room to himself.

And sometimes in the silent depths of his own heart.

There were two churches in the village of Glynderi, the one picturesque with its slim Gothic lines and tall spire, the other squat and solid and less attractive in appearance. The one was Anglican, the other nonconformist.

Only a handful of people from the village and surrounding farms and a few of the forty servants from the house of Tegfan ever attended the church, though everyone paid tithes to it—in cash rather than produce since the new law passed a few years earlier. It was a bitter grievance with the people. And what made it worse was that the tithe money did not go to the church but to the man who had the living in his possession.

Their tithes, like their rents, enriched the owner of Tegfan and Glynderi and the farms and all the land most of them had ever traveled in the course of their lives. The Earl of Wyvern.

Almost everyone from the village and from the farms for miles around attended the chapel. It was the spiritual center of the community and the social center too. And the center of music and song, of course, so essential to the Welsh soul. The Reverend Meirion Llwyd's sermons were always at least twice as long as the Anglican vicar's. But in addition to length they always had enough *hwyl,* or fiery, almost hypnotic emotion, that his congregation could have listened and responded for as long again. The fact that the Anglican service was over well within an hour of its start whereas their own frequently lasted far closer to two was no inducement to any chapel member to switch allegiance.

And then, of course, there was always the best part to look forward to when the service was finally over, though no one ever put it quite that way. There was the gathering in the street outside if the weather was fine or crowded into the porch and the back pews or even spilling into the Sunday schoolroom if it was raining. It was a gathering for fellowship, for the exchange of news and opinions, for the sharing of gossip. For people who worked long, hard hours through the week, many of them on farms too far distant from each other or from the village to allow for much company, Sunday morning was the time to look forward to, the time to cherish. The best morning of the week.

Glenys Owen, kitchen maid at Tegfan, had never felt quite so important in her life as she did on this particular Sunday morning. This morning she had come to chapel, bringing with her the news that the Earl of Wyvern had arrived unexpectedly from London in the middle of the night and thrown the whole household into consternation. Glenys had not yet seen him herself but he was there right enough.

"Praise the Lord," the Reverend Llwyd said. He was standing at the top of the stone steps leading down from the porch to the street, shaking hands with his departing congregation. He raised both arms as if in benediction. "Praise the Lord for bringing him safely home."

Not everyone agreed.

"After all this time?" Glyn Bevan, a farmer, said. "I wonder what for, then?"

"He has never shown much interest in the place before," Gwen Dirion, a farmer's wife, remarked to Blodwyn Jenkins, who kept the general store next to the chapel. "Glad to get away from here, he was."

"And never came to see his poor old mam," Miss Jenkins said, nodding about to include others in her remark, "until she was in a wooden box. Too late it was then."

"Geraint Penderyn." Eli Harris, the harness maker, turned his head to spit into the dirt roadway, perhaps forgetting for the moment that he was wearing his Sunday best and should therefore be on his Sunday-best behavior. "Come here to show off his fine clothes and his fine English ways and his fine English voice, I suppose. Come to lord it over us, is it? It do make me sick to my stomach."

"Eli," Mrs. Harris said reproachfully, glancing furtively at the minister.

"Well, it do, woman," Eli said, half-sheepishly, half-defiantly.

"Penderyn," Ifor Davies, the cooper, said. "Who broke his mam's heart, as Blodwyn has said, and does not care the snap of his fingers for us. A cheek, I do call it, mind, coming down here to sneer at us all."

"Not that any of us treated his mam very well for many years, mind, to be fair," Mrs. Olwen Harris said with ruthless honesty, nodding about at the other women for approval. "Not until we *knew,* that was."

"Geraint Penderyn," Aled Rhoslyn, the village blacksmith, said almost pensively, not talking to anyone in particular. "It is not the best time for him to come down here, is it? He may be sorry that he did. And so may we."

"Perhaps," Ninian Williams, a farmer, suggested, his hands spread over his ample stomach, "we should wait and see why he has come and what he intends to do. He has every right to be in his own house, after all. Perhaps we should give the man a chance."

"Yes, Dada." Ceris Williams, small and slim and dark and mild-mannered, rarely spoke in public. But she possessed a certain courage that occasionally impelled her to speak out. "I was only fifteen when he came for his mam's funeral. That was ten years ago. I felt sorry for him then because he seemed to feel so out of place and everyone was watching him so closely, more prepared to find fault than to welcome him home. Perhaps we should not judge him now that he is the Earl of Wyvern. Perhaps we should wait and see." She blushed furiously, bit her lip, and lowered her eyes.

"Perhaps we should at that," Aled said, his eyes fixed on her, their expression softened. "But we will not expect too much, is it? He has been the earl for two years, after all, and things have got worse here since then rather than better."

Ceris looked up and held his gaze for a few moments, her own eyes filling with a longing that was quickly hidden when she lowered them again to the ground at her feet.

"Wait and see? Give him a chance?" Marged Evans's voice was incredulous and taut with fury. "I do not need to give him a chance. For two years he has had his chance. That is long enough. Too long. Can Eurwyn be given a second chance? Eurwyn is dead, thanks to Geraint Penderyn, Earl of Wyvern." She almost spat out the name, her back straight, her bosom out, her chin up. As always Marged, tall, lithe, and beautiful drew both eyes and attention.

"Eurwyn committed a crime, Marged," the Reverend Llwyd said firmly, ever courageous despite her obvious anger.

She turned it on him, her cheeks flushing, her eyes flashing. "A crime," she said. "A crime to try to stop his people from starving. Oh, yes, a crime, Dada. A capital crime, as it turned out. A crime for which he died. My husband died, leaving behind him a farm to be run by three

women, by his wife and his mother and his grandmother.
Eurwyn died because Geraint Penderyn cares for no one but
Geraint Penderyn. And we are to give him a chance? A
chance for what, pray? To raise our rents again? To force the
tithes from us even if we starve as a result? To force us to
pay ever more and higher tolls at the gates so that we cannot
go to and from market or bring the lime we need to fertilize
our fields? To force us from our land into the workhouse?"

The Reverend Llwyd, Marged's father, raised one hand
again. "It is not for us to break the law, even to right a
wrong," he said. "Two wrongs do not make a right. We must
leave the righting of wrongs to the Lord. 'Vengeance is
mine, saith the Lord.'"

There was a chorus of murmurings from the gathered
congregation, which had not this morning broken up into
several smaller groups, as it usually did. But it was not clear
who was murmuring assent and who was indicating dis-
agreement. The two combatants stood facing each other at
opposite sides of the crowd, the father on the chapel steps,
the daughter on the street.

"Well, sometimes, Dada," Marged said, uncowed, "the
Lord needs a helping hand. And here are two." She raised
two slim hands, callused palms out. "I say that if and when
the Earl of Wyvern shows his face in Glynderi or on any of
our farms, we give him the welcome he deserves."

"Which can be interpreted more than one way, mind,
Marged," Miss Jenkins said.

"I know how I will welcome him if he dares to come to
Tŷ-Gwyn," Marged said.

"He has a right to go there, Marged," Ninian Williams
reminded her. "Your farm belongs to him just as mine does.
Just as all the farms around by here do. It would be best to
be polite and to wait and see."

"Perhaps," Aled said, "we would not be feeling quite so
angry if he were anyone but Geraint. We think of Geraint as
a person. It is easier to focus our displeasure and our
protests just on owners generally. It is too bad he has
decided to come back here just now. I don't like it."

"But he *has* come and he *is* Geraint Penderyn," Marged said, drawing her cloak more closely about her. "I am going home. Are you coming, Ceris?"

Ceris glanced at Aled to see if he would say more. But he had turned away. "I will go on ahead with Marged, then, Mam," she said, turning toward her mother and smiling too at her father before stepping out into the street to begin the long walk home along the river and up into the lower hills—one and a half miles for her, two for Marged.

The crowd outside the chapel split, according to age and gender, into its more usual smaller groups.

Chapter 2

Marged and Ceris had been close friends for most of their lives despite the fact that they were almost as different from each other as it was possible to be. But they had one thing in common that perhaps accounted for their relationship. They both believed passionately in goodness and right.

Marged shortened her stride to match that of her smaller friend. "Aled has an incurable sense of fairness, you know," she said. "He will not immediately turn to violence. He was one of Geraint's few friends when we were children. He was one of the few who bothered with him when he came back here ten years ago. He will give him a chance now. You must not worry that he will die as Eurwyn died."

Ceris bowed her head, so that for a few moments the brim of her bonnet hid her face. "I do not worry about Aled Rhoslyn," she said. "He is nothing to me, Marged."

Marged sighed. "The old story," she said. "I am your friend who knows you almost as well as you know yourself, Ceris. Perhaps better in some ways. Why are you still unmarried and living with your mam and dada at your age if Aled means nothing to you?"

"I have not found the right man," Ceris said.

"You have," Marged told her. "That is the trouble. He will not go to burn Geraint in his bed tonight, you know. More is the pity." She laughed briefly.

"You do not mean that, Marged." Her friend looked at her reproachfully.

"No," Marged admitted. "Not quite, I suppose."

"But it does not matter, don't you see?" Ceris's voice and face were unhappy. "Aled is committed to disobedience, to worse than disobedience. As soon as he agreed to represent Glynderi—"

"On the committee?" Marged completed the sentence for her. "The less said out loud about that the better. So far it has been kept so secret that no one who ought not to know about it does. Let us pray it stays that way. None of us know who the other members are. Perhaps it would be better to pretend we do not even know Aled is a member. Perhaps it would be better not to talk about it openly among friends."

"Aled was more than a friend," Ceris said with unusual candor. "I know it in my heart, Marged. Even if I must never talk about it, even if I must pretend even to myself that I do not know it, I do know it. Aled represents this area on the committee that is to decide what we can do to show our displeasure to the landowners and perhaps to draw the attention and sympathy of the government in London. There, it is said. I cannot love such a man. I cannot."

Marged sighed again. "Then it is better to suffer oppression and injustice in silence?" she said. "It is better to be driven from our land and our means of livelihood? It is better to watch children starve? It is better to see families forced into the workhouse, where they are separated from one another and where they are slowly starved? Where their spirits are broken even before their bodies die?"

"Oh, Marged." Ceris looked up at her, tears in her eyes. "You have learned it from your dada, that way of talking you have. You make it sound like a glorious thing to fight against oppression. You make it sound cowardly to refuse to use violence. But violence does nothing but breed more of itself. Look what happened to Eurwyn. Ah, I am sorry. I ought not to have said that."

"Eurwyn would rather be dead than alive and at home now, afraid to act on his convictions," Marged said. "And I am proud of him even though I have been left alone without him. Yes, I am, though it was cruel. Ah, it was cruel, the way he died. And nothing from Geraint Penderyn, from the Earl of Wyvern, though I lowered myself to write him letters and remind him of a time when I had befriended him. Oh, yes, I could almost wish that Aled would go and burn him in his bed tonight."

"No, you do not, Marged," Ceris said.

"I did say *almost*." Marged was tight-lipped and angry. They lapsed into silence.

She did not want him back at Tegfan, Marged thought. She had been hurt too deeply by him. When he was a child and smaller than she even though he was two years older, she had befriended him. She had championed him even though it was her father who, with the deacons, had driven his mother from chapel. She had continued to champion him throughout his boyhood after he had been sent away to England and never came back or wrote letters to any of his former friends. She had always been one for causes, she thought rather bitterly now.

Clouds were moving across the sky from the west, heavy clouds. It would rain later. She drew her hood up over her head and wished her cloak was not so old, so close to being threadbare. There was so little money for anything but the bare necessities. But then for some there was not even that much.

Even when he came back to Tegfan for his mother's funeral, she had been prepared to take his part, even though he was silent and morose and arrogant in manner and spoke nothing but English—in a very cultured way. She had told herself and everyone else that he was merely shy, that he needed time. And she had been very eager at the age of sixteen to fall in love with his handsome face and figure. He had been unexpectedly tall and attractive—and attentive.

Until he had made it very clear to her one day that he saw her as nothing better than one of his London whores. And the next day, when she had thought he came to the manse to apologize, he had talked exclusively with her father and had ignored her apart from one cold and insolent look.

It was the last time she had seen him, she realized now.

He had had his revenge for his slapped face and unrequited lust that afternoon. He had ignored her groveling pleas for Eurwyn. And Eurwyn had died.

Geraint Penderyn, Earl of Wyvern, had killed her husband.

"Oh, Marged." Ceris fell back, panting. "I cannot keep up with your pace, girl. You will have to go on ahead."

Marged slowed her pace again with a smile of apology. Ceris had always contended that the Earl of Wyvern had never received her letters. She herself would not excuse him so easily.

And now he was back. Oh, yes, if he dared to come near Tŷ-Gwyn, though it was his and she only paid rent on it, she would know how to welcome him. She could hardly wait. And yet for all that she wished he had not come. She wished he had been content to keep his person and his wealth and his consequence and his—oh, his *Englishness*—in London for the rest of his life.

"Do you really think there is going to be trouble?" Ceris sounded desperately in need of reassurance.

"I sincerely hope so," Marged said. "It is high time. Other parts of West Wales have not been as slow and as cautious as we have. Perhaps the arrival of the Earl of Wyvern will have one positive result."

"Rebecca?" Ceris asked unhappily.

"If someone brave enough will play her part," Marged said. "I would do it myself except that no man would accept a woman as Rebecca. Ironic, isn't it? I thought that perhaps Aled—".

"Oh, *Duw*, no!" Ceris wailed. "Not that he is anything to me, of course."

"Perhaps now that Geraint Penderyn is here in person,

people will be able to see that the enemy is very real," Marged said. "Perhaps now someone will be goaded into leading the protest. There are enough of us, heaven knows, who are willing and eager to follow."

"Us?" Ceris stopped walking, having reached the lane that led to her father's farm. "*Us*, Marged? Surely you would not—"

"Oh, yes, I would," Marged said fiercely. "I have to be the man at Tŷ-Gwyn, Ceris. I have to stand in place of Eurwyn for his mam and his gran. Well, then, I will stand in place of Eurwyn in other matters, too. I would like to see the man who will stop me."

Ceris sighed. "Oh, Marged," she said, "how wrong you are, girl. Home for dinner now, then, is it?"

"Yes." Marged smiled. "Home for dinner. Home to wait and see what will happen. But not for long if I have anything to say in the matter."

She turned to stride onward up the grassy hill track to the white longhouse that had been home since her marriage seven years before to Eurwyn Evans.

Ceris stood at the end of the lane, watching her go. Poor Marged. There was so much bitterness in her, so much hatred. And so much potential violence—as there was in so many people these days. Even Aled . . . Sometimes she wondered if she was the one who was wrong. But it seemed so clear to her that violent protest would only bring more suffering. And hatred had never mended any bridges.

But her thoughts were interrupted before she could turn in the direction of home. Someone hailed her from a short distance across the hill, and she waited for him to come up to her. He was neither a very tall nor a very robust man, but he was dressed smartly in a greatcoat and boots, and he was removing a top hat to reveal smooth fair hair. He was good-looking, Ceris thought, if not exactly handsome.

"Good morning, Mr. Harley," she said in English.

"Good morning, Miss Williams," he said. "And a fine morning it is too. I decided to take a walk after church."

She smiled at him. He frequently took walks after the Anglican service, and their paths often crossed. Deliberately, she believed.

"I am not ready to go home yet," he said. "I suppose you would not care to stroll with me for half an hour, Miss Williams?"

"I have to help my mother with dinner, Mr. Harley," she said, making an excuse as she always did when he issued such invitations. But she was still feeling somewhat upset over the morning's events. And she was twenty-five years old, she reminded herself, and would no longer allow herself to love Aled. Could she do better than Matthew Harley? He was English, which fact she must not hold against him. He was also the Earl of Wyvern's steward, a man of some importance. A man who would be able to support a wife in some comfort—she shook off the thought as unworthy of her. He was a man who must not be blamed for being tough over rents and tithes and other matters. He was merely doing a job.

He had already bidden her a good morning and turned onto the downward path she had just walked with Marged.

"Mr. Harley," she called impulsively, and when he turned back to her she had no choice but to continue. "Perhaps later this afternoon? Perhaps you would like to come to tea? Mam would be pleased. And we could take a walk afterward."

"Thank you," he said. "I should like that." He touched his hat to her and continued on his way.

She was left feeling breathless and almost panic-stricken. What had she just started? She was not at all sure she even liked him. She felt almost repelled when she imagined him touching her—or kissing her. But that was only because for years she had thought of no man that way but Aled. It felt like being unfaithful to invite another man to tea, to suggest walking out with another man. And that was ridiculous.

Besides, he was only coming for tea and a little walk. There was nothing in that.

*   *   *

For two days after his arrival at Tegfan, his large Welsh Carmarthenshire estate, Geraint Penderyn, Earl of Wyvern, did not venture beyond the house and park. It felt strange to be back.

He had other estates in England and other grander houses, including the one in London. And yet this one felt strangely large and empty despite the presence of servants. He should perhaps have brought some friends down with him. He had not thought of it at the time.

Of course, the house really was unfamiliar to him. He had lived in it for only a few weeks at the age of twelve before being packed off to England and the waking nightmare that had faced him there. Tegfan had been bewildering and intimidating. His grandfather had been terrifying. His mother had been absent. He had not been allowed to see her. Despite his twelve years and despite the fact that he had been a bold urchin from infancy, he had begged and pleaded for her. And cried for her.

They had been as hard as nails, his grandfather and the servants appointed to look after him for those few weeks.

And he had lived in this house for three weeks at the time of his mother's funeral. Three weeks before fleeing back to London and vowing never to return, a bewildered boy caught between two worlds. And in love for the first time—and the only time—and gauche and foolish. And very unhappy.

During those two days of rain and heavy clouds, he stood a great deal at the window of his bedchamber, gazing broodingly out over the rolling land of the park and across the distant river, or wandered about the house, or paced through the stables, or strode over soggy grass and among dripping trees. Wishing he had not come. Wondering why that snippet of a conversation between strangers had impelled him to such uncharacteristically impulsive behavior. Wanting to go beyond the park. Wanting to return to London and the familiarity of his life there without further ado.

On the third day he rode over to Pantnewydd, the

neighboring estate, smaller than his own, its lands less prosperous, its house less grand. Sir Hector Webb lived there with his wife, Geraint's aunt, his father's sister. They had not met many times. There was no closeness between them. Understandably, he supposed. Tegfan was unentailed. For twelve years after the death of her brother, Lady Stella had fully expected that the estate would be willed to her and her husband.

And then Geraint had stepped suddenly and unwillingly between them and their expectations.

He was given a correct, if somewhat frosty welcome. He was regaled over tea with an account of the shameful goings-on at a neighbor's estate a few nights before, when a mob had burned down Mitchell's hayricks merely because his bailiff had been seizing goods in lieu of unpaid tithes among the farmers there.

"As if it were the right of every man, woman, and child to refuse to pay lawful taxes on the grounds that they cannot afford them," Lady Stella said. "I have always said this is a barbaric country in which to live."

"Before we know it, we will be back to the Rebecca Riots of thirty-nine," Sir Hector said. "The leaders of that should not have been left with the impression that they had won. They should have been hunted down and hanged, or transported for life at the very least."

"They won?" Geraint asked politely.

"Three new tollgates there were," Sir Hector explained. "All erected to catch the farmers hauling lime from the kilns and evading other gates. The mob pulled down all three, the one at Efailwen several times when the trust kept replacing it. Eventually the trust took all three gates away and no more was said. It was a fatal show of weakness, as I said at the time."

"At least with Jones and Tegid you do not have to worry about trouble on your land, Wyvern," Lady Stella said grudgingly. "They have never stood for any nonsense and all your people know it."

Bryn Jones was his bailiff, Geraint knew. He had met the

man just that morning and not much liked him. Huw Tegid had used to work with his grandfather's gamekeeper and was quite possibly the gamekeeper himself now. Geraint knew precious little about his Welsh estate. He had always deliberately avoided knowing anything about it, although he had been at pains to learn everything there was to be learned about his other estates.

"I appointed Harley as my steward at Tegfan because he was the best man available," Geraint said. "I have never had cause to question his running of the estate." Almost the only thing Geraint knew about Tegfan was that it was prosperous.

"You would do well to leave everything in his hands even if you plan a lengthy stay," Sir Hector said. "He is a good man."

"And after all," Lady Stella added, an edge of malice to her voice, "you were not educated to run an estate, Wyvern."

It was not strictly true. His education from the age of twelve on had been devoted to little else. What his aunt meant, of course, was that he had not been raised from birth to run an estate. Geraint inclined his head, rose to take his leave, and did not dignify her remark with an answer.

It was the fourth day before he ventured beyond the park to the village and the farms. He felt strangely reluctant to meet people he might or might not know. Almost shy. He wondered how many he would remember. He wondered how many would remember him. Though he could not expect that they would have forgotten him, he supposed ruefully. His was the sort of story on which local mythology could be expected to thrive for a century or more.

He went first to call on the Reverend Llwyd—the Anglican vicar had already waited on him at Tegfan. It seemed the courteous thing to do, to call first on the nonconformist minister, whose chapel most of the villagers had used to attend and probably still did. And it seemed not quite the thing under the circumstances to hold a grudge.

The Reverend Llwyd looked older and thinner and not as tall or as formidable as he had used to appear. He still dressed severely in clerical black. He wore wire spectacles now. Geraint had to admit to himself that he rather enjoyed looking down at the man and receiving his bow and his formal speech of welcome—delivered in English. He rather enjoyed making a stiff acknowledgment of the minister's greeting and taking the offered seat in the manse parlor. He could remember the time when he had been afraid of the man. The Reverend Llwyd had driven his mother out of the chapel when she had appeared there large with child—with himself. She had already been turned away from Tegfan. It was the Reverend Llwyd and his deacons who had made it impossible for her to live in the village or to get work at any of the farms. It was they who had driven her onto the upland moors.

"It is an honor to have you back in our midst," the Reverend Llwyd was saying now. He was squeezing his hands together and nodding his head. "Praise the Lord that he brought you safely here. The road offers many perils to the unwary traveler."

Geraint had been half-afraid, half-hopeful that it would have been Marged who had opened the door to him a few minutes before. But Marged was only two years his junior. She must be twenty-six now. She would no longer be here at the manse. She was probably not even in Glynderi.

"I trust Miss Llwyd is well," he said. She was probably no longer Miss Llwyd.

"Marged?" The minister stopped rubbing his hands. "Well indeed, I thank you, my lord, the dear Lord be praised. Busy, of course. Always busy. It do not seem right for a woman to be doing a man's work, but she do refuse to come back here to live with her dada, though she would be very welcome, I always tell her. But she do feel responsible for Eurwyn's mam and gran, and I can only honor her for that."

"Eurwyn?" Geraint raised his eyebrows. She was married, then? He had known she must be by this time. The slight sinking of the heart that he felt was involuntary.

"A nasty business, that." The Reverend Llwyd looked

almost flustered and he drew off his glasses to polish them
with a large handkerchief. "It was handled in the only way
possible, of course, by the authorities. It is a pity the
outcome was so tragic, but it was no one's fault. These
things happen. They are in the Lord's hands."

Eurwyn *Evans*? Old Madoc Evans's son? The child
Geraint had kept himself well beyond reach of Madoc's
boot after once being kicked painfully in the backside with
it. Marged had married his son? And he had died in some
tragedy?

"She lives on the farm?" he asked.

"At Tŷ-Gwyn, yes," the minister said. "The White House,
that is," he translated, perhaps assuming that the Earl of
Wyvern had forgotten every word of Welsh he had ever
spoken. "Still white it is, my lord. Marged whitewashed it
just last spring. She is a good worker, I will give her that."

He tried to picture Marged living on a farm, doing the
work of a man. Whitewashing the longhouse. Refusing to
move back home because there were two other women who
presumably could not carry on without her help. Marged,
who had loved books and music, who had played the harp
well enough to draw tears to the eyes and yearning to the
heart, and whose singing voice had been unequaled in a
country of lovely singing voices.

But yes, he could imagine that it was true. There had
never been anything soft or shrinking about Marged. Quite
the opposite. She had been the first child to adopt him when
he was seven and she was five and she had spied him hiding
in a hedgerow behind the village, wistfully watching while
she gathered berries with a crowd of other children, all
singing and laughing. He had been a mere waif, with skinny
arms and legs and rags and bare feet. She had smiled at him
and spoken politely to him as if he were a real person and
had offered him a palmful of berries.

She had continued to be his friend even after her father,
the Reverend Llwyd, had explained to her that Geraint
Penderyn was not a suitable playmate for the children of

Glynderi. And even at the age of five she had done so openly, defying her father, scorning to deceive him.

Aled had become his friend too. Aled and Marged. Until he was torn away from them and forbidden to have any further dealings with them, even by letter, though his mother had taught him to read and write.

He got to his feet now to take his leave of the Reverend Llwyd and received with a curt nod the man's bow and his effusive thanks for the honor of the visit.

Chapter 3

He had intended making one or two other calls in the village. One in particular. Aled Rhoslyn had succeeded his father in his blacksmith's business a few months before Geraint came home for his mother's funeral. And he still was the village blacksmith. His forge was beside the chapel. Geraint had intended to call there.

But he found himself unexpectedly reluctant. One of his few good memories of childhood was Aled's friendship. But time had passed. They would have grown apart. Geraint was content with his life as it now was, and he had a number of close friends. But he did not want to be confronted with the knowledge that his first friendship with someone of his own gender no longer existed.

Perhaps some other day. He walked past the blacksmith's forge and was aware of faces at windows the length of the village street and nodded to the one curtsying woman he passed—he did not recognize her. But he did not stop anywhere. He had walked to the village. He found himself walking now beyond it, away from the park and the house. He found himself walking along beside the river and turning onto the rough path that led gradually upward into the hills. He followed almost instinctively a route that he must have walked a thousand times when he was a child.

He knew where Madoc Evans's farm was, more lately Eurwyn Evans's, now Marged's. He had passed it numerous times, though he had never been beyond its gate. It was while standing on the bars of the gate one spring day, watching a new calf walk about the yard on spindly legs, that he had encountered the boot of Madoc Evans, who had come up the lane behind him, unheard. Ragamuffins from the uplands were not welcome near the farms of the respectable.

Geraint paused after he had walked perhaps a mile. Was he going to call on her? He had hoped she was not at the manse or in the village. He had hoped she had married and moved away onto someone else's land. He had hoped never to see her again. And yet, having heard that she was at Tŷ-Gwyn, he had turned his footsteps immediately in that direction.

He turned to look back the way he had come. The gradient had not seemed steep, and yet he was high up already. He was assaulted with the familiarity of the scene below him—the river, flowing straight until it bent to curve around and into the park of Tegfan; the trees and smooth lawns of the park, and the large stone house; the village stretched out along the river; the farms dotted about in the lowlands and on the hills, the fields, bare now in early spring, but each looking different from every other; the pastures, in which a few sheep and cattle were grazing.

He felt a sudden and unexpected wave of longing again—the same feeling he had had on the pavement in London when he had overheard the snippet of a conversation in Welsh.

But I miss the hills. . . .

The hills had been a part of his childhood, a part of him. He had missed the hills, he remembered now, for weary years before forgetting them entirely, suppressing all memory of them until that meaningless encounter with two Welsh drovers had brought it jolting back. And the hills had beckoned again.

It had been much higher in the hills he had lived with his mother. He turned to look upward, but there was no clear view to the top. He would never again go up there. It was a place he did not want to see.

Would he go higher at all today? He looked broodingly about him. He could not see Tŷ-Gwyn, but he could see another farmhouse, built of stone, its roof neatly tiled with slate. It had been thatched when last he saw it. He thought for a moment. Mr. Williams. He was not sure he had ever known the man's first name. He had been a large and formidable-looking man. And yet occasionally when he had passed Geraint on the path, he had reached into a pocket and handed him a coin. Once, when he must have been on his way to market, he had given the boy a bunch of turnips and told him to take them to his mam for their dinner. And then, when Geraint had been scurrying away with his treasure, he had called him back and added two large brown farm eggs as an afterthought.

Mr. Williams had had a young daughter who used to run and hide when she saw Geraint coming, though he could remember her smiling shyly at him once or twice from behind her mother's skirts.

The Williams farm was his now, the Earl of Wyvern thought, if indeed it still belonged to the same man. Just as the Evans farm was his, and all the farms he could see from his vantage point, for as far as the eye could see. Perhaps he would call at the Williams farm this morning and then return home. He had no real wish to see Marged. And yet it seemed that his feet worked independently of his brain, for they carried him past the entrance to the short lane that would have taken him to the stone farmhouse, and led him upward.

And so ten minutes later he found himself again outside that gate, gazing in at the farmyard and the house of Tŷ-Gwyn. It looked so much the same that for a moment he felt disoriented. It was a longhouse, something so out of fashion that he had never seen one in England. It was one long, low building, the entrance to one side of the center, the house occupying the longer half, the cow barn the other. Animals and humans were housed together during the winter, separated by the passage from front door to back. The building was thatched and whitewashed. It was old-fashioned and certainly no symbol of wealth. And yet it was as neat as the proverbial pin.

His impression was formed in a mere moment. He did not have a chance to stand there and observe more fully. It was not a boot from behind that disturbed him this time, but the sight of a figure in the farmyard. She must have been feeding the single pig, which was in an open pen. It seemed she had even paused to talk to it or pet it. Or perhaps not. Perhaps it was the sight of him at the gate that had turned her utterly still.

He opened the gate and stepped inside onto the neatly swept path that led past the plot that would soon be planted to vegetables and into the yard itself. He walked along the path.

She did not move. She wore a plain and faded dress, which was covered by a large apron, slightly soiled from the morning's work though still crisp and white. She wore no cloak or hat, despite the chill of the breeze. Her light brown hair was pulled back from her face and confined in a simple knot at the back of her neck, though a few errant tendrils were blowing about her shoulders and face.

She was tall, as he remembered her, and well shaped. And as proud as she had ever been as the minister's daughter. She was standing with straight back and lifted chin and face devoid of all expression.

He knew instantly from that expression, or lack of expression, that she had not forgotten. At the age of eighteen he had been an unhappy, confused, and insecure boy, still not quite sure in which of two worlds he belonged. He had finally been allowed to return home on the death of his mother only to find that it was not home, that perhaps it never had been. Naively, he had expected people to welcome him, to rejoice in his change of fortune, to be apologetic for the way they had once rejected him and his mother. He had been very ready to forgive. But he had met reticence and suspicion and even some open hostility. Except in Aled and in Marged.

Marged. She had grown into a lovely sixteen-year-old. She had been beautiful and accomplished. She had played her harp for him and sung to him and had brought flooding back to him all his memories of Wales and of Welsh music. She had smiled at him and walked with him and held his hand and even kissed him. He had tumbled inevitably and deeply into love with her. He had been so desperate for love.

Too desperate. One afternoon up in the hills he had made an utter idiot of himself by pulling her to the ground and pawing her and trying with fumbling and totally inexperienced hands to get beneath her skirts. His head had been ringing from her resounding slap moments later and she had been running from him. The next day, when he had gone to the manse to apologize to her, she had treated him so coldly and been so much on her dignity and he had been so terrified and so embarrassed that he had turned utterly craven and directed all his conversation toward her father and had ignored her completely apart from one long and languid and insolent perusal of her body when her father was not looking. It was the mask behind which he had hidden all his hurt and guilt and insecurity. It was the mask he had worn for everyone else in the village except her and Aled. And now for her too.

He had returned to London the following day. He had not seen Marged since. And her look told him now that she had not forgotten. And that perhaps she had not forgiven, though it had been ten years ago and she must have realized during the intervening years what a gauche puppy he had been then.

He stopped six feet away from her. She was a woman now, he noticed. More beautiful than she had been as a girl.

"Marged," he said quietly.

*   *   *

She had been expecting him. Or if not exactly that, at least she had been aware since Sunday that he was at Tegfan, that Tŷ-Gwyn and all the land for miles around belonged to him, and that he might come at any time. She had prepared herself for his coming. She had prepared herself so that she would not be taken off guard.

And yet when she looked up from feeding old Nellie and saw him standing still and quiet at the gate, she felt rather as if a great fist had landed against her stomach with all the weight of a great arm behind it.

He opened the gate without invitation—he did not need an invitation—and came inside, walking slowly up the garden path and into the farmyard toward her. She watched him come, helpless to stop him, unable to move. He was dressed as she supposed English gentlemen of wealth and fashion dressed—such gentlemen were not in the habit of passing this way. He wore a long dark cloak with a single cape at the shoulders and had removed a tall hat. Beneath the cloak she could see a dark, full-skirted coat, ending several inches above his knees, and a dark green waistcoat and white shirt with starched collars and dark neckcloth. His dark, slim trousers hugged his legs. There was not a detail of his dress to be criticized.

And not a detail of the man himself either. He must have grown another few inches after the age of eighteen. He had been slim then and graceful. He was still slim, but he was a man now and not a boy. His shoulders and chest were broad. His waist and hips were slender. His dark hair was not as long as it had been when he was a child or as unruly as it had been when he was eighteen. It was expertly styled but still thick and curly. His eyes seemed bluer, more intense.

His face had changed. It had thinned into the face of a man. An aristocratic man, handsome, hard, and ruthless. It looked like a face that rarely if ever smiled or showed any other strong emotion. It was a disciplined, cold face. She could see nothing in it of the big-eyed, bold, soulful waif he had been 20 years before.

She hated him with an intensity that surprised even

herself. She hated him because she had loved him and had
made a fool of herself over him. Because he had let her
down and shown her arrogantly and cruelly the gap in their
stations. Because he was responsible for Eurwyn's death.
Because he had come now to fill the role of the authority
figure who had always most angered her in her life. Because
he was the Earl of Wyvern. Because he was Geraint
Penderyn. Because she had loved him at the foolish age of
sixteen and because even then—especially then—love had
hurt. Because even though she had prepared herself for his
coming, her apron had become soiled and her hair had been
buffeted by the wind and she had a visible patch on the
sleeve of her dress. Because she was twenty-six years old.

She hated him.

"Marged," he said quietly.

He rolled the *r* of her name in the Welsh way. He
pronounced her name correctly. And yet the Englishness of
his voice was apparent even in the one word. And how
dared he call her by her given name? She was Mrs. Evans
to strangers, and he was a stranger. But of course he was the
Earl of Wyvern and she was merely a tenant farmer, one
who paid him rent and tithes. He was putting her in her
place, very firmly in her place, by walking into her farmyard
uninvited and by calling her Marged.

Well, then.

She kept her back straight and her chin high and bent her
knees in a deep curtsy, grasping the sides of her dress as she
did so. "My lord," she said, speaking deliberately in
English, "what an honor, to be sure."

His expression did not change at all. And yet she knew
he had understood that her subservience was deliberate
mockery.

He knew that battle had been engaged.

How she hated him.

He was unwelcome. He could see it in her eyes, could sense
it in every line of her body. The foolish curtsy and her
words, spoken unexpectedly in English, merely confirmed

the fact. He did not realize until that moment how much he had hoped she had forgotten that foolishness of ten years ago. Or perhaps she had forgotten. Surely she had. It was just that circumstances had changed. Ten years had passed. She had been married and widowed during those years. He was the Earl of Wyvern now. She would expect him to have changed. And she would be right.

But he was disappointed. She had been his first friend. His wonderful friend. That was how he had described her to his mother that first day, when he had bounded back up the mountain, his mouth stained purple from berries. *I have a wonderful friend, Mam.* His mother had held him tightly, his face pressed against her too thin body, and smoothed her thin fingers gently through his curly hair.

"I hear that you run the farm yourself," he said now in English. "I hear that your husband passed away. I am sorry about that, Marged."

Her jaw tightened and her eyes grew hard. It was an expression he remembered from her childhood, though it had usually been used then against those who would have driven him away or scolded her for playing with him.

"I run the farm myself," she said, "with a little help from laborers when I can afford it. Did you think it impossible for a woman to do? I have always paid the rent, even this year. And the tithes."

Even this year? What was significant about this year? he wondered. He did not ask. But he understood her bristly manner suddenly, her belligerence. And it was so typical of Marged as he remembered her. She was afraid he had come to question her ability to run a farm herself. Her hackles were up.

"Perhaps," he said, "you could show me the farm." He looked about the yard and at the house. It all looked very well kept to him.

For a moment she did not move. She continued to look at him with her hard eyes and unreadable expression. And then she dipped into her curtsy again. "Certainly, my lord," she said, "I am your servant."

If she had been, he thought with a flash of annoyance, he would have put her in her place in a moment. He did not tolerate insolence from subordinates.

"The pigpen is too large for our needs," she said, indicating it with a sweep of one arm. "My father-in-law built it years ago. But one does not rebuild a stone pigpen to accommodate one's needs. We have only Nellie now, and she is still here only because on my marriage I made the mistake of naming her and making a pet of her and now cannot bear the thought of slaughtering her."

She turned toward the house. And yet, he thought, it would be wise surely to buy or breed more pigs. When he had been a child, all the farmers had had half a dozen or so. Bacon and ham had been a staple food, though not with his mother and him, of course. He followed her across the yard toward the house. There were a few chickens pecking away at some grain in one corner. He could see some sheep grazing in a meadow to one side of the yard.

"The cows are still being kept inside," she said. "I will be letting them out soon, but one can never assume that spring is here to stay merely because there has been some nice weather. I would not wish to put the calves or the milk at risk."

She spoke briskly, impersonally, entirely in English. She walked with long, purposeful strides and no enticing swaying of the hips. And yet she looked utterly feminine, nevertheless.

He stepped after her through the front door and into the dark, cool passageway beyond. The cow barn was to his right. One cow lowed contentedly. Geraint counted ten stalls. Five of them were occupied. Three of the cows had calves with them. Although there were the inevitable smells of a barn, it was clean and orderly, he saw. The straw on the ground looked fresh.

"The stalls were all full five years ago," she said. "We have had to sell half the herd gradually."

He did not ask why.

"They look well cared for," he said. "You do all the work with them, Marged? And all the milking?"

"My mother-in-law does most of that," she said. "There are other things for me to do and only a certain number of hours in each day."

He had seen no sign yet of the mother-in-law or the grandmother.

She led him through the passageway and out into a lean-to built onto the back of the house. It was a dairy, he saw. The dirt floor and the slate surfaces of the work area were clean. There were both butter and cheese in the making.

"You sell the produce?" he asked. He had used to envy the children of farmers, on their way to market with their parents, the carts in which they rode laden with produce.

"When there is a market for it," she said. "There have been strikes in the coalfields and at the ironworks. There is no money there now for Carmarthenshire butter and cheese. And prices have fallen."

"Have they?" He looked at her. "That is a pity."

"Yes," she agreed, her voice tight with anger, "it is."

As if he was responsible for the shrinking market and the drop in prices.

"And your crops?" he asked. "You hire laborers to put them in for you?"

"I do it myself," she said. "Plows are not so hard to use if one has well-trained horses. Ours are getting old, but they are good. I work the land myself. At harvesttime I need help."

He had seen men pushing the heavy plows behind the horses or oxen, struggling to keep the furrows straight and uniformly deep. He did not believe for a moment that plows were not hard to use. Was she too stubborn to hire a man to do the work for her? Did she have to prove to every man about Glynderi and Tegfan that she was their equal?

He reached out on an sudden impulse and took both her hands in his. He turned them palm up and looked down at them. It was only as he did so that he realized that touching her was not such a good idea. Holding the backs of her hands cupped in his palms suddenly seemed unwisely intimate. And he had had to take a step closer to her in order to do so. He was holding her thumbs back with his own, he realized.

He looked up into her eyes. Another mistake. She had always had the steadiest eyes he had ever known. He could not remember ever trying to stare Marged down, but it would have been a useless game, one impossible to win. And he remembered now how those gray eyes had always been fringed by long lashes, several shades darker than her hair. They had not changed.

"Calluses," he said softly, tightening his grip as he felt a tremor in her hands.

"You know the word and its meaning," she said equally softly. There was no suggestion of sarcasm in her tone, though it was there undisguised in her eyes. "They come from hard, honest work, my lord."

She licked her lips when his eyes lowered to them, though he knew she did not do so with any intention of being provocative. He felt his breath quicken even so. Belatedly, he released her hands.

"My lord," she said, "would you care to step into the kitchen and take a cup of tea with us?"

Why did she hate him so much? he wondered. Could a boy's fumbled attempts at seduction have made her so angry even ten years later? Or was it merely the fact that he was now wealthy and she was not? The possibility that Marged of all people could be so mean-minded annoyed him. He inclined his head curtly.

"Thank you," he said.

For a few moments longer she stared into his eyes, unconcealed resentment and hostility in her own. And for those same moments he stared back, angry himself, on the verge of asking her straight out what he had done to offend her. But he had learned years and years ago, perhaps from his birth, but certainly from his twelfth year, not to open himself deliberately to disappointment or hurt or rejection.

He recognized danger with Marged and closed himself off against it.

And then she turned and strode off back down the passageway to the low doorway leading into the kitchen of the house. He followed her and found himself standing on the flagstones of the kitchen floor, turning toward the large open fireplace. Sitting in the inglenook beside the fire was an elderly woman, whom he could not remember seeing before. She was nodding her head, presumably in acknowledgment of his appearance. In front of the fire, the Mrs. Evans he remembered—Madoc Evans's wife—was bobbing a curtsy and directing her flustered gaze at his feet.

He inclined his head to them both and bade them a good morning.

"His lordship is doing us the honor of taking a cup of tea with us, Mam, Gran," Marged said, still speaking in English. "Do take a seat, my lord." She motioned him toward a bare wooden settle close to the fire and turned toward the dresser to lift down cups and saucers.

Geraint sat.

Chapter 4

She was furious with herself. She had been proud of the way she had been able to mingle contempt and courtesy and of the impersonality of her manner. She had been delighted to sense that he understood but did not know quite what to do about it.

And then he had startled her by taking her hands in his and turning them palm up and looking down at the calluses. Her first reaction had been horror and shame. Until she married Eurwyn she had always taken pains to dress and behave as much like a lady as she knew how. She had read as widely as she was able and had learned several accomplishments. She had thought that perhaps she would try to persuade the old earl or his steward to open a school so that she could teach the children from the farms and village. But she had been flattered by Eurwyn's attentions and offer of marriage and had accepted. He was a man she had admired. Most of the calluses had come after his death, though she had worked hard even before that.

She wore her calluses with pride. And yet her first reaction to the knowledge that *he* was looking down at them was shame and embarrassment. Shame that she had to work hard for a living. Embarrassment that she did not look like a lady.

Her second reaction had been one of acute physical awareness. An awareness of the warmth and strength of his hands against the back of hers. An awareness of his closeness. He really was taller than he had been ten years before. And broader. And he smelled—expensive. She had looked up into his face and he had raised his own eyes almost at the same moment. He had always had the bluest eyes she had ever seen.

When he had spoken, she had managed somehow to think of a fittingly cutting reply. But in reality she had been mesmerized by his eyes and then acutely aware of the fact that their gaze had dropped to her mouth. For a moment she had felt as if her heart would beat its way right through her bosom and be exposed to view. She had thought he was going to kiss her. *But she had done nothing to try to prevent its happening.*

And then he had released her hands. But not before he must have felt her tremble. She knew he must have felt it. His grip had tightened.

She was furious with herself. Furious that she had felt shame. Furious that she had felt and responded to the pull of his masculinity.

He was the reason there was no pig but Nellie on the farm. He was the reason there were only five cows left and their calves. And only a few chickens. And fewer sheep than there had ever been before. And no new clothes for almost two years now. He was the reason she could not hire a man to do the heavy work on the farm. She did not know if she would even be able to afford someone at harvesting time. He was the reason Eurwyn was not here to do the heavy work himself.

And yet she was one of the fortunate ones. Somehow they were still here at the farm and still functioning, she and Mam and Gran. Some people were not still on their farms. The Parrys, for example, driven out finally by the newest raise in the rents, living up on the moors, hoping somehow to pick up enough casual work that they could avoid the dreaded and final move to the workhouse. And there were plenty more living on the brink, in debt, unable to absorb even one more small raise in the rent or one more poor harvest or fall in market prices.

Geraint Penderyn was responsible for it all. And yet she had felt shame to have him see her ruined hands. And she had been attracted to his male splendor.

She spread a cloth on the kitchen table and set out cups and saucers while her mother-in-law poured boiling water into the teapot and set the cozy over it so that the tea would steep. Marged made no attempt to make conversation, though she could feel the tension while Geraint asked politely, in that very cultured English accent of his, after the health of the other two women and they answered in monosyllables. She enjoyed his discomfort, though he kept talking. Gentlemen, of course, were trained to converse even when there was nothing whatsoever to say.

She did not glance at him. And yet she was aware that he looked all about the kitchen—at the open fire with the bread oven in the chimneypiece beside it and the large pot and kettle suspended by chains over it; at the plain table with its simple wooden benches; at the dresser and the cupboard bed in which she had slept with Eurwyn and now slept alone; at the door into the combined parlor and bedroom, where the other two women slept; at the spinning wheel, which occupied her during the evenings when there was no other work to do; at the harp.

She knew that his eyes lingered on her harp. She had used to play it even as a child. She had sneaked Geraint into the manse one day when her father was out visiting and had played and sung for him. She could remember now her amazement at his rapt expression and at his insistence that she play and sing over and over to him. She had sneaked him in often after that, just as he had sneaked her onto the forbidden territory of Tegfan park, confident that he knew where all the gamekeeper's traps were set and could take her on a safe path. She had taught him to sing with her. He had had a pure and sweet soprano voice.

"Do you still play, Marged?" he asked now, bringing her eyes to his at last.

She picked up the teapot, though her mother-in-law had been about to do so, and began to pour the tea. "When I have the time," she said. "Not often." She concentrated on keeping her hands steady and cursed herself because the effort was necessary.

"Oh, but she do play lovely, our Marged," old Mrs. Evans said from her seat in the inglenook. "And she sings like an angel."

Gran did not do much these days except rock in her chair and gaze into the fire. She did not even knit now, her fingers having become too bent and too stiff.

"Then I must hear her," he said, meeting her eyes as she handed him his cup and saucer. His own were as cold as ever and yet there was something in them that hinted at a challenge. "Sometime."

When hell is dripping with icicles, Marged thought, but she said nothing. She sat down and picked up her own cup of tea. It should have been a rare luxury to sit thus in the middle of the morning, but she would far rather have been at work. He was sitting where Eurwyn had liked to sit. Her own fault—without thinking she had indicated that particular corner of the settle. It did not matter.

Except that she could not stop herself from comparing the two men. Eurwyn had been heavyset, ruddily handsome. He had rarely worn anything but work clothes and had laughed at her for wanting to wash them almost every day. She would wear them out in no time with her scrubbing, he had told her. And he had always drunk his tea in noisy sips. She had hated to sit listening to him. She had always tried to occupy herself with something that would make a noise and drown out the sounds. It had been a silly irritation that she had never been able quite to quell.

Geraint—the Earl of Wyvern—was slim and quietly elegant and immaculate. He had removed his cloak and set it on the settle beside him. Even his boots appeared to have picked up none of the dust of the path. He conversed with apparent ease, though Marged guessed that he felt the discomfort the rest of them were less adept at disguising. Eurwyn had never seemed to feel the need to keep a conversation going. He had spoken only when he had had something to say, though he had not been a morose man. Geraint drank his tea silently.

He was without a doubt the most handsome and the most attractive man she had ever met, Marged decided. And the thought angered her. If his whole life had not changed suddenly at the age of twelve, if he had not been educated as a gentleman, if he had not inherited the wealth with which to dress expensively, would he be any more attractive now than Eurwyn had been? Or any other man of her acquaintance?

Yes, an annoyingly honest part of her mind admitted. Even as a child, as a thin and ragged and frequently dirty waif, he had been beautiful. She had fallen in love with his beauty at the age of sixteen. With nothing else. There had been nothing else to love. Well, she was ten years older now. Ten years wiser. Beauty alone could no longer seduce her.

And heaven knew she had reason enough to hate the man behind the beauty.

He was rising to take his leave, nodding to her in-laws, thanking them for the tea, turning to her with a look of inquiry, commanding her with his eyes and his whole aristocratic bearing to see him on his way. He picked up his cloak and his hat from the settle.

She walked to the gate with him in silence, her chin up. She had called herself his servant earlier, but in reality she was no man's servant. He might own the land on which they walked and he might in a few years, if rents continued to rise and prices continued to fall, force her out, but at the moment it was her land. She had worked for it. She had earned every callus on her hands.

He opened the gate and stepped out into the lane. He

closed the gate, turning toward her in order to do so. He looked at her, and she would not look away from his eyes.

"I am sorry your husband died, Marged," he said. "But you appear to be doing very well here on your own."

Something snapped in her. She threw back her head and glared at him. "You are sorry," she said almost in a whisper. But the fury could not be controlled. Her eyes flashed. "You are sorry! You may take your sorrow, Geraint Penderyn, and stuff it down your throat. Go away from here. I have paid my rent and this farm is mine until rent day next year. Go away. You are not welcome here."

He looked startled for a moment. But he did not retaliate. She would have liked nothing better than a fight, which she could not possibly have won. But he kept his gentlemanly calm.

"No," he said quietly. "I realized that from the start, Marged."

He put on his hat—it succeeded only in making him look even more elegant—and turned away from her. She watched him walk down the lane and itched to hurl some choice epithets after him. She knew a few despite the fact that she was her father's daughter and was a regular chapel goer. She would have loved to hurl more than epithets, but her hands were empty. Besides, it would be lowering to yell with shrill hysteria or to throw missiles.

She was not sorry for her outburst. If his skin was so thick that he had not got the message during his visit, then he would know now. He would know to stay away from her and Tŷ-Gwyn.

She tried not to think of the fact that Tŷ-Gwyn belonged to him and that the annual rent day seemed to gallop up faster each year.

It was the first and the worst of such visits that Geraint paid to his tenant farmers during the coming days. But worst only in the sense that Marged had been his friend and almost his lover once upon a time and now seemed to hate him with an intensity in excess of the facts. No, it was not that she *seemed* to hate him. Her unexpected outburst when he was leaving Tŷ-Gwyn, just after he had tried to sympathize with her and compliment her, had cleared away any doubt he might have had. She hated him.

All the other farmers he visited were polite. A few of them were almost friendly—the Williamses, for example. And their daughter too, still pretty, still shy, and still unmarried. Ceris Williams had poured tea for him and found it impossible to converse with him beyond monosyllabic answers to his questions, but she had smiled kindly at him. He found himself hoarding the few smiles he was favored with. Most of the people he visited were polite and little else. With a few he felt hostility bristling just behind the politeness.

It seemed that the past few years had not been kind to farmers. There had been more rain than usual and damage had been done to the crops. Market prices were down for almost all farm products. A few farmers stated, as Marged had done, that they were carrying fewer livestock than formerly. Clearly no one was prospering. Geraint felt rather ashamed that he had avoided learning anything about his estate in Tegfan. He had appointed the best steward he could find to look after it for him and had closed his mind to a place and a past he preferred not to remember. But he should have at least have read reports from Tegfan. He should at least have known that his farmers were struggling. He could hardly blame them for showing some resentment at his appearing suddenly, well-dressed and clearly not suffering financially at all.

Also he had grown past his naïveté of ten years before. Ten years ago he had expected to come home to find everyone rejoicing in his good fortune. It was rather like a fairy tale for the discovery to be made twelve years after the birth of a penniless waif that he was the legitimate heir to an earldom and three vast estates—although his mother, of course, had always told him to hold his head high as she held hers because she had been married to his father, the earl's son, before he had been killed, though she had no proof and no one would believe her. In fairy tales everyone always rejoiced at the reversed fortunes of the Cinderella-type characters. But he knew now that it was not so in real life. He knew that his people must resent him just because of who he was.

He was going to have to stay in Tegfan, he thought reluctantly as the days passed. He thought of spring approaching in London, bringing the Season and all the giddy round of social activities with it. But he would have to let it proceed without him this year. He was going to have to stay to convince his people that he was not the enemy, that he did not look down upon them with smug satisfaction because he had now been elevated above them. He was going to have to find out about his property and the true state of his farms. It would not be difficult to do. He was very knowledgeable about his other estates and had a reputation as a fair and approachable master, he believed. He had real friends among his English tenant farmers.

He was going to have to stay.

Of course, there were people he had still not called upon at the end of those few days of intensive visits. One of them was Aled Rhoslyn. Geraint had felt reluctant to renew his acquaintance with his former friend and partner in crime. But if he was to stay for longer than a mere week or so, then the encounter could not be avoided forever.

Finally one afternoon he walked to the village and stepped inside the blacksmith's forge. He had heard a hammer ringing on the anvil from well down the street. The sound was almost deafening once he was inside. Aled had his back to the door. He was hammering out what looked to be a metal wheel rim. A boy at his side, apparently a young apprentice, drew his attention to the customer and faded nervously into the background.

Aled had not changed a great deal. He certainly had not shrunk in size. He was still only two or three inches taller than Geraint, but he was broader, with the powerful arms and shoulders necessary to his trade. He still had rather too much fair hair on his head and hazel eyes that seemed always to be smiling. His face was still good-humored and good-looking.

Geraint observed him as he glanced over his shoulder and then set down his hammer and straightened up and turned slowly, wiping his hands down his large leather apron as he did so. It was obvious from his expression and his whole manner that he was as reluctant for this meeting as Geraint. There was no noticeable hostility in his eyes, but there was a wariness there, a certain embarrassment.

"Aled," Geraint said, "when are you planning to start the hard work for the day?"

Aled smiled slowly. "I did not want to be out of breath and sweating when you came calling," he said. "I thought I would do some light chore while I waited." But he hung back rather awkwardly.

Geraint walked toward him, his right hand extended. He was absurdly nervous, afraid of one more rejection. And this one would hurt most, apart from Marged's. "How are you?" he asked.

Aled looked at his hand before taking it. But his clasp was firm enough when he did. "Well," he said. "And you?"

Geraint nodded. "You are married?" he asked. "There are half a dozen eager little blacksmiths on the way up?"

Aled laughed, but he flushed with what looked suspiciously like embarrassment. "I am not married," he said.

"Then you must have learned to run faster than you used to," Geraint said. It had always been a source of pride to him as a child that he could outrun his friend even though Aled had been a year older and a head taller and a stone or two heavier.

Aled laughed. And looked awkward.

Geraint spoke from impulse. "You have a great deal of work to be done this afternoon?" he asked. "Can it be left? Come and walk with me in the park."

Aled looked down at the wheel rim on his anvil. He pursed his lips, and Geraint could see that he wanted to refuse, that he was reaching for an excuse.

"We can even walk about there openly without having to skulk about among the trees avoiding mantraps," Geraint said. "We will no longer be trespassing."

Aled grinned, genuine amusement in his eyes. "Why not?" he said. "Welcome home, man." He lifted the heavy apron off over his head.

And yet, Geraint thought ruefully as they left the forge together and walked down the street in the direction of Tegfan park, Aled was uncomfortable. He would a thousand times rather be back in his forge than on his way for a stroll with his former friend.

Aled Rhoslyn had not really expected Geraint ever to return to Tegfan, even though he was now the Earl of Wyvern. It would be too difficult for him to face the strange facts of his childhood and boyhood. The child Geraint had never been disliked as much as he had thought. He had been pitied more than anything, as had his mother, although, of course, the strict moral code by which most of them lived as nonconformists had forced them to reject the latter publicly. Most of the children had secretly admired the bold and almost charismatic little ragamuffin.

Most people had not disliked him during his boyhood after the earl had somehow made the staggering discovery that his long-dead son had been legally married to Gwynneth Penderyn when the two of them had run off together. They had been married before the conception of their son. A few of the meaner-minded, of course, had been spiteful with envy and a few others had not been slow to notice that Gwynneth Penderyn—she was never known by her married name of Marsh and Geraint had legally changed his name back to hers as soon as he reached his majority—was sent to live alone in a small cottage on the estate and was never either invited to the house or visited by Geraint.

Most people had not disliked him during his brief visit after the death of his mother. But everyone, almost to a person, had felt awkward with him, not knowing quite whether to talk to him as if he were Geraint Penderyn or to show him deference as Geraint Marsh, Viscount Handford. The fact that he had been both had led to an impossible situation.

But Geraint had always felt disliked. Not that he had ever been self-pitying about it. But he had built defenses, of which Aled, as his one close friend apart from Marged Llwyd, had been aware. The defense of not caring a fig for anyone as a child. The added defense of aloofness as an eighteen-year-old and the firm hiding behind his newly acquired Englishness and his gentleman's manners.

Aled had not expected him to return. And over the years he had somehow managed to divorce in his mind his feelings for Geraint as friend and his feelings for the Earl of Wyvern as owner of the land on which he and his acquaintances and neighbors lived and worked. The Earl of Wyvern was that impersonal figurehead who represented the aristocracy, the English owners who cared nothing for Wales or the Welsh except as a source of wealth to themselves. Matters had come to crisis point. The whole system seemed designed gradually to squeeze out the small farmers and replace them with those who could better contribute more and more to enriching those who were already rich.

Aled had never thought of himself as a leader or as an agitator. He had been content to let Eurwyn Evans be both. But Eurwyn was dead and Glynderi and its neighborhood had needed a leader, someone with both firm convictions and a level head, and several people had approached him to take on the position and join the secret committee that had formed to organize protest in almost the whole of northern Carmarthenshire. Marged had asked him and he had remembered that Marged had suffered a great loss.

And so he had agreed. And had somehow blanked his mind to the fact that he had committed himself to organizing protest against his friend among others. He walked now beside Geraint beyond the village and onto the driveway leading to the house of Tegfan and then off it and across a wide lawn—and knew with a dreadful discomfort that Geraint was both his friend and his enemy, and that probably it was going to be impossible for him to remain both those things.

"Aled," Geraint said suddenly, and it was only then that Aled realized they had been walking in silence, "don't."

The few words they had exchanged had all been spoken in English, Aled realized. Just as they had been ten years ago.

"Don't what?" he asked uneasily. If they must talk, let it be on safe trivialities.

"Don't treat me as if I were the Earl of Wyvern," Geraint said.

"But you are." He knew what Geraint meant but did not want to know.

"I am Geraint Penderyn," his friend said, and there was a hint of frustration in his voice.

Aled remembered the talk outside the chapel on Sunday and Marged's suggestion that everyone make the earl feel unwelcome if and when he visited. Apparently he had visited and had been made to feel unwelcome. A village blacksmith tended to hear about such things.

"Yes," he said, "and the Earl of Wyvern too."

"We used to fight," Geraint said unexpectedly. "Wrestling, not boxing. Almost every time we met. You always won. I believe there were no exceptions. Do you want to try to retain that record, Aled?"

Aled looked at him in amazement. "Now?" he said. "Don't be daft, man." His eyes took in Geraint's immaculate clothes.

But Geraint had stopped walking and was stripping off his coat. "Yes, here," he said, and there was the tightness of anger in his voice—and a familiar gleam of recklessness in his eyes. "Come and fight me, Aled. Let's see if you can still put me down. No, don't back away and look at me as if you think I should be consigned to bedlam. Fight me, dammit, or I will slap your face and make you fight."

Chapter 5

The world had taken leave of its senses, Aled thought, watching as white shirtsleeves were rolled up sinewy arms. He had not wrestled since he was a boy. He was twenty-nine years old and a respected workingman. And there had been no provocation. There was no reason to fight. Not that they had ever needed a reason when they were children beyond that simple fact—they had been children.

He shrugged out of his own coat and dropped it to the grass. He was taller, heavier, better muscled, he thought, looking critically at his opponent's body. It should be no more difficult now than it had ever been to win the fight. Though he had never won anything else with Geraint, he thought ruefully. The younger, smaller, scruffier boy had always somehow been the leader. Where he had gone—and it had very often been where he ought not to have gone— Aled had followed along behind.

They fought for a long time, in silence except for their breathing, which grew progressively more labored. They circled each other, engaged each other, tripped each other, rolled over each other, put seemingly unbreakable holds on each other, broke apart, jumped to their feet, circled each other, and began the process all over again. It was sheer luck, Aled had to admit, that finally sent Geraint tumbling at an awkward angle so that Aled's heavier body could bear his shoulders to the ground and hold them there before he could twist free.

And then they were lying side by side on the grass, staring upward and panting to recover their breaths.

Geraint chuckled after a minute or so. "One of these days," he said. "One of these days, Aled. Ah, thank you, man. I have needed that for a long time."

He was speaking Welsh. He sounded quite like the old Geraint, Aled thought. The cultured English accent disappeared when the language changed.

"You needed humiliating?" Aled switched languages too and joined in the laughter. "I could have spat in your eye, man, and saved us both some time and energy."

Aled knew what was coming in the short silence that ensued. And he knew he was quite powerless to avoid it.

"What have I done?" Geraint asked him, still in Welsh. He was no longer either laughing or panting. "Is it just that I was Geraint Penderyn and am now the Earl of Wyvern? Is that all it is, Aled?"

Aled grunted. "You cannot expect people to be comfortable with you, man," he said. "Just look at you, or at the way you looked fifteen minutes or so ago anyway. No one was ever comfortable with your grandfather either. You must remember that."

"And why did you know," Geraint asked him quietly, "exactly what I was talking about? It is more than discomfort, Aled. There is hostility. Why? What have I done? Apart from not showing my face here for the past ten years. Is that it? Is it?"

"You are imagining things, Ger," Aled said. "You always had a vivid imagination."

"Goddammit," Geraint said, "we were friends, Aled. You and Marged and I. Marged told me to get away from Tŷ-Gwyn. She told me I could shove my sympathy for her down my throat—I believe she was itching to suggest a different location. She told me I was not welcome. And you tell me I have a vivid imagination. Don't make this lonelier for me than it has to be, man. What have I done?"

Aled sat up and draped his arms over his knees. He drew a deep breath and let it out slowly. Why the bloody hell had Geraint come home? And wouldn't he be listening to a blistering reprimand if the Reverend Llwyd could listen to the language of his thoughts.

"Made it almost impossible for anyone to live here," he said shortly.

"What?" Geraint shot up into a sitting position beside him and glared. "I have not even been living here myself, Aled. How could I have been making it impossible for anyone else to do so?"

"Yields and prices have been going down," Aled said, "and rents have been going up. Tithes now have to be paid in money, not goods, and enforcement has been stricter. Poor rates have gone up and yet the poor are worse off than ever with the building of the workhouses. The turnpike trusts have been putting up more tollgates and making it more expensive for farmers to transport their goods than to produce or buy them. Trespassing and poaching are being more strictly controlled and punished than ever before. Need I go on?"

He did not look at his friend's face, but he could tell that Geraint was looking aghast.

"But I know nothing about any of this," he said. "None of it is my fault."

Aled turned his head at last and looked at the Earl of Wyvern with surprise—and for the first time with some contempt. "Ah," he said. "I have work to do. If you will excuse me." He reached for his coat and would have got to his feet, but Geraint's hand clamped on his arm.

"Ignorance is no plea, is it?" he said. "But I cannot be blamed for all those things, Aled. Tithes are the church's, not mine, and I did not make that new law about cash payments. I did not make the new Poor Law or conceive the idea of workhouses. Those grievances at least cannot be laid at my door."

"Are you sure, Ger?" Aled got to his feet despite the staying hand and shook the grass from his coat before putting it back on.

Geraint stayed where he was. "You have me at a disadvantage," he said. "I know nothing about Tegfan, Aled. I have avoided knowing anything about it. I do not know what I am doing here now except that I passed two men on the street in London who were talking Welsh to each other."

"Perhaps," Aled said, "you should have stayed away. Perhaps it would have been better for you and better for the people here." He himself would have found it far easier to fight against the impersonal earldom of Wyvern in its capacity as owner of Tegfan.

Geraint was on his feet too before Aled could walk away. He was rolling his shirtsleeves back down to his wrists. "No, you are not striding off on that note," he said. "You owe me another bout, Aled. You know you won that one by sheer luck, just as you won all our fights as boys. Every one of them a lucky win. How many times did we fight? A dozen? Fifty? A hundred? There will be at least one more. And I make it a rule only ever to wrestle with my friends. Give me time, Aled. Give me time to find out the truth and to decide what I am going to do about it."

Damn! Aled did not want the issues muddled. He could already feel conflict of interest weighing heavily on his shoulders.

Geraint was holding out his right hand again. "Agreed?" he said. "A week? Perhaps two? And then you can decide whether or not to sever your friendship with such a blackguard. Come on, man. You have not lost that fairness of mind that I always admired, have you?"

Damn! Aled took the offered hand and tightened his grip. "I really do have work to get back to," he said.

Geraint stood back and let him pass. But Aled heard him laugh as he strode off in the direction of the village, feeling all the hopelessness of the conflict between the pull of

friendship and the pull of loyalty to the people he represented.

"Perhaps I will challenge you to a boxing match next
time," Geraint called after him. "I have some small skill at
the sport, I believe. I will relieve you of some blood via your
nose, Aled."

Aled smiled despite himself but did not acknowledge the
challenge.

Geraint became gradually aware that he was not alone. It
was not that he heard anyone or saw anyone beyond the
disappearing figure of Aled Rhoslyn. It was just a feeling he
had, an instinct he had developed years and years ago and
had been unaware until now that he still retained. There
were trees not far away, ancient trees with huge trunks.

"You had better come out from there," he said conversationally in Welsh. "It would be more advisable than forcing
me to come and get you."

He was not sure who or quite what he would be facing.
For several moments there was continued silence. And then
a rustling heralded the appearance of a small, thin, untidy,
shabbily dressed lad perhaps eight or nine years old. Staring
at him, Geraint felt strangely as if he were looking into a
mirror down a long time tunnel. Except that the boy's hair
was straight. He was standing on one leg, scratching it with
the almost nonexistent side of the shabby boot he wore on
the other foot.

"You had better come closer," Geraint said, clasping his
hands formally behind his back. The boy shuffled a few feet
forward. "Much closer. One inch beyond the tip of my
fingers if I were to stretch my arm out in front of me."

The boy came to stand perhaps two feet beyond the
indicated spot. He stood very still, his dark eyes fixed on
Geraint's. Geraint knew exactly how the boy felt, just as if
the boy were his mirror image and he was the real
flesh-and-blood figure. The child's heart would be beating
so painfully that it would be pounding in his ears and
choking his throat. He would be considering escape. From

the corners of his eyes, without betraying himself by letting them dart about, he would be scouting out escape routes. But he would know that there was no escape.

"Well?" Geraint asked. "What are you doing here?"

"I was playing," the child said in a piping voice. "I got lost."

Exactly the excuse he himself had given the only time he had been caught—fortunately by one of the gardeners and not by any of the gamekeepers. Even so, by the time he had been allowed to take his leave, his backside had been so sore that he had not been able to walk normally and he had still been unable to sit down by the time he had scrambled up to the moors and the hovel that was home.

"Got lost hunting rabbits?" Geraint asked.

The boy shrugged and shook his head.

"You know who I am?" Geraint asked.

The boy nodded and Geraint recognized the bold, fixed look in his eyes as one of unadulterated fear.

"And who are you?" he asked.

"Idris," the boy said.

"Idris? Just Idris?"

"Idris Parry."

"Idris Parry," Geraint said, "has no one taught you how to address adults?"

"Idris Parry, *sir*," the boy said.

"And where do you live, Idris Parry?" Geraint asked. He hoped the answer would not be the one he fully expected.

"With my mam and my dada," the child said, his voice less bold. "And my sisters."

"I asked where," the earl said.

The child pointed vaguely toward the hills. "Up there," he said while Geraint inwardly winced. "Are you going to send me away, sir?"

Transportation. For poaching. The child had learned young the risks he took, just as he himself had learned.

"Please, sir, will you beat me instead?" he asked quickly, and Geraint knew just what it had cost the boy to show such a sign of weakness. "I got lost. I was just playing."

"Well, Idris." Geraint reached into a pocket. "There used to be wicked mantraps here, traps that would hurt your leg like a thousand devils and hold you fast until someone came to let you out. I think it altogether possible that they are still here. You are going to have to be very careful about where you play, aren't you?"

The child nodded.

"Are you to be trusted?" Geraint asked. He had selected a coin neither too small to be useless nor too large to cause undue suspicion. He held it out to the boy. "Give this to your mam, Idris. And it would be wise to tell her that it was given to you somewhere else by someone else."

The child suspected a trap—as an earlier child had suspected one the first time Mr. Williams had offered him money. He suspected that the coin was a bait to draw him near enough to be grabbed. Geraint tossed it into the air, and the boy caught it deftly.

"Be off with you now," Geraint said. "And watch for traps."

"Yes, sir." The boy was on his way already. But he stopped dead in his tracks and looked back. "Thank you, sir."

Geraint nodded curtly. He was feeling sick to his stomach. What on earth was a family doing living up on those moors with a child so ragged that he seemed not to possess a single whole garment? But at least there *was* a family, if the boy had been speaking the truth. A mother and a father. At least they were not living there because they had been made outcast from the chapel and from the community. At least the child was not a bastard.

But he still felt sick at the reminder that there was such poverty in the world. It seemed so much more personal on Tegfan land than it ever appeared on the streets of London.

Staying away had been selfish, he thought. Deliberately keeping himself ignorant of Tegfan affairs had been an unpardonable self-indulgence. He hoped it had not lost him Aled's friendship or caused the permanent hostility of his people.

They *were* his people. He had realized that from the moment of his return, or perhaps even from the moment of that brief encounter on a London street.

They were his people.

Choir practice at the chapel was the one event of the week that regularly drew a large number of people together, except at the very busiest times of the year. Singing was the one passion and the one accomplishment that united most of the people of West Wales, or of any part of Wales for that matter.

Marged had conducted the choir since her girlhood in order to relieve her father of one of his many duties. Though perhaps it was misleading to describe her as the conductor, she often thought. A Welsh choir, unless it was competing at an *eisteddfod,* really did not need to have someone stand in front of it beating time or forcing changes of volume or tempo. A Welsh choir simply sang from the diaphragm and from the heart and sang as a choir. Welsh singers loved nothing better than to listen to one another's voices and the harmony of the other parts as they sang.

Marged conducted in the sense that she began the practice, putting an end to the noisy chatter as everyone exchanged news of all that had happened since Sunday, and choosing the hymns they would sing the following Sunday and the order in which they would sing them. When they sang she sat and sang with them while Miss Jenkins thumped away at the keyboard of the ancient pianoforte in the Sunday schoolroom.

They sang for an hour while Marged admitted to herself that they came together weekly not really to practice but to enjoy the singing and the company. After the hour was up, they would talk and gossip as avidly as they did after morning service on Sunday.

She was still angry. Perhaps angrier with *him* than she might have been because she was angry with herself. She had not been able to stop thinking of him since his visit. She had even dreamed of him. And so all her thoughts of him had to be focused on her hatred of him and her deep resentment that he had come back to Tegfan. Why had he not done the decent thing and stayed away?

He was, of course, the main topic of conversation as soon as she had indicated that the practice was at an end. Almost all of them had seen him. Most of them had encountered him in one way or another. Several of them had had personal calls from him.

Everyone was agreed that he looked very grand, that he behaved like a gentleman born, that his speech was more English than the English spoke, that his manner was stiff and stern. A few ventured to suggest that he had been courteous during his visits and interested in seeing the farms. Perhaps there would be changes now that he had come in person and seen for himself. Most were suspicious and angered by his aloof manner and his neglecting to ask them about any problems or complaints they might have.

"He offered me *sympathy* on the death of Eurwyn," Marged said finally, unable to keep out of the conversation any longer. "And then he complimented me on the way I have run the farm alone. Almost as if he was telling me that Eurwyn was of no account, that I am better off without a criminal as a husband." She was so furious that her voice was shaking as well as her hands.

"Ah," Ifor Davies said, "that was not well done of him at all, *fach*."

"And you may depend upon it, mind, that when he visited us on the farms he had his eyes about him to see who could be squeezed for more rent next year," Gwen Dirion said. "I am not sure we should trust him for all his fine manners."

"And he is, after all, only Geraint Penderyn," Eli Harris commented.

"I do not see why we should stand meekly by and allow the *Earl of Wyvern* to step into our farmyards and inside our homes whenever the mood takes him," Marged said, still angry. "I do not see why we should give him the right. Perhaps it is time we gave him a taste of his own medicine."

"Marged," Aled said, "perhaps we should wait and see. He does, after all, have the right to see what is his own."

She turned on him, her eyes flashing. "And you, Aled Rhoslyn," she said. "You are supposed to be our leader. You are supposed to be working with the committee to help us make an organized and effective protest against our owners. We have heard nothing yet about what exactly we are supposed to do."

"This is not the time or the place, Marged," he said.

"Then what is the time and where is the place?" she asked. "Tell us that, Aled. And what are we going to do? Pull down tollgates, as is happening elsewhere? It worked three years ago. It is the gates that are the final straw for most of us. And soon it will be time to haul the lime to fertilize our fields. How are we going to afford the tolls?"

"Oh, Marged." Ceris had got to her feet as if she was about to leave, but she sat down abruptly again. "Don't talk of violence, girl. Oh, please don't." She did not look at Aled.

"The committee is working on it," Aled said. "It is not easy. And we should not be talking about it openly here, either. We are having difficulty finding someone to lead such a movement. We need someone to take the part of Rebecca."

"How about you, Aled?" The challenge came from Morfydd Richards, the wife of a farmer three miles off in the hills.

But Aled shook his head, clearly uncomfortable. "I would follow such a movement if it was orderly and the decision of the committee," he said. "I could not lead it, Morfydd. I do not have the gift of authority. Rebecca would have to command a large number of men and that is not an easy thing to do."

"And women, Aled," Marged said. "She would have to command a large number of men *and women*. Is there no one with enough courage, then? Eurwyn would have done it." Her voice was bitter. "Well, I do not believe we should wait for the committee or for Rebecca. I believe we should show our displeasure now. Without any further delay."

"But how, Marged, *fach*?" Ifor asked.

"Oh, no violence, please." Ceris was clearly dismayed.

"One can show displeasure without violence," Marged said. "One can be a nuisance without being violent or unduly destructive. All the milk delivered to Tegfan one day could be sour. Or it could be spilled accidentally from the cart over the front steps and terrace as it is on its way to the kitchen. The stable doors could be left accidentally open one night long enough for all the horses to get out and wander away. A thousand and one things could happen if we had the imagination to dream them up."

There were a few titters of laughter and some open bellows of amusement. And then imaginations began to soar.

"The sheep could break out of the pasture at night and decide to graze on the flower beds."

"There could be spilled tea or pig swill or something by clumsy old us when he comes calling."

"There could be string across the driveway when he is riding down it and some sound to startle his horse to make it break into a gallop. Oh, *Duw*, I would like to see that one."

"Too violent, man, for God's sake. He might break a leg. And the man on his back might land with a thud on his backside."

There was general amusement over this exchange.

"Well?" Marged said. "Who is with me?"

A few people, most notably Ceris, were definitely not. A few were willing to give it a try provided no one's safety was put in jeopardy, including the Earl of Wyvern's. Most were enthusiastically in favor of showing their displeasure and their frustration—and their fear—in some active manner.

Marged, it seemed, was in charge.

Aled advised waiting. "Give it a week or two, Marged," he pleaded. "Perhaps he will change a few things now that he has seen for himself. And perhaps by that time someone will agree to be Rebecca and we can work on a larger scale in a far wider area."

But Marged was not willing to wait. "For more than two years, since Eurwyn's arrest, I have waited," she said quietly, the anger gone, grim determination having taken its place. "For several months, since the formation of the committee and your appointment to it, Aled, I have waited. For almost a week since Geraint Penderyn's return, since the *Earl of Wyvern's* return, I have waited. I have waited long enough."

There was a murmuring of assent from all about her.

"Well." Aled got to his feet. "You will do what you must do, Marged. I will wait to see what the committee decides. Will I walk you home, then, Ceris?"

"No, thank you, Aled." Ceris still did not look directly at him, though she spoke quite firmly. "I will not take you out of your way." She left the schoolroom hurriedly and alone and did not even look at Marged.

If it were not for Geraint Penderyn and his like, Marged thought bitterly, there would not be this unhappiness and this dissension among them. All any of them wanted was peace to live their own lives and to earn an honest and dignified living. But that right was fast being denied them, and she for one was going to see that they did not go under meekly.

It seemed childish to be thinking of tricks to play on the Earl of Wyvern. But they had precious few ways in which to protest.

Chapter 6

Matthew Harley knew that the chapel choir practiced on Thursday evenings. And he knew that Ceris Williams was a member of the choir. He had not arranged to meet her after practice, and he knew that very possibly she would leave with Marged Evans. But he hung about in the village street anyway, on the chance that she would come out alone and would allow him to walk her home.

He was surprised when his hopes were realized.

"Yes, thank you," she said after he had greeted her and offered to see her home.

She even took his arm when he offered it. It was something he had not done during their Sunday walk. These Welsh women, especially these chapel women, were funny. Straitlaced. Skittish.

But he needed a woman, possibly a wife. He did not believe that Ceris Williams, or any other woman on the estate, could be had without marriage, though he had considered Marged Evans. She had been a widow long enough to be restless and might be ripe for a few tumbles. But Marged Evans was not really his type. She was too spirited, too outspoken. Ceris was far more palatable. She was pretty, docile, beddable. And he certainly needed a woman.

Ceris Williams had been the blacksmith's woman, though Harley did not doubt that she was still a virgin. But there had been a break in that courtship recently.

"I enjoyed tea on Sunday," he said, "and our walk."

"Yes." She smiled, though she did not look up at him. "So did I."

"I have hoped," he said, "that you will allow me to call on you again. Will you?"

She did not answer immediately. She was the right height for him, he thought. She made him feel tall. He wished he could take her walking in the hills and have his pleasure of her without having to consider marriage, but he doubted it was possible.

"Yes," she said. "Thank you."

Her unexpected acquiescence was a balm to his bruised feelings. He knew that he was generally disliked on the estate. It was to be expected. He had a job to do and he did it without flinching. Unpopularity had never bothered him. The feeling of power his job gave him had always been adequate compensation. But now he was being threatened. His employer had come from London after two years of showing no interest at all, and he was starting to ask questions, to intrude where he was not needed or wanted.

Harley found it irritating.

"The Earl of Wyvern has been visiting his tenants since his return home," he said. "Has he visited your father?"

"Yes," she said. "He drank tea with us."

"And how does everyone feel about his return?" he asked. He hoped everyone felt as badly about it as he did. Perhaps the earl would return to London if he felt no welcome at all.

But he asked the question idly. Really he was quite happy just to be walking with a woman. With this particular woman.

*   *   *

Geraint walked to church on Sunday morning despite the fact that he had had a great deal of exercise during the morning. Actually it was the *chapel* to which he walked. He was too late for the Anglican service, which started half an hour before the nonconformist one. He convinced himself that it was chasing sheep that had made him late, but if he was honest with himself he would have to admit that he had been looking for some excuse to go to the chapel instead of to the church. The sheep had merely provided the excuse.

He grinned to himself as he strode down the driveway, the wind buffeting him and threatening to dislodge his hat. And he realized that it felt good to smile, to feel amused. Even the wind felt good. There had been precious little to feel cheerful about for the last week, especially the last couple of days.

His gardeners certainly had not been amused to find that a whole flock of sheep had broken out of the pasture during the night and were grazing contentedly on the lawns before the house. He had rather liked the look of them himself when he had gazed down on them from the window of his bedchamber. They had made for a pleasantly rustic scene. But the sight of gardeners and grooms trying to shoo them away and merely causing them to wander in a bewildered circle instead had caused him first to grin and then to pull on his boots to go down there.

It had been his idea to send for the dogs, but only after he had done some sheep chasing himself. And even then he followed the flock and the dogs and the irate head gardener all the way to the pasture and watched the gate being securely shut. It was hard to know how such a secure clasp could have come accidentally undone. Most likely someone had been careless enough to leave the gate unlatched. Or so the gardener had said, menace in his voice. And he would find out who the culprit was too.

Geraint had commented that no harm was done. The sheep had merely been grazing peacefully on the grass. There were no flowers yet for them to destroy. His gardener had given him a hard, tight-lipped, almost pitying look. And the reason was now obvious. As he had set out for church, Geraint had noticed a whole army of gardeners sheepishly scooping up sheep droppings from the sacred expanse of the Tegfan lawn. He grinned again, enjoying the pun.

But he sobered as he reached the village and could see ahead of him along the street several people entering the chapel. This was not going to be easy. He had never attended the chapel as a boy—he had been kicked out of it when he was still inside his mother's womb. Sometimes, unknown to his mother, he had lurked outside it on Sunday mornings, usually to one side or at the back rather than on the street, listening to the singing, learning the hymns, hoping to attract Aled's attention or Marged's when the service was over. He should have hated the chapel, but he had always perversely longed to be a part of it.

He had never attended a service there. And now he felt even more self-conscious than he had expected to feel. His grandfather had always attended the church when he was at Tegfan. It would be assumed that he would do likewise. He would not be welcome here. He had not felt particularly welcome in any of the homes he had visited in the past week. Even Aled had told him it would have been better if he had not come. And now he knew at least some of the reasons for the hostility he had felt everywhere beneath the surface courtesy he had been accorded by everyone—everyone except Marged.

He had a great deal of work ahead of him.

The chapel seemed alarmingly full to him when he stepped into the doorway between it and the porch. He was unaccustomed to seeing churches with apparently no empty pews. But this seemed to be one. There was nowhere to sit. And yet it was too late to retreat. A few heads had turned to see who the newcomer in the doorway was, and without looking directly at anyone, he was aware of eyes widening and eyebrows rising and elbows digging at neighbors. During the few seconds he stood there hesitating, he guessed that at least half the congregation became aware of him. The buzzing of muted chatter diminished significantly.

And then he saw an empty place. Inevitably it was close to the front, no more than three or four pews back. But it was either that or stand where he was through the service or turn and leave. Neither of the last two seemed a viable option. He walked down the aisle.

Throughout his life he had been conspicuous. He had never quite been part of a group. First there had been his outcast nature in Glynderi, then there had been the ghastly years at school, when he had been a Welsh waif among the sons of English gentlemen, and most recently there had been his position as a peer of the realm and one of its most wealthy and propertied members. He was used to being stared at. And yet he could not remember an occasion when he had felt quite so conspicuous or quite so alone.

Instinctively his spine stiffened and his features hardened into impassive and haughty lines.

He seated himself in the empty space next to a woman and stared at the pulpit, willing the Reverend Llwyd to make his appearance soon. He should, he supposed, turn his head casually from side to side and nod affably at any of his people who were looking back at him—it felt as if everyone was. But he felt almost as if his neck would snap in two if he tried turning his head.

And then he became aware, when it was too late to acknowledge the fact naturally, that the woman beside him was Marged. He did not—could not—turn his head to confirm the fact. But he could *feel* that it was so. She was wearing a blue dress. That much he could see out of the corner of his eye. It was absurd that he could not simply turn, nod politely, and face the front again.

At last the minister came from the vestry, the congregation stood, and the pianist thumped out the opening bars of the first hymn. If Geraint had been in any doubt, it fled immediately. Although the whole chapel was suddenly filled with the rich sounds of four-part harmony, the soprano voice of the woman beside him could belong to no one but Marged.

He would not sing himself. *Could* not sing, though he

held a hymnbook open in his hands. Nostalgia, bitterly
sweet, making his throat and his chest ache with unshed
tears, was washing over him.

But I miss the hills. . . .

*Oh, God, oh Duw, I have missed Wales. I have missed
home.*

It seemed to Marged that she had felt nothing but bitter
hatred for a week—since last Sunday when Glenys had
brought the news from Tegfan that the Earl of Wyvern was
home. She pulsed with hatred now and felt all the unhappy
incongruity of such an emotion while she sat in chapel and
tried to concentrate her soul on the love of God.

But she could not feel God. And her body was overpow-
ering her soul. What she could feel was the heat of Geraint
down her left arm and side. When they had sat down after
the first hymn, Mrs. Griffiths on her other side had sat
closer, forcing Marged to sit closer to *him*. She had to be
very careful to keep her arm pressed to her side so that
she would not touch him. But there was the heat of him. And
the smell of him, that same expensive smell she had noticed
at Tŷ-Gwyn. A musky smell. She had not known any man
who wore any sort of cologne. But he did. And yet it was not
a strong perfume and it was definitely not effeminate. It
seemed a part of him and of his undeniable masculinity.

He had been at Tegfan for a week. For a week he had
established his lordship over them all, visiting them dressed
in clothes so splendid that their own shabby garments
appeared mere rags in contrast, treating them to his own
brand of coldness and arrogance that quite put the old earl
in the shade. Yesterday his bailiff and a few of his hefty
servants had called at Glyn Bevan's farm and confiscated
one of his horses and some of his cows because Glyn had
not paid his tithes. How was Glyn to plant his crops without
enough horses? And how was his wife to prepare sufficient
butter and cheese for market without enough cows?

And yet he had dared to come to chapel this morning, to
spoil the one day of the week when they could all come

together to worship and relax and enjoy a friendly chat afterward. And he had dared to sit beside her and ignore her. And ignore everyone else. He had nodded in acknowledgment of her father's greeting from the pulpit, but he had looked neither to left nor to right. He had not joined in the singing. Probably he had forgotten every word of Welsh he had ever known. And yet the whole service was conducted in Welsh—except for that brief greeting to the Earl of Wyvern.

Why had he come? To make them all uncomfortable? He had succeeded.

She noticed, without looking directly at them, that his hands were well cared for, that his fingernails were well manicured. His fingers were long. She could remember telling him as a child that he should be a harpist or a pianist. There had been a great deal of music in him.

And unwillingly she remembered Geraint as he had been, a bold little urchin, always up to mischief either for its own sake or out of necessity. He had explored Tegfan land for the sheer excitement of avoiding the mantraps the gamekeepers set and of evading capture. But he had done it too in order to snare rabbits and catch salmon from the salmon weirs—so that he and his mother would not starve. He had climbed trees and scrambled over fences and bounded across streams and raced up and down hills with energy and a certain wild grace. He had been thin and ragged and frequently hungry and yet had talked ceaselessly and laughed and sung as if he had not had a care in the world. The hungrier he had been, the merrier he had laughed. He had been good at disguising his feelings, at avoiding being pitied.

She had pitied him and admired him and followed him and scolded him and fed him—he had always taken half home to his mother.

She had loved him. She had worshiped and loved him. With the love of one child for another.

He had been taken from a life of indescribable poverty to one of unimagined wealth. He had been taken from her. She had rejoiced for him and wept for herself. She had made excuses for him when he did not write or come home for the holidays—even when word had it that he did not even write to his mother. She had found reasons, good reasons, why he did none of these things. She had continued to love him.

And her love for him had blossomed, briefly and gloriously—and ultimately painfully—into the love of a woman for a man when he had finally come home, grown up and handsome beyond belief and displaying the magical transformation that six years in England had wrought in him.

The pain of that love had never left her. And of his betrayal. It was terribly wrong, she thought, to think of the love of sixteen-year-olds as puppy love, as something less serious than real love, whatever real love was. She had loved Eurwyn. She had grieved terribly at her loss of him. Part of her would always love him and grieve for him. But that love and that grief had not been more painful, for all that, than the first love and the first grief.

That thought, which blossomed into her conscious mind in the middle of her father's sermon, surprised Marged and alarmed her. But it was true, she knew. There was no point in denying it. It was true.

And the object of that first love was seated silently and stiffly at her side. She had loved him from the age of five to the age of sixteen. She had grieved for him for a number of years after that. And now for two years she had hated him. She had hated him in his absence. But the hatred was intensified many times now that he was here in person.

Geraint. Ah, Geraint, how could you have changed so much?

She wondered how much damage the sheep had done. It was a shame it was not later in the year, when there would have been flowers and more destruction to be done. But then she did not want to be destructive or violent. Merely a nuisance. She hoped he had been annoyed. She hoped he would be more than annoyed in the coming days.

The Reverend Llwyd kept Geraint talking at the top of the chapel steps after service was over, and Ninian Williams joined them there. Everyone else stood about in groups in the street, Geraint noticed, as they always had done, though it seemed to him that their gossip was quieter, more self-conscious than it had used to be. It seemed to him that everyone studiously avoided looking at him, as if they were afraid to be caught staring.

It had not been a good idea to come. But he had hoped that by attending chapel he would be able to demonstrate his good will, his desire to be a part of the lives of his people, though he knew that both his strange past and his present position would always keep him apart from them. There could be friendly relations, though, he hoped, as there were on his English estates.

But it was not going to be easy. And perhaps it had been a mistake to come today, so soon. Aled had been right in what he had said. Geraint had spent two days discovering that rents had been raised quite steeply for the past five years in a row. There did not seem to be any good reason for quite such a rise. Matthew Harley, his steward, had explained that there were too many potential farmers in Wales and too few farms. If one could not pay the rent, therefore, there was always another able and willing to do so.

It did not sound like a good enough reason for raising rents. To Geraint it sounded more like greed.

And he had discovered something he was ashamed of not having known sooner. The living of Glynderi parish was in his possession and therefore all its tithes were paid to him. He had a bailiff with a sound reputation for gathering outstanding tithes. Apparently Bryn Jones was the envy of all the neighboring gentry. It seemed to Geraint rather as if he were the beneficiary of double rents. Tithes had originally been devised as a way of financing the church, had they not? Yet almost all the people of Glynderi and its surrounding farmland attended the chapel while almost no one attended the Anglican church and the Earl of Wyvern received the tithes.

Something was wrong. It would have been farcical if it were not also deadly serious.

The road trust that had the responsibility of repairing the roads on his property and the right to set up tollgates was partly owned by the Earl of Wyvern. But for the past two years—since Geraint had inherited the title—the trust had been leased out to a company that could more efficiently look after the roads and collect the tolls. Until the leasehold expired, the earl and the other landowners who held the trust had no control over its operation.

And poaching on Tegfan land was still punishable by transportation. It was still discouraged by the presence of several gamekeepers and the strategic placement of man-traps. The salmon weir on the river as it flowed through the park still hoarded all the salmon for the use of an earl who rarely set foot on the estate and even then was only one man in possession of only one stomach.

His discoveries had shamed Geraint.

He conversed politely with the minister and with Ninian Williams on the chapel steps while he watched Marged talking in a group that included Mrs. Williams, Ceris, and several other women. He wished she was not quite so hostile to him. It would have been good to have two friends here still—Marged and Aled. Though he was not sure of Aled, either. Aled had not come near him this morning.

Someone was calling for silence and waving his arms above his head to draw everyone's attention. Ianto Richards, Geraint saw, one of the farmers he had visited during the week. He was laughing and red-faced.

"Hush this noise for a minute, then, is it?" he said when he had finally succeeded. "And let a man get a word in edgewise. Morfydd's mam is having her eightieth birthday this week on Thursday. And she has not been over the doorstep since last summer on account of her legs. Morfydd and I would be very pleased if you would all come by our house in the evening to help us celebrate. It is choir night, but the choir can practice for Mam to hear. Ninian has offered to carry Marged's harp over. He has not offered to carry Marged, mind."

There was a burst of laughter.

"*Duw,* man, how will you get us all in?" Ifor Davies asked.

"We will squeeze you in with a shoe lift," Ianto said with a laugh. "If everybody will come, we will find room for you all. Won't we, Morfydd, *fach?*"

"We will that," his wife assured everyone, her voice raised loud enough to be heard. "We want every one of you to come. For Mam's sake, is it, then?" Her eyes swept over the crowd and up the steps to include the minister and the other two men standing there. But she looked hastily away when her eyes encountered the earl's.

"And we will all bring food as well, Morfydd," Mrs. Williams said. "It is too much for you to feed all us lot, girl. We will help out, is it? And fancy your mam being eighty already. How time do fly, indeed. She has lived to a good age, mind."

The crowd was beginning to disperse, Geraint noticed. Marged was saying something to the group of women and then she turned away to stride along the street. She was holding her shawl about her shoulders with both hands. The blue dress swayed pleasingly about her hips and legs.

He acted hastily and without any real wisdom, especially considering the fact that there was still a large audience. He touched his hat to the Reverend Llwyd and Ninian Williams, bade them a good morning, though morning had passed into afternoon during the long sermon, skirted around the crowd still standing on the street, and hurried along it, not toward home but away from it in pursuit of Marged.

Chapter
7

He caught up to her at the end of the street just where it became a path proceeding along beside the river. The wind was in their faces. She had not heard him come. She turned a startled face toward him as he fell into step beside her.

"A woman should not be left to walk home from chapel alone," he said.

Her face flushed. But her lips thinned and her eyes grew arctic as he watched. "Thank you," she said to him in English, "but I would prefer to walk alone."

"Than with me," he said. "That is how your sentence ended even if the words were not spoken. What have I done to you, Marged?"

He knew what he had done to her, what he had done to all his dependents. He had made life hard for them, unnecessarily hard. He never behaved hastily. His education and training had taught him that every coin has two sides and that both must be examined with care before one commented on the whole coin. But he would make changes, he was sure of it. He could not imagine finding any reason why he should not. Tegfan was a very prosperous estate. And even if it were not, he was a very wealthy man.

"You have denied me my freedom to walk alone," she said.

"We were friends," he said. "You and Aled were my only friends."

And yet how could he expect either of them to be his friends now? The improbability of it struck him fully even as he spoke. Another thing his training had taught him was that one could expect friendship only from people of one's own station, and sometimes not even from them. There were still men—mostly men he had known at school—who despised his background even though his birth and lineage were impeccable. Though not quite, he supposed. His mother had been a commoner, a mere governess, even if she had been his father's legitimate wife.

"That was a lifetime ago," she said. "Longer even than that."

"It was what happened when I came home?" he asked. "You cannot forgive me for the liberties I tried to take? You were a very desirable girl, Marged."

She laughed, though she did not sound amused. She was matching him stride for stride along the path, he noticed.

"It was a long time ago," he said. "Ten years."

"Yes," she said. "Ten years. Another lifetime."

"Your singing voice has matured," he said, changing the subject. "It is even lovelier than it used to be. *You* are even lovelier than you used to be."

He was not quite sure what he was trying to accomplish. Perhaps he was trying to make her soften, to make her smile, to make her show pleasure in a compliment. But he knew he was being clumsy. He was not usually clumsy with women. Perhaps because he did not usually feel awkward or on the defensive with women.

She stopped walking and turned to him, her back straight, her head thrown back, her face tense with anger.

"What is it that you want?" she asked. "But I need not ask, need I? You think to get from me what you almost got but did not quite get last time you were here? Perhaps if I smile nicely enough it will not even be on the hard ground in the hills as it was then. Perhaps it will be in the earl's feather bed in the earl's grand bedchamber. Or am I being foolish? Whores do not merit being taken to the earl's bed, do they? You will not find whores for your pleasure in this part of the world, *my lord*. You should have stayed in England for that."

He reacted instinctively. He held himself erect and stared at her coldly. "Have a care, Marged," he said, his voice quiet and under rigid control, "and remember to whom you speak."

But she was not to be cowed. "Oh, I do not forget," she said, her voice a passionate contrast to his own. "I do not forget who you are, my lord. Murderer!" She turned with a swish of her skirts and started up the path toward Tŷ-Gwyn and the hills.

He did not pursue her farther. He stood looking after her, startled and frowning. *Murderer?* She might have called him a number of derogatory things with some justification, but he had certainly not expected that. It sounded very dramatic, but it had no meaning. She was obviously very angry over something, though, and there was no point in following her. There was no chance of holding a rational conversation with her in her present mood.

He turned around and stood staring down into the water of the river for several minutes. Marged had always been one to espouse a cause, especially when it was more someone else's cause than her own. She was probably angry over the way he was squeezing every last penny out of his people, herself included. He could hardly blame her. And he would not use ignorance as an excuse, even to himself.

He would change a few things after a little more careful investigation, and then perhaps he would redeem himself somewhat in her eyes.

He wanted to redeem himself, he thought. Especially in Marged's eyes. He had had mistresses and flirts in the past ten years. Twice he had considered marriage. Once he had been on the very brink of making his offer. But he had loved only once in his life. And could love very easily again.

The same woman.

The realization surprised him. And disturbed him.

She was right. He wanted to bed her. But he wanted to impress her too. He wanted her respect and her liking and her friendship. And perhaps more than that again.

But she hated him. Perhaps for personal reasons, perhaps for broader reasons. And she had called him a murderer. What the devil had he murdered in her life? Her faith in him?

Could one restore faith when it had once been lost?

One could but try, he supposed.

He had been *flirting* with her. He had walked at her side, his body straight like an iron bar, his face like granite, his blue eyes roaming over her as if she had no clothes on, and he had paid her those ridiculous compliments.

Were English ladies so easily pleased, so easily deceived? So easily seduced? For flirtation was too mild a word. He had been attempting seduction, just as he had ten years ago. Except that she was no longer the naive girl she had been then. Not by any means.

How dare he. Oh, how dare he!

He had known exactly what he was doing, sitting next to her in chapel without a word or a glance in her direction, just letting her feel his warmth and smell his expensive cologne. He was a master seducer—he had improved in ten years. He must have known that tension had built in her to such a degree that she could not afterward say even what the text of her father's sermon had been, let alone its contents. She could not even remember what hymns they had sung, even though she had chosen them herself last week.

Marged fumed for the rest of the day. She could do little else. It was Sunday. No unessential work could be done on a Sunday. While she had lived at home with her father, there were not even any hot meals on Sunday and no dishes were washed. Sunday was a day of rest, a day in which to recoup one's energies for the hard week ahead.

After dinner, when Gran was already nodding in the inglenook by the fire and Mam was settling opposite her, Marged drew her shawl over her shoulders and went out walking. She took some Welsh cakes with her, freshly baked the day before, and some butter and cheese, and strode upward into the higher hills until she was on the bare moors. They had been common ground once upon a time. All the farmers had grazed their flocks there during the summer. Now they belonged to Tegfan, and only Tegfan sheep were allowed to fatten themselves on their scrubby grass.

But there were buildings up there too, if they could be dignified by such a name, ugly little sod huts with sparse thatch to keep out the cold and rain. There were not many, fortunately, but enough to testify to poverty and despair and suffering. Their inhabitants usually left for the workhouse eventually.

The Parrys had never been good farmers. Eurwyn had often used to cluck his tongue over the inefficiency and waste and lack of organization so evident on their farm. They had never been prosperous. But they had not been bad people, either. They had been honest and proud and there had always been love within the family.

Now they were living on the moors and there were not many farmers in a financial situation to be able to offer Waldo Parry any regular employment. There were three children, and Mrs. Parry was expecting another. It was one more evidence of their impracticality, Marged thought. The new baby must have been conceived after they were forced off their farm. But then, who was she to condemn an unhappy man and woman for indulging one of the few pleasures left to them?

Marged felt the old pang of regret that in five years of marriage and almost nightly intimacies she had never conceived a child of her own. She suppressed it, as she always did.

She made her deliveries, sat for a while with Mrs. Parry

while one of the little girls hovered at her side and then climbed onto her lap, and continued on her walk. She strode across the moors, breathing in the spring air, gazing about her at hills that stretched to the farthest horizon in all directions. The hills of home. She could not imagine living anywhere else. The hills were a part of her.

She missed Eurwyn with a sudden pang so intense that she stopped walking and closed her eyes. She missed Eurwyn and she missed being married. She had never felt any wild passion for her husband, but she had liked him and admired him and loved him too. She had liked those brief nightly intimacies. They had become very much a routine part of her life, not consciously enjoyed, though never disliked either.

It was a part of her life that had ended when Eurwyn was taken from her. Now sometimes she tossed in her bed, unable to sleep, yearning for the physical touch of her man. And now at this moment she yearned. She ached. Not just in her emotions but in her body. Her breasts felt tender and her thighs ached and she throbbed in that place where Eurwyn had joined his body to hers for a few minutes each night.

Oh, Eurwyn, I want you back. I need you, cariad.

What had brought that on? she wondered, opening her eyes and walking resolutely onward. She had put grief and longing behind her long ago. They were destructive emotions when carried on too long. There was too much living to be done to bury oneself in the past.

But she knew what had brought it on. Geraint Penderyn, the Earl of Wyvern. Who had killed Eurwyn and asked her only this morning what he had done to her. Who had tried ten years ago to seduce her and had tried again just this morning. Who had . . . Ah, there was no point in enumerating his offenses over and over again.

Sheep let loose on his lawn! It was a pitiful protest. If only Aled and his committee would get moving. If only they could find a Rebecca. Did no man have Eurwyn's courage?

And then she saw that she was not the only person strolling in the upper hills. A young man and woman were

walking toward her some distance away, hand in hand until
they spotted her and released each other. Foolish people, she
thought. As if she would mind seeing such an innocent sign
of affection.

They were Glenys Owen and one of the grooms from
Tegfan. Marged did not know his name—he was not from
Glynderi. And it was obvious from Glenys's flushed face
and the indefinable air of dishevelment about both of them
that they had been indulging in a little more than just
walking. Marged smiled and greeted them and could feel
only envy. Her father often preached from the pulpit about
the wicked hills. Hasty marriages following upon summer
courtships in the hills were far from uncommon. But
Marged was envious.

And then she had a thought. She did not know where it
came from unless it was the sight of Glenys combined with
her angry thoughts about Geraint and the recent memory of
her accusing him of being unwilling to take his whores to
the earl's bed.

The earl's bed.

"Glenys!" She turned and called after the disappearing
couple, who were hand in hand again, she noticed.

They both turned to gaze back at her.

"Glenys," she called. "May I have a word with you?"

Marged had once taught Glenys in Sunday school. The
girl had shown little aptitude for reading, but she had been
sweet and affectionate and had often stayed after the other
children to chatter about nothing in particular. She came
back now toward Marged. Her young man stayed where he
was.

It was a foolish idea. But then all ideas for making
nuisances of themselves to the Earl of Wyvern were foolish
ones. Until there was a Rebecca, they could do little else but
annoy him.

"Glenys," she said, "do you ever have reason to go to the
Earl of Wyvern's bedchamber?"

Glenys stared blankly at her. It really was a stupid

question. Fortunately the girl did not read any meaning into the unintentionally suggestive query.

"Oh, no," she said. "I am just a kitchen maid, Mrs. Evans."

"But you know where it is, his bedchamber?" Marged felt herself flushing.

"Yes," the girl said, frowning.

No, it would not do. She should have thought more carefully before calling Glenys back so impulsively. It would be asking too much. Even if the girl did have reason to go near his room on occasion, it would be dangerous. She might be caught red-handed, or else it might be traced back to her. No, the idea was not a good one at all. Not as good as tomorrow's. Tomorrow there was to be a large delivery of coal to Tegfan. But that coal, every lump of it, was to suffer an accident on his lordship's driveway. It was to be spilled out in every direction.

She smiled in some embarrassment at Glenys. "It does not matter," she said. Unless . . . It was madness. Sheer madness. But sometimes madness was necessary when there were great injustices to be fought. That was what she could remember Eurwyn saying on one occasion. "No, wait."

Glenys, half turned back to her young man, looked politely at her.

"Glenys," she said, "could you show me where his bedchamber is? Could you show me how to reach it? Without being seen?" She listened to her own words, appalled.

"His lordship's bedchamber?" Glenys sounded mystified, as well she might.

"You have heard about the sheep?" Marged asked. "Your brothers must have told you, I am sure. They were both with me last night. And you were in chapel this morning."

Glenys smiled, her eyes dancing with amusement. "We all thought Mr. Vaughan would start foaming at the mouth this morning," she said, naming Tegfan's head gardener.

"But none of us knew that the sheep did not get out by accident. There is a good joke it was, Mrs. Evans."

"There will be more," Marged said. "You heard too what happened to Glyn Bevan yesterday?"

Glenys sobered. "Yes," she said. "Oh, I do hate that Mr. Jones, I do. He loves his job. A person ought not to love such a job."

"No," Marged said. "Can you show me the room and the way to it, Glenys? Without getting yourself into any trouble at all? It will be just another joke, I promise."

Glenys swallowed and then nodded.

Marged laughed as they parted a couple of minutes later. "Watch for the coal delivery tomorrow," she said. "It should be amusing."

But it was not amusement she wanted to feel. And indeed it was not amusement she felt. It was excitement. And determination. Soon he would know that it was not just a series of clumsy accidents that was making his life less than comfortable. Soon he would know himself to be the victim of hatred.

It would happen the night they planned to let the horses out of the stables. Friday night. She would do it that same night. Before the night was over he would know.

Finally Marged directed her steps downward. It must be almost teatime.

It was not a good week for Geraint.

He talked to his steward, and Matthew Harley chose to be indignant and to take offense at the suggestion that there was something wrong at Tegfan and on its farms. He pointed out that the estate was the most prosperous in West Wales and was the envy of every other landowner. He explained with some pride that other stewards and even some landowners had visited him to ask his advice on a wide range of topics concerning estate management. He pointed out that tithes and road trusts and the poor rate were beyond his power to control but that rents certainly were not. By raising rents annually, he had ensured the continued prosperity of Tegfan and the continued superiority of the farms.

"How so?" Geraint asked, questioning that last point.

There were many more farmers than there was land for them to rent. It was a competitive business. If a man with land could not afford his rent, he was proving that he was a poor manager. It made perfect business sense to see that he was replaced by a better man. The knowledge that they might be replaced by someone better able to run their farms was incentive enough to keep everyone working hard.

It sounded reasonable. It sounded admirable. But Geraint had always suspected that business was often an impersonal thing, ignoring the human factor. He could not shake from his mind the image of Idris Parry, thin and ragged and poaching on his land. And the memory of what it felt like to live in stark, frightening poverty.

He talked to his neighbors. One of them, who was also in full possession of the tithes of his parish, stared at him in incomprehension when Geraint raised the matter. Tithes were a part of the whole establishment of the church. Church and state would collapse without them. And if one man refused to collect them on the grounds that he did not need them, then the whole fabric of society might crumble.

"One might almost call such a man a traitor," the neighbor said severely.

It seemed extravagant to Geraint. But it was a disturbing idea that perhaps he was not free to act alone on a matter because it was something that concerned the whole of society. Perhaps at least he could see that the tithes were spent on the church—or, better still, on the chapel.

And all his neighbors were agreed that rising rents were desirable for all concerned. They trotted out arguments so exactly like Harley's that Geraint realized anew why he was so envied in his steward. He could find no one sympathetic to the idea of lowering rents or at least freezing them for a few years until there had been a few good years for crops and until the demands of the market had improved.

"It is a mad idea and one you had better not institute,

Wyvern," Sir Hector Webb told him sharply. "You would not be popular with your relatives and friends, and your tenants would see you only as a weak man. They would not respect you for it."

"It is just the sort of thing I would expect you to suggest," Lady Stella said coldly. "You are still one of them at heart, are you not, Wyvern? But you must remember that according to Papa's will, I will inherit Tegfan if you fail to marry and produce a legitimate heir." She put slight emphasis on the adjective.

"Your aunt is right, Wyvern," Sir Hector told him. "I would not take kindly to your wasting her inheritance."

Geraint merely nodded. He refrained from arguing or from reminding them that he was only twenty-eight years old and perhaps capable of producing a dozen sons.

Life was not going to be easy.

Chapter

8

He sought out Aled again, early one evening, entering the forge just when Aled was finishing work for the day and dismissing his apprentice. They walked into the park of Tegfan as they had before.

"You were right," he said, bringing to an end the meaningless exchange of talk that had occupied them for a few minutes. "Things have not been well done since I inherited Tegfan. And I cannot plead ignorance, though I have been deliberately ignorant. My problem now is seeing a solution."

Aled maintained a silence.

Geraint told him about his visits to his neighbors. "And it seems that I have no power over the road trusts at all," he ended by saying. "Although I draw lease money from them, their actions are beyond my control. And even when the lease is due for renewal, mine is only one voice among many. I would be outvoted."

Aled still said nothing and Geraint sighed.

"But the problem is mine, not yours," he said. "You do not have a great deal of respect for me, do you, Aled?"

His friend shrugged and looked intensely embarrassed. "I can understand your situation well enough to know that I would not wish to be in your shoes," he said.

"I will do what I can," Geraint said. "When rent day approaches I shall do my best to see that there are no raises at the Tegfan farms." He sighed. "But that will help only a few farmers out of hundreds in this part of Wales. It is a problem not only here but all over, is it?"

"Yes," Aled said shortly.

"And what happens," Geraint asked, "to the farmers who are driven off their land when they cannot afford the rents? They have to become laborers? They are employed on my own lands? Foolishly it is a question I have not yet asked Harley."

"Perhaps it is he you should ask, then, Ger," Aled said.

Geraint nodded. But he had a sudden thought. "You know a family by the name of Parry?" he asked. "They live up on the moors, I believe."

"Yes," Aled said, his jawline tightening. "I know them."

"It is a last resort, moving up there," Geraint said, "as I know from experience. What happened to them?"

He was afraid that he knew the answer. He almost wished he had not asked.

"Not all of them find work as your laborers," Aled said dryly.

Geraint closed his eyes and balled his hands into fists at his sides. "I will do something," he said after a few moments of silence. "Before rent day comes along there will be some changes. I am very much the enemy, aren't I?"

"The numbers of those who were prepared to give you a chance has dwindled since the incident with Glyn Bevan," Aled said. "It was not well done, Ger. He has little ones."

"Glyn Bevan?" Geraint asked with some dread.

"A farmer cannot last very long when his horses and his cattle are taken from him," Aled said, "and all in the name of a church he does not even attend."

Tithes? But Geraint would not even ask what had happened. Obviously it was something that must have occurred since his own return to Tegfan, and therefore it was something he ought to know about. It seemed that his estate was running very well without him. He was almost superfluous—as he had set out to be two years ago, of course, when he had realized he was the owner of land he had poached on as a child. Land that brought back memories he did not want to harbor.

Yes, there were going to have to be some changes.

"Aled," he asked, "what do you know about the, er, accidents that have been happening during the past week?"

"Accidents?" Aled looked instantly wary.

"Sheep grazing on the lawn before Tegfan," Geraint said. "Coal tipped all over the driveway. Milk spilled all over the terrace. Mice in the dining room during dinner and the cat just happening to have escaped from the kitchen."

"I imagine they are just that," Aled said. "Accidents, man. They happen—even to peers of the realm."

"I have the feeling," Geraint said, "that the list is going to get longer as the days go on."

His friend shrugged and Geraint nodded.

"At least," he said, "whoever is organizing them appears to have a sense of humor. At least no hayricks have been burned yet. Rebecca does not roam these parts, Aled?"

His friend looked startled. "Rebecca?" he said. "Who is she?"

"If I did not know you," Geraint said, "I would be under the impression that you are remarkably stupid, Aled. But I do know you. I would say conditions are ripe in these parts for her visits. Would you not agree?"

But Aled was tight-lipped again.

"Perhaps she has some justification too," Geraint said. "But I would not take kindly to her visits. Perhaps you know someone to whom to pass along that message, Aled."

"No," his friend said. "I don't."

"If I were not who I am," Geraint said, his voice brooding, "I might even follow her myself. Make myself into one of her daughters, perhaps. It is just the sort of thing I would have done as a boy, isn't it? No, not quite. When I was a boy it would have been more like me to be Rebecca herself. With you as one of my daughters." He grinned, but Aled was not amused. His face had paled.

"It is no joking matter," he said. "Anyone who dares to be Rebecca has an instant price on his head. He is in danger of capture by the law and of betrayal by his followers. But yes, it is just the sort of thing you would have done. Thank goodness it is impossible."

Geraint laughed. "You sound as if you care, Aled," he said. "I was beginning to wonder. And *is* it impossible? Maybe that is just what this whole impossible situation needs, someone from my side to come over to your side—it *is* your side, isn't it?—and force the issue a bit."

"You are mad." Aled bent down, scooped up a clump of soft earth, and threw it at his friend. It hit his shoulder and scattered down the front of his coat.

"Man," Geraint said, brushing at himself and making the mess worse, "I should have you arrested for assaulting a peer of the realm. Or perhaps I should merely let my valet loose on you. I had better let you go home for your dinner. You are not quite comfortable with me, are you? But you are too loyal to an old friend to give me the cold shoulder." He grinned. "So you give me a slightly muddy one instead."

"It will give your valet something to do to earn his living," Aled said, grinning too.

"Shall I tell him it was another, ah, accident?" Geraint asked, and they both chuckled.

He watched Aled make his way back to the village and still brushed absently at his coat. They had ended their encounter on a light note, both sensing perhaps that their friendship was treading thin ice. And it was very obvious that Aled knew all about the accidents that were not accidents at all. Geraint hoped somehow that his friend was not involved in them. They were a nuisance more than anything, but they disturbed him because they suggested that there were people who did not like him. An understatement, doubtless.

More disturbing, perhaps, was the knowledge that at the moment he did not much like himself.

For years, all through his school days, he had wished fervently that the old earl, his grandfather, had never discovered that his birth had been legitimate. He had often yearned to have his old life back, poverty and moorland hovel and near starvation and all. And to have his mother back. He had loved his mother with a fierce protectiveness. Those years had passed. He had grown accustomed to his new life and eventually he had come to like it, to identify fully with it.

Today, now, this moment was the first time in years he had wished he could go back. He had come to see privilege as responsibility too. One did not feel guilty about a privileged life when one also accepted the responsibilities that came with it. He had thought that he had done so. But he could see now that he had not at Tegfan. It had not been enough to appoint an efficient steward. He had abdicated his responsibilities and people had suffered as a consequence. And yet he saw now more than ever before that people of his class could not act as individuals for all their privileges. If they did not act as a class, as a unit, they might all crumble.

He did not feel proud of his class at that moment. And he did not particularly want to belong to it. He felt a strong nostalgia for those childhood days when only his own survival and his mother's had been of importance to him.

Yes, he thought, he could not blame these people—*his* people—for disliking him. If he were still one of them, he would dislike him too. And he might well decide to do something about it. Help accidents to happen, perhaps. Or worse. If he were one of them, perhaps he really would lead them as Rebecca to larger, more organized, more forceful protests.

If he were one of them.

But he was not.

He turned his steps toward the house, feeling a growlingly familiar weight of depression. And he thought about

Aled and their strained friendship. And about Marged and her open hostility.

And about an eightieth birthday party to which he had inadvertently been invited. Tomorrow evening, he thought. Everyone in the community had been invited. Marged was to be there with her harp.

Marged.

In what hidden corner of his heart had he been carrying her for ten years?

Life was hard on the farms of Carmarthenshire. Each part of the year and, indeed, each part of the day brought its chores, enough to occupy both men and women, and often children too. And there was always the weather to contend with, and always the threat of poverty and possible ruin to bring constant anxiety. The spirits of the farmers and their wives and of other workmen had been bowed over the years. But not broken.

They believed strongly in community and in chapel and in music. They knew how to enjoy themselves when the opportunity presented itself.

Old Mrs. Howell, Morfydd Richards's mother, had raised eight children, not counting the two who had died in infancy, and had worked side by side with her husband on their farm. For years she had been the leading contralto in chapel and for years she had brought home the solo prize for contraltos at every *eisteddfod* within a radius of twenty miles from Glynderi. For years there had been no Welsh cakes and no *bara brith* to match hers. Her talents as a cook were largely responsible for the fact that her husband had been almost as round as he was tall, people had used to say with affectionate humor. And no other woman had been able to spin wool quite as good as Mrs. Howell's.

Her eightieth birthday was something to celebrate. There was scarcely an able-bodied adult or child who did not trudge to the Richards's farmhouse in the hills above the river three miles from the village on the Thursday evening. And a merry gathering it was too, even though there were scarcely enough chairs to accommodate the elderly and scarcely enough space to hold everyone else standing.

"But never mind, though," Dylan Owen said, setting an arm about Ceris Williams's shoulders. "It do give one an excuse to get fresh."

There was a great deal of chuckling as Ceris smiled and ducked out of the way.

"We could all get inside tidy, mind, Ianto," Ifor Davies said, laughing, "if we moved the table outside."

But there was a chorus of protests. The table was laden with food to such a degree that plates had to overlap one another. Mrs. Howell and Morfydd had been baking for two days, and not a woman guest had arrived without at least one plate of baking in each hand.

The farmers and their families ate sparingly and plainly throughout the year, but they knew what was due a party. They knew how to feast when there was good reason for a feast.

"Or if we put Marged's harp in with the cows," Eli Harris suggested.

"Don't listen to him, Marged," Olwen Harris said, digging an ample elbow into her husband's ribs. "Eli do love a little bit of harp music. All the way up here he has been saying that if no one else brought it down for you, he would."

"It was brought here at my request," Mrs. Howell said from her place of honor beside the fire. "We will have music tonight and song to raise the thatch off the roof. Sing for our supper it will be, is it?"

Mari Bevan slapped the back of her young son's hand as it tried to slide a jam tart off the table.

"Ow, Mam," he protested.

"It is a good thing this room is crowded," Glyn Bevan said sternly from some distance away. "It would be your backside getting tanned if I were over by there, boy."

Idris Parry, invisible beneath the white cloth that covered the table and fell over its sides almost to the floor, licked the jam out of his own tart and caught crumbs of pastry with his free hand.

"I hear you are going into the business of catching and caging mice, Dewi," Ifor Davies said to Dewi Owen, Dylan and Glenys's brother. "It will make your fortune, will it?"

There was a general burst of laughter.

"A pity you lost them under the table at Tegfan, mind," Ifor said. "I hear that the old cat there had a decent supper."

The laughter grew louder and merrier.

But the Reverend Llwyd cut it short. "It has come to my attention," he said, raising both arms, not an easy feat in the crowded farm kitchen, "that certain members of my congregation have taken it upon themselves to show the Earl of Wyvern that he is not welcome here. You must know that I am as unhappy as anyone to see that he has been acting with some greed in the past few years, but what he has done is his lawful right. It is not our lawful right to punish him."

"It *is* our lawful right as Britons, Reverend," Aled Rhoslyn said as Marged drew breath to make some retort, "to be free to live our lives without fear of ruin and starvation and to earn our living with the honest labor of our own hands. When those in power try to deny us that right, then we have the right to assert ourselves."

"Here, here," someone said.

"Amen," someone else said.

There were murmurings of assent from all around.

"*Duw,* Aled," Ifor Davies said, "I thought you were Penderyn's friend. I saw you go off walking in the park together just yesterday."

"I was not talking about anyone in particular," Aled said. "I was talking about those in power. That nameless mass of aristocrats and gentry who believe we exist only for the purpose of making them richer. Perhaps some of them, some individuals, might change if they can see what is happening, if they can see that we are people."

"No," Marged said fiercely. "They are all the same, Aled. And it is time that we showed them we can be pushed only so far and no farther."

"I can be pushed as far as a tollgate," someone said. "I pay my rent and my tithes and my taxes, and then I find I cannot even travel the roads about my home without paying for the privilege. I do not know where the money is going to come from to haul the lime when May comes. There is almost no butter to sell and no one to sell it to."

"And you would have to pay the tolls in order to take it to market and to bring yourself and your horse and cart home," someone else added.

"It is the gates we want down," a third man said over the swell of grumblings around him. "Gates first, I say. And if the idea of getting together all the farmers of this part of Carmarthenshire to do so is not going to work, then maybe I will have to start doing it myself."

"It will not come to that, Trevor," Aled said. "The committee has a definite plan, with dates and places set and which gates are to go first. Give it another week or two, man, and we will be on the march. All the men here who want to join us will have the chance, and a few hundred men from other places too."

"And women, Aled," Marged said. "It will not be all men. When the first gate is pulled down, I am going to be there."

"Oh, hush, Marged," Ceris said, obviously close to tears. She turned and pushed her way past neighbors and friends until she could let herself out through the door.

"It was well said," the Reverend Llwyd said, his eyes on fire as he gazed at the closed door. "It is the God-given function of women to give life and nurture it, not to destroy. And it is not the work of men to destroy, either, even when what they destroy is wicked. The Lord will punish wickedness in his own good time. 'Vengeance is mine, saith the Lord.'"

"Well, the Lord is a little slow for me, Dada," Marged said.

Everyone packed into the room looked from one to the other with interest. Their minister and his daughter often disagreed in public. They were alike in many ways, but it was a likeness that led to certain conflict. Their opinions on most topics differed.

However, enjoyment of the scene was cut short when a knock on the door heralded a late arrival. Silence, at first incredulous and then decidedly uncomfortable, spread through the Richards's farm kitchen when the woman closest to the door opened it and the Earl of Wyvern stepped inside.

It was all intensely embarrassing, as he had known it would be. All the way up the hill his steps had lagged. He knew that he would not be welcome. If he had not known it a week ago, he knew it now. And it was worse even than he had thought.

Yesterday he had sent food up to the Parrys—he had found himself unable to go in person. And with the messenger he had sent a request for Parry to present himself to his steward for work as a laborer on the home farm. Harley had explained that it was not his policy to hire on farmers who had lost their farms, since that very fact usually indicated that they were indolent men. But Geraint had fixed him with a blue stare and pointed out that this would be one exception.

The food had been sent back and with it a polite refusal of the offer of work. Waldo Parry, it seemed, was not a man who accepted charity. Or not at least from the man who had destroyed him in the first place, Geraint thought. He had been puzzled and angered—until he remembered that on the few occasions when the old earl had sent clothes and food to his mother, she had always returned them even though she and her son might be shivering in rags and have stomachs painful with emptiness. She would not accept charity from a man who would not acknowledge that she was his lawful daughter-in-law and Geraint his lawful grandson, she had explained on one such occasion, hugging him in her thin arms and shedding tears against his cheek.

His other attempt yesterday at showing goodwill had failed just as miserably. He had pondered long and hard the idea of sending back the horses and cows that had been confiscated from Glyn Bevan—it *had* happened since his return to Tegfan, he was ashamed to discover—and had rejected it. It might set up all sorts of confusion in the minds of the rest of the farmers and might justifiably infuriate those who had paid their tithes. Instead he had sent a message informing the farmer that he might borrow free of charge the services of one of the Tegfan workhorses at seeding time and harvest and whenever else he had need of it.

It had been a clumsy move, he had to admit now. But it had been a sincere attempt to try to alleviate suffering that he was at least partly responsible for causing. The answer had come. Glyn Bevan would not have occasion to make use of any his lordship's property or possessions, thank you kindly.

They complained of his treatment of them, Geraint thought in a flash of anger and frustration, but they would not allow him to make amends.

But he was not going to go away. And he was not going to hide away either. Help them he would, one way or another. Things were going to change on the Tegfan estate and on the estates around it if he had any say in the matter.

And so he went to Mrs. Howell's birthday party. He had, after all, been included in the invitation, even if his inclusion had been unintentional. And even if he had not, surely it was the correct thing to do for a landlord to pay his respects to a woman on such a landmark occasion.

Marged was to be there, he thought as he approached the house. The thought had been there, hovering in the back of his mind, ever since he had decided to come. She would have nothing to do with him. It would be far better for his peace of mind to stay away from places where she was likely to be. But he knew that it was the sure knowledge she would be there that had influenced his decision to come.

He would see her again—in a place where perhaps she could not openly snub him. Though one never quite knew with Marged.

Even then, when he reached the farmhouse, he was not

sure he would have had the courage to go inside. He paused outside the door, hearing the sound of voices. But then he saw, out of the corner of his eye, the fluttering of fabric. He turned his head to see that someone was standing at the far side of the farmyard, close to the chicken coop. A small woman. Ceris Williams, he believed, though he could not see quite clearly in the darkness. But she had seen him and curtsied to him. He inclined his head in return.

And so he had no alternative but to lift his hand and knock on the door. And when it opened and he saw the kitchen crammed with people, all of them with turned heads to see who the late arrival was and all of them falling silent with amazement and embarrassment, his course was set. He had to step inside, take off his hat, and acknowledge with nods all those whose eyes he met.

Chapter
9

He had spoiled the party, he thought a few minutes later after Ianto Richards had rescued him by coming forward to welcome him. He made his way to the fireplace where Mrs. Howell was seated—a path opened before him as if by magic—and wished her a happy birthday and talked to her with the conversational skill learned long ago and practiced so often that it had become almost second nature to him. And then the Reverend Llwyd was at his side and engaging him in conversation.

The silence had dissolved into the buzz of conversation again. But it was a self-conscious conversation, Geraint thought. For such a large gathering and such an occasion, and in the presence of such a feast as he could see loaded onto the table, it did not appear to be a merry party. It had been before his arrival, he would wager, and would continue to be after he took his leave.

He must take his leave. He had done his duty. He had made his point. Now it was time to leave the occupants of the house to enjoy themselves. Aled, he noticed, had kept his distance and had kept his eyes averted. Some friend he was.

He remembered suddenly running home to the moors one day, excited with the news that there had been a wedding in the chapel and that everyone was going to the house of the bride's father to feast. There had been two long tables of food set up outside the house. He had managed to snatch up a large bun that had fallen to the ground and Mr. Williams had spied him and tossed him a handful of small coins. He had shown his mother his treasures and had broken the bun carefully in half to share with her.

It was almost the only occasion when he had seen his mother cry. She had sat holding him, telling him about the parties she had attended as a girl, when she had been the daughter of the minister—the one who had preceded the Reverend Llwyd. They had been the most wonderful of occasions, she had told him, pain and wistfulness in her voice. Not only because of the food and the merriment, but because of the laughter and the company and the wonderful sense of belonging, of being with people who cared.

Yes, he thought now. He had been outcast then because the people who cared had put limits on their caring, cutting off those they believed had transgressed their stern moral code. And he was outcast now—perhaps more justifiably so. But even so, he had tried and was trying to show friendship and the willingness to reach out in sympathy and they were giving him no chance.

But before he had the opportunity to take his leave, Mrs. Howell spoke up.

"Marged, *fach*," she said, "sit down at your harp, girl. It is time for the singing. A few folk songs on your own, is it? And then we will have a *gymanfa ganu,* a singing together. We will sing to be heard across the hills. We will sing to be heard by Eurwyn's gran, who cannot travel any more than I can these days, and by his mam, who stayed at home to keep her company. Come, *fach*."

Marged smiled and kissed her cheek before seating

herself and drawing the harp toward her. She completely
ignored him, Geraint noticed, though he was standing close.

"I would rather have the *gymanfa ganu* right away, Mrs.
Howell," she said. "But for you I will sing folk songs."

She spoke in Welsh, the first that had been spoken since
Geraint's arrival. Aled was the only one—and Idris—with
whom he had spoken Welsh since his return to Tegfan.
Perhaps everyone thought that he had forgotten the language he had heard and spoken every day for his first twelve
years. Marged's choice of language now was perhaps a
deliberate snub.

He knew that her singing voice was still lovely. He had
heard it in chapel on Sunday. But there was something about
harp music and something about the Welsh folk songs she
chose that made it sound hauntingly lovely tonight. He
listened enraptured and felt again that tightening in his chest
and aching in his throat. Had he really believed until very
recently that he could live happily in England for the rest of
his life? Had he really believed that he could ignore his
Welsh heritage?

Had he really believed that Marged was just a bittersweet
memory of his past?

He stayed for the *gymanfa ganu* even though he kept
telling himself that he should leave so that everyone else
could relax and enjoy the singing and the feast that was to
follow it. He kept telling himself that he would stay and
listen to just one more hymn—he would not sing himself,
though he remembered the tunes and even most of the
words. But the harmony all about him was just too soothing
to his rough and battered nerves. And after a while everyone
seemed to forget his presence and relax anyway.

Aled slipped outside during the singing. He stood quietly
outside the door for a while, allowing his eyes to grow
accustomed to the dark. She might have gone home, but he
did not think she would do that without a word to her
mother and father. And then he saw the lightness of her

dress down by the gate leading into the pasture. She was standing with her arms along it, her back to him.

"Ceris," he said softly as he came up behind her. He did not want to startle her.

She set her forehead down between her hands and said nothing.

"You will be cold," he said. He noticed for the first time that she had not brought her cloak with her. He shrugged out of his coat and set it about her shoulders. She whirled around then, perhaps to shrug free of his coat. But he did not drop his arms. He kept them about her and tightened them, bringing her close against him. She did not struggle. She rested her forehead against his chest and sighed.

He turned his head to rest his cheek against the top of her head. It had been so long.

"There is one thing I regret more than anything else in my life," he said. "I should not have been so concerned about paying off my father's debts and getting the business back on its feet before marrying you. I should have listened to you when you pleaded with me to marry you, poverty and all. You would have been my wife now. We would have had some little ones together."

She did not say anything for a long while. He held her to him, listening to the singing from inside the house, feeling that happiness was this, this fleeting moment. And unhappiness was the same moment.

"I am glad you were so stubborn," she said. "I am glad we never married, Aled."

He swallowed awkwardly. "I love you, *cariad*," he said.

"No," she said. "It is something other than love that rules your life, Aled. It is hatred and the desire for revenge. It is the desire for destruction and violence."

"It is the desire for a better life," he said, "and the conviction that we have a right to it. It is the belief that I owe it to myself and to my neighbors and to my unborn children—if ever I have any—to do something to bring about that better life. It is something I cannot allow others to do for me, *cariad*."

"Neither could Eurwyn," she said bitterly. "But he died and left Marged and his mam and gran to manage without him. And no one has a better life as a result of what he did."

He lifted one hand to cup the back of her head. "It is what you are afraid of?" he asked softly. "That I will die and leave you alone? It is better, you think, not to marry me and not to have my little ones if I recklessly court death?"

She was crying then and trying to pull away from him. But his arms closed about her like iron bands. And he kissed the top of her head, the wet cheek that was exposed to him, and finally the wet face she lifted to him. He kissed her mouth with hunger, parting her lips with his own.

"Tell me you love me," he whispered against her lips. "It has been so long since I heard you say the words. Tell me I am your *cariad*."

But she struggled then and freed herself and turned back to face the gate, his coat held about her shoulders with both her hands.

"No," she said. "You are not my love, Aled. And I do not believe Marged is my friend any longer. I am sorry for it. Marged is causing mischief and you are talking of breaking down tollgates with perhaps hundreds of men to make a mob. Someone will get hurt. It may be you or it may be Marged. But worse, it may be someone else, hurt because of you or Marged. I cannot love you any longer. No, let me put it differently. I *will* not love you any longer. But you knew that. We have argued it out before. Let there be an end now. No more scenes like this. It is over."

"And yet," he said, "you still love me."

"You were not listening." She released her hold on his coat and let it slide to the ground.

"Ah, yes," he said sadly, "I was, *cariad*."

She said nothing more. And he could think of nothing more to say either. She would not give up her conviction that protest and violence were never justified, and he would not give up his conviction that they were and that if he wanted to see change and thought someone should do something about effecting it, then he must be willing to do his part. He could no longer stand back and let the Eurwyns of this world do his fighting for him. He must fight for himself.

Even if it meant giving up the one good thing in his life that had given it meaning and direction for the past six years. For four of those years he had worked long, hard hours in his forge, making himself worthy of her, making for her a secure future and preparing a comfortable home. And now for two he had taken the course best calculated to drive her away forever.

But there was nothing he could do to change that. For if he could not offer her his integrity, then he had nothing worth offering at all.

He stooped down to pick up his coat and set it over the top bar of the gate. And he turned to walk back to the house. He stopped, though, when he reached the door and looked back. She had not moved except that her head had gone down again. He could not see clearly in the dark. He could not see if her shoulders were shaking. But he had the impression that she was crying again. Or perhaps, like him, she was too deeply dejected to cry.

He changed his mind when his hand was already on the latch of the door. He strode away from it and instead took the downward road home. It was a chilly night, but he scarcely noticed the absence of his coat.

Ceris did not move for a long time. She was trying to conjure up another face, another body, other hands, another kiss. Anything to dull this raw pain. And to ease the guilt.

He had come calling twice in the past week and had talked politely with Mam and Dada before asking them if he might take her walking—as if she were a girl instead of a woman of twenty-five. But Mam and Dada had been pleased—as pleased as they could be when they wished she would settle her differences with Aled and marry him. And as pleased as they could be when he was English and when he worked for the Earl of Wyvern. But, as her father had said, it was an honest living. He could not be blamed for what he was required to do.

She had walked out with him twice, and on the second occasion—just two evenings ago—he had taken her home and stood outside with her and asked if he might court her. They were his exact words. She had said yes.

He had asked if he might kiss her and she had said yes again. And so he had, drawing her against his body, his hands at her waist, and setting his lips against hers. She had felt him grow instantly hot and had stepped back hastily.

But she had agreed to the kiss and to the courtship. He had behaved correctly and courteously. And she had acquiesced. In effect she had agreed to consider marriage with him.

And yet now, what had she done? Would there be no end to this—passion?

Or to the guilt? She had felt guilty saying yes to Mr. Harley—to Matthew. Guilty because for so long she had thought of herself as Aled's. And now she felt guilty because she had allowed Aled to hold her and kiss her. Guilty because she had agreed to a courtship with Matthew.

You would have been my wife now. We would have had little ones together.

I love you, cariad.

And yet you still love me.

She could feel the power of his arms and the hunger of his mouth. She could hear his voice loud in her memory.

And she tried desperately to think of the man she had agreed to consider marrying.

The whole tone of the party had changed. For everyone, though soon enough everyone else adjusted to the unwanted presence in their midst and resumed their conversations and their joking. It was different, of course. There was more self-consciousness in the merriment, but even so the evening was not ruined—for everyone else.

Marged could not return to even a semblance of normality. She experienced all the expected feelings—shock that he had had the gall to come, indignation that he should try to spoil one of the few evenings of enjoyment they ever indulged in, a more personal fury, hatred. But there were other feelings too, more disturbing because they were apparently uncontrollable—a grudging admiration for his handsome face and figure and his immaculate dress, a very physical awareness of him, a feeling that every move she made, every word she spoke was open to his scrutiny and therefore must be perfect.

When Mrs. Howell asked her to play the harp and sing, she did so for him. Oh, not willingly. She kept her eyes away from him and tried to focus her mind on Mrs. Howell, but all the time while she sang she wondered if he liked her playing, as he had used to do, if he found her voice pleasing, if he remembered the songs she chose. She wondered if her hair was as smooth and as shiny as it had been when she left home. She wondered if she looked all of the ten years older than she had looked at sixteen. *He* looked older, but then age had only improved his appearance. But he had told her she was lovelier than she had been and that her voice had matured and was lovelier.

The more she tried to ignore him and focus on the singing about her and the occasion they had all gathered to celebrate, the more she felt as if only he was in the room with her.

She hated the feeling.

She had hoped he would have the decency to leave before or during the singing. And then she hoped he would leave when supper began. Surely he did not intend to eat with them. But he did so, held perhaps by the fact that her father and Ninian Williams made conversation with him. And then Ceris. She was offering him a plate of food and smiling shyly at him and talking with him. And he was bending his head to hers, to hear what she was saying above the din of the room, his hard blue eyes almost gentle on hers. Marged felt a pang of something unpleasant and recognized it for what it was.

She was appalled. *Jealousy?*

She went to the table and spent some time choosing the foods she would sample, concentrating on the choice as if it was a matter of some importance. And she winked at Idris Parry, whom she spied beneath the table. She had noticed him there earlier. He had sneaked into the house, though he had had no need to do so since his parents had been invited. They had been too ashamed to come, though. Ashamed of their poverty and shabbiness.

She felt a special partiality for Idris. She was fond of the little girls too and they were far more affectionate when she went up onto the moors with food for the family. Idris was a wild little imp, who roamed free and was rarely at home. But her heart ached with tenderness for him.

She reached out to take a scone, but her hand remained suspended over the platter. How strange that she had never noticed the similarity before. It was so strong that it was almost like looking back over time. They even looked alike. Idris was almost like a reincarnation of Geraint as he had been. That was why she was so fond of him?

The thought saddened her immensely.

And then the Owen brothers arrived, one on each side of her, and proceeded to examine every item on her plate and discuss between themselves, over the top of her head just as if she was not even there, exactly how many pounds each item would add to her weight.

"Roly-poly she will be by next Sunday," Dewi said. "She will be able to roll down the hill to chapel and save the energy of walking."

"But a nice soft armful she will make for some lucky man, mind," Dylan said.

"Well, it will not be you, Dylan Owen," she said sharply. "And you had better be standing to one side of the path when I come rolling by, Dewi, or I will flatten you." She picked up the largest scone on the platter and deposited it ostentatiously on top of the other food on her plate.

"Fuming she is," Dewi said. "Look out for Marged when she is mad, Dyl. It would be safer to wave a red flag to our dada's bull."

"We had better keep her happy, then," his brother said, picking up a jam tart and adding it to her pile. "Enjoy yourself, Marged, and do not burst at the seams."

Marged found herself giggling. She kept up the banter with them for half an hour while they ate, and other young people joined them. She deliberately kept her back to Geraint and hoped that perhaps before she turned he would have taken his leave without her even noticing. Though she would have known, she thought. She could feel him behind her almost as if he had a hand against her back, though he was still standing close to the fire, some distance from the table.

Finally people began to leave, especially those with young children, though several of the youngsters protested loudly. She would slip away with them, Marged thought. If the Earl of Wyvern was going to stay to the end, then she would leave. Once numbers had dwindled, those remaining would gather in one group about the fire. She had no wish to be drawn into a group that included him.

Unfortunately, she had to approach the fireplace in order to take her leave of Mrs. Howell and Morfydd, who was standing behind her mother's chair.

"It has been lovely," Marged said, bending over the elderly lady to kiss her cheek again. She straightened up. "Thank you, Morfydd. I will leave my harp here, if you don't mind, and ask Mr. Williams to bring it home tomorrow or when it is convenient to him."

Both Morfydd and her mother were effusive in their thanks for the music and in their assurances that the harp could stay as long as Marged wished. The children would be kept away from it and no harm would come to it.

"I will carry it up to Tŷ-Gwyn now," a voice said from behind Marged. She closed her eyes briefly. "And see you home at the same time, Marged. Women should not be out alone in the hills at night."

She could not refuse any more than she had been able to refuse outside chapel on Sunday. But twice within a week! She had been teased after Sunday by the group who had joined her in planning the pranks at Tegfan and carrying them out. This could lead to more than teasing. It could lead to gossip.

But it was not the gossip she cared about. It was being alone with him in the hills at night. Though even that was not her primary concern. Did he not understand that he was the last man on earth . . . Ah, it sounded like a cliché.

She tried. "It is quite unnecessary for you to go out of your way, my lord."

"It will be my pleasure, ma'am," he said, sounding for all the world as if he were preparing to escort an English lady home from an English ball.

He was ready to leave by the time she had drawn on her cloak and raised the hood over her head. He lifted her harp and followed her out into the night.

Chapter 10

It was a walk of over a mile, first across the crest of a hill and then upward. It was a dark night, with not much moonlight to light the way, and they had not brought a lantern. She found herself hoping that he would not be as surefooted as she, though the thought seemed absurd when she remembered him as a child. And she hoped that he would find himself unequal to the task of carrying her harp the whole distance. It was a heavy instrument and awkward to carry. She hoped that soft living would have him puffing and taking frequent rests. But he carried it with apparent ease.

They did not talk. They walked side by side in the darkness and in silence and she wondered if the air between them really did pulse with tension, or if only she felt it. She had never been more thankful to be the owner of a harp. Would he have insisted on escorting her home if there had not been the harp? She imagined what it would be like now, walking together across the lonely hills, if there was nothing to burden his arms. And she became more breathless than the walk and the climb could justify.

She tried to think of Eurwyn and succeeded better than she had hoped. There had always been work to occupy both of them for most of their waking hours. And the longhouse had always been occupied by his mother and grandmother as well as the two of them. She had loved those few occasions when they went out together and could walk home alone together, relaxed and comfortable. It had happened so rarely. She had liked to walk with her arm linked through his. He had not been a fat man, but he had been large and solid. She had always felt softly feminine, protected, almost fragile with Eurwyn. They were not images of herself that she cultivated, but sometimes it had felt good to believe that her man would protect her from all of life's harms.

Sometimes she had wished that he would stop in the darkness and kiss her. She had even suggested it once, not long after their marriage. He had been almost embarrassed. Eurwyn had not been a romantic man. What happened between a man and his wife to give them both ease should happen only at a certain time of day and only in their bed. He had never stated that in words—Eurwyn had never been able to talk about intimate matters—but it had been his belief.

She had loved him for his firm beliefs and principles, for his solidity, for the gentle affection he had shown her even though he had never put it into words, even during his courtship of her.

And then they were home and she was opening the gate into the farmyard so that the Earl of Wyvern would not have to set her harp down in the dust. And she was aware of him again, alive and there with her while Eurwyn was long dead, nothing to her but a memory. She hurried across the yard to open the door into the passageway and then the one into the kitchen. It was in darkness. Her mother-in-law and Gran would have been in bed for an hour or more.

She had felt very alone with him out on the hills. She felt even more alone with him when he had followed her into the kitchen and set her harp down in its usual place—even though the other two women were so close in the next room that they might hear a whisper.

He straightened up and turned to look at her, the planes of his face looking even more chiseled and even harsher than usual in the dying embers of the fire. They were alone, and he was no longer burdened with the harp. And they were standing no more than three feet apart.

She was very aware of the cupboard bed just behind her.

She turned sharply and led the way back out into the passageway. She could hear a few of the cows moving restlessly in the straw.

He turned in the doorway to look at her. It was quite dark there, but they had been walking in the dark for longer than half an hour. Their eyes were accustomed to it.

Eurwyn had used to kiss her when they were in bed together. Never at any other time except a few times when he was courting her. His lips had always used to be soft and warm against hers. And then he would turn her onto her back and draw up her nightgown. She would settle him in the cradle of her thighs and feel his weight pressing down on her. And then he would come inside and they would be man and wife together for a few silent minutes. There was never any great excitement, but just that—the being to-gether, the being one as a man was supposed to be one with his wife. And then afterward his kiss again and his arm beneath her head and his apology. Always his apology for bothering her when she must be tired.

Her body had been so empty without his. Her heart had been empty without him. Now, coming home together after the rare treat of a party with their friends and neighbors, they would have gone to bed together and have had the closeness of each other for the rest of the night.

The man who was standing in the doorway reached out and took her hands in his, as he had done on a previous occasion. But instead of looking down at the calluses this time, he raised them one at a time to his mouth and set his lips against her palms. She felt the warmth of his breath. He set her hands together, palm to palm, and held them there as if to keep his kisses warm. He looked into her eyes, though she could not see for sure that he did so. What little light there was, was behind him.

"Good night, Marged," he said so softly that it was a mere whisper of sound.

And then he was gone while her palms were still pressed together and tears would have blurred her vision if there had been anything to see.

Good night, Marged.

They were the only words either of them had spoken since leaving Ianto Richards's house, she realized. The house behind her felt empty and she knew that the bed would be cold. She yearned and yearned for a man's touch, for a man's loving. But they were all mixed up together, her longing for a long-dead husband and her yearning for the man who had betrayed her.

Good night, Geraint. The tears spilled over, hot onto her cheeks. *Damn you. Oh, damn you.*

He was cautiously hopeful. He could not pretend that he had been welcomed with open arms at Mrs. Howell's party the evening before, but neither had he been openly rejected. Everyone had been polite. A few had made the effort to talk with him. Perhaps with some persistence and some patience on his part, eventually he would make them see that he was not the eternal enemy. Once that happened, there could be dialogue. He could find out where the real problems lay and try to find solutions.

Even Marged had seemed less hostile. He had spent a largely sleepless night thinking of Marged, wondering what she would have done if he had lowered his head and kissed her lips, as he had wanted to do. And wondering where the one kiss would have led if she had been receptive to him. Part of him wished he had put it to the test. His body was on fire for her. Part of him was glad that he had not tempted fate, that he had an almost tender memory of the end of the evening.

Of course, he must not be overoptimistic. He had not

failed to notice that Aled had disappeared during the singing and had not returned. Aled had avoided him. Perhaps because he had not wanted to be trapped into having either to show open friendship or to openly snub his friend.

Were they friends? Geraint was not sure. He doubted Aled was sure either. And he guessed that neither of them really wanted to find out at the moment.

But Geraint felt hopeful. For a few days there had been no "accidents." And tomorrow he had an appointment with the man who had leased the toll roads and gates from the trust of which he, Geraint, was part owner. He was going to see if something could be done about lessening the burden on the farmers. It seemed they had two particular grievances. They paid tolls on the vast quantities of lime they had to haul for fertilizing their fields, and they paid frequent tolls because there were several different trusts in Carmarthenshire and they all had their gates and their charges.

Surely something could be arranged. Surely landowners like himself would consent to paying tolls on the roads too—it seemed only fair. And perhaps too they could lower the cost of the lease so that the man leasing from them would not be out of pocket for easing the burden on the poor.

It was going to mean several meetings with several people, and some of them—like his aunt and uncle—would doubtless be resistant at first. But he could get them to see sense. He had never lacked for persuasive powers.

He went to bed that night quite early and slept soundly after his sleeplessness of the night before. He woke up later, feeling angry, wondering what sort of drunken brawl was going on in the street outside until he remembered that he was at Tegfan, in the country. But what the devil *was* going on outside? He could not have been sleeping for longer than a few hours. It must be the very dead of night. And yet he could hear yelling voices and the crunch of boots on the gravel of the terrace. He could hear at least one horse whinnying.

He looked down from his window a few moments later on a scene of chaos. There was plenty of moonlight tonight.

He could see the stable block over to his right. A couple of grooms were standing outside it, one hopping about as he tried to pull on a boot, the other seeming to have a hard time getting his arms inside the sleeves of a shirt. Other grooms were dashing after disappearing horses, in various states of undress.

It did not take a genius to understand what had happened. By some strange chance—doubtless an *accident*—the stable doors had been left open as well as all the doors into the horses' stalls, and the horses had bolted. No one could be blamed. Accidents happened, after all.

Geraint's jaw hardened and he felt fury ball inside him. And disappointment. And frustration. It would take his men perhaps the rest of the night to round up the frightened animals—they had clearly not wandered out of those unlatched doors. They had been driven out.

He turned and strode toward his dressing room.

They were fortunate that at least they were not hampered by the darkness. It took them less than an hour to round up all but two of the horses. One of those was Geraint's own. It and the other missing one were nowhere to be found.

"Leave it," Geraint said wearily to his head groom sometime later when the two of them were at the northern end of the park, uphill from the house, and could see down and across a whole expanse of land. Nothing was moving except for a few servants, halfheartedly searching for the missing animals. "Tell the men to go back to bed. We will find them in the morning, or more likely they will return on their own when they discover they are ready for their morning feed."

The head groom did not argue. He made his way back downhill, leaving Geraint where he was.

The trouble with foolish pranks like this, Geraint thought, was that one dared not show how furious one was. For that was just what the pranksters hoped to provoke. They would like nothing better than to have him storm into the village tomorrow and about the farms, breathing fire and brimstone, demanding confessions. He would play right into their hands by doing that. But the impotent feeling of knowing that there was nothing he could do merely fed his fury.

He watched the grooms return to the stables. He watched one of them come from behind the house and dart quickly, doubled over, across a stretch of lawn and into the trees opposite. The same groom reappeared a few moments later higher up, just below where Geraint was standing. He stopped and looked back, gazing downward, shielded by the trees just below him. Geraint frowned.

As a boy he had learned to move quickly and silently. Often his safety and his very freedom had depended on his being able to do so. It was amazing how some skills never quite left one even if they had not been used a great deal for many years. It did not take Geraint even a minute to descend the slope and to come up behind the still-motionless figure of the lad.

Except that he was not a lad. He was dressed in breeches and a man's jacket, but he was hatless, and his long hair was twisted into a knot at the nape of his neck.

"The show is over," Geraint said softly. "Everyone is on the way back to bed."

The lad spun around and gazed at him in dismay.

"I believe I told you last night that it is dangerous for a woman to be out on the hills alone," he said coldly.

She did not try to run away. Doubtless she realized it would have been pointless. Neither did she speak. She lifted her chin and stared back at him.

"What do you know about all this, Marged?" he asked.

Still she said nothing. He saw scorn in her eyes, and perhaps hatred too.

"You were a part of it?" he asked. "You were one of them?"

He waited for her to reply but she did not answer him.

"Tell me who your leader is," he said. "Tell me who has organized all this. There is a modicum of humor in it all, I suppose, but I have ceased to be amused. Who is he?"

She still did not speak, but the corners of her mouth turned up into a smile that was not really a smile.

"Why?" he asked.

The half smile faded and now the look of hatred was quite naked.

"Why do you hate me?" he asked her. He could feel his temper rising and fought to keep it under control. "Marged, I was a boy with a boy's cravings and a boy's gaucheness. I thought you were willing and did not stop to ask you or to consider that perhaps it was unwise even if you were. For this must you hate me for the rest of my life?"

Her nostrils flared and her eyes flashed and her hands curled into fists at her sides. At last she spoke.

"You did not even answer my letters," she hissed at him. "When I had groveled before you, you would not even say no."

"Your letters?" He frowned.

"I begged you to show mercy on Eurwyn," she said. "You would not even deign to answer me."

Oh, God!

"What happened to your husband?" He could scarcely get the words past his lips.

"You do not even know, do you?" she said, scorn and fury mingled in her eyes and her voice. "You washed your hands of him and did not even care to find out what happened to him afterward. He died in the hulks. He did not even get as far as Van Diemen's Land to begin serving his seven-year sentence of transportation. He died on the ship. He was a strong man, a healthy man. But he could not survive those inhuman conditions. He died. My Eurwyn died like a vicious, depraved criminal."

She was not crying or hysterical, but he could tell from the clenched fists and the tautness of her posture that she was reliving the agony of her loss.

"Marged—" He reached out a hand toward her.

She leaned back sharply. *"Don't touch me!"* she said to him. "What did you need with all the salmon? You were not even living here. There were hungry people. The harvest had been bad. Eurwyn cared. We were not hungry. But he cared about those who were." She laughed suddenly. "He died because of some salmon. Your salmon. And because you would not intervene to save him."

"Marged—" he said.

"You killed my husband," she said. "You did not put a bullet through his heart, but you killed him. And you ask me why I hate you? There is no one in this world I hate as I hate you, Geraint Penderyn. Are you going to have me arrested now? Perhaps I will live to see Van Diemen's Land, as Eurwyn did not."

"I will see you home," he said.

"I will see you in hell first," she said.

"You need not walk at my side," he said. "You need not make conversation with me. You need not see me. But I will see you safely home."

She stared at him for a long while before turning sharply and striding away in the direction of home. He followed behind her, keeping his distance, keeping her in sight so that he might protect her from any danger that presented itself.

He watched her let herself in through the gate when she reached Tŷ-Gwyn and stayed where he was until she had entered the house without looking back at him.

He still did not know quite what had happened, though it was not difficult to piece together the main events. Eurwyn Evans must have been caught poaching for salmon on Tegfan land. He had been arrested and taken before the nearest magistrate for trial. He had been found guilty and sentenced to seven years transportation. And he had died in the hulks.

Marged had written to him, begging him to intervene on her husband's behalf. He could have done so. He was not a magistrate, but it was on his land Eurwyn had been caught. All he needed to have done was to have written to the appropriate authority explaining that Evans had been fishing with his permission.

But he had never read the letters. His steward at Tegfan had been instructed not to bother him with estate business, and his secretary in London had been instructed to intercept anything that came directly from Tegfan and deal with it himself. He did not know if Marged's letters had been presented at Tegfan or sent to London. He did not know which servant had withheld them from him. But it did not matter. Whoever it was had done so on his instructions.

It was his fault that the letters had not reached him.

It was his fault that Evans had been transported.

It was his fault the man had died.

Yes, he had in effect killed Marged's husband.

By the time he arrived home, Geraint was bone weary. Even so he doubted that he would sleep. But he must lie down. Perhaps somewhere between now and dawn sleep would catch him unawares and give him some moments of oblivion.

But when he had undressed and entered his bedchamber and threw back the covers to climb into bed, he found himself staring down at black ashes over which a pitcher of water must have been dashed.

Geraint began to realize the enormity of the problem.

His efforts to come to some arrangement with the other owners of the road trust and the man who had leased it from them came to nothing at all. No one was willing to budge an inch. And everyone was downright angry with him for even suggesting that change was necessary. Was it not enough that the lower classes were seething with discontent? Was it not enough that in other parts of West Wales the rioting and gate breaking had resumed after three years and even in their own area Mitchell's hayricks had been burned?

It was time to stand firm, not time to display even the slightest sign of weakness or wavering.

Besides, Geraint came to realize, the trust of which he was part owner was only one of several in the county. Even if he could gain concessions for his people in the immediate area of Tegfan, they would find the same oppressive tolls to pay as soon as they ventured farther afield—as they must in order to reach markets and in order to haul lime.

In fact, he came to realize that the whole problem was too large for him. If he lowered rents on his land, countless farmers on other people's land would still be suffering. If he gave back the tithe money in services to his people, no other landowner would do so for theirs. The poor would still grow poorer and the workhouses would become increasingly places filled with human despair. He toured the one in Carmarthen with Sir Hector Webb and an alderman of the town. They displayed it with pride. It haunted his dreams for the coming nights. The upland hovel he had shared with his mother had been paradise in comparison. At least they had been together and at least they had been free.

Eurwyn Evans had not been fishing for salmon. He had been trying to destroy the salmon weir that trapped all the fish on Tegfan land and denied the people of Glynderi and the farms beyond one source of food. He had been caught and tried—Sir Hector had been one of the magistrates involved—and sentenced to transportation.

Geraint instructed Matthew Harley to have the weir destroyed. His steward protested but found himself impaled by the cold blue gaze of his employer. There was no love lost between the two of them, Geraint thought ruefully as he left the man's study. Harley had had the sole running of the estate for two years and had done an admirable job when judged only by impersonal criteria.

Huw Tegid made similar objections to removing all the mantraps set up on Tegfan land. They were the best deterrent there was to poachers. There were not enough gamekeepers to patrol every corner of the land, and none of them liked to work nights, when poaching was most likely to occur. Like the steward before him, Tegid found himself facing an employer who chose not to argue with him but merely to look at him.

But Geraint felt frustrated. He would make changes on his own estate and gradually conditions would improve. Gradually his people would come to trust him. But it would all happen on a pitifully small scale. For the first time in ten years he felt again a confusion of identities. He was the Earl of Wyvern. In two years in England he had grown comfortable with the title. Now, after a mere couple of weeks in

Wales, he was Geraint Penderyn again as well as the earl. He felt with his people. He felt angry with them. It seemed to him as if his real enemies were people like his aunt and uncle, the lessee of the turnpike trust, his steward, his gamekeeper, and—himself.

His two identities were in conflict with each other.

Chapter

11

There was a small forge attached to the stable block of the house though it did not have a full-time blacksmith. When there was work to be done, the Glynderi smith was summoned.

Geraint sat in the forge one afternoon watching Aled shoeing one of the workhorses. They did not converse a great deal—the noise of the forge made conversation difficult—but the silence was companionable enough. Geraint relaxed into it. It must be good, he thought, to have a trade, a skill, something one did well and enjoyed doing, something that occupied most of one's time. He imagined that Aled was a happy man. He wondered, though, why his friend was not married. He was twenty-nine years old. But then Geraint was not married either and was only a year younger. His thoughts touched for a moment on Marged but veered firmly away again. He had spent a week avoiding thoughts of Marged—without a great deal of success.

Aled stretched, his work done. A groom led away the horse, the last of the day.

"I should have charged admission to the show," he said, grinning.

"I could sit and watch work all day," Geraint said, "and never grow tired. I can recommend it as a wonderfully useless occupation."

"You will have to go watch your cook making your dinner, then," Aled said. "I am done here."

"Sit down and relax for a while," Geraint said. "I want to talk to you." He got up himself and strode to the adjoining door into the stables to call to a groom to fetch him two mugs of ale.

"And me a good chapel man," Aled said.

"It is a good restorative, man," Geraint told him. "Think of it as medicine."

Aled seated himself on a rough workbench. "At least you choose to talk to me today instead of fighting me," he said. "I see that Wales is civilizing you again, Ger."

"Again?" Geraint laughed. "I was a marvelously civilized little urchin, wasn't I? Do you remember the ghosts?"

They both laughed at the memories that came flooding back. Poaching at Tegfan had been so bad at one time that the gamekeepers had been put on night patrol. Geraint and Aled had played ghosts one night, dressed in two old nightgowns, one Aled's sister's and the other Marged's. They had wafted through trees, wailing horribly whenever they had spotted a gamekeeper. It had all been Geraint's idea, of course.

"I feel the hair stand on end at the back of my neck when I picture what would have happened if we had been caught," Aled said.

They talked and laughed, reminiscing, until their ale came. It felt almost like old times, Geraint thought. And although he could not be quite sure that they were friends, still he felt closer to Aled than he felt to any of his friends back in London. It was a surprising and rather disturbing thought.

"Aled," he said at last, and his friend's instantly wary expression showed that he understood the conversation was moving past the preliminaries. "I have given orders to have the salmon weir destroyed and the mantraps removed from my land. There will be other changes as time passes. But they will not be enough. Most people here have closed their minds against me. And even if we could make a little haven of this part of West Wales, the injustices and the suffering would go on elsewhere."

Aled drank his ale and avoided Geraint's eyes. He looked distinctly uncomfortable.

"Something drastic has to be done," Geraint said. He realized as he talked that the thoughts had been germinating in his mind for days. Now they were taking definite shape as he talked. "Something is being done in other areas. Rebecca Riots. Why are there none here?"

Aled looked at him then, amazement and anger mingled in his expression. "Is that what this is all about?" he said, indicating his glass of ale. "You are looking for an informer? How in hell would I know why there are no Rebecca Riots here? And what *are* Rebecca Riots, pray? I have a tidy walk home. I had better get started."

"No!" Geraint said. "Sit there, Aled. You have been like a bloody eel since I came home, wriggling and slippery to the grasp. If there are no Rebecca Riots here, there ought to be. I hate the thought of destruction as much as the next man, but there is no surer way of attracting outside attention, I believe. Any riot confined to one man's land will be seen as his problem. Any riot concerning the public roads will be taken far more seriously. And perhaps it will bring about change for the better."

"And perhaps it will lead men into a trap to their deaths or to hard labor half a world away," Aled said, his voice still tight with anger.

Geraint leaned forward and held his friend's eyes with his own. "A trap of my setting?" he said. "Come, man, you know me better than that."

"Do I?" Aled frowned. "You are a stranger I used to know, Geraint, a long time ago."

Geraint leaned back in his chair. "In one way I have

changed," he said. "I have learned to read men's minds by listening to the tone of their voice as well as their words, and by watching the expression on their faces and the language of their bodies. There are plans in the making, aren't there? And you know about them. Are you one of the leaders, Aled? I would imagine you are, though you lack the fiery spirit to be the main leader, I believe. Are the plans very close to fruition?"

"Bloody hell," Aled said. "That is exactly where you have escaped from. You are the very devil. What kind of a story are you making up? And which magistrate are you going to take it to? Webb?"

Geraint was rocking on the back legs of his chair. He ignored Aled's words. His eyes were narrowed in speculation. "I wonder what the delay is," he said. "And I wonder if the pranks that were happening at Tegfan until they culminated in wet ashes in my bed last week were a result of the frustration of waiting. Marged was never very patient, was she? As soon as she had an idea she always had to carry it through now if not yesterday. I have realized that Marged must have been the mastermind—the mistress mind?—behind those accidents. But I suppose it would have to be a man to lead Rebecca Riots. The area would be larger and a larger number of men would be involved. A woman would not be accepted. Is that it, Aled? Are you all waiting for a leader? For a Rebecca?"

"Damn you," Aled said. "You had a lively imagination as a child. I see that by now you are creating fairy tales with it. Not truth, but fantasy."

Geraint held his eyes. The front legs of his chair had been returned to the floor. "You have one," he said. "You have a Rebecca. You are looking at her."

Aled went very still and his face paled. "You're mad, Ger," he almost whispered. "I always said you were mad. I was right."

"And I am right too, aren't I?" Geraint said. "It is a Rebecca you are lacking. Look back in your memory, Aled. Who is more likely to relish such a position than I?"

Aled seemed to have forgotten that he knew nothing about Rebecca Riots. "It would be absurd," he said. "The riots are a protest against landlords. You are one of the biggest landlords in Carmarthenshire."

Geraint nodded. "And I grew up as one of the poorest of the poor," he said. "I know both worlds, Aled. They should be able to coexist in peace and harmony but do not. I want them to do so but have been frustrated in my approaches to both worlds. I feel stuck firmly in the middle and impotent to change anything. But as Rebecca I could. I am accustomed to leading. I did it from instinct as a boy, and I have done it from training as a man. A rabble is not easy to lead or control. I could do both. And I know how to attract attention. As Rebecca I could write letters to the right people—to government figures, to Englishmen who are sympathetic to the poor and influential in Parliament, to certain newspapers."

"*Duw* save us," Aled said, still pale, "you are serious."

"Yes." Geraint nodded. "I am. But I need a bridge from one world to the other, Aled. There is an organization already in place, plans already made. There are, aren't there? And you know about them and can bring me in."

"You are mad," Aled said again. "Do you think anyone would accept you as leader, Ger? You are the *enemy.*"

"No more than a few people need know," Geraint said. "Who is making all the plans? A small group, at a guess. Some sort of committee? I imagine that if they are wise they emphasize secrecy at every turn. If there are informers it is as well to give them as few people to inform against as possible. Rebecca's identity would probably be kept from the rank and file, wouldn't it?"

"This is your fairy tale," Aled said. "You tell me."

"What sort of disguise does Rebecca wear?" Geraint asked.

"From what I have heard," Aled said, "of distant riots, you understand, she usually wears a flowing white robe and a long blond wig and she blackens her face."

"Blackens her face." Geraint thought for a moment. "Not

a very good disguise for her followers who might be close enough to have a good look at her. A mask would be better, something to pull over the whole head beneath the wig."

"You would be recognized anyway," his friend said.

"I think not," Geraint said. "The disguise is a good one for hiding form and figure. Everyone will assume that I am someone from another town or village, someone they have never met before. And who in his right mind would even dream that it might be me?"

"Your voice?" Aled said.

"You are the only one to whom I have spoken Welsh since my return," Geraint said. "Do I speak it with an English accent?"

"No." Aled frowned.

"Rebecca will speak only Welsh. And it is no problem to deepen my voice a little just in case," Geraint said, doing just that. "No one will know. And no one would guess that I would disguise myself in order to lead my own people against me, would they?"

"Even those who knew you were mad as a boy would not realize that you are totally insane," Aled said. "You are, Ger. I am surprised that someone has not chained you to the wall of one of your elegant London mansions before now."

Geraint grinned. He had not felt so vibrantly alive for—he could not remember for how long.

"In the meantime," he said, "I am going to have to halt reform on my own land. I don't want anyone to become confused and perhaps pity me. The destroyed weir and mantraps will have to do for now."

Aled straightened up on his bench suddenly and looked wary again. "Oh, *Duw*, Ger," he said, "you had me going there for a while. That was an amusing fairy tale."

Geraint chuckled. "Too late, Aled," he said. "I saw the truth in your face, and I saw the excitement in your eyes. You need a Rebecca and you know I am the perfect choice—perhaps the only choice. Are you on the committee? And don't ask what committee."

Aled stared at him.

"Take me to them," Geraint said. "They can all hide behind disguises if they wish. You can keep the location a secret from me. You can even blindfold me. But let me talk to them."

He watched as Aled closed his eyes and paled again.

"Aled," he said, "why would I be setting a trap for you? You are the only thing I have resembling a friend here. Marged hates me bitterly and I understand why now. You can go and see for yourself that the salmon weir has gone. Is that not proof enough for you that I mean well? Will you not trust me?"

Aled was looking at him again, his eyes troubled. "I dare not trust you," he said. "There are too many people dependent upon my judgment." He grimaced. "But I suppose those very words show that I am wavering. Damn you, Ger, why did you not stay in England where you belong?"

"I think I came because you need a Rebecca," Geraint said quietly. "Do you believe in fate, Aled? Seemingly insignificant events can be enormously significant in retrospect. Two men passed me on the street in London, talking Welsh. One of them was saying something about missing the hills. And here I am. For almost three weeks I have thought that perhaps it was a dreadful mistake to come. Certainly my return has brought me no happiness. But now I know why I was made to pass those men and overhear a snippet of their conversation. I was sent here to be Rebecca."

"By Satan," Aled said.

"Perhaps." Geraint looked steadily back at him. Silence stretched between them. "Well?"

"You used to talk me into trespassing for the sake of trespassing," Aled said. "You talked me into playing ghosts that one night. You talked Marged and me into hiding you in that cupboard in the schoolroom one Sunday afternoon before Sunday school. You talked me into participating in every mad scheme you ever dreamed up, Ger. Why not this one too?" There was no amusement in his voice, only a sort of irritated frustration.

"Where? When?" Geraint jumped to his feet.

"Soon." Aled got more slowly to his. "I'll let you know, Ger. But I wouldn't get my hopes too high if I were you. You will not find the other members of the committee quite as gullible as I am."

"Aled." Geraint held out his right hand, as serious as his friend. "You will not regret trusting me, man. I'll not let you down."

"I'll fight you to the death if you do," Aled said quite seriously. "Assuming I am free to fight, of course."

They clasped right hands.

Matthew Harley paid an afternoon visit to Pantnewydd. He called at the office of Sir Hector Webb's steward, but as usual he soon found himself walking outside in company with Sir Hector himself. The two men had a mutual respect for each other, and Harley had always realized that Sir Hector—and through him, Lady Stella—used him in order to gain news of Wyvern in England and in order to oversee the estate that would perhaps be his wife's one day. It had always seemed to Harley that Sir Hector was more his employer than the Earl of Wyvern.

"He ordered me to have the salmon weir destroyed," he explained to Sir Hector when they were well launched into the topic they had come together to discuss. "And he has had Tegid take away all the mantraps."

"Fool!" Sir Hector said viciously. "Does he expect to be better respected for it? Does he not realize he will be merely laughed at and seen as a weak man?"

"With all due respect, sir," Harley said, "I do not believe he fully understands the situation. He is trying to be popular. He has attended their chapel and a birthday party for an elderly lady on one of the farms."

"Fool!" Sir Hector said again.

"I suppose it is understandable," Harley said. "He was, after all, one of them as a child. It must be difficult—"

"My brother-in-law was a greater fool than his son!" Sir Hector's voice had lost none of its viciousness. "But that is not the point now. He must be controlled, Harley. Once these Welsh farmers have spotted a weakness, they will exploit it. Before we know it, we will be having Rebecca Riots in this part of the country as well as in others. And it will all be Wyvern's fault."

"Perhaps," Harley said, "he will take warning from all the accidents that have been happening at Tegfan lately. He must have realized by now that they are not really accidents at all."

They had been strolling along beside the hedge surrounding the sheep pasture. But Sir Hector stopped and looked inquiringly at Tegfan's steward. He laughed shortly when he had heard the account of the "accidents."

"If we are fortunate, Harley," he said, "his feelings will be hurt and he will crawl back to England and allow his estate to be run by those who know how to run it. *If* we are fortunate. In the meanwhile we need to keep a careful eye on the situation. The people are restless and word travels. There are gates being pulled down in Pembrokeshire and Cardiganshire and even in this county. Do you have any informants?"

"I have never needed any," Harley said.

"Then it is time you did." Sir Hector began to walk again back in the direction of the house. "They are not difficult to come by. Someone who is in your debt. Someone who has a grudge against his neighbors." He looked assessingly at the other man. "Some woman. You are a fine enough young fellow, Harley. Get some woman panting over you. Women are loose-tongued as any man could wish when they fancy themselves in love."

Harley thought of Ceris Williams, whom he was officially courting. He had found himself unexpectedly hot for her during the last couple of weeks. In addition to being pretty and sweet-natured, she seemed taken with him. She held his hand when they walked and listened attentively to what he said. She returned his kisses. She had even allowed him last night to fondle her breasts through the fabric of her dress, though she had pushed his hands away at first.

He did not doubt that he could use her as an informer. But

the problem was—did he want to? He did not like the idea of mixing business with pleasure, and Ceris Williams was definitely pleasure. He even thought he might be falling a little in love with her. But then business—his position, the power he had enjoyed—had always been more important to him than any pleasure. And both were threatened at the moment, threatened by the presence of his employer at Tegfan and by the tense situation with the farmers.

Sir Hector Webb chuckled. "That silenced you," he said. "Thinking of all the Welsh maidens you can tumble and milk for information, are you, Harley?"

"I will keep a close eye on the situation, sir," he said. "I'll keep you informed."

"Good man." Sir Hector slapped a hand on his shoulder. "These London beaux are all the same, you know. They know nothing about anything and think they know everything about everything. I'll not forget who really runs Tegfan and has kept it such a prosperous estate. And Lady Webb will not forget, either."

"Thank you, sir," Harley said.

Marged had kept herself busy for almost two weeks. She had let the cattle out to pasture and had cleaned the barn with such thoroughness that her mother-in-law declared it was as clean as the kitchen. She had prepared the plow for the seeding and she had wandered slowly back and forth across the field, picking up the heavy stones that never failed to accumulate as if by magic every spring. It was heavy and backbreaking work that had used to exhaust even Eurwyn. He had never allowed her to help. Now she did it almost alone except for a little uninvited help from young Idris Parry, who spent a whole afternoon keeping up to her pace so that he could chat nonstop. So much like Geraint as he had used to be! She gave him some food to take up to his family and offered a few coins she could ill afford. He refused them.

She worked harder than she needed to. At first she was driven by fear. He had thought perhaps that she was a mere onlooker rather than a participant in the accidents that had been happening. But if he had seen her on that slope, the chances were good that he had seen her come from the direction of the house. Once he returned home and saw his bed, he would know. And perhaps he would guess that she was the leader he had asked her to identify.

She did not believe he would have her arrested. He would make himself look too foolish. But telling herself that with her mind and convincing her body that it was so were two quite different matters. She feared prison with an icy fear. She feared the hulks. She feared a foreign land and slave labor—perhaps chains, perhaps whips.

She lived with terror night and day and despised herself and held herself so stonily calm and aloof that even Gran noticed and asked her if she was feeling ill.

After several days the fear subsided. But in its place came a loathing even stronger than she had felt before. She could not bear to see him ever again. She could not bear to see him alive and handsome and—yes, and suffocatingly attractive while Eurwyn was long in his grave. Though he was not even there. She did not even have the comfort of a grave to attend. Eurwyn's remains were somewhere on the ocean floor. She could not bear to see the Earl of Wyvern and remember that she had wanted him the night he had taken her home and kissed her palms.

She even avoided chapel on the first Sunday, persuading her mother-in-law to go for a change instead. Someone had to stay at home with Gran. It was a convenient excuse. She did go on the second Sunday, but shrinking inside with dread. He did not come.

And she went to choir practice on the Thursday following. It was unlikely she would encounter him between Tŷ-Gwyn and the chapel. She had heard that he had had the salmon weir removed from his land. Perversely, she did not want to believe it. Or she did not want to believe it had anything to do with her or Eurwyn. She did not want him to do her any kindness. Anyway, it had come two years too late. It would not bring Eurwyn back.

Singing was a balm to the soul. She had always known it
and it was proved again. Even singing to herself while she
was about her daily work was soothing. But singing with
other people, hearing the richness of harmony all about her
and lending her voice to it was as wonderfully soothing as
a bathe in the river on a hot day. More so. She prolonged the
practice, singing more hymns than they needed for the
coming Sunday.

No one objected.

But when she finally signaled the end of practice, Aled
jumped to his feet and held up his hands for silence.

"I have something of importance to say," he said. His face
was pale and set, Marged noticed. "Those of you who do not
wish to hear it may leave now. There will be no compulsion
put upon anyone as there is in some other places."

Marged's heart leapt and began to beat uncomfortably.
This was it, then. She could tell from Aled's voice that it
was not the usual news of delay that he was about to impart.
She looked fixedly at him as a few people got to their feet

and left the schoolroom, among them Ceris, who hurried out, her eyes directed at the floor.

"Well," Aled said when the door had closed again, "the time has come. All is planned. The night after tomorrow. Every man who wishes to follow me should meet me down by the river after dark."

"Gate breaking?" Dewi Owen asked. "Which one is to go, Aled? Or which ones? I am with you every step of the way, man."

"I cannot say which," Aled said. "The less you know the better, Dewi. I am sorry but that is the way it must be."

"Rebecca?" Marged leaned forward in her chair. "There is a Rebecca, Aled?"

"Yes." He nodded curtly. "We have found a Rebecca, Marged."

"Oh, who?" She found that she was agog with eagerness.

He shook his head. "I cannot say that either," he said. "It is safer for everyone if almost no one knows his identity."

She was disappointed. "But he is not from here?" she asked. "No, he cannot be. But is he anyone we know? Anyone from close to here?"

"Aled is right, Marged, *fach*," Ifor Davies said. "It is better we do not know. No one can squeeze out of us what we do not know, girl."

"But is he suitable?" She could not let it alone. "He is not someone who has been pressed into it against his will, Aled? Or someone who is merely a daredevil with no sense of responsibility? Or someone who is ruthless and will do more destruction than is necessary?"

"He will do, Marged," Aled said. "He will be the best Rebecca there has been, I believe."

She raised her eyebrows. Aled was not given to wild enthusiasms. This was praise indeed.

"I will show my support of him and my trust in him by being one of his daughters," Aled said. He smiled faintly. "Charlotte."

Charlotte was, by tradition, Rebecca's favorite daughter. The leader's right-hand man. Rebecca must indeed be someone Aled believed in. Marged was more curious than ever.

"Bring with you crowbars or anything else that will help destroy gates and tollhouses," Aled said. "But no guns or anything else designed specifically to harm people. There is to be no violence shown to any people. Rebecca has made it a firm condition of her service to us, and I support her wholeheartedly."

"*Duw,*" Eli Harris said, "but there are a few gatekeepers I would not mind putting the fear of God into—with my fists or something a little more convincing."

"Rebecca will not tolerate a rabble," Aled said. "He will expect a disciplined army and he will demand obedience. Anyone who cannot accept that would do better to stay at home."

Eli grumbled to himself, but he appeared to have no supporters.

Rebecca, Marged thought, was winning her respect with every passing minute. She hoped Aled was not exaggerating. But where had this man been hiding all this time?

"I am all for you, Aled, and for Rebecca," she said. "At least something will be done to speak loudly and clearly to the government. At last the likes of Geraint Penderyn, *Earl of Wyvern,* will have something rather more serious to bother him than a few stray mice and escaped horses and ashes in his bed. I can hardly wait to see how he reacts."

Aled looked steadily back at her. "I imagine he will be very angry, Marged," he said.

She smiled brightly at him. "I hope so," she said. "*Duw,* but I hope so."

He had forgotten the feeling. He had lived with it for years, this combination of excitement and fear, the one inextricably a part of the other. He had been a child then, poaching for a living, thrilled by the sheer delight of snaring food for himself and his mother, titillated by the knowledge that sure punishment awaited him if he were caught.

He was a man now and realized that for many years life

had been tame. Not that he had not enjoyed it, but it had been without challenge. His boyhood exuberance returned to him as if the intervening years had fallen away. There was a new challenge on which to focus all his energies. He was to lead the Rebecca Riots in this part of Wales. There would be perhaps a few hundred men to lead and control and keep safe. There was his identity to be kept secret from both sides—from both the authorities and the men he led. There was his own safety to be guarded against possible informers. There were always large rewards offered for the capture of a Rebecca, he had been told.

And there was the fear. Definitely the fear. Fear that he would be unable to control his men and that he would be merely creating a mob that would wantonly destroy property and perhaps harm people. And fear of being caught. Transportation for life—that was what lay in wait for any Rebecca who was caught. None had been yet. Perhaps in this case, since he was a landowner and an aristocrat and would be seen as someone who had betrayed his own class and perhaps his country—in his case, perhaps the ultimate penalty.

Geraint had made his appearance before the committee, conducted to their meeting blindfolded, as he had suggested, by a grim Aled. He had been kept behind a screen in a darkened room. For longer than an hour he had made his case and answered questions and withstood a thorough grilling. He had lost hope. They were not going to accept him. But they had. Perhaps they thought they had little to lose. If he failed, if he was somehow trying to set a trap, they would be safe. He had seen none of them except Aled. It was clear to him that they had even disguised their voices.

He had set his conditions. Only tollgates and tollhouses were to be destroyed. There was to be no damage to private property. There was to be no harm done to any person. No one was to be coerced into joining the rioters, as was happening in other areas. No one was to carry a gun. And one gate was to be exempt. There was a gate on Tegfan land, the Cilcoed gate, kept by an elderly woman, Mrs. Dilys

Phillips. He had given her the word of the Earl of Wyvern that he would protect her from all harm.

And so he had a third identity. He was Geraint Penderyn and the Earl of Wyvern—and now Rebecca. He was to become Rebecca for the first time on Saturday night. His disguise had been found for him and was safely stowed away in a derelict gamekeeper's hut at the northern tip of the park. He had studied the rituals that were always observed at a gate breaking. They were foolish rituals, perhaps, as was the whole idea of Rebecca and her daughters, but he knew that sometimes ritual had its function in giving form and orderliness to a situation that was fraught with dangers. He thought Saturday night would never come.

He found himself unable to settle to anything for the intervening days but wandered restlessly about the house and park. He found it difficult to eat. He found it almost impossible to sleep.

He was excited and afraid.

She was terribly afraid. Perhaps more afraid than she had ever been in her life. But, no, that was not true. She had been more afraid when Eurwyn had been out trying to destroy that weir. And her feelings at his trial and afterward had gone beyond fear. Fear was a dreadful emotion when it was accompanied by utter helplessness.

There was an element of excitement and exhilaration mingled with this fear. And this time she was not helpless. She was doing something. She was in control of her own destiny.

Her mother-in-law and grandmother always went to bed early. Sometimes Marged regretted the fact. Evenings could be long when they were spent alone. But tonight she was glad. She dressed quickly and quietly in the old breeches and jacket she had cut down from Eurwyn's size to her own. She pulled a woolen cap over her head and then stooped down by the fire to blacken her face with some of the cooled ashes she had mixed with a little water.

Wet ashes. Her hand paused for a moment over the dish.

But she would not think about *him* or about what she had done to his bed. She had not seen him for two weeks and she could not be happier. It seemed that the less than warm welcome he had received from them all and the "accidents" that had befallen him had had the desired effect. He had retreated into the house and park of Tegfan. Perhaps soon he would retreat all the way to London. Perhaps the riots that were to start tonight would drive him away.

She could not somehow imagine Geraint running from danger, though. But then she was remembering him as a daring urchin. She did not know anything now about the state of his courage. Except, she thought unwillingly, that it must have taken courage both to go to chapel and to go to Mrs. Howell's birthday party. She had not thought of it that way before. And did not want to think it now. Or to think of him.

She slipped out of the house quietly, closing both the kitchen and the outside doors slowly, hoping that her absence would go unnoticed. She did not want the other two women involved in what she had decided to do. It would be unfair. They had suffered enough anxiety with Eurwyn.

She hoped she was not too late. She wanted desperately to be part of this first mass demonstration. She wanted to be a part of all of them, even though they would become progressively more dangerous as the authorities were alerted to trouble. It was a very dark night. Heavy clouds hid the moon and the stars. It was better so. And yet bounding downhill was not an easy thing to do. She hoped she would be in time.

She was. They were gathered at the river beyond Glynderi, perhaps twenty-five men, and more joined them within the next few minutes. They were all on foot except for the one figure on horseback, wearing a dark flowing robe and a dark woman's wig. His face was blackened. Rebecca, Marged thought for a moment, and her heart beat faster. But he rode closer to her and looked down at her.

"Marged?" he said in Aled Rhoslyn's voice. "You should

not be here, girl. Go home now where it is safe, is it? It is enough that Eurwyn worked for the cause."

It was Aled, of course, looking grotesque but somehow menacing as Charlotte. Rebecca was from somewhere else. And Rebecca, if tradition was being followed, would be clad recklessly in white.

She shook her head. "I am not going anywhere but with you, Aled," she said. "You will not drive me away. Unfortunately it is gates we will pull down and not Tegfan, but Geraint will know after tonight that he has powerful enemies. I am one of those enemies and I will not cower at home."

"We will be walking for many miles over the hills," he said. "It will be a long, hard night, Marged."

"And chapel in the morning?" she said, smiling broadly at him. "I will not have any of my choir missing, mind, and staying in their beds to catch up on sleep."

"Well, then," he said, wheeling his horse away from her, "don't complain to me of blisters."

He had not exaggerated. He led them straight into the hills and over the crest—and through valleys and over other hills. Miles and miles of walking. Most of the time he walked with them, leading his horse by the reins. There was not a great deal of talking. They picked up more men as they went and two more "daughters." There must have been more than a hundred of them eventually, Marged guessed, all moving together and so quietly that no one standing close by who did not know of their presence would have suspected it.

And then suddenly it seemed that they were to join forces with another group at least as large and as close-packed and as quiet as their own. Marged, who was walking almost at the head of her own group, close to Aled, felt a thrill of excitement and fear again. At the head of the new group, seated on a large dark horse, was a figure dressed in a flowing white robe and a long blond wig. Even the face looked white—masked, Marged realized, rather than black-ened.

Rebecca!

She sat motionless on the horse, appearing to tower over the crowd on foot and even over her mounted and darker daughters.

Who was he? Marged wondered, staring at him. He looked even more grotesque than Aled. And many times more magnificent. Aled rode forward with the other daughters from their group and they took up their positions to either side of Rebecca.

And finally she raised both arms upward and outward. White sleeves fell like wings from her wrists to her sides. It was an unnecessary gesture since there had been no noise to hush. But it was a commanding gesture. The silence became almost a tangible thing. Marged could almost hear the beating of her own heart.

"My daughters," she said, "and my loyal children, welcome."

It was a rich male voice, speaking Welsh. A voice that seemed not to be raised and yet spoke clearly enough to be heard by the farthest man in the crowd. It was a voice that sounded accustomed to command.

"I will lead you to a gate," Rebecca said, "a gate that ought not to be there, taking as it does the freedom of passage away from my countrymen. You will destroy that gate, my daughters and my children, and the house of the gatekeeper. You will destroy them when I give the command. You will not harm the gatekeeper or abuse him with words. My followers are courteous people who perform a necessary service for their families and neighbors and friends. If anyone wishes to turn back, now is the time."

No one moved. There were low murmurings of assent.

He was magnificent, Marged thought again. They were a rabble with destruction in mind. But he was converting them with very few words and in a very short span of time into an army with a noble purpose. He had them all eating out of his hand, herself included. She felt at that moment that she would follow him to hell and back if he asked it of her.

"Lead on, Mother," Aled said.

"We will follow you, Mother," a few of the other daughters said.

Marged found that her heart beat faster at the foolish ritual, which somehow at this moment did not seem foolish at all.

And then Rebecca lowered her arms, and they were all making their way down from the bleak hillside on which they had gathered. Down toward the road and a tollgate, though it was invisible in the darkness. In the darkness it was hard to see even the ground ahead of one's feet. The horses ahead and the hundreds of men on either side were mere shadows in the darkness, felt more than seen. The only thing that could be seen with any clarity was Rebecca's white garments. Marged fixed her eyes on them.

Who was he? He was someone from another valley, another village. The chances were that his name and face would mean nothing to her even if she heard the one and saw the other. She knew he was no one from near Glynderi. He had not come with them. Besides, she would recognize a man with such a commanding presence no matter how well he was disguised, if she knew him at all. It was hard to believe that in everyday life he must be a farmer or a tradesman. Or perhaps a lawyer. She knew that the few men who had been arrested for participating in Rebecca Riots had all been defended by such able lawyers that none had yet been convicted. Those lawyers were rumored to be Rebeccaites themselves. Perhaps one of them was actually a Rebecca. He spoke perfect Welsh—almost as if he were an educated man.

And then suddenly, without any warning, they were on the road and turning to walk along it. Marged could feel its harder surface beneath her feet. And the dark shadow ahead of the horses suddenly resolved itself into the distinctive outline of a tollgate across the road and a squat house beside it.

The horses stopped and the crowd closed in behind. Marged was almost at the head of it. There was an eerie silence. And then Rebecca raised both arms again.

At the same moment there was light. Only a thin thread of it, but it was startling to eyes that had looked into nothing but almost total darkness for a few hours. The door of the tollhouse had opened and a man and woman had come out, huddled together. The man held a lantern aloft. In its light Marged could see that both were terrified.

The reality of it all hit her powerfully then. What they were doing, what they were about to do suddenly had a human face. And the danger of the moment was so apparent that she thought the beating of her heart would make it impossible to catch her breath. There were hundreds of men all about her, angry men, as she was angry. Men who were perhaps looking for a scapegoat. It would need only one spark to ignite a fire of violence and revenge. Rebecca had appeared commanding up in the hills. But the real test had come.

Now.

Rebecca spoke, her voice as quiet and as clear as it had been earlier. She ignored the gatekeeper and his wife. "My daughters," she said, "there is something in my way. What is it?"

Aled was the one who replied. "It appears to be a gate across the road, Mother," he said.

"But why is it there? I wish to ride on with my children but cannot."

Marged recognized the ritual she had heard of. It sounded very much more menacing in reality.

"It is there to stop travelers like you and me, Mother," Aled said. "It is there to force money from us, the money we have already paid to our landlords in rent and tithes and poor rates."

"It is there to impoverish us and force us from our land, Mother, and into the workhouse." Another daughter took up the story.

"It is there to prove to us that we Welsh are not free in our own country, Mother," a third said.

A fourth spoke up. "Shall we destroy it for you, Mother?"

Marged felt a stirring about her as men grasped clubs and

crowbars and axes more tightly and prepared to surge forward. But Rebecca had not lowered her arms.

"In a short while, my daughters," she said. "But we will not be hasty." For the first time she looked at the gatekeeper and his wife. "This is your home, my friends?" She spoke to them with quiet courtesy.

The man pulled himself together. "You will not get away with this," he said. "Powerful men own this trust—the Earl of Wyvern, Sir Hector Webb, Mr. Maurice Mitchell. You will be caught and punished."

"Our quarrel is not with you and your good wife or with your personal possessions," Rebecca said. "My children are not patient, but they will obey their mother. They will wait for ten minutes while you remove your possessions from the house and make your way to the nearest habitation for shelter. Ten minutes."

The man took a step forward, seemingly prepared to take on the whole army of them. But his wife plucked at his sleeve and dragged him back toward the house.

"Don't do anything stupid," she said. "Let us hurry, then, Dai."

His arms must be tired, Marged thought several minutes later, watching Rebecca from behind. They were still raised and spread. He looked like the statue of an avenging angel. And the control he held over the crowd was amazing. She could feel the tension all about her, the eagerness to be at the job they had come to do. And yet no one moved and the few who spoke did so in whispers.

The gatekeeper and his wife reappeared before the ten minutes had passed, their arms laden with bundles. The woman would have stumbled away into the darkness, but the man stood his ground and glared up at Rebecca.

"My wife has an oak chest in by there," he said. "It is too heavy for us to carry. I will hold it against you for the rest of my life." He spat in the dirt at his feet.

Rebecca spoke with continued courtesy. "Charlotte, my daughter," he said, "choose two of my children who are on foot, if you please, and direct them to carry out this good woman's oak chest and set it down with care some distance from the house."

Aled turned and pointed to the Owen brothers. They scurried into the house to do Rebecca's bidding.

"And now, my children," Rebecca said when the job was done, raising her voice only slightly, "you will destroy this obstruction across the road and the house beside it." Her arms swept downward.

And then at last there were noise and movement as more than two hundred men surged around the house and the gate. Marged went forward with them, raising the club she had brought with her.

This is for you, Eurwyn, *cariad*, she thought as she brought it down on the top bar of the gate. This is for you. And this is a blow against him. For your sake I will never stop hating him.

It was over in a matter of minutes. The gate was down and strewn in several pieces across the road. The house was a mere heap of rubble. Several men were sweeping the bits clear of the road so that horses and vehicles and pedestrians might pass unobstructed.

Chapter 13

Marged joined in the general cheer. She did not believe she had ever felt so exhilarated in her life. It was a blow for justice, for freedom, for the dignity of their lives. Dylan Owen was slapping her on the back, as excited as she.

"Now we have shown them, Marged," he said. "And we will continue to show them."

She smiled back at him, but she became aware suddenly that one of the horses had moved up close to her other side. She looked up, startled.

Rebecca leaned down from his horse's back and set a hand beneath her chin to keep her face turned up. It was some sort of a woolen mask, she saw, hugging his face tightly, with only small slits for his eyes, nose, and mouth. Long blond ringlets cascaded down about the mask and over his shoulders. It was impossible to know what the man behind the mask looked like and would be impossible even in daylight, Marged believed. She felt unaccountably frightened. There was such a contrast between the effeminacy of the woman's attire and the power the man had shown tonight.

"Is it possible," he said, his voice low and soft and quite audible despite the noise by which they were surrounded, "that one of my children is a real daughter?"

"Yes." She looked directly back into his eyes, which gleamed darkly through the slits of the mask. "And there are a few others here too. We represent all the women who feel as strongly as the men that it is time to protest against oppression but who have been kept at home by the orders of fathers or husbands or by the needs of children."

"Ah. Brave words, my daughter," he said.

She felt almost as if she were just that for a moment. She felt absurdly pleased by the implied praise.

He released her chin and raised his arms again and called for silence. Amazingly he got it after only a few moments. "My children," he said, "enough for tonight. Next time we will destroy more than one of these abominations. My daughters will tell you where and when. I have been proud of you tonight. You have behaved with courage and determination—and discipline. Go now. Most of you have a long walk home."

It seemed almost anticlimactic. And it really was a long walk home. Marged smiled at Dylan, determined not to show her weariness. But a hand came to rest lightly on her shoulder and she turned to look up again at Rebecca, who had not moved off. He took his hand away and offered it to her, palm up.

"Come, my daughter," he said. "Take my hand and set your foot on my boot and ride up with me."

The prospect was unaccountably frightening. He was not her enemy. He was the leader she had hoped and prayed for. Even better than Eurwyn would have been, she thought treacherously. He had won her respect and admiration and loyalty tonight. But he looked ghostly and yet massively real all at the same time. And it was the dead of night. And she did not know who he was.

"I am not afraid of the walk home," she said, "even though I am a woman."

She could have sworn that his eyes smiled at her. "Then

ride up here for my sake," he said. "I am a woman in need
of company so late at night."

She smiled then. And certainly it would be pleasant to
ride for a part of the way, until their paths took them in
different directions. Of course, by then she would be
separated from her friends and would have to walk the rest
of the way home alone. But she was certainly not going to
give in to a fear of the dark.

She set her hand in his and lifted her foot to rest it on his
boot in the stirrup. The next moment she was seated
sideways on the horse's back in front of the saddle, his arms
like a safe barricade on either side of her while he gathered
the reins in his hands.

He held his horse still until everyone had disappeared into
the darkness. Only then did he give it the signal to start.
Marged sat very still, fighting breathlessness so that he
would not notice. One thing had been very clear from her
brief contacts with Rebecca and the ease with which she had
been lifted onto the horse.

Rebecca was a very powerful man.

All three of his identities had merged in the course of the
night. His education and training had reinforced the natural
ability to command that he had possessed even as a child.
Yet tonight he had used that training and that ability to assert
his Welshness, his identification with his people. He felt
passionately throughout the night the rightness of what he was
doing. He felt a deep love for the people whom he commanded
and a deep commitment to their cause. And he found that
the role of Rebecca suited him. The role of woman and
mother served to remind him that it was a cause for which
he fought and that it could be done with dignity and a
measure of compassion.

It was a night he frankly enjoyed. It took him back to
childhood years and made him realize just how much of his
identity he had been forced to give up at the age of twelve,
and how much he had finally given up voluntarily in order
to retain his sanity. He felt almost as if he had been living

a suspended life for sixteen years and was now vibrantly and gloriously alive again.

He watched as a few hundred men broke down the tollgate and the keeper's house—by tradition Rebecca and her daughters did not participate in the actual destruction.

And then he saw Marged. He would not have been quite sure, perhaps, if he had not seen her dressed in the same garb the night his horses were let loose from the stables and he found wet ashes in his bed. She was wearing a cap tonight and he could see from the brief glimpse he had of her face that it had been blackened as almost everyone else's had. But she was undoubtedly a woman. Undoubtedly Marged.

His first instinct was to keep his distance. How impenetrable was his disguise? But he had ever been bold as a boy. If the disguise could not fool Marged, then perhaps it would not fool someone else—someone who might betray him. Conversely, if it could fool Marged, then it could fool anyone.

And so he put it to the test, leaning down from his horse's back, cupping her chin with his hand so that she would be forced to take a good look at him, speaking to her with his voice only a few inches from her ears, bending his head so that she could see him despite the darkness.

She did not know him.

His exhilaration and boldness grew as he dismissed the men and sent them on their way home. It had been a brief encounter. What if it were a longer encounter and at even closer quarters? He had been careful about detail. He had even made sure that he did not wear his usual cologne and that none of it lingered on any of the clothes he wore beneath Rebecca's robes. But was there a detail he had neglected, one that would betray him?

It was something he did not need to put to the test. It was something it might be dangerous to put to the test. And even if he could deceive her, it would perhaps be unfair to do so. She hated him with very good reason.

But temptation was something he had never been able to

resist as a boy, and the years of discretion that had intruded since that time had fallen away in the course of the night. The more daring an enterprise, the more likely he had been to try it as a child. It was a miracle he had never come to any grief more painful than that blistering spanking he had had at the hands of one of the gardeners at Tegfan.

He leaned down again and touched Marged on the shoulder.

And talked her into riding with him.

And watched the men disappear into the darkness on their way home, trying to calm his breathing as he did so. He had no excuse to be breathless. He had not participated in the exertions of the last half hour.

But he was beginning to realize that perhaps he had made a mistake. His arms, bracketing her body though not quite touching her, burned with her body heat. His thigh felt singed where it rested against her knee. He could smell ashes and sweat and woman—an unbearably erotic perfume.

Marged. Ah, Marged.

"Where do you live, my daughter?" he asked her.

It was incredibly difficult to turn her head sideways and look into his eyes when she was this close to him. They were light eyes, gray or blue—it was impossible to tell which. He looked even more solid from close to, even larger than life. And strangely masculine despite the grotesque woman's garb and the mask.

"On a farm beyond Glynderi and Tegfan park," she said. "Do you know the area?"

"I know it," he said. "When we have passed the village you must direct me to the correct farm."

"Oh," she said, realizing his intent, "you must not take me all the way home. It is late and I would not take you out of your way."

"Ah, but it would be my pleasure," he said. "What is your name?"

"Marged Evans," she said. Sitting sideways on a moving

horse was not easy. She had never done a great deal of riding. He must have sensed the fact. His right arm came firmly about her waist, and she felt instantly safe.

"Well, Marged Evans," he said, "perhaps as you said earlier, there were other women out tonight, but I did not see them. Why did you come? It was strenuous and dangerous business."

"I do a man's job at home," she said. "I run a farm. My mother-in-law looks after the house and milks the cows and does some of the work in the dairy, but I do everything else. I do not shrink from hard work."

"Where is your husband?" he asked.

"Dead." The horse was moving upward into the hills and was throwing her balance sideways. She tried to stay upright, but her shoulder touched his chest and then pressed heavily against it. And his arm held her against him. She had not been mistaken. He was very solidly male.

"I am sorry to hear it," he said softly, and she felt that he meant it. She felt warmed by his sympathy. "You came out, then, to prove that you are any man's equal?"

She chuckled. "Yes, I suppose so. I had to come. I have the same grievances as everyone else. I also have a personal grievance."

"Ah," he said, and his arm tightened as his horse scrambled over uneven ground. She lost the battle with her neck muscles and her head came to rest on his shoulder among the blond ringlets of his wig. "Is it also a private grievance?"

"No," she said, "not really." Who better to tell than Rebecca? "My husband died in the hulks while being transported to Van Diemen's Land. He had been sentenced to seven years for trying to destroy the salmon weir at Tegfan. The Earl of Wyvern never even lives there."

"I have heard he is in residence now," he said.

"Yes." She could hear the bitterness in her voice. "But I wish he had stayed away. His coming has brought it all back fresh again. I used to know him when we were children. We used to—play together. I thought to appeal to that old friendship after my husband was sentenced. I wrote to him—twice. But he did not help. He did not even answer my letters."

For a moment she felt his cheek against the top of her head, but he did not keep it there. "I am sorry," he said softly. "It must have been a dreadfully painful time for you."

She swallowed but did not answer. This was not good for her, this being cradled by a man's arm, her head on his shoulder, feeling his sympathy. It was not good at all.

"Who are you?" she asked him.

He chuckled. "I am Rebecca, Marged," he said.

"But who is the man behind the mask?" He was someone she had never met. She knew that. But he was someone she would like to meet. She would like to see him in his everyday clothes. Was his physique as magnificent as it felt through the robes? Was his face handsome? What color was his hair? "Where are you from?"

"There is nothing behind the mask," he said. "There is only what you see. And I come from the hills and the valleys and the rivers and the clouds of Carmarthenshire."

She smiled rather ruefully. "You wish to keep your identity a secret," she said. "That is understandable. I should not have asked. But I would not betray you, you know. I admire what you did tonight and the way you did it more than I can say. I will follow you in the coming nights as often as you call us out."

"That is high praise indeed," he said.

They were moving downhill. It would have been easy for her to sit upright again. But his arm held her to him, and she did not struggle against it.

They lapsed into silence. But she was not embarrassed by it. Her initial fear at his closeness and at her precarious position on the horse's back had passed. They were alone in the dark hills, but she was not afraid of him. Leaning against him, no longer looking at his disguise, she could feel that he was only a man. And he was a man she trusted. He was Rebecca.

And yet other feelings came gradually to replace the fear.

An awareness of him as a man. An awareness of the fact that she was cradled against the chest of a stranger, her head on his shoulder, his arm about her waist, his inner thigh pressed against her knees. And that they were alone together in the hills on a dark night.

But still there was no fear and no embarrassment. Only a guilty enjoyment. It had been so long. Until recently she had felt guilty about thinking of other men, wanting other men. She had felt disloyal to Eurwyn. She had felt still married to him. But lately she had admitted to herself that he was dead, that her loyalty to him while he lived had been total, but that she still had a life to live. She had started to feel her emptiness, her need of a man. And yet she had been unable to feel interest in any of the men who had signaled that they might be interested in her.

She had a mental image suddenly of a man standing in darkness before her, his back to the doorway of Tŷ-Gwyn. Of that man taking both her hands in his and raising them one at a time to kiss the palms. And of the shameful way she had wanted him. Shameful because she hated him. She shivered and pressed her head harder into Rebecca's shoulder.

"You are cold?" his voice asked against her ear.

"No." She shook her head slightly. "Am I taking you very far out of your way?" But she knew she was. They had walked for miles earlier before they came up with him.

"No," he said, but she knew he lied.

They were silent again. And she closed her eyes and frankly enjoyed her closeness to him. And the feel of him, strong and broad-shouldered. And the smell of him. He smelled—clean. And the knowledge that he was someone worthy of her respect and loyalty. She enjoyed the pleasant desire he aroused in her. He made her feel that she was back in the land of the living. He made her aware again of her femininity. He made her know that one day she would really desire and really love again.

It seemed a strange end to a night that had been devoted to violence and hatred.

*   *   *

Guilt and pleasure warred within him. She really did not
know who he was. She did not even suspect. He could tell
from the way she snuggled against him, all her weight
resting sideways against his chest, her head nestled on his
shoulder, that she trusted him utterly. It was foolhardy. She
was alone in the middle of the night with an apparent
stranger and trusted him to do her no harm.

And yet it was no man she trusted, he knew. It was
Rebecca. She admired and respected and trusted him
because he was Rebecca. He had told her there was nothing
behind the mask. He had lied more than she realized.

He remembered suddenly the way she had leaned away
from him, revulsion in her face, when he had reached for her
that night the horses had been let out and she had been
telling him about the letters she had sent him pleading for
her husband. *Don't touch me!* she had told him.

He should have left her to walk home with the Glynderi
contingent.

But he had not done so and now he was committed to
taking her all the way home. He would not do it again.
Indeed, he would persuade her before letting her down not
to join any of the Rebecca Riots in future. He would
command her as Rebecca not to come. It was just this one
time, then. And they must be more than halfway home
already.

And because it was just this one time and because they
were more than halfway home, he allowed himself to enjoy
her closeness. It had been so long. And no one would ever
convince him that young love was ridiculous and of no
account. He had bedded his share of women and considered
others as a wife, but he had never loved any of them as he
had loved Marged. He had never suffered the pain of loss
with any of them as he had suffered it with her.

He had loved her. And though he had not thought of her
constantly or even often during the past ten years, he had
thought of her occasionally and always with a pang of
nostalgia and regret for the gaucheness that had killed his

chances with her. It was partly Marged who had made him resolve never to return to Tegfan and never to know what was happening there.

And now he held her in his arms again, and like a dream, she rested against him, relaxed and trusting. Although he was no longer a young boy with a young boy's foolishness, he knew that in the future he would continue to remember her occasionally and that when he did, it would be tonight he would remember.

And then landmarks began to look familiar as they loomed out of the darkness. They were almost home. He felt both relief and regret. Relief because enjoyment was beginning to turn to active desire. Regret because he knew there would never again be a night like this one.

He skirted past both the village and the park. He almost made the mistake of turning up into the hills toward Tŷ-Gwyn. He caught himself in time.

"We have just passed Glynderi," he said. "You must direct me from here, Marged."

She turned her head to look about her, and he realized that she must have had her eyes closed.

"Oh," she said, "it seemed such a short distance coming back." Perhaps he only imagined that he heard regret in her voice.

He chuckled. "Distances have a tendency to feel shorter when one is on horseback," he said.

"You must ride often," she said. "You ride easily. Turn right here up into the hills."

He turned right and did not comment on what she had said.

"Your mother-in-law will be worried about you?" he asked.

"She does not know I am gone," she said. "At least, I hope she does not. She had enough worries with my husband. She deserves to live out the rest of her life in peace."

"You should not even take the chance of worrying her,

then, Marged," he said. "What if you were caught? Who would run the farm for her?"

"Somehow the Lord provides," she said simply. She laughed softly. "I am a minister's daughter, you know. When my husband was taken, I wondered the same thing. But somehow we manage without him. We have to do what we believe in in this life, I am firmly convinced. We cannot always be wondering what will happen if things go wrong. That is the surest road to cowardice."

It was not going to be easy.

"I married Eurwyn because he was the sort of man who followed his convictions," she said. "I loved him for it. I never whined and insisted he think of me first before going into danger. And I never blamed him for leaving me alone."

He felt a stabbing of jealousy for the long-dead Eurwyn Evans, the man she had loved. And the wistful desire to be so loved himself. But such love had to be earned. He had done nothing to earn it.

"A little farther on," she said, pointing. "At the top of the next rise."

They rode the rest of the distance in silence. When they reached the gate and the shape of the longhouse could be made out through the darkness, she stayed where she was.

"Here?" he asked her.

"Yes." Her voice was low, almost a whisper against his ear.

Chapter
14

She was as reluctant to end the night as he was, he realized. She was no more ready to say good night than he.

"Marged," he said, "I do not doubt your courage or your commitment to the public cause or your personal grievance. I honor you for what you have done tonight."

"But," she said. "I hear a *but* in your voice. Don't say it. Please. I have admired and respected you so much tonight. Don't spoil it by talking about a woman's place. A woman's place is not always at home. Her place is where she must be. And I must be with my people during these protests, sharing the exertion and the danger—and the exhilaration with them. I must be with you. With Rebecca, that is. Don't forbid me to go."

Damnation! All his resolve was melting away. "And if I did?" he asked her. "Would you obey?"

She did not answer for a few moments. "No," she said at last.

"Rebecca must demand total obedience of her children," he said. "It is necessary for the success of our cause and for the safety of all. I suppose, then, I must not issue a command that cannot be obeyed. Doing so would merely place us both in an impossible situation, wouldn't it?"

"Yes," she said. And then more fiercely: "Thank you. Oh, thank you. I knew you were a man I would like almost more than any other."

His heart turned over at the compliment, though he knew that it was a compliment for Rebecca rather than for the man behind the mask.

"Come," he said. "It is time you were safe in your bed." He dismounted, holding her firmly in place with one hand as he did so. Then he reached up both arms and lifted her to the ground.

She stood in front of him, staring up at him. His hands were still at her waist, he realized, though he did not remove them. She looked absurd and rather endearing with her cloth cap covering all her hair and with her blackened face.

He lifted one arm and took off the cap. Any hairpins she had been wearing to hold her hair in place must have come away with it. Her hair cascaded over her shoulders and down her back in thick waves. He had not seen her with her hair down, he realized, since she was a child.

"I must look a mess," she said.

He was touched by the vanity of the words, so rare with Marged. She did look a mess. And strangely lovely.

"It is the blackening that really does the trick," he said.

"Oh." She brushed the knuckles of one hand ineffectually over one cheek. "I had forgotten that. So you have seen me with part of my mask removed. Let me see you. It is dark and I would never know you to identify."

"Marged," he said, taking her hand in his and drawing it away from her face, "I am Rebecca. There is no one behind the mask." He was about to carry her hand to his lips, but realized that it might be too familiar a gesture. He squeezed it instead. "Good night," he said. "I will stand here until you are safely inside."

"Good night," she said, returning the pressure of his hand. "Good night, Rebecca. And thank you for riding so far out of your way."

He released her hand, but she did not turn away from him fast enough. She paused long enough to smile at him. Too long. He set his hands at her waist again, drew her against him, and kissed her.

He could feel nothing but her lips, trembling against his own—the wool of his mask kept his face from touching hers. But it was enough. Too much. He deepened the kiss, parting his lips over hers, licking at them with his tongue. Marged! Love, he was discovering, could lie dormant for ten years but did not die. It could flower again with one kiss. Flower into a more intensely glorious bloom than before. Yes, it was like the flowers of springtime, blooming out of plants seemingly dead at the end of a long winter.

"Oh," she said, her eyes and her voice dazed when he lifted his head. Her hands were stroking across his shoulders. "Who are you? Who *are* you?"

"Go in now," he said. "Go now, Marged."

She gazed into his eyes for a moment longer and for the first time he saw a frown between her brows and doubt in her eyes as if she were recognizing him. But she shook her head and turned away. Before he could assist her, she was through the gate and hurrying across the farmyard to the house. He could scarcely see her by the time she opened the door, but he thought she turned to wave to him. He lifted a hand in response and kept it there, motionless.

If only he had not been so foolish as a boy, he thought. If only he had not cut himself off from Tegfan so ruthlessly that even a personal letter from the woman he had loved had not made it into his hands. She could love him again. He had seen it in her face and heard it in her voice and felt it in her kiss. If only he had not done things to make her hate him, he could woo her back. But those things were irreversible. He could not bring her husband back to her. And if he could, he would lose her anyway.

He would do it gladly, he thought with a jolt of pained surprise, if only it were possible. He would bring back the husband she had admired and loved. And so cut himself off from her forever. It would be enough to know that she was happy.

And that perhaps she would remember him with some kindness.

He stood at the gate for a long time before turning back to his patient horse and swinging himself back into the saddle.

She was in chapel at the usual time on Sunday morning. She sat very erect, looking straight ahead instead of giving in to curiosity and looking about to see how many of last night's Rebeccaites had managed to get themselves out of bed in time.

She realized that she had had no more than four hours of sleep. What surprised her was the fact that she had had that much. She had not expected to sleep after scrubbing her face and undressing and climbing into the cupboard bed, exhausted as she had been. There had been too much teeming around inside her head.

But she had found as soon as her head was on the pillow and the blankets up beneath her chin that there was only one image in her mind after all. There was Rebecca's face covered by the pale mask, surrounded by the blond ringlets. And Rebecca's light eyes, beautiful and compelling. Eyes that for a moment before she had come inside had had her reaching for something in the recesses of her memory that just would not come into her conscious mind.

And Rebecca's mouth, warm and inviting and wonderful—and giving the startling lie to any lingering myth that there was no man behind the mask.

She had relived his kiss and the memory of the feel of him, burrowing farther beneath the blankets and keeping her eyes firmly closed, unwilling to let go of the magic of it. She had been kissed again after so long. She had been desired again. And she had desired. A man she had never seen without the disguise, a man she would not know if she passed him in the village. But there had been desire between them.

And she would see him again. Perhaps never to talk again. Perhaps he would never look at her again. But she would see him. And follow him as Rebecca wherever he chose to lead her. Because she admired and trusted him.

Because she had fallen a little in love with him. She had smiled at the thought. And fallen deeply asleep.

She wondered now if it was wicked to be sitting in chapel after such a night. She had been part of a mob that had destroyed a tollgate and a tollhouse. She was a criminal in the eyes of the law. And she had kissed a stranger and desired a man who was not her husband. Oh, yes, she had desired him. She had wanted to lie with him, all the disguises stripped away. She had wanted him in her bed and in her body, man and woman together.

But she would not feel ashamed.

And then someone sat in the empty seat next to her, Eurwyn's place that no one had taken since his death. Except that one Sunday. And again today. Without turning her head, she knew. She could feel that it was he. And she could smell the distinctive musk of his cologne. She stiffened with resentment.

"Good morning, Marged," he said very quietly.

So he had decided to notice her this morning, had he? She considered ignoring him, but she was in chapel. Not that that should make any difference. If she acknowledged him only for that reason, she was being very hypocritical. She turned her head to find his blue eyes steady on her. They gave her a jolt of awareness.

"Good morning, *my lord,*" she said equally quietly.

It was the limit of the communication between them, and he did not try to walk home with her after chapel as he had the time before. It would have been difficult, anyway. She drew Mrs. Williams and a reluctant Ceris away from the crowd far sooner than usual after service, linked her arms through one each of theirs, and marched them off homeward, talking determinedly about the spring flowers blooming wild along the banks of the river.

But he had ruined her morning. She had been unable—

again—to concentrate on any part of the service though it had sounded as if her father had been fuller of *hwyl* even than usual if the chorus of responses from the congregation during the sermon was anything to judge by.

And what was worse, he had ruined last night for her. She had tried to ignore her awareness of him by concentrating her mind and her emotions on Rebecca and their ride home together and their shared kiss. But it had not worked. Not as well as it had the night before when she had gone to bed.

He had merely been a stranger being gallant. And taking advantage of the situation a little at the end by stealing a kiss. Though there had been no theft involved, of course. He must have known that she was pathetically willing. It had been nothing more than that for him. Perhaps he even had a wife at home, wherever home was.

Only she had felt the magic.

And damn Geraint Penderyn for making her see that sooner than need be. Yes, she would use the word again quite deliberately in her mind.

Damn him!

Ceris walked with Marged but did not participate at all in the conversation. She had always known her friend's views and had always sympathized even if she could not agree. Marged after all had lost a husband cruelly. It was enough to make any woman bitter. If it had been Aled . . .

But Marged had gone beyond talk. She had joined Rebecca last night, as had Aled, and they had gone to smash a tollgate. A legally erected tollgate. She knew they had gone. Her father would have gone too if the distance had not been so great. But he was no longer a young man and found it difficult to walk great distances. Aled had advised him against going, he had explained last evening to Mam and her. But he would go another time, when it was a gate closer to home.

Ceris marveled at how well rested Marged looked. No one would know that she had been up for most of the night and marching through the hills and breaking down a tollgate.

She herself had not slept at all. Worse, she had been sick with worry all night. What if they hurt someone? Or killed someone? What if they were caught? What if some of them were hurt or killed? Or thrown in prison to await trial as Eurwyn had been? She had felt sick for every one of them, especially those she knew. She had visualized them one at a time in her mind, all those men she knew had gone. And Marged.

She had not thought of Aled. And she had thought of no one else. Her father had told them that Aled was playing the part of Charlotte, Rebecca's favorite daughter. The one who would be closest to Rebecca. The one who would be in most danger.

She had still been sick with worry this morning. Had they really done it? Had they all returned safely? And then in chapel she had seen that no one was absent except Miss Jenkins's elderly father, who sometimes stayed in bed on a Sunday morning although they lived right next door to the chapel.

Marged was there.

And Aled was there. Her legs had felt like jelly as she walked behind her mother to their pew. Thank God, oh, thank God, Aled was there. He had come back safely.

And then of course, just when relief should have helped her to relax so that she could concentrate on worship, the guilt hit her. She had worried all night and all morning over Aled—and had not spared a thought for Matthew. She had put Matthew off when he had wanted to walk with her last evening. She had been afraid he would see something.

She had thought she was growing fonder of him. She *was*. She enjoyed his company. He talked to her about his childhood in England and about life there. He opened up a different world to her imagination. She was trying to enjoy his kisses. She *did* enjoy them. And she was trying not to flinch from some rather more intimate touches. Aled, after all, had done more than just kiss her. There had to be more than just kisses between two people when they were courting.

And she had agreed to be courted.

He was showing interest in her, making her feel that she mattered to him as a person. He was asking her about her life and her people. He had even asked her about Aled and why they had broken up.

"Well," he had said, not pressing the point when she had given him a vague answer, "all I can say, Ceris, is that I am glad you did and that I never thought him worthy of you."

She was glad he had kissed her then. She could not have responded in words.

She was trying very hard to fall in love with him. She had thought she was close. And yet all last night and all this morning she had thought only of Aled.

She wondered in some despair, as she walked home after chapel, not participating in the conversation Marged and her mother were holding, if she would ever stop loving Aled. One should be able to stop loving someone of whom one disapproved. One should be able to fall in love with someone one liked. But love did not work that way.

Sometimes she wished—although she had denied it to Aled at Mrs. Howell's party—that they had married before all this had started to happen. And sometimes she wished that on one of those occasions when they had walked up into the hills together and their embraces had grown hot, one or other of them had not stopped the embrace before it went too far. Sometimes she wished that she had known Aled in the biblical sense at least once in her life. And that she had at least one of his little ones to hold in her arms.

And God forgive her for the sinfulness of such thoughts.

Perhaps if she married Matthew and knew with him what she had never known with Aled, and perhaps if she had a child with him—perhaps . . . Did love work that way? she wondered. She had no way of knowing—yet.

"Ceris," Marged said, speaking to her directly at last and forcing her friend's wandering thoughts back to the present, "you are walking out with Mr. Harley? I have known it for some time—everyone knows it by now—but we have not been exactly the closest of friends lately, have we?"

She smiled rather awkwardly and Ceris noticed that her mother had walked on up the lane to the house, leaving them alone together.

"Is it wise?" Marged asked.

"Wise?" Ceris became instantly wary.

"Well, he *is* the steward at Tegfan," Marged said, "though he cannot be blamed for what he has done there, I suppose. He is merely doing a job. We all know where his orders come from." Her voice hardened.

"He is courting me," Ceris said. "I—I like him, Marged."

"But he is the Earl of Wyvern's steward," Marged said, "and loyal to him. You know what is going on here, Ceris. What if you say something to him that you ought not?"

Ceris did not often lose her temper. But her eyes blazed now. "You think I would?" she said. "You think I would stoop that low, Marged, just because I will not support what you are doing?"

"No!" Marged looked stricken. "I meant inadvertently, Ceris. Without realizing it. I—oh, forgive me. I did not mean—"

Ceris's anger died as quickly as it had flared. She stepped forward and hugged her friend impulsively. For some reason, they were both in tears.

"He is a good man, Marged," she said. "I may marry him if he asks. I am twenty-five years old and l-lonely. But I would never betray my people even if I cannot support what they do. I would never say anything to put you in danger or Dada or . . ."

"Or Aled," Marged said. "Oh, Ceris."

Ceris blinked away tears. "What happened last night?" she asked miserably. "Was anyone hurt? Was a gate destroyed? Was anyone recognized?"

"A gate was destroyed," Marged said. "We have a wonderful Rebecca, Ceris. He has complete control and uses it wisely. He allowed the gatekeepers to leave in peace and gave them time to take their possessions with them. And

Aled supported him throughout. He was very—brave. It is not an easy risk to take."

Ceris paled. "Aled is nothing to me," she said quietly. "I am walking out with Matthew Harley. But Marged, I will say nothing. You must not fear betrayal from me."

"I did not." Marged's voice was contrite. "Friends again, Ceris? I have missed you."

Ceris nodded. "Me too," she said.

Sir Hector Webb called at Tegfan during the afternoon with his wife. Geraint, who was busy in the library writing letters, had them shown to the drawing room and joined them there a few minutes later.

"I suppose you have heard what has happened?" Sir Hector said almost before they had finished greeting one another. His look was thunderous, Geraint noticed.

"Happened?" he asked politely.

"It is disgraceful," Lady Stella said from her place on the sofa.

"The tollgate near Penfro was pulled down last night," Sir Hector said. He had not seated himself. He was pacing the floor. "And the house too and everything in it. The keeper and his wife were fortunate to escape with their lives. As it was, they were threatened and beaten."

"Indeed?" Geraint raised his eyebrows and took the chair opposite the sofa. "Were there many persons involved? I trust they were apprehended. They must be made a public example of."

"It was a lawless rabble," Sir Hector said. "Several hundred strong, all wielding guns and axes and knives. And of course it was led by a man calling himself Rebecca. And no, no one was caught. That is always the trouble with these Rebecca Riots. There is so much countryside and so many gates. It is almost impossible to know where and when they will strike next."

Geraint's eyebrows rose again. "And so we sit back and allow ourselves to be made fools of?" he asked, his voice cold and haughty. "And will it be our hayricks and our stables and our houses next? I think not, Hector."

"I am thankful to see that you are as outraged as we are, Wyvern," Lady Stella said. "From the way you have been talking about tolls and tithes and rents, we wondered if you would be sympathetic to the mob."

"It is one thing to give some favor freely, Aunt," he said. "It is another to have it taken by force. We can allow no such thing. What measures are to be taken, Hector? Has the army been summoned?"

"I have talked with others since this morning," Sir Hector said. "We will request that soldiers be sent, of course. In the meanwhile we will have special constables sent to the area. But it will not be easy. We will rely heavily on informers. We will offer a reward for the capture of anyone who takes part in the riots—fifty pounds is one suggestion, with one hundred for one of the leaders, or daughters as they are foolishly called, and five hundred for Rebecca. What do you think, Wyvern? Are you willing to pay your share of the cost?"

"It is a great deal of money," Geraint said.

"You can afford it." His aunt made no attempt to hide the contempt in her voice.

"I meant that it should not be long before we round up the ringleaders and put an end to this insanity," Geraint said. "Surely informers will flock to claim their reward."

"It is obvious you have not been in this part of the world for a long time," Sir Hector said. "They are a foolish and stubborn people, the Welsh peasantry. And as closemouthed as clams. They would prefer to protect one another than to make their lives a little more comfortable with blood money."

"Someone will surely talk," Geraint said. "It will take only one."

"Or one caught red-handed," his uncle said. "A man might trade information for the assurance that he will not spend the next seven or so years of his life at hard labor in a foreign land."

"I will do my part, certainly," Geraint said. "By this time tomorrow my people will know that it would be wiser to let the Penfro gate be the first and the last they will ever attack. I thought I was prepared to take a closer look at rents and to take a more lenient view of tithes. I thought I was prepared to see a lowering of the tolls to help my farmers. But they have just alienated my sympathy."

"Well," Lady Stella said, "that is something, at least."

Sir Hector cleared his throat. "Far be it from me to criticize, Wyvern," he said, "but I predicted this as soon as I heard about your salmon weir and the gamekeeper's traps. It never does to show even a hint of weakness to these people."

"I can see that now," Geraint said humbly. "But it will not happen again, you may rest assured. It does not amuse me to be spat upon." He turned to Lady Stella as he rose to his feet and approached the bellpull. "You will be ready for tea, Aunt."

Chapter 15

Geraint was careful the next morning not to call on Aled first. He visited a few of the farms before going to the village and paid a few calls there before stopping at the smithy. This morning he was no longer the newly arrived earl, making an effort to get to know his people and even to show some friendliness toward them. This morning he was the stern, thin-lipped aristocrat, asking questions, issuing warnings, hinting of rewards.

The Reverend Llwyd surprised him.

"I will ask you to leave, my lord," he said, rising to his feet and speaking with great dignity when Geraint tried to enlist his help in encouraging informers to come forward. "Anyone who can ask that one man betray another in the name of law and justice is not welcome in this house. Both the one who can ask it and the one who betrays are an abomination in the sight of the Lord."

"Even when they would be helping to put an end to violence and destruction?" Geraint asked haughtily, getting to his feet too.

"I do not condone violence," the minister said. "Neither

do I condone betrayal of a fellow mortal. And I do not condone the oppression of the poor by the rich, neither, mind, my lord. But it is the Lord God"—he shook his finger in the direction of the ceiling—"who sees sin in whatever form it shows itself. And it is the Lord God who will punish. 'Vengeance is mine, saith the Lord.'"

Geraint left. The Reverend Llwyd had just won his deep respect. And yet every man has his blind spot, he thought. The minister obviously believed that some sins ought not to be left in the Lord's hands. Pregnant, unmarried women could be driven from the chapel and from the community and left to live or die by their own devices.

He went to the smithy next. Aled turned from the anvil, eyeing him warily as a customer sidled from the shop. He wiped his hands on his apron.

Geraint went through his litany for the benefit of the wide-eyed apprentice, who was cowering in a corner trying to make himself invisible. But finally Geraint looked significantly at his friend and nodded almost imperceptibly in the direction of the boy.

"Gwil," Aled said, "home for dinner now, is it? And tell your mam sorry you are a little early."

Gwilym took to his heels without further encouragement.

"There are letters on the way to London," Geraint said quickly. "And letters on the way to every landowner in the area, myself included."

Aled nodded. "You have been prompt," he said.

"It is to be Wednesday night, then, and two gates?" Geraint said. "We must make doubly sure that secrecy is maintained. This push for informers may bear fruit."

"I doubt it," Aled said. "You are insulting my countrymen, Ger."

"And my own." Geraint grinned briefly. "Aled, Rebecca has coffers of gold."

His friend looked at him blankly.

"Money has been sent from the coffers to the Penfro gatekeeper and his wife to compensate them for the loss of their home and livelihood," Geraint said. "The same thing will happen in future. And money has been sent or soon will be to people who are suffering badly from the way the Earl of Wyvern and other landowners treat them. Charlotte will doubtless be asked about it. I mention the existence of the coffers so that your jaw will not hang and make you look stupider than usual." He grinned again.

"Is it necessary, Ger?" Aled frowned. "None of the committee will be able to contribute."

"I have not asked for help," Geraint said. "They are the coffers of *Rebecca* and I am Rebecca. I must go, or anyone who is timing me will think I am flaying you—alive. Wednesday, then."

Aled nodded curtly.

Marged was doing another backbreaking round of the field that would be sown to wheat soon. She had ignored some of the smaller stones during the first round, convincing herself that they were too small to matter. But with the larger stones gone, the smaller ones had suddenly looked bigger themselves and they had stared accusingly at her every time she was busy about something else in the farmyard.

So she was picking stones again. She had been at it since early in the morning. By early afternoon she was feeling hot and stiff and dirty. Dirt was encrusted under her fingernails, she saw with distaste. And the soil of the field must be on her face, rubbed there by the back of her hand, with which she frequently and ineffectually pushed back tendrils of hair that had worked themselves loose from her bun.

There was going to be a bath tonight despite the inconvenience of hauling and heating all that water. And clean clothes. And relaxation before the fire until bedtime. But tonight seemed a whole era away. She straightened up to look across the field, trying to convince herself that she was halfway.

And then she turned her head sharply toward the yard. Her nostrils flared. He looked so immaculate that she wondered if he did anything else at home *but* soak in a tub of hot water and send down his clothes for laundering and ironing. And of course he had just the sort of short curly hair that hardly moved in the wind. He probably did not know what sweat felt like. Or soil—though he had felt it constantly many years ago beneath his bare feet.

He was standing by the gate into the field, watching her. There were two other women on this farm. If this was a social call, he might have knocked on the door of the house and entertained himself with Mam's conversation and Gran's for however long he had decided to favor them with his company. But oh, no, it was she he had to take from her work.

She rubbed her hands hard up and down her dirty apron and strode toward him. She could not have felt dirtier or scruffier or uglier if she had tried, she thought. And with every stride her anger mounted because it mattered to her that he was seeing her this way. It did *not* matter. She did not care how he saw her or what he thought of her.

"What on earth are you doing?" he asked in that hateful cultured English voice.

"You have caught me playing instead of working," she said tartly. "I am picking stones off the field when I could be doing some real work like feeding Nellie. What does it *look* as if I am doing?"

"Marged," he said, "this is man's work."

"Oh, of course." She smote her forehead with the heel of one hand. "How foolish of me. I shall go to the house without further delay and call out all the men who are sleeping in there or in the barn."

He stared at her with his cold blue eyes and impassive face. She did not care what he thought of her insolence or what he would do about it. And then he swung off his cloak and slung it over the rough wood of the gate. He hung his hat over the gatepost and pulled off his frock coat.

"What are you doing?" Her eyes widened.

His coat joined his cloak over the gate. He was undoing the buttons of his waistcoat. "It would seem," he said, "that there is only one man available to do the job."

Marged snapped her teeth together when she realized that

she was gaping. "Oh, no," she said. "Oh, no, you don't. I don't want your help. Get off my land."

He looked at her coolly as he rolled up one immaculately white shirtsleeve above his elbow. "The last time I checked, Marged," he said, "it was my land."

"I have paid my rent on it," she said. "I was not even a day late."

But she had lost her audience. He was striding out into the field. His boots were so highly polished that he could probably see his face in them when he bent down, she thought. And he was walking into a bare *field* with them? His trousers were dark and obviously very expensive and hugged his legs well enough to show that they lacked nothing in shape or muscle. His shirt was flapping in the breeze but was anchored at his very slim waist, where it was tucked into his trousers. Even when the breeze died for a moment, the breadth of his back and shoulders prevented the shirt from collapsing about him. The hair on his arms was as dark as that on his head.

Marged caught the direction of her thoughts and snapped her teeth together once more. She strode after him. This was *her* farm and this was *her* job. But by the time she came up to him, he was already bending down and picking up stones and tossing them into the wagon that she would have the horse pull away when the task was done or when it was full. Well, she thought vengefully, leaning down beside him and resuming her work without a word, she hoped he would get filthy. She hoped that his back would get so sore from the unaccustomed manual labor that he would be unable to straighten up when he was finished. She hoped he would never come back, for fear that she would have some other heavy task awaiting him.

And damn him, he was moving faster than she. And he was picking up two stones with each hand, except for the larger ones, as Eurwyn had used to be able to do.

She could not believe how quickly they finished. They worked for perhaps a couple of hours, stopping only at the end of every second row to drink from the water jar she had brought out with her after luncheon, not speaking a word to each other. And it was done. She had expected to work until dark and even then perhaps not be quite finished.

And then, when they were back in the yard together, she watched as he prepared one of the horses and led it out to the field, hitched it to the wagon, and led it to the stone pile, which he must have seen for himself at one corner of the distant pasture. Eurwyn had used the stones to build some walls. His father before him had used them to build the pigpen.

Marged was tempted while he was gone to rush into the house to wash her hands and face, to comb her hair, and to change her apron. But she would be damned before she would do anything to make herself look more attractive in his eyes.

Besides, she thought, watching him in some satisfaction as he brought the horse back, he was not looking very immaculate himself any longer. His boots were dull with dust and caked with soil, his trousers looked gray rather than black, and his shirt was liberally stained with dirt. And there were circles of wetness beneath his arms. His face and hands looked grimy.

She had wondered at one time whether he would look so splendid if he were not dressed so immaculately. She had her answer, she thought grudgingly. Geraint would be beautiful even if he still lived up on the moors, scratching a living mainly from poaching. But she was glad he was dirty and sweaty. She hoped that he felt uncomfortable. She hoped that tomorrow he would be too stiff to move.

He came and stood in front of her, rolling down his shirtsleeves as he did so. And he spoke for the first time in hours. "What do you know about the destruction of the Penfro gate on Saturday night?" he asked.

Her heart skipped a beat, but she had prepared herself for this.

"The Penfro gate?" She raised her eyebrows.

"Rebecca brought glorious destruction to it," he said. "But I suppose you know no more about it than anyone else in Glynderi or on any of the farms?"

"No," she said.

He nodded curtly. "I thought not," he said. "I would have you know, Marged, that the men who join Rebecca play a dangerous game."

"But there are no men here," she said. "What does this have to do with me?"

He was buttoning his waistcoat with dirty hands over a dirty shirt. And it looked so deliciously expensive.

"And it will become more dangerous," he said, "as more players are added. Special constables. Soldiers. Do I make myself clear?"

"Yes," she said. "You are issuing a warning that I am to carry to the men living about here." She looked directly back into his eyes. She would not allow him to play cat and mouse with her.

"Anyone who is caught," he said, "will be dealt with harshly. You know all about that, Marged."

She breathed in very slowly through her nose. Oh, yes. And there would be no mercy. She knew all about that too. His eyes were icy cold.

"Anyone who is willing to put an end to it," he said, "would be doing everyone else a favor. And would be compensated for any—unpopularity he might have to endure. Or she."

She was not quite sure she was hearing him correctly. But oh, yes, she was. "An informer?" she whispered. "You are looking for an informer?"

"Shall we call him—or her—a friend of the people?" he asked.

She should have looked back at him as coldly as he was looking at her. She realized that afterward, when it was too late. But then she would not have denied herself the satisfaction of what she actually did, though it was less wise. Before she could think, before he could know what she was about to do, her hand whipped across his face, turning it sharply to one side, and causing him to lose his impassivity and wince quite noticeably.

"Get away from here!" she cried. "Get out."

He picked up his frock coat, drew it on, and buttoned it, watching her all the while. His cloak followed. And then he picked up his hat. She watched, fascinated, as one of his cheeks reddened into a scarlet hand. And she thought of Rebecca as he had been at the Penfro gate, both arms raised, holding a few hundred impatient men in check while he talked courteously to the gatekeeper and his wife and gave them time to remove all their personal belongings from the house and make their way to safety. She thought of him bringing her home. And kissing her.

And yet this man, cold and arrogant and cruel, and others like him were prepared to use their wealth and their power to persuade someone to inform on him. It would take only one. She understood then why Rebecca had refused to tell her who he was or where he lived and why he had refused to remove his mask even in the darkness. Torture would not drag the information from her, but he was wise to trust no one.

The Earl of Wyvern turned to leave without another word to her. She watched him go. But she could not let him disappear without saying the words that stuck in her throat but must be spoken if she was to retain her self-respect.

"Geraint," she called, and realized too late that she had used his given name.

He turned.

"Thank you," she said, tossing back her head. "Thank you for the help." She was pleased to hear that she sounded more as if she were telling him to go to hell.

He nodded and touched his hat to her and was on his way.

He felt dirty. He looked down at his grimy hands and grimaced at the sight of ten blackened fingernails. His shirt felt uncomfortably wet under the arms. He could smell

himself. His boots—he looked down at them and winced—
might well be irredeemable. His cheek was still stinging.

One thing was clear. He could not pay any more calls
today.

But he grinned unexpectedly. He felt rather wonderful.
He had enjoyed the morning visits, much as he had expected
them to be distasteful. It had given him a perverse sort of
pleasure to tyrannize all the people who had expected him to
by a tyrant and who had repulsed all his efforts to be
otherwise. And it had amused him to look into blank, stupid
faces—only Marged had offered any variation on that
theme—and to remember many of the same faces blackened for disguise and the arms belonging to the faces
smashing a gate and a house.

It seemed so long since there had been any real excitement in his life. This suited him perfectly, this playing a
dual role.

And Marged. He fingered his cheek rather ruefully for a
moment. He had given up feeling guilty for bringing her
home and holding her close on Saturday night. And even for
kissing her. If she was going to be reckless enough to follow
Rebecca and then to ride home with a stranger and allow
him to kiss her—and even kiss him back—then she must
bear the consequences. Far from feeling continued guilt, he
had enjoyed just now looking into her eyes, keeping his own
cold, and imagining the look on her face if she knew that it
was he, Geraint Penderyn, Earl of Wyvern, who had kissed
her.

Probably at this moment he would have two stinging
cheeks instead of one, plus two black eyes and a smashed
nose. He could remember once when he had persuaded her
to sneak into Tegfan park with him and he had been
surprised by a mantrap that had been moved to a new
location and had almost caught his leg in its steel jaws. She
had hauled him away, and though it was he who had almost
been hurt, not her, she had pummeled him with her fists and
kicked his shins with her shod feet—and then cried all over
him.

He grinned once more. He was feeling more and more like that boy again.

And then his little reincarnation suddenly appeared, tripping along at his side. Idris Parry. Geraint looked down at him in some surprise. He would have expected the child to keep his distance after their encounter in the park.

"Idris," he said, "how are you?"

"I am to have new boots," the child said.

"Are you?" Geraint glanced down at the pitiful shreds of boots the boy wore. It was amazing that they stayed on his feet. "That will be pleasant."

"And my sisters are to have new dresses," the child said.

"Very nice," Geraint said.

"My dada has money," Idris said. "And I know why. And I know where it came from."

"Oh?" Geraint made his voice chilly. He hoped the father had not been that indiscreet. All they needed was to have a blabbing child in Glynderi.

"My dada has money because he went with Rebecca," Idris said while Geraint closed his eyes briefly. "And the money came from Rebecca."

Geraint stopped walking and gazed sternly down at the child. He clasped his hands at his back and found himself hoping that his face was not too noticeably dirty.

"What is this, Idris?" he said. "Do you realize what you are saying and to whom? Do you realize that you could get your father into serious trouble if I believed you? Do you realize that he could be sent away for a long, long time and you would be left with only your mother and your sisters?"

"I wanted to go too," the child said, "but Dada would not let me. He told me he would take the strap to me if I followed him."

Geraint took a deep breath and stooped down on his haunches. "I should think so too," he said. "Now listen to me, Idris. I do not want to hear you telling such stories about your father again. And I do not want to hear of you telling them to anyone else. If I do, I might be tempted to take a strap to you myself for lying. And I have big muscles and a heavy hand. I will pretend I have not heard you today. Do you understand me?"

"But I did go out," Idris said. "And I saw her."

"Her?"

"Rebecca," the child said. "I saw her."

God damn it all to hell! "She probably looked very frightening," he said. "In future you will know to stay safe in your bed at nights, Idris." What were the parents about, allowing the child to wander at night? And yet he remembered that he had done it himself, eluding his mother while she slept.

"I want to help her," Idris said. "I want to help her because she helps us to fight against the bad men. And because she gives money to people who are poor. And because she is not what she seems to be." He was looking directly into Geraint's eyes, his own wide and guileless.

And dear God in heaven, what was this?

"I want to help her if I can," the child said again. For the first time he looked almost frightened. His next words were whispered. "I know who she is."

Dear Lord God!

"Then it were best that you kept the knowledge to yourself, lad," he said. "Go home to your mam now. It looks as if it might rain." It did not.

"Yes." Idris nodded. "But I want to help her. If there is anything I can do."

Geraint rested his hand lightly on the boy's head. He was not sure what kind of communication was passing between them. Not sure at all. Or perhaps he just did not want to know.

"Go home now," he said quietly.

But before he straightened up, he did something that took him quite by surprise. He wrapped his arms around the thin and ragged little figure and hugged him close.

"Life can be dangerous for little boys," he said, "even when they are very brave little boys. Wait until you grow up, lad, and then you can show the world your mettle."

He felt almost embarrassed when he finally stood up. But

the little urchin did not linger. He was off up the hill again, bounding along with all the energy of childhood.

But before he did so, he gave Geraint one wide-eyed look that could surely not be misinterpreted. It was a look of pure devotion.

Hell and a million damnations!

Chapter 16

Tuesday was wet and windy. But Wednesday was sunny and even warm, and the gentler breeze dried the ground by noon. The sky was clear and blue. The only trouble with the weather, Marged thought as she stood at the pigpen, her arms along the top of it, keeping Nellie company, was that it would be a light night with moon and stars.

Aled had passed the word along yesterday that tonight they would march with Rebecca again.

It would be a great deal easier to cross the hills. They would be able to see where they were setting their feet. But it would be a great deal easier too for them to be seen. Word had it that the Earl of Wyvern and Sir Hector Webb and the other landowners had called out special constables and that they had sent for soldiers. And of course they had issued threats and were searching for informers.

Marged felt far more nervous than she had felt the first time. She found it difficult to settle to anything all day. Her nerves were tense with fear. Fear for herself and fear for her friends. *Anyone who is caught will be dealt with harshly,* he had said. *You know all about that, Marged.*

She shivered and tickled one of Nellie's ears. Yes, she was mortally afraid of being caught, of being locked in prison, of being tried and sentenced, of . . . But fear was not going to hold her back. Fear was necessary for one's own safety, Eurwyn had told her once. But it could also be one's greatest enemy, making one a coward, preventing one from doing what one knew should be done.

No, it was not going to hold her back.

But she feared too for Rebecca. Mrs. Williams had heard—probably from Mr. Harley—that they were offering a reward of five hundred pounds for his capture. Five hundred pounds! It was a vast fortune. Would anyone be tempted? Anyone who knew who he was? There must be some people who knew. But a betrayer would not have to know his identity. He would only have to betray the time and place of the next gate smashing and be sure that constables were lying in wait.

They would catch Rebecca and others too as a bonus.

"Nellie, love," she said, rubbing the pig's snout and straightening up resolutely, "there is butter to be churned and you are keeping me gossiping here. For shame!"

She punished the butter inside the dairy to alleviate her fears. But it was not all fear. There was the inevitable excitement too. Saturday night had been incredibly exhilarating. Although there had been destruction, it had all been done in such a disciplined manner that it had not seemed a thing of horror. And they had accomplished something, she believed. They had shown that there were limits to which the poor could be pushed without fighting back. They had shown that they were not without spirit and courage.

And there was the other excitement too. She had to admit it to herself. She would see him again. Rebecca. She had been so very impressed with his air of command, with his dignity, with his compassion for the gatekeepers of Penfro. And she had hugged to herself since Saturday her memories of him as a man. It had been a magical ride they had shared and a magical kiss. She knew she would remember both for the rest of her life.

Her hands stilled on the butter churn. She was behaving like a young girl over her first kiss. But it was not a happy comparison. She thought of the eighteen-year-old Geraint kissing her sixteen-year-old self and the wonder of it and the conviction that the love she had felt would brighten all the rest of her life. And she thought of him as he had been on Monday, handsome and virile in his shirtsleeves while he picked stones, cold-eyed and autocratic as he spoke afterward about Rebecca and her followers.

She did not want to think about Geraint. She wanted to think of Rebecca. And she wanted tonight to be a repetition of Saturday night. But she knew that something so wonderful could not be repeated—just as there had been no repetition when she was sixteen. The next time she had met Geraint he had tried to . . . Somehow, thinking back on it now, it did not seem so very dreadful. He had tried to make love to her. At the time she had known nothing. She had had her head and her heart full of sweet romance and kisses and young love. She had known nothing about the yearnings of the body, nothing about the carnal act of love. She had been sickened and terrified.

She wondered what would have happened if she had known more. Would she still have stopped him? Would he have stopped? Would they have loved, there on the hillside? And what would have happened afterward? Would that have been the end of it? Or the beginning?

"Marged? What is the matter, girl?" Her mother-in-law's voice brought her back to reality with a start, and she realized that she was clutching the butter churn and staring into space.

"Oh." She laughed. "I am taking a breather, Mam, that is all. Is Gran still sleeping?"

"You go in and have a cup of tea, *fach*," her mother-in-law said. "There is some warm in the pot and nice and strong. I'll take over here, is it? You are working too hard, Marged."

Marged relinquished her place at the butter churn with

some guilt and some relief. "A cup of tea sounds lovely, Mam," she said. "Thank you."

She must expect nothing of tonight except a long, hard march and the smashing of a gate at the end of it. And a long, hard march home. She must not think of the danger. And she must not expect that Rebecca would even notice her tonight, let alone give her a ride home. And kiss her.

It would be enough just to see him and to dream of how he must look beneath the rather bizarre disguise.

Except that she knew it would not be enough at all.

Some special constables had been sworn in by the magistrates of the area. A few more had been sent from Carmarthen. Geraint knew that more attacks were expected this week. The logical gates to attack were the ones along the same road as the Penfro gate. Constables had been quietly posted at two of them in the hope that at least one of them would be the next target.

And so tonight the gates to go would be two on the road south of Glynderi, across the river. They were strategic gates. The farmers had to travel south to the lime kilns. Many of them would have to pass these two gates. And they belonged to two different trusts—two tolls to pay even though there were no more than two miles between the gates.

He wondered tonight what he had stirred up. His fellow landowners were outraged and determined at all costs to stamp out the protests. The constables had guns. So would the soldiers if and when they came. Perhaps he had begun something that could only lead to violence and defeat. After all, very few protests or uprisings against the established ruling classes ever succeeded. The chances were strong that this one would not.

But he must pin his hopes on the fact that this time the protesters had a champion among the ruling classes, although neither side knew it yet. His fondest hope was that one of the London newspapers to which he had written as Rebecca would find the information intriguing enough to send down a reporter. If a London newspaper would print the truth and combine it with the rather romantic story of Rebecca and her daughters, perhaps public sympathy would be enlisted. And if any of the carefully chosen public figures to whom Rebecca had written decided to ask questions, or even to come down to investigate, then perhaps they too would see the truth.

It was a slim chance. They were just as likely to see the truth from their own standpoint as members of the ruling class. But if the information he gave them as Earl of Wyvern somehow tallied with what they would learn from the people themselves, then perhaps . . .

Certainly he had a better chance this way of attracting enough attention that something would be done. The people alone, even banded together with a Rebecca at their head, were virtually helpless. He alone, as the Earl of Wyvern, was merely an eccentric and annoying gentleman best ignored.

No. He rode toward the agreed meeting place, not in Glynderi, but two miles south of the river, stopping only once among some densely packed trees he had chosen in advance for the purpose to unroll his blanket and don the garb of Rebecca. No, he must not begin to wonder now or to worry about what he might have unleashed. He must go on. And he had to admit that it was exciting to go on. For four days he had lived for this moment.

He wondered if Marged would come tonight. Part of him hoped that she would remain safely at home. Part of him—perhaps a larger part, if he was strictly honest with himself—hoped that she would come.

He stopped when he reached the meeting place, holding both his horse and his person motionless despite the fact that moonlight bathed the bleak and open hillside and he would be in full view of anyone who happened past. But he knew that his followers expected courage and daring and dignity of their Rebecca. Well, then, he would give them what they wanted. Besides, he would be just as visible if he pranced about and ducked and weaved.

Finally they came, large groups from the east and the north, a smaller one from the west. But at least as many men as on Saturday night and perhaps more. It seemed that they had not been scared away by the warnings or the knowledge that there were constables in the area. He felt a wave of pride for his people. His daughters rode up beside him, all of them silent. Apart from Aled, he did not know the identities of any of the others, just as they did not know his. It was better so. Only the members of the committee knew who he was.

And Idris Parry, an inner voice reminded him.

Apart from one sweep of his head from right to left, he kept his head high and his eyes forward. It had been impossible to tell from that one glance if Marged was in the crowd. But he would bet a fortune that she was. It would be a matter of pride with Marged to go wherever the men went. And to strike every possible blow against the Earl of Wyvern.

He raised his arms slowly and waited for all the murmurings to die away. He knew from his education and experience not to yell over the noise, muted as it was, and so lessen the sense of power and authority he sought to project. He waited for total silence.

"My children," he said, using the voice skills that he knew carried the sound a great distance without the necessity of yelling. "Your mother welcomes you and thanks you for coming to give her your help. There are two gates that disturb me and that must come down this night. You will remove them, my children, when I give the signal."

There was a murmuring of assent.

"Lead the way, Mother," Charlotte said.

"We will follow," another daughter added.

He lowered his arms when the murmuring had died away again, and rode forward, Aled on his right, another of his daughters on his left.

It should have been easier tonight, he thought when they came down to the road and turned left toward the tollgate already visible in the distance. Tonight he knew that he could control his followers and that they could accomplish what had to be done quickly and efficiently. But his heart pounded like a jackhammer in his chest. And perhaps it was just as well, he thought. Perhaps the night he was relaxed and confident would be the very night when danger would strike and he would not be ready for it.

At the first gate there was a gatekeeper with a wife and an infant. The woman was hysterical, the child loudly crying, and the man terrified and sniveling. Geraint had to direct that four of his followers help remove the family's belongings and set them far enough away from the house that they would not be damaged. This was the worst part, he thought as he sat motionless facing the gate, his arms aching from being raised for so long. He did not enjoy creating terror in innocent people. He did not enjoy making them homeless in the middle of the night even though he knew that tomorrow they would be well compensated from the coffers of Rebecca.

But finally the personal belongings were safe and the family had disappeared and he was able to bring his arms sweeping down and to watch as his followers destroyed one of the symbols of their oppression.

Marged, he saw, was working on the gate as she had the last time, wielding blow for blow with the men on either side of her. She did not look up at him.

At the second gate there was only one elderly man as gatekeeper. He neither sniveled nor raged, and he had so few personal belongings to fetch from the house that Geraint felt a stabbing of pity for him. He went limping off into the darkness, his bundle over his shoulder, before Rebecca brought down her arms and his home was destroyed within a few minutes.

Geraint felt slightly less exhilaration tonight. And perhaps that was as well too. This was not a game he played. He was not a boy any longer. He was a man. And it was serious business he was involved in. Unfortunately, in serious business there were always people who suffered. He did not like causing suffering. He did it only because it seemed necessary, but he would not allow any more than he must.

"My children." He raised his arms and waited for silence. He had thought that first night that he might not achieve it since the men's blood was up after such destruction. But he had found that the raised arms and the firm expectation of obedience to his will had brought it. It happened again.

"My children," he said, "you have done good work tonight. Rebecca is proud of you. Go home now but be careful. We have enemies. Your mother will call you out again soon and you will come to her assistance."

He held his horse still in the middle of the road as he had done the last time while the men dispersed and went their several ways. Marged went with the men from Glynderi. He watched her go. Their eyes had not once met tonight. He had made no attempt to ride close to her or to single her out for attention. He was not sure it would be wise to try to repeat what had happened on Saturday night. He did not want to tempt fate. And she might have had time to realize since Saturday that it was not wise to pursue any sort of flirtation with a stranger. He did not want to approach her and be rejected. Being rejected as both Geraint Penderyn and Rebecca might be just too much for him.

And yet he watched her go with regret and wondered if he should go after her.

A little farther along the road her group turned upward into the hills. She stopped for a moment to look back at him. The moment stretched and she half lifted a hand in a gesture of farewell.

He raised his own arm upward, palm in, and moved it slowly toward himself—a slight gesture of beckoning that she could interpret as she would.

She stood where she was a moment longer and then came walking back toward him. He did not know if she had said anything to the others, but they kept walking upward after a couple of them had stopped briefly to look down at her.

She stopped beside his horse and looked up at him.

It was too late to send her back. And he knew in his heart

of hearts that he did not want to. But he felt the difference between tonight and Saturday. There was very definitely a difference.

He reached down a hand for hers and looked into her eyes, shadowed beneath the brim of her cap. "Come," he said.

She looked at his hand for a few moments before placing her own in it and her foot on his boot. She felt it too, then. She knew this was different. But like him, she knew it was too late to go back. And perhaps like him, she did not really want to.

She sat before him on the horse's back. Without turning her head to look at him, she took off the cap and stuffed it in a pocket of her jacket while she shook her hair free. She took a handkerchief from the same pocket and scrubbed at her face with it. Unwise moves, both. She was making herself beautiful for him.

Ah, Marged.

Then, still without looking at him or saying a word, she leaned sideways against him and burrowed her head into his shoulder.

He gave his horse the signal to move.

Perhaps she should not have stopped and looked back. He had made no move to seek her out or to speak with her tonight. Perhaps he had not wanted any further involvement with her. She was as bold as any man in many ways, but she had never taken the initiative in seeking out any man. Perhaps she had made a mistake.

But she knew she had not. She had known as soon as she turned that he was watching her. And she had known by his gesture, slight as it was, that he wanted her to come. And she had known as soon as she was at his horse's side and looking up into his eyes that he wanted her to ride with him again.

But she knew more than that. She knew that it was different tonight. She knew that tonight he had beckoned to her as a man and that she had come as a woman. She knew that a great deal more had happened on Saturday night than had been apparent and that a great deal more had happened during the intervening days than she had realized. She knew tonight that she had desired him on Saturday and every day and night since. And she knew quite consciously that she desired him tonight. She leaned her weight against him and nestled her head on his shoulder and closed her eyes and felt the heat of him and the strength of him. She smelled the clean smell of him.

She did try for a few moments to tell herself that she could not possibly desire a man she had never seen without the grotesque disguise, a man she did not know. She did not even know his name or his occupation or his marital status. She tried to tell herself that the daughter of the Reverend Meirion Llwyd could not possibly be indulging in and reveling in these feelings of pure physical desire for a man who was not her husband. She had never had feelings quite so intense even for Eurwyn.

But she did not fight for long. For the first time she understood the temptations that led women into sin. And sin did not even feel sinful tonight. Besides, they were just feelings. No one would be hurt by them. He would take her home and kiss her again and she would have the rest of the night in which to dream of these moments. Not as many as last time—they had worked much closer to home tonight.

She knew he was feeling as she felt. There were the physical layers of a disguise between them, but when her eyes were closed she knew that there were no barriers at all between their hearts. Or perhaps she was glamorizing the situation too much, thinking of hearts. But she knew that he desired her. She knew that she had not merely made a fool of herself by turning back to him.

She did not know where they were. She had kept her eyes closed. When his horse slowed and then stopped, she opened them and found that they were in darkness, among trees. Just south of the river, she guessed. Close to home. She wished they had five more miles to go. Or ten.

He lifted his shoulder, bringing her head closer to his. She closed her eyes again when she realized he was going to kiss her, and turned slightly so that she could lift an arm about his other shoulder.

There was something almost unbearably erotic, she thought, about feeling the warm, soft flesh of his mouth against her own but only the wool of his mask surrounding it. He kissed her with parted lips as he had done before. Eurwyn had never done that. Neither had Geraint—she closed off the thought. And he traced the seam of her own lips with the tip of his tongue, something that shocked her and sent raw pain—no, not really pain—shooting down through her body to set up a throbbing between her legs.

"Oh," she said when he was finished.

But he did not immediately ride on again as she expected or kiss her again as she hoped. He was looking at her, but it was too dark among the trees to see his eyes clearly. And the moon and stars had disappeared, she realized. Clouds must have moved over.

"Shall we get down, then?" he asked her, his voice low and husky against her ear.

She was not so naive that she did not understand him. Or so dazed by his kisses or her own desire that she did not understand all the implications. It was something that had horrified her as a girl of sixteen. It was something she had deplored in others. It was something she would not have thought herself capable of even considering.

"Or shall I take you home?"

Take me home. Oh, yes, take me home. "We will get down," she heard herself whispering.

He held her steady while he dismounted and then lifted her to the ground, as he had done the last time outside her home. He kept his hands on her waist, as he had done then, and kissed her briefly on the lips.

"You are sure, Marged?" he asked her.

Her legs felt boneless. Her heartbeat thudded in her ears. "Yes." She was still whispering.

Chapter

17

He released her in order to tether his horse and lift a bundle from its back, and then he took her by the hand and led her farther in among the trees until it was so dark that she did not believe she could even see the end of her nose. She stretched out her free hand ahead of her.

"Here." He stopped walking and held her hand firmly while he appeared to be spreading on the ground the bundle he had drawn from his horse's back. "Lie down."

Looking back the way they had come, she could see the lighter grayness of the world outside the forest. Here it was blacker than night. She lay down. It was a blanket or a cloak that was beneath her.

When he came down beside her and cupped her face with one hand and found her mouth with his own, she drew in her breath sharply. His mask was gone. She raised her hand to his face. And so was the wig. He had short, thick hair. Wavy. He opened her mouth with his own, and his tongue came slowly and deeply inside. She heard herself moan.

She was wearing breeches, she thought suddenly. It was going to be awkward. But he did nothing about them for the moment. He was unbuttoning her jacket and then her shirt. And his hand was coming inside, over her shoulder, down the valley between her breasts, and then around to cup one of her breasts, to feather his fingers over it, to rub his palm over her nipple, to pinch it gently.

Oh. Eurwyn had never . . . "Oh."

His mouth was moving down over her chin, down her throat, trailing hot kisses to her breast, opening over its tip and closing again. His tongue rubbed the nipple.

"Ah." She arched up against him. Both her hands held his head, her fingers pushing into the thick curls.

And then his mouth was on hers again and she could feel his fingers dealing with the buttons on her breeches. She lifted her hips when she could feel that they were all open and reached down a hand, helping him to slide them off along with her undergarments. She felt the cool night air against her bare flesh. She felt as if she were on fire.

She did not help him with his own clothes. He still wore Rebecca's robe, and she guessed he wore some kind of breeches beneath. He did not completely remove them. She could feel the fabric against her legs as he came onto her and eased them wide. When he put himself against her, she discovered that she was swollen and throbbing and wet. But she could feel no embarrassment, only the aching urgency of the moment. His hands came beneath her to cushion her.

"Marged," he said against her ear.

She did not know his name to reply. It did not matter. *"Cariad,"* she whispered to him. *My love.*

He came in slowly. But he came deep. She felt stretched wide by him, filled with him. She had never imagined . . .

She had always lain still. Willing and receptive, but still and impassive. She could not be either this time. When he withdrew and slid inward again, she pivoted her hips and tightened muscles she had not known she had in order to draw him far in, in order to feel him there. And then she relaxed while he withdrew again, and lifted and pulled inward when he returned. She had felt rhythm before, but someone else's, someone doing something to her, pleasurable, but not involving her. This time his rhythm became her own, so that soon she was gasping with him and slick with sweat with him and moving with him to that outpouring of energy and tension that she had always faintly envied in her husband.

"I can't. . . ." She was frightened suddenly. Suddenly she wanted to turn back, to make different decisions, to give different answers. She did not want to move into this new world.

"You can." He spoke softly against her ear, though he was breathless from his exertions. "You can, Marged."

And he held deep in her when she expected him to withdraw and so broke her rhythm and the sudden defenses she had thrust up in her panic. She was impaled on him and had no choice but to give him what his body demanded. Her own body's surrender. Not the acquiescence she had always given in her marriage, but surrender. Of her body. Of her heart. Of her whole self.

But just at the moment when terror threatened to engulf her, wonder caught at her instead. For with the warm springing of his seed deep inside her she felt him surrender exactly the same things to her.

They had made love, she thought hazily and foolishly. They had not just coupled. They had made *love*. She had never before really understood the meaning of the term.

She had made love with a stranger.

With Rebecca.

Incredibly she was sleeping. It was a chilly night and the ground was hard, but she lay on her side, pressed in to his body, her head on his arm, her hand clutching Rebecca's robe just below his shoulder. He had pulled the edge of the blanket up over her. And she was sleeping.

He was moved by the trust in him she must have to sleep in his arms. And to give herself to him though she did not know who he was. It seemed to him so typical of Marged to behave with such reckless generosity.

He fought sleep himself. He was sated and utterly

relaxed, but he dared not sleep. There was danger in the fact that he had all the trappings of Rebecca with him when two tollgates had been destroyed a mere few miles away. Though that was not the danger that most concerned him. If he fell deeply asleep, he might not wake until after dawn. And Marged would see with whom she had lain and loved.

He had not intended this to happen. He really had not. Even when he had beckoned her to come back to him, he had not planned this. He had not *planned* anything. Perhaps he had expected a repetition of Saturday night. Even when he had felt the difference, after she had come back to him, he had thought only of kisses. Even when he had stopped by the trees among which he had changed into his disguise earlier, he had not planned this.

Had he?

Why, then, had he stopped here? He could hear himself asking her the question—*Shall we get down, then?* And then, so that he would not pressure her into doing anything she did not want to do—as he had tried to do at the age of eighteen—*Or shall I take you home?*

And yet it was not really a free choice he had given her. He should have fought the temptation to take her in the guise of a stranger. And yet she had given herself freely to a stranger. He might be anybody. He might be a married man for all she knew.

Marged. He rubbed his cheek lightly over the top of her head. Her hair was warm and silky. She had given herself with passion, as he would have expected. There had been a suggestion of innocence too. She had been frightened at the end by the force of her own passion. Perhaps Eurwyn Evans had allowed it to lie dormant inside her. But he did not want to think about her marriage—or how it had ended.

She stirred and her head went back along his arm. She was looking up at him. He wondered if her eyes had grown accustomed to the darkness. His own had not. But it had been reckless to remove his mask and wig.

"Who are you?" she whispered. "Surely you can tell me

now. Surely you must know that you can trust me, that I will never betray you."

He found her mouth with his own and kissed her. "I am Rebecca," he said.

"Give me a name at least," she begged him. "A first name. A name to think of you by."

He wondered what she would do if he simply gave her his name, all of it. For a moment he was tempted. He would hold her very tightly while she raged and fought. And then he would love her again. But it would not be that simple. She blamed him for her husband's death, and she was justified in doing so. And he had deceived her tonight just about as badly as a man could possibly deceive a woman.

"Rebecca," he said softly against her lips. "Think of me as Rebecca."

She sighed and smoothed her fingers through his hair and cupped one of his cheeks with her hand. "Rebecca," she said hesitantly, "are you married?"

"No," he said.

She sighed again. "Why not?" she asked him. "There must be lots of foolish women in your village to have allowed you to remain free. Why have you not married?"

"I have been waiting for you," he said, and realized even as he said it that there was a large measure of truth in his words.

"Ah." She moved her thumb across his lips. "But you will not even trust me with your name. Will you leave your mask off when we go back out into the night?"

"No," he said. "And we must go back out, Marged. We ought not to have stopped. It might be dangerous. The alarm might have been raised by now."

"Ah, must we go home?" she said. "I wish we could stay here forever. How foolish I am."

He rolled away from her in order to adjust his clothing and feel around in the darkness for his mask and his wig.

"And how selfish I am," she said. He could hear that she was pulling her breeches back on. "I am close to home. You still have a long way to ride. No, I am not fishing or trying to trap you. But I know you have a long way to go. If you lived close, I would know you. And I do not know you." She chuckled suddenly. "Except in the most biblical of senses. Why am I not ashamed? I am not, you know. Are you?"

"No," he said. He stooped to gather up the blanket and reached for her hand. He was not sure his answer was strictly true. "Come."

There was no sign of movement beyond the trees. The night was darker than it had been earlier. He was both glad and sorry for it. Glad because he could not easily be seen and sorry because he could not easily see. He mounted his horse and reached down a hand to bring Marged up in front of him. She snuggled immediately against him, wrapping both arms about his waist. He headed cautiously for the bridge across the river.

"You must be careful," she said. "Did you know that they are offering five hundred pounds for your capture?"

"Indeed?" he said. "I am worth that much?"

"No one will inform against you," she said. "Besides, no one knows who you are. The only real danger is that you will be caught. And I have added to that danger."

"No." He kissed the top of her head, feeling with regret the barrier of his mask that prevented him from touching her hair.

"He called on everyone on Monday," she said. "He even came to Tŷ-Gwyn."

"He?" The bridge had been safely crossed. He turned his horse upward into the hills.

"The Earl of Wyvern," she said. "He had the gall to help me with the stone picking on one of the fields. And then he questioned me and threatened me and hinted that I would be serving my people by informing against them."

"That was not nicely done," he said.

"I should have remained icily aloof," she said. "But I was furious. I slapped his face. But I was not sorry afterward. I am not sorry now."

"He was probably sorry," he said.

"He just looked at me with those cold eyes of his," she

said. "He has changed so much. He used to be full of—oh, how do I describe it? A passion for living."

"You used to like him?" he asked.

"I loved him," she said. "He was a wonderful child. He lived in such dreadful poverty and yet his spirit was quite unbowed. He was cheerful, energetic, daring—oh, a hundred different things. And he used to sing, with the sweetest soprano voice. Such heavenly music from a ragged and impish little rogue." She chuckled, though there was sadness in the sound. "I used to love him. I find it hard to believe that he is the same person. I would not wish to see you in his power. He is hard and ruthless. He does not show mercy. I do not like you riding in this area."

"I will be careful." They were riding up the last part of the slope between Ninian Williams's farm and Tŷ-Gwyn. He could not talk easily. There was an ache in his throat. She had spoken of Geraint Penderyn, the child, with such wistful tenderness in her voice.

He did not speak again until he had lifted her to the ground outside the gate to the farmyard. He kissed her warmly.

"Marged," he said, "you must be careful too. I would rather you did not come out again."

"Would you?" She lowered her eyes. "I should not have looked back tonight, should I? You did not mean to spend time with me tonight, did you? I am sorry. But I did not go for that reason. I went because I had to. I will go again for the same reason. I will not come near you again. I am not trying to put an obligation on you merely because I have lain with you."

"Marged." He drew her close against him. "I may have got you with child. Have you thought of that?"

"Strangely, no," she said. "I was married for five years and never conceived. I have always thought I was unable to."

"If you are with child," he said, "I will not leave you in disgrace. You must tell me. If all else fails, you can communicate with me through Aled Rhoslyn. But it would not be a good situation, Marged. It would not make you happy."

He was trying desperately to be sensible. He was trying to force *her* to be sensible.

She looked up at him suddenly, smiling brightly. "I thought men were supposed to take their pleasure and feel no responsibility for their consequences," she said. "You are tenderhearted, Rebecca. Go now. You must go. And be careful."

He lowered his head to kiss her again, but she had turned away and was opening the gate. She hurried through it and closed it behind her. She was still smiling at him.

"Good night, Marged," he said.

"Good night." Her smile was too bright. *"Cariad,"* she added, and turned to flee across the yard toward the house.

"Good night, *cariad*." He formed the words with his lips, though he did not speak them aloud.

There were special constables in the area. They were staying, apparently, at Tegfan, four of them, housed in the servants' quarters. But they had been seen walking about the park, deep in conversation with the Earl of Wyvern. And Glenys Owen had reported to her brothers that they had dined with him.

They called at almost every house in Glynderi and at almost every farm, asking questions, demanding that each man account for his whereabouts on the night when two tollgates and houses had been pulled down by Rebecca and her children. They offered immunity to anyone who would confess to having been there but who would give them the names of Rebecca and perhaps some of her daughters. No one could give them any assistance at all, of course. Every man had been in his bed, where he belonged at night, and every man's wife would vouch for the fact.

Marged heard all about it from Ceris, who called at Tŷ-Gwyn two days after the attack. The constables had not been there themselves, having ascertained, no doubt, that there were no men living there. Ceris was pale and shaking and huddled inside a shawl, even though the weather had turned warm. Marged took her into the empty cow barn and they leaned against the partition between two stalls.

"It must stop now," Ceris said. "Surely it will, Marged. Someone is going to get caught."

"I don't believe it will stop," Marged said. "This is what we wanted, Ceris—to attract attention. There would be no point in doing what we have done if no one took any notice of us. We want the government to take notice. We want them to ask questions, to find out why it is happening. We want the gates down permanently, and we want the government to know that the gates are only one grievance out of many."

Ceris put her hands over her face, and Marged heard her take a deep and ragged breath.

"At least it is not the Earl of Wyvern himself going around this time," Marged said. "He must have been discouraged by the reception he had on Monday."

But she could not whip up the appropriate anger against Geraint. And she could not get as excited as she ought about Ceris's news. She was too selfishly wrapped up in her own emotions. It was selfish, she knew. The greater cause was all that mattered, and yet all she had been able to think about since Wednesday night was the fact that he did not really want her.

Her heart had felt so leaden for almost two days that she felt that she was dragging it about on the soles of her feet with every step she took.

If she was with child, he would not leave her in disgrace. She might communicate with him through Aled. She supposed he meant that he would marry her if she was pregnant. Only because she was pregnant. Not for any other reason.

It would not be a good situation, Marged. It would not make you happy.

His words had repeated themselves so many times inside her head, that she felt dizzy with them. And yet she had told him—and she had meant it—that she did not lay any claim to him merely because she had lain with him.

She had lain with him! With a stranger. She could hardly believe that she had done such a thing and that she had felt so little shame—and still felt almost none. It had felt so right. As if they belonged together. She had never had a stronger sense of belonging even with Eurwyn. And yet it was ridiculous. She did not even know his name. She did not know what he looked like, where he lived, what he did for a living. She knew nothing about him except what she had learned about Rebecca. She could think about him only as Rebecca. But he was not Rebecca. She did not know who he was.

And yet she loved him. It was a foolish idea. It was the natural defense the mind made against sin, she supposed. It seemed less sinful, what she had done, if she could persuade herself that she loved the man with whom she had sinned.

She loved him.

It would not be a good situation, Marged.

He did not love her.

And yet he was an honorable man. He had given her a choice before lifting her down from his horse. And he had agreed to take responsibility for any consequences of their folly.

"Marged." Ceris laid a hand on her arm. "You look tired, girl. Will you at least stop going now? You have made a point. You have proved to everyone that you are as brave as any man and that you are willing to stand up for what you believe in. But you have Eurwyn's mam and gran to look after. Don't go again."

"Everyone has someone to look after, Ceris," Marged said. She was tempted not to go out again. It might be better to hold her memories intact, not to have to go through the pain of finding herself ignored. But as she had told him, she had other reasons for following Rebecca. More important reasons. "I will go."

They had reached an impasse. But before either of them

could say more, there was an interruption in the form of a knock on the outer door. Since it was open, Marged could lean her head out into the passageway and see that it was Aled.

"Come in, Aled," she called to him. "We are in the barn here, Ceris and I." She would have avoided the meeting for both their sakes if she could, but it was impossible.

"Hello, Marged," Aled said, striding into the barn, his wary look at variance with his firm stride. He nodded in Ceris's direction. "Ceris."

Ceris had scurried a little farther into the barn. "Hello, Aled," she said, not quite looking at him.

"I had something I wanted to talk over with you, Marged," he said.

Ceris moved, drawing her shawl more tightly around herself as she did. "I'll be leaving, Marged," she said. "Mam will be needing help with the wash."

But Marged held up a staying hand. She remembered with shame the way she had suggested just a few days ago that Ceris might perhaps, however inadvertently, say something she ought not to Mr. Harley.

"Don't leave, Ceris," she said. She looked at Aled. "You can speak in front of Ceris. She is my friend."

Ceris stood where she was, and Aled, after a moment's hesitation, nodded.

"Have you heard of the coffers of Rebecca?" he asked Marged.

She frowned and shook her head. "No," she said, but her stomach lurched just at the sound of his name.

"There is a fund," he said, "to help those in need. Some goes to the gatekeepers who lose their homes and their livelihood. Some goes elsewhere."

Oh, what a wonderful idea. She wondered whose it had been and who financed it.

Aled cleared his throat. "Rebecca has directed me to call on you," he said. "You need a laborer on the farm, especially with the seeding coming up."

She stared at him.

"And Waldo Parry needs a job," he said. "His wife has another little one on the way. I suppose you know."

She nodded, not saying anything and not taking her eyes off his face.

"I am to ask you to accept this money to pay him for working for you," he said, patting a pocket and looking downright embarrassed. "We all know how proud you are, Marged. We all know that you are capable of running this farm as well as any man. But you could use the help. And Waldo will end up in the workhouse if he finds no job this spring. I do not know who else can afford to offer him employment. You know what happens in the workhouse. He will be separated from his wife and she will be separated from her children. And they will all come close to starvation. Do it, girl. For them, is it?"

Marged was very much afraid that she was about to disgrace herself. If she moved or tried to open her mouth, she would end up bawling. He cared! He did care. She did not for one moment believe that his primary concern was for Waldo Parry. He could have persuaded anyone to take Waldo on. But he had chosen her. Because she needed help. Because he cared.

She nodded.

Aled looked surprised and relieved. "Good. Then it is settled," he said, taking a package out of his pocket and handing it to her. "This should be enough for six months' wages. You will speak to him, Marged? It would be better, perhaps, if he did not know the story behind his new job."

Marged nodded again.

Aled looked uncertainly at Ceris and cleared his throat again. "Will I walk you home, then, Ceris?" he asked.

She stood for a long time without moving. But then she nodded and stepped forward. "Yes," she said. "Thank you."

She hugged Marged as she passed. "I am so happy that you will have help and that Waldo will have work," she said. "Perhaps some good will come of all this after all."

Marged nodded and made no attempt to leave either the barn or the house with the two of them. She stood where she was, looking down at the package in her hand. She used her free hand after a minute or two to swipe at a couple of tears that had escaped from her eyes and were trickling down her cheeks.

Chapter 18

She had agreed to allow him to walk her home, but she had pretended not to notice his offered arm. She held her shawl with both hands and kept her eyes on the path ahead of them. She kept two feet of clear space between them. And she made no attempt at conversation.

They had used to hold hands when they walked, except when they were among the hills, off the beaten track, when often he had set an arm about her shoulders and she had set one about his waist. Her eyes had always sparkled at him and there had always been a brightness in her face, a smile on her lips. She had always chattered to him about anything and everything.

He thought about three smashed gates and the letters Geraint had written and sent to local landowners and to various people in England. He thought about the odds against success and the odds in favor of capture and punishment. There were constables actually posted at Tegfan—there at Geraint's invitation. Aled's childhood admiration for his friend had returned and doubled in force over the last couple of weeks. He was as daring as ever, but now there was a sense of purpose and a sense of responsibility to temper the daring. Geraint was no longer reckless. Except perhaps where Marged was concerned. Aled knew they had ridden off home together on both gate-breaking nights. But Geraint had fixed his aristocratic blue stare on his friend when Aled had suggested to him that it was perhaps unwise.

Aled thought again about what they had done and what there was still to do—all the uncertainties and all the dangers. And for that he had given up *this*. He turned his head to look at the woman he had loved with single-minded devotion for six years. Sometimes it seemed a poor exchange.

"You are stepping out with Harley, Ceris?" he asked. He had not meant to ask the question. He knew the answer but did not want to hear it from her.

"Yes," she said.

He felt deeply wounded, as if he were hearing it for the first time. But he could not leave it alone.

"You care for him?" he asked.

"Yes." There was a dullness to her voice—so unlike Ceris.

"And he is good to you?" He did not want to know how good Harley was to Ceris, God damn his soul to hell.

"Yes," she said. He thought their poor stab at conversation was at an end, but she continued after a short silence. "He is courting me."

Well, he had invited it. He should not have asked the first question. Courting was rather more serious than stepping out. Courting was a preliminary to a marriage offer and to marriage itself.

He wanted to say something. He wanted to tell her that he wished for her happiness. Or that he was glad she was getting on with her life. Or that he was pleased she had chosen a man who would be able to provide well for her. Or that he envied Harley. But there were no words he could force past his lips.

They had reached the end of the lane leading up to her father's house. It was the place where he had always kissed her whenever he was not going to go into the house with her. They both stopped walking, though he had expected her to keep on going.

"Aled." She looked up into his eyes—the sparkle in her own was all gone, leaving only sadness and beauty behind. "Marged says that R-Rebecca is a good and a compassionate leader, if those qualities can belong to a man who also destroys property. But I can see that she is at least partly right. Was it his idea to compensate the gatekeepers who lose their homes and jobs? And to help the poor? Was it his idea to help Marged and Waldo Parry, both at the same time?"

"Yes." He nodded. "It was all his idea, Ceris. It is not something that is part of the usual role of Rebecca."

"I know," she said. "And you are his right-hand man, his Charlotte. Did you volunteer to call on Marged?"

"He asked me," he said, "and I agreed." He smiled briefly. "I did not expect it to be as easy as it was. Marged is about as proud as it is possible for a woman to be."

"Aled," she said, "perhaps I have done your cause some injustice. Perhaps it is doing some good. If only it were not also doing a lot of evil." She sighed.

Hope had revived painfully in him for a moment. But there was no hope. Besides, another man was courting her.

"I must go and help Mam with the wash," she said.

He nodded and smiled at her and turned away. But when he had taken several steps down the path and assumed that she was on her way to the house, her voice stopped him again.

"Aled," she called.

He turned and looked at her. Her unhappy eyes had grown luminous.

"Be careful, *car*—" she said. She lifted her shoulders and tightened her hold on her shawl. "Be careful."

Cariad. She was going to force herself to love Harley and to marry him. She was of an age at which she needed a home of her own and a man of her own and little ones. But being Ceris, she would not go with her heart when her heart led her away from her deeply held principles.

But she loved him.

Perhaps if he asked her to wait . . . This would be over one day, settled one way or another. If he was still free then, perhaps . . . But no. Nothing would have changed. He would still be a man who had fought in the Rebecca Riots, and she would still be a pacifist.

He nodded. "I will," he said, and turned back to continue on his way back down to Glynderi.

It was going to become far more tricky and far more dangerous, of course. There were constables, not in Glynderi, but right in Tegfan itself. There was a firm promise of soldiers. The temptation was to lie low for a while, to postpone further action until the fever to catch Rebecca had died down. And until the landowners had got over their outrage at the letters they had all received from Rebecca, clearly enumerating the people's grievances and the conditions under which they would suspend further destructive action.

The Earl of Wyvern was one of the most furious. He grumbled to the constables and mumbled to Matthew Harley and raged to Sir Hector Webb and Lady Stella about gratitude for favors given and how he would know in future to keep his favors to himself. He was sorry he had ever set foot back in Wales, but he would be damned now if he would leave before the trouble had been settled and Rebecca caught and punished.

It was too soon for there to have been any response from England. But Carmarthen and Swansea newspapers had boldly published the letter that had been sent to each of the landowners. Perhaps copies of those articles would be published elsewhere—perhaps in England, perhaps in London. They could use all the publicity they could get.

No, it was not the time to hold back. It was not the time to become cautious. Everything so far was happening according to plan. They had known the dangers would become greater with every appearance of Rebecca. It was not the time to run and hide.

Friday, Geraint had agreed with Aled, and two gates west of Glynderi since all the vigilance of the constables was being focused east and south. But everyone was going to have to be far more careful about leaving their homes and returning to them. And they must gather at a place more distant from the village. But Friday would remain the night for their next attack.

As he cut himself off more and more from his people—he rarely left the park and always wore a grim expression whenever he did—Geraint came more and more to identify with them. His Welshness returned to him almost as if the sixteen years of his exile in England had never been. He walked about the park of Tegfan, breathing in Welsh air and gazing about him at rolling Welsh hills, and knew that he was home at last after a long, long absence. What had he said to Marged when she had asked where Rebecca was from?

I come from the hills and the valleys and the rivers and the clouds of Carmarthenshire.

Perhaps he had not realized at the time how much he spoke the truth. And it angered him intensely that his people were not free to live lives of work and contentment and freedom in their own homes, in their own country.

Oh, yes, he would continue to fight for them even if the danger doubled, as well it might.

But with the reassertion of his Welsh identity came the need to go all the way back, to find his roots, his beginnings. To face the pain.

His mother. She had always appeared beautiful to his child's eyes with her dark wavy hair and blue eyes, like his own. But she must have been beautiful by any standards, he thought now. It was hardly surprising, perhaps, that Viscount Handford, his father, had been so smitten by her when she was Lady Stella's governess that he had been reckless enough to elope with her and marry her, though she was only the daughter of a nonconformist Welsh minister.

For the first time since his return, Geraint went to see her grave in the Anglican churchyard. And his father's grave. They had been buried side by side. GWYNNETH MARSH, VISCOUNTESS HANDFORD, the inscription on the headstone read. His mother. She did not sound like his mother.

"Mam," he said softly.

He had seen her only once alive after that strange morning when the Earl of Wyvern, his grandfather, had appeared in person up on the moors and had spoken to his mother until she was in tears and Geraint had launched himself at the man and punched him and kicked him until servants pulled him off and held him. Only once, on the morning he was leaving Tegfan and Wales for school in England. A brief, deeply emotional farewell. A good-bye, though he had not realized it at the time. He had never been allowed to write to her and he guessed that she had not been allowed to write to him.

He had had to be ruthlessly purged of everything from his first twelve years of existence that made him unworthy of being the Earl of Wyvern's heir.

"Mam," he said again, and his eyes moved to his father's grave. He knew little about the man who had been killed only weeks after his son's conception, beyond the fact that he had been handsome and daring and full of laughter. And that he had loved Gwynneth Penderyn, Geraint's mother.

Geraint wondered about the loneliness of his mother's life for the eighteen years following the death of his father. For twelve of those years she had had only him and had loved him fiercely. For the last six she had had—no one? He did not know about her last six years. The pain and the emptiness of not knowing stabbed at him and reminded him that he had put them aside with everything else when he had left Wales forever—or so he had thought. He had felt the deep guilt of his neglect of her, though he had been only a boy and had been given no choice at all. But still there had been the guilt. She was dead, and he would never be able to tell her that he loved her constantly through the years of their separation.

"Mam." He knelt down and rested a palm against the turf beneath the headstone. He hoped there was a heaven. He hoped she had been with his father there for ten years, though time would be meaningless in such a place, he supposed.

It was the middle of the afternoon and he had nothing in particular to do and nowhere in particular to go. But he did not want to go back to Tegfan. Someone there was always seeking him out for some purpose and there was always the chance of visitors, especially these days. He did not want to talk with anyone. His heart was too heavy with remembered emotions. He stood up and looked around—and up.

He had told himself on his return that it was one place he would never go. It was too much a part of his deepest nightmares—the isolation, the ostracism, the hunger and cold, the bareness of home, his mother's loneliness and unhappiness, masked for his sake, but always known to him. He did not want to go back. But it was the only place to go. If he did not go back, he thought suddenly, then he would never really be able to go forward.

And so he went, trudging determinedly uphill, his head down. Perhaps there would be nothing to find except the remembered contours of the bleak upper moorland. Perhaps it would all look familiar yet different. Perhaps he would be able to look about him and breathe in the fresh air and know that it was all gone, all in the past. And that his mother was gone and at peace. Perhaps he would not find any ghosts at all. And those hovels were built of sod and thatch and could not be expected to last long against the elements of the uplands.

But the hovel in which he had lived with his mother had not gone. Not completely. It had been built against an outcropping of rock and had been sheltered from too rapid deterioration. One side of it had collapsed and the thatch was sparse and almost black with age, but it was still recognizable as a wretched habitation. And there was still a doorway to the interior.

He stood some distance away, looking at it, for a long

time before approaching the doorway and peering inside. There were only darkness and mustiness to greet him.

He had never felt this dread as a child. Children were so very adaptable, he thought, especially when they had known nothing else. It had not seemed abnormal or even very terrible to him as a child to live here in such poverty that it was amazing they had survived. It was only in retrospect that it had become a place of horror, a subject for his nightmares.

And yet he had known love here. The only love of his life. His mother. Perhaps that was why it had become a dreaded place, suppressed from his memory and surfacing only in his nightmares. Perhaps it was not so much the poverty and the bleakness that haunted him but the love— the total, unconditional love he had received here. Perhaps this was the place where the riches of his life had been. For sixteen years he had had everything in his life *except* love.

He had dreaded coming back because something deep in him had known that doing so would reveal his present poverty to him.

He moved to one side of the hovel, to the side still standing, and rested his arm along the dirty thatch of the roof. And his head sank onto his hands. If only they had let him write to her, even once.

He wept.

She did not waste any time. She made a quick explanation to her mother-in-law and then threw a shawl about her shoulders and made her way up to the moors with long, mannish strides.

She wanted to share her exuberance and her good fortune.

She had to go carefully, of course. She was not sure if the Parrys would reject the offer if they knew the truth. Perhaps not, but even so it was probably as well if as few people as possible knew about the coffers of Rebecca.

So she told Waldo Parry that she had set aside a little money and had now decided to use it to hire help, certainly for the summer and perhaps permanently. She hoped he was available and would be willing to help her. She hoped some other farmer had not beaten her to it. She knew how much his services were coveted.

He had had a few offers, he told her. Nothing that he fancied until now. He would enjoy working for her, though, and he knew how much she and her in-laws needed a man about the place. Mrs. Parry smiled and nodded and looked suspiciously bright-eyed. The little girls sat and gazed from their father to the visitor and back again as each spoke. Idris stood in the doorway, darting glances all about and drawing attention with strategic shuffles to his new boots until Marged complimented him on them.

It looked as if Rebecca had already partly taken care of the Parrys. The little girls, Marged noticed, were wearing new dresses. How did Rebecca know of them? she wondered. Through Aled? Doubtless he had someone in each community reporting to him. Or perhaps it was the committee itself, acting in the name of Rebecca, which was helping where there was need.

But it was Rebecca himself who had decided to help her. She did not doubt it. She hugged the thought to herself as she left the Parrys to their pride and their newfound joy— which, of course, they had not shown in full measure while she was there with them. But she did not feel like returning home just yet. She wanted to be alone to feel the full extent of her own joy.

Nothing really had changed. He had still warned her quite clearly that he wanted no permanent connection with her, that if he was forced to marry her it would not be a good situation. But the point was that he *would* marry her if her condition made it necessary for her to ask and that he *did* care. Perhaps he would never look at her or speak with her again. Perhaps she would never ride with him again. Or make love with him again. And it would be painful. She had no doubt about that. But she would hug those facts to herself and she would remember for the rest of her life her brief and glorious fling with romantic love.

She strode across the top of the hill, letting the wind take her unconfined hair, and relived that night of love. She relived every kiss, every touch. She relived their union and the unexpected passion of it. She had not known it could be like that. Not that she would ever admit that it was better than it had been with Eurwyn. With Eurwyn there had been warmth, affection, marital closeness. With Rebecca there had been . . . Oh, there were not words. Marged lifted her chin and closed her eyes and drew in a deep breath.

She was in love with Rebecca—deeply in love. And she could not feel sorry that she had known everything with him. Even if, by some strange quirk of fortune, she was with child. She felt a moment's stabbing of panic. But he would not leave her in disgrace, he had said. And how wonderful it would be—oh, *Duw,* how wonderful—to find that after all she could have a child of her own. His child.

She opened her eyes again and smiled. She did not know who he was. She had never even seen his face. And yet she was wishing for his child?

Her steps had brought her in a different direction from the one she had taken a few Sundays before. She was close to where Geraint had used to live with his mother. The hovel was still there, she knew, though it was in very bad repair. She did not often come this way. She usually avoided the memories. And she should have done so today. She did not want to think about Geraint. She wanted to focus her thoughts entirely on Rebecca. She would at least see him soon—tomorrow night again. Her heart beat faster at the thought.

And then she was aware of something at the far side of the old hovel, something that did not belong there—the flutter of dark fabric from behind the far wall, the suggestion of something darker than the thatch on the far side of the low roof. She felt fear for a moment—it was a very bleak and lonely spot. But she had never been one to flee fear. She walked slowly closer, stepping as quietly as she could.

By the time she stepped cautiously past the old house, far enough that she could see what was behind the side wall, she was no more than eight or ten feet away from him. His cloak was thrown back over his shoulders. His arms were spread, elbows out, along the roof and his face was hidden in his hands. He was hatless.

Although his cloak was fluttering in the wind, he was standing quite still and silent. Obviously he had not heard her come.

Her first instinct was to leave—and fast. She felt the familiar welling of hatred and resentment. She had no wish to see him ever again. And the thought struck her that if he had his will, he would destroy her new love as he had destroyed the old. He was Rebecca's enemy. He had constables at his house sworn to catching Rebecca. He was not himself a magistrate, but she knew he would rejoice in the capture and would press for the stiffest penalty the law would allow.

She had heard that any Rebecca who was caught would be transported for life. If he did make it to Van Diemen's Land alive, he would never return. Never.

She actually turned to leave. But she looked back over her shoulder. He was so still. What was he doing? He was the same person, she thought unwillingly, as that little boy who had lived here with his mother. That little boy she had loved with a child's adoration.

She stepped closer to him, close enough to touch him. She lifted one hand, saw it trembling, and closed it on itself. But she opened the hand again and touched it lightly to his shoulder.

"Geraint?" she whispered.

He spun around so quickly that she took an involuntary step back, terrified. Her hand stayed suspended in the air. But then she gazed at him, horrified. His eyes were filled with tears and both they and his cheeks were blotched red. He had been crying!

"I am sorry," she said, still whispering. Her hand fell to her side. She had some idea of turning and fleeing.

But before she could make her escape, both his arms came out and grabbed her. He hauled her against him and held her there with arms like iron bands. For a few moments she was terrified. She could scarcely breathe, and her nostrils were assaulted by the expensive musk of his cologne. She thought he meant to do her some mischief.

But it did not take her longer than those few moments to realize that he was in deep distress. There had been the tears and the signs that he had been crying for some time. And she could feel now the wild beating of his heart and the irregular gasps of his breathing.

"Don't fight me. Don't fight me," he ordered her fiercely. And yet she knew that his words were a veiled plea for help.

She was horrified anew at the situation. And she should fight, she knew. If he was suffering for some reason and her fighting him would make his suffering more acute, then she would be having some small measure of revenge on him. He had not moved a single finger to lessen her suffering. She should pull away from him, say something cutting, laugh in his face, and walk away.

She wriggled against him until she could free her arms to wrap about his waist. And she turned her head to rest her cheek against his shoulder. She relaxed against him, giving him all the silent comfort of her warmth and her softness.

She closed her mind to what she ought to do.

He was Geraint.

She felt his cheek come to rest against the top of her head.

Chapter
19

It took him a few minutes to realize exactly what had happened. She had come upon him when he had least expected to see anyone, and she had caught him at his most vulnerable. He was almost never vulnerable. He had built a hard shell about himself long ago, probably from the very earliest years of his life.

He held her tightly and drew strength and comfort from her warm, relaxed body. She had her arms clasped about his waist and her head on his shoulder. She had not fought him—he could hear the distant echo of his voice commanding her not to. Neither had she turned limp and impassive in his arms. She was deliberately offering him the comfort of her presence.

It had seemed natural to him to turn to her, though it had been an unconscious, instinctive thing. She was, after all, Marged. And he was her lover. He had loved her just two nights ago with his body. But she did not know that. He was her enemy.

He lifted his cheek from her head and loosened his hold. He supposed there was no way of hiding the fact that he had been crying. He could not remember the last time he had cried. Not at his grandfather's funeral or even at his mother's. Perhaps when he was at Tegfan at the age of twelve and they would not allow him to see his mother.

Marged drew back her head and looked up at him, though she did not immediately drop her arms from about his waist.

"Can you imagine a greater cruelty," he asked, "than driving a poor pregnant woman out of a church and out of a community and forcing her to live her life as an outcast, so abjectly poor that she does not even know if she will be able to feed her child on any given day? And of doing such a thing in the name of Christianity?"

She gazed at him for a while before finally lowering her arms though she did not step away from him. "No," she said. "I don't believe I can."

"Even if she had been guilty," he said. "Don't the devout members of your church realize that love is what Christianity is all about? Just simply that? Nothing else. Only love." He was no expert on Christianity, but it seemed to him that that was the Gospel—the good news. Not the rigid, judgmental application of a code of rules and laws.

She did not answer him. Perhaps she thought he was not the person to be preaching love and Christianity.

He had to move. He had to get away from that house. But not alone. He shunned aloneness now as he had shunned company when he had left the churchyard earlier. He had always been alone, so very alone. He took her hand in his, willing her not to pull away, and drew her up the steep slope beside the house onto the top of the outcropping of rock. There was a view from up there, an unobstructed view of rolling hills and valleys that stretched for miles. And there was wind. It buffeted them, sending her dress and his cloak billowing out behind them.

She did not pull away. Neither did her hand lie quite limply in his. She curled her fingers lightly about it.

"She used to joke sometimes," he said. "'At least we have a back garden with a view,' she used to say. 'The best in the country.'"

They stood looking at the view. She said nothing. Their shoulders did not quite touch.

"She was my father's wife," he said quietly. "She gave birth to my father's son. She kept me alive and gave me all the love I have ever known and taught me all the important things I have learned in my life. She was my mother, my mam, and yet suddenly when I was twelve she became a contaminating force in my life. So much so that I must never see her. I must never even write to her or receive a letter from her. She was Welsh and a product of the lower classes—a lethal combination. They spoke of her—on the few occasions when she was mentioned at all—with contempt. I was encouraged to despise her."

"Did you?" Marged asked.

"No," he said. "Never for a moment."

It was perhaps the one comfort he could feel. But he had never been able to tell her that. When he finally saw her again, she was dead.

"Marged," he said, "they gave her a cottage to live in. She must have lived there for six years before her death. Was she quite alone?"

"No," she said. "Not quite. Many people tried to make amends. My father and the deacons and their wives called on her. Admittedly they would not have done it if they had not discovered that she had been legally married, but it took some courage. A few people called more than once or twice. I believe Mrs. Williams became her friend. I—I called on her several times. She would never go back to chapel."

He realized suddenly that he was gripping her hand very tightly. He relaxed his hold.

"I was not allowed to return here or to write to anyone," he said. "My past was to be obliterated as if it had never been. I became Geraint Marsh, Viscount Handford—though my grandfather and everyone else called me Gerald—an English gentleman whose life began at the age of twelve."

He turned without conscious thought to lead her down from the rise and to stroll across the hills with her. It seemed natural to share his thoughts and his pain with her. After all, she was his lover and his love. But the thought was not a conscious one.

She felt rather as if she had stepped out of time. What was happening did not quite belong in this time or this place. With her mind she could tell herself that she did not need to hear this or anything else that would somehow make him appear human to her. She could tell herself that he was her enemy, the man she hated more than anyone else in this world. If he suffered, he could never suffer enough for her liking. She could remind herself that she loved another man now—and that they had been lovers, however briefly. She loved a man who was this man's sworn enemy. She could remember that she had walked across the hills rather than go home because she had wanted to think and to dream about Rebecca.

But sometimes the mind has only a little influence over one's whole being. She walked with him and held his hand and listened, not only to his words but to his pain, and she could not think or feel any of the things she should think or feel.

He was Geraint and he needed her.

"I always assumed somehow that I would come back," he said. "Back home to my mother. When my education was finished. I thought they would be satisfied then. I thought I would be my own man. I thought I would come back to her and love and care for her during her declining years as she had loved and cared for me during my growing years. Even when I knew she was dead, I thought I was coming home. I thought I would assert myself and stay here." He drew a deep breath and exhaled audibly.

She found herself wanting to take a step closer to him so that she could lean her head on his shoulder. She resisted the urge. He was the Earl of Wyvern, she reminded herself.

"It was not home," he said. "There was no home. Anywhere. Nowhere where I belonged. No one I belonged to."

"Your grandfather—" she began.

"No," he said.

She remembered the handsome, arrogant, self-assured, very English young man who had returned from England for his mother's funeral.

"Marged," he said, "for what it is worth after so long, I am sorry for what happened. Deeply sorry. I selfishly grabbed for comfort where I thought—without any good reason—it was being offered. But I did care. You were still my wonderful friend—that was how I described you to my mother the day you befriended me and plied me with blackberries. Do you remember?"

She swallowed but still heard a gurgle in her throat. She fought tears. "Yes," she said.

He stopped walking and turned to her. "And I am sorry for this too," he said, lifting her hand in his own, though he did not release it. "I have kidnapped you and forced you to listen to an outpouring of self-pity. I am not given to such outpourings, Marged. You were in the wrong place at the wrong time. You will wish me to the devil—where I belong." He smiled rather wanly.

Yes, she must wish it. She bit her lower lip. He was not Geraint. Not any longer. He was the Earl of Wyvern. *Why did you ignore my pleas for Eurwyn?* she wanted to ask him. *Why did you forget then about our wonderful friendship?* But she did not want to hear his answer. Not now. She was feeling too confused and upset.

"Come," he said, and he brought her hand through his arm and finally released his hold on it. "I will walk you home."

It was on the tip of her tongue to tell him that she had walked far enough with him already. Too far. She could see herself home. But she could not say that either. Hatred, she was discovering, was too powerful an emotion. Too like love. Sometimes the two were indistinguishable. Perhaps if she had not loved him, she would never have hated him. She would merely have disliked and despised him.

Her heart ached with hatred and with the memory of love. It was only after they had walked for a few minutes in silence, back toward the path that would lead downward to

Tŷ-Gwyn, that she felt resentment. She was twenty-six years old. She was no longer a girl to feel such confusion of emotions. She loved Rebecca now—or the man behind Rebecca's mask. There was even the chance, however remote, that she carried his child inside her. When one loved one man, one ought not to be able to feel any tenderness at all for any other. Especially when that other man was not even worthy of one's liking or respect.

And yet there had always been Geraint. And still was, it seemed. Always, all the time she had been married to Eurwyn, all the time she had loved him, there had been Geraint. And now that there was Rebecca—though there was no present or future tense in that relationship, only the past—even though it was a passionate relationship for her and an all-consuming one—even now there was Geraint.

"There will be the seeding to do soon," he said at last. He sounded like the Earl of Wyvern again, remote, haughty, rather cold. "And lime to haul for fertilizing. Do you need help, Marged? Can I send a man or two from the home farm?"

She felt a welcome surging of anger—and of smug satisfaction. But mostly anger. She had had help. She had had a man of her own. But that man was gone, thanks to the Earl of Wyvern.

"No, thank you," she said coolly. "I have all the help I need. I have hired Waldo Parry to work for me."

"Have you?" he said. "I am glad, Marged. I was under the impression when I saw you picking stones off the field that you could not afford to hire anyone."

How dared he!

"I have afforded my rent each year," she said, "and my tithes. What other money I have and how I spend it are my concern, *my lord.*"

"Quite," he said, and they walked on in silence for a while. But he was not finished with her. "Marged," he said when they were a short distance from Tŷ-Gwyn, "I would hate to see you lose your help almost before you have him. If Waldo Parry—or any other man of your acquaintance—is a follower of Rebecca, it might be as well for you to warn them that I am hot on their trail. It is a mere matter of time before the whole foolish trouble is at an end."

"And there will be no mercy on any of them," she said. "I know that. But you cannot make me tremble with fear, Geraint Penderyn. If I knew any of Rebecca's followers, I would encourage them to continue what they are doing. Perhaps I would even become one of them myself. And perhaps I would see Rebecca as a hero, as someone to be admired and respected. Someone to be followed."

She did not care about the recklessness of her words. She had promised herself on a previous occasion that she would not allow him to play cat and mouse with her.

"He is a criminal, Marged," he said. They had stopped outside the gate and he was looking at her with his hard blue eyes—eyes that had been tear-filled and beautiful up on the moors just a short while before. "He has no way of winning."

"Sometimes"—she leaned a little toward him and looked directly into his eyes—"people, both men and women, would prefer to fight a hopeless cause than not to fight at all. Sometimes the worst that can happen to a person is that he lose his self-respect or his soul. Or hers. Don't threaten me, my lord, or try to make me run in a craven panic to warn off anyone I may know who marches with Rebecca. You are wasting your breath."

He nodded slowly, his eyes never leaving hers. "Yes," he said, "I can see that. Be careful, then. Far more careful than you were the night you put wet ashes in my bed. I caught you then, remember?"

She had just told him that he could not make her tremble with fear. But she felt cold with it as he took her right hand in his, raised it to his lips, and kissed the palm as he had done with both hands on a previous occasion. *He knew.* Not just about the ashes—of course he knew about those. He knew that she followed Rebecca. He was warning her that he could easily catch her, as he had that night. And that he would not help her when he did.

Was he warning her in the hope that he would not have to catch her and see her punished? Was it his way of acknowledging that he had once cared?

He turned without another word and continued on his way down the hill. She watched him go, the man who was so much a part of her that not even hatred, not even her love for another man could quite dislodge him.

She could not love him, she thought, frowning slightly for a moment. She had loved him once, then Eurwyn, now Rebecca. That at least made sense—one man at a time. She could not have loved him while she loved Eurwyn. But she knew she had. She certainly could not love him now while her passionate love for Rebecca was so new and so wonderful—and so painful. But she knew that she did in some strange, strange way.

In some way she would always love Geraint Penderyn. Unwillingly and with denial on her lips and in her mind at every turn. But in this moment of painful truth she knew that he would always be there—in the depths of her heart.

Where she did not want him to be.

But where he was and always would be.

Matthew Harley was taking a Friday afternoon off. It was something he rarely did, though he was entitled to it and to far more spare time than he ever took. Usually he did not look for time off. He was happiest when at work. But work was no longer satisfying. He had even wondered if he should start looking for a post elsewhere.

Except that he did not want to go elsewhere. He had begun to think of Tegfan almost as his. He had made it as prosperous and efficient as it was. He had made a reputation for himself. He had won the respect of every landowner in Carmarthenshire. He did not want to have to begin again somewhere else.

It did not seem fair to him that he would always be someone's steward, that he would never own land for himself. But then life was not fair and he had never been one to complain about what could not be helped. But he had

begun to think of Tegfan as his own. He had begun to
believe that the Earl of Wyvern would never want to live
there himself. He had two larger estates in England, after all,
and he was known as a man who preferred life in London to
country living, anyway.

It had seemed safe to Harley to give in to the fantasy that
Tegfan belonged to him. It had never mattered that he drew
only a salary from it and not all the profits. Money had
never meant a great deal to him provided he had enough for
his needs.

But Wyvern was back and it seemed that he was going to
stay. And he had become tougher lately and had fallen more
in line with what was expected of him in this part of the
British Isles. It was he who was conferring with Sir Hector
Webb and the other landowners on what must be done about
the threat the Rebecca Riots was posing. It was he who
was talking with the special constables, planning strategy
with them.

Harley had hoped at the start that Wyvern would return to
England soon. He still hoped it though it was seeming less
likely than it had. And he hoped for a way of reasserting his
own importance. If only somehow he could be the one to
trap the mob, particularly their Rebecca! His mind returned
sometimes to that conversation he had had with Sir Hector,
when the baronet had suggested that he find an informant.

Harley spent the Friday afternoon with Ceris. It was a
beautiful day, and warm. They took a picnic up into the hills
behind Tegfan—inside the park so that they could be alone
together. But he could not think seriously of informants or
riots or even his own frustrations as a steward on such an
afternoon and in such company. He put it all out of his mind.
He would think about it some other time.

"Now tell me," he said, lying back on the grass after they
had finished eating, and setting one arm over his eyes to
shield them from the sun while he reached for her hand with
the other. She was seated on the grass beside him, her knees
drawn up, her dress pulled decently down so that he was
given not even a glimpse of her ankles. "Did you cook all

those cakes and biscuits yourself? Or was it your mother?" He smiled, though he did not remove his arm to look at her.

"I baked them all myself," she said primly. "Mam was busy making the cheese. Did you think I was incapable?"

"Not for a moment," he said. He had tried very hard not to fall in love with her. When he had started to think about leaving his present employment, he had started to think too about England and a more suitable bride. His parents would not appreciate a Welsh peasant for a daughter-in-law. His grandfather was a baron. "Come down here to me."

She had turned her head to look down at him when he withdrew his arm to look. He tugged on her hand and then reached up his other arm to her waist. She came down rather awkwardly, half across him. But she kissed him as sweetly as ever, her lips pouted softly and closed. He felt the familiar rush of heat and tightening in the groin. He set his arms about her and turned her until she was lying on the grass and he was bent over her.

"I will swear on a stack of Welsh Bibles," he said, "that I consider you the best cook in Wales. Will you marry me?"

He heard his own question with some surprise. But he did not want to retract it.

He watched her eyes grow huge and rather sad and bright with tears. And he felt a stabbing of pain because she was going to reject him. It was the blacksmith, he thought. He did not know what had happened there, but it was the blacksmith.

"I should like that, Matthew," she said softly.

He gazed down at her. He had not realized quite how lonely his life had been. He pictured her, neat and pretty, in his cottage, waiting for him at the end of each working day, the house filled with the smells of cooking. And seated beside his hearth during the evenings, busy at her loom or with her needle. And in his bed, waiting to give him the comforts of her body. Kissing him farewell in the mornings. How had he ever thought that the sort of female companionship he got at brothels on occasion was all he needed or wanted?

He kissed her and prodded at her lips with his tongue. They trembled and parted to allow him access to the soft flesh behind, though she kept her teeth together. He fondled her breasts through the cotton of her dress—lovely full, firm breasts. And he pressed his palm down over her ribs and stomach and abdomen until he could push his fingers down between her legs and feel the heat of her there. He felt her stiffen before she relaxed again.

He kept his hand where it was as he lifted his head and looked down into her flushed face. "Are you a virgin, Ceris?" he asked. He did not know quite how he would feel if the answer was no.

"Yes," she whispered.

He tightened his hand a little. "Let me show you how pleasant it will be to lose it," he said. "Here, Ceris, in the warm sunshine? And on Sunday I will have the banns called in church for the first time."

He watched her gnawing at her lower lip while her eyes roamed over his face. "If it is very important to you, Matthew," she said. "But if it is all the same to you, I would prefer to wait."

"For a marriage bed?" It *was* very important to him. He was hard and throbbing, and denying himself would cause several minutes of acute pain. She had not said no. And he would make it pleasant for her. He knew how, even though he had never broken in a virgin. "The marriage bed it will be, then."

He lay down beside her and set his arm over his eyes again. He tried to focus his thoughts on something other than his arousal.

"Thank you, Matthew," she said.

"What do you know about the Rebecca Riots?" he asked her.

"Nothing," she said very much too quickly, her voice breathless.

Ah. "It seems very possible," he said, "that there are rioters here in and around Glynderi as there are everywhere else."

"No," she said. "I think not, Matthew. I would know. There has been no mention. Everyone is law-abiding about here. No one has reason to be so foolish."

It pained him to know that she would lie to him when she had just agreed to be his wife. Though he had known that she would. He ought not to have introduced the subject. He had not meant to. He should drop it. He should take her back home. If he kept her out much longer, her parents would imagine that he was doing to her what he had just asked her to let him do.

"I suppose you are right," he said. "I have told Wyvern as much. It is a waste to keep constables here, I have told him, when they could be used to better effect elsewhere."

"Yes," she said. "It is foolish."

"Those men from other places," he said, "and their Rebecca—it was thought by some that they might be out again last night. There are those of us who know that almost certainly it will be tonight. A trap is being set for them if they but knew it. The Earl of Wyvern has one or two reliable informers, and we know exactly where they will attack next. There will be a reception committee awaiting them there. I believe we can hope to catch the leaders at the very least—Rebecca, Charlotte, some of the other so-called daughters. We will nip this thing in the bud tonight. It is a good thing that no one from around Tegfan is involved."

No, he did not imagine it. He was holding her hand. It turned cold and clammy in his grasp. And he was furious with her and furious with himself for ruining the afternoon. It was tonight, then. He had guessed correctly. Whom would she try to warn? The blacksmith? And what sort of a hell of a night would she have, imagining all the various traps her people might be walking into?

He hated himself for teasing her. When she was his wife it would be as well if he did move away from here so that her loyalties would not be divided. When she was his wife, she was going to be his. All his. He was going to have all her loyalty and all her love for himself.

But a thought came to him suddenly. What if he took it a

little further than teasing? If he was right, and if he had
scared her sufficiently that she would try to warn someone,
he could discover the identity of at least one follower of
Rebecca. It would be difficult to prove, though, that she had
called on that person for that particular reason. He frowned.
He would have to prevent her from giving her warning too
early. If there really was to be an attack tonight and she
arrived too late to warn her friends, would she follow them,
hoping to prevent disaster? Was Ceris brave enough to do
that? And did she care enough? He thought so. With any
luck she would lead him and a few constables, and perhaps
even Wyvern, to a gate smashing and to Rebecca himself.
And he would be the one everyone would have to thank
for it.

But he would be using Ceris to trap her own people. And
he was in love with Ceris. He wished fervently that he had
not touched on this subject at all.

He scrambled to his feet and stood looking down the
slope to the house for a few moments. Then he turned and
reached down a hand for hers.

"It is time I took you home, Ceris," he said.

"Yes." She allowed him to pull her up and busied herself
brushing grass from her skirt and picking up the empty
picnic basket. Her face was like parchment. Even her lips
looked bloodless.

"We will call at Tegfan first," he said. "There is something I must do there. It will take only a few minutes. And
then home." He smiled. "I will come inside with you and we
will tell your parents our news, shall we?"

"Yes, Matthew." She made a pitiful attempt at a smile.

Once inside her father's house, he would be invited to
stay. He would do so, even staying past his welcome if
necessary. Past the time when Rebecca and all her followers
could be warned to abandon tonight's outing.

Chapter
20

It was a night that was sometimes almost light and sometimes almost pitch-black. Clouds had moved over the sky since the afternoon, though they were not in a solid mass. Sometimes the moon and stars beamed down; sometimes they were obscured.

Idris Parry made his way uphill with dawdling steps in the direction of home. He kicked a few stones as he went and then remembered that he was wearing his new boots and had been warned to take care of them. He stopped to take them off and hang them about his neck by the laces. He felt more comfortable in his bare feet, anyway.

How boring it was to be nine years old! He wished he was old enough to join in all the excitement with Rebecca. It was not fair that only men were allowed to go—and Mrs. Evans. He had considered going himself—he had just been watching all the hushed excitement of the gathering—but a boy his size would be spotted in a moment, even on the darkest night, and he would be sent home. Or, worse, his dada would be called and he would have his trews pulled down and his backside walloped in sight of everyone else. In sight of Rebecca.

Rebecca was Idris Parry's idol. Before going to the meeting place, Idris had hidden outside the old gamekeeper's hut, where he had waited patiently for over an hour until Rebecca had come and fetched his bundle before riding off with it. On the first night Idris had been fortunate enough to see Rebecca return to the hut, still wearing the disguise. Perhaps he would not have known her identity otherwise.

Now there was nothing to do but go home and sleep for the rest of the night while Rebecca and his dada and most of the other men from round about were out having fun.

But Idris stopped suddenly and crouched down at the side of the path. His ears sharpened and his eyes darted about. He had spent enough nights outside, trespassing and poaching, that he knew when there was someone else out too and close by. There was someone now. He had been walking carelessly. He had to look about to get his bearings. He was close to the lane leading to Mr. Williams's farm.

It did not take Idris more than a few minutes to move around silently until he saw who it was. It was one of the special constables from Tegfan. Idris had seen him there with the others, talking with the earl—with Rebecca. What a joke that had been! But what was the man doing here? Was he hoping to catch Mr. Williams going out with Rebecca? Dada had said that Mr. Williams could not go because his legs were bad.

And then Idris heard footsteps coming from the farm and ducked down well out of sight. If it was Mr. Williams, then he was too late to go with Rebecca anyway. But it was Mr. Harley—up here courting Miss Williams, although she liked Mr. Rhoslyn better.

And then Mr. Harley stopped and spoke quietly. "Are you still there, Laver?"

"Yes," the constable said equally quietly.

"I have to hurry back to the house to alert Wyvern," Mr. Harley said. "Perhaps he can round up more constables in a hurry. I don't believe I am mistaken. It must be tonight.

Follow her if she leaves the house. Don't let her out of your sight. I'll wager she will try to warn someone or, better still, try to go after them to warn them. I'll catch up with you as soon as possible."

"Yes, sir," the constable said. "Two people went down a while ago—a man and a lad. It would seem a strange time to be going out to be sociable."

"Yes, indeed," Mr. Harley said. "I'll be back, Laver." And he strode off downhill.

That would have been Dada and Mrs. Evans going down, Idris thought. But *who* was going to leave the house? *Who* was going to lead Mr. Harley and the constables to Rebecca and her followers? Miss Williams? But Miss Williams did not hold with the gate breaking. Of course, she was sweet on Mr. Rhoslyn, and Idris knew who Charlotte was. Was Mr. Harley using Miss Williams to lead him to Rebecca?

Rebecca would be sent to the other side of the world for the rest of his life and would be chained and whipped and made to work harder than hard if he was caught, Idris had heard his dada say. And the same thing would happen to Dada, though not for quite so long a time. And to Mr. Rhoslyn and Mr. Harris and Mr. Owen and Mrs. Evans. Idris felt panic like a heavy and giant hand against the back of his neck.

And then Ceris Williams appeared. She had a shawl clasped about her shoulders with one hand while the other hand held up her skirt at the front so that she would not trip over it as she hurried along, head down. She sped downward, bathed in moonlight as one of the gaps in the clouds spread overhead. The constable moved like a shadow after her.

Idris's mind had calmed. He knew where Rebecca and the other men were going. He had heard Charlotte tell them in a low voice which direction they would be taking. Idris was not sure of the exact gates, but he could guess. He could get there before the pursuers. He could save them in time.

He could do something for Rebecca after all.

He got to his feet and sped off across the hill, still in his bare feet. It was perhaps fifteen minutes later, far too late, that he suddenly realized that his mind had not been working clearly after all. If it had, he would have thought of tripping noisily and cheerfully after Miss Williams and chattering to her loudly while warning her quietly that she was being followed.

But it was too late. He sped onward.

And what was going to happen when Mr. Harley went looking for the Earl of Wyvern? But Idris could not afford to start worrying about that.

Rebecca was being extra cautious tonight. It had been arranged that the special constables in the area would be sent to hide out in certain tollhouses south and east of Tegfan. But the operation was not very well coordinated. Although all the landowners were cooperating together, none of them had been appointed overall leader. The constables' billets were scattered about, and some of the men liked to follow their own initiative rather than take orders from men who seemed to know no better than they did where Rebecca might turn up next.

So one never knew if one was going to ride up to a gate west of Tegfan only to find oneself peering down the barrel of a gun.

He had the safety of a few hundred men to consider—and at least one woman. He had seen Marged almost immediately tonight, though she had kept her distance and had not once met his eyes. He could not afford to think of Marged until the night's work was safely completed, or to consider whether he would take her home tonight. Or make love to her.

He put the image of her and the decision to be made firmly from his mind.

All went well at the first gate. There was no one there except a gatekeeper with a heavy limp who informed Rebecca that she could have his gate and his house and welcome to them provided she did not lay a hand on him.

"Bloody gates," he said, shaking his fist at the one he had

been employed to tend. "More trouble than they are worth. I take more abuse here than my wages make up for. And the house is so drafty that I might as well sleep in the middle of the road."

He caused a general burst of laughter from those close enough to hear when he offered to help pull everything down. But no one was fool enough to put a club or an ax in his hands.

The second gate was a different story. It was closer to Tegfan. The gatekeeper had lived in Glynderi for a while. Charlotte warned all Glynderi people to make sure that their faces were well blackened and that they kept their distance from the house until the keeper was gone. But that was a warning that was given each time to the people who would be working close to home.

There was another problem. The spies who had been sent on ahead to scout out the house and surrounding area, as they always did, came back to report that there were two constables with guns inside the house.

There was a murmuring among the men close enough to Rebecca to overhear the report. It seemed they would have to retreat and come back another night.

"We can find another gate, Mother," one of the daughters said loudly enough to put heart back into the men. "There are plenty of them close by."

"We have destroyed one gate tonight, Mother," another said. "It is enough to cause serious annoyance. We will follow you another night."

Rebecca raised her arms and silence fell. This was the moment for which Geraint had taken on leadership. Soon perhaps all the remaining tollgates would be manned by armed guards. If they turned back now, a few hundred unarmed men discouraged by two men with guns, then they were beaten. And yet the safety of every last one of them was in his hands.

"My children," Rebecca said, "we have been asserting our right to freedom—freedom of movement within our own country, freedom from oppression by the owners of the

land, who would bow us down to the ground with the
burden of taxes in various guises. There is a gate on the road
below us that your mother finds disturbing. It will not be
easy to remove because it is guarded by two men and two
guns. Are we to be daunted?"

"No!" a few bold voices said quite firmly. They were
followed by a chorus of agreement. If he had demanded it at
that moment, Geraint knew, they would have rushed the
gate for him, leaving a few dead behind them when they left
again.

Rebecca did not lower her arms. "We will make a wide
circle about this gate," she said. "No one is to be seen or
heard. You will wait, out of sight and silent, my children,
and let your mother do the talking. You will not show
yourselves or put yourselves in any danger until I give the
clear signal. This is understood?"

"Yes, Mother," Charlotte said while there was a swell of
agreement from the men gathered around.

"Go now, then," Rebecca said. "My daughters will lead
you. I will wait for ten minutes." She lowered her arms
slowly and watched her daughters and her children move off
into the darkness, all perfectly disciplined. This sort of
situation had been discussed and planned with the daughters. Now was the time to see if it worked.

Charlotte was the one daughter who stayed close to
Rebecca. And with them stayed the men—and one woman—
from Glynderi. Marged was close by. Perhaps it was the
most dangerous place for her to be, but Geraint felt the need
to have her within his sight. He looked at her consideringly
for a moment, but he knew it would be pointless to order her
to go back.

She looked up at him and their eyes met for the first time.
He saw the flash of her teeth in the darkness.

Damn the woman—she was enjoying this.

She should be afraid, she knew. And perhaps she was in a
way. Certainly there was an almost tangible tension in the
men gathered about Rebecca and Aled, the only two on

horseback. A few hundred others had melted away into the darkness and were forming a wide and silent circle about the tollgate and tollhouse below—and about the two men with guns who were lying in wait for them there.

For the first time there was real danger. Some of them could be captured with those guns. Some of them would be killed. And yet instead of retreating, they were going to go forward.

But she was not afraid. Not really. Rebecca was sitting on his horse's back, quite still, quite calm and confident. And she trusted him. Perhaps it was foolish, this almost blind trust she had felt from the first moment, before there had been any question of more personal feelings. But she did trust him. And instead of fear in its most mind-numbing form, she felt exhilaration and the anticipation of adventure.

She met his eyes for the first time and knew, despite the mask, that he was considering speaking to her, advising her or commanding her to go back home, where it was safe. But she knew too that he would not say the words. He would know that she would refuse and that the necessity to exact obedience from all his followers would put him in an awkward position. And so he would not speak. They had met—incredibly—only twice before, but there were certain things they understood very well about each other. She smiled at him.

He had noticed her, he had considered her safety, and he had respected her right to decide for herself what she was going to do about it. It was enough. He had made clear that he wanted no continued involvement with her. But he had also proved to her that he cared. And that fact had been confirmed in just that one considering glance.

No, she was not really afraid. But she could hear her heart beating in her ears as she waited silently with everyone else. Even Rebecca and Aled did not speak to each other. Ten minutes seemed longer than an hour.

But they passed eventually. Rebecca raised one arm, bent at the elbow.

"We will move forward," he said. "But you will stop

when I give the word, my children. Only your mother must be seen from the road below."

He was going to show himself. And there were men with guns below. And perhaps more lying in ambush. Did they know that there were not? But if there were, those men would have seen them by now and raised the alarm. Marged hoped he would keep back out of gunfire range. Her heart was beating harder and more painfully.

They walked silently for a short while until they approached a rise that Marged guessed would bring them in sight of the road. Rebecca raised a staying hand. And then rode on alone, slowly, to stop again at the top of the rise.

At the same moment clouds scudded by and the moon beamed down.

"Ho, there below!" Rebecca called, and held his horse quite still. He estimated that he was beyond the range of any shot from the house. He wondered if the people inside could feel the silence pulsing outside.

After his second call, the gatekeeper came out slowly and looked uneasily about him. And then he looked up and saw Rebecca on the hill. He took a step back toward the door.

"Stay where you are," Rebecca commanded him. "And call the others outside too."

"There is just me," the keeper called in a thin, nervous voice. "I have no family. And I have no quarrel with you, Rebecca."

"Call them out," Rebecca said. "With their guns. You are surrounded by three hundred men. It will be safer to surrender." In other parts of the country there were always guns among the rabble. It would be assumed that they too had guns. It was safe to expect that their bluff would not be called.

"There is no one else here," the gatekeeper said after one nervous glance over his shoulder.

"They have until the count of ten before I ask my children to close in," Rebecca said. "One."

The gatekeeper looked up and down the road and uneasily about at the hills.

"Two."

"There is no one with you," the man called. "And there is no one with me."

"Three."

They came out when the count reached six—two constables, each with a gun in his hand.

"Walk to the middle of the road and set the guns down," Rebecca said, "and then go back with your hands raised. One of you can then return to the house and bring out the other guns." He was guessing.

"There are no other guns," one of the constables called, his voice angry. He too looked around at the silent hills. "You are bluffing, whoever you are."

"Seven."

Four guns lay side by side on the road and three men stood with their arms raised above their heads when Rebecca's voice was in the pause between nine and ten.

Rebecca raised both arms and the gatekeeper's hands shook visibly. "My children," she said, raising her voice to be heard among the hills, "I see before me a gate that is obstructing the free passage of your mother and your brothers and sisters. And three men who have thought to defend it. They are doing what they are employed to do. They will not be harmed. They will leave the scene now, and you will come down, my children, when I lower my arms and destroy this gate and this house."

The three men below looked about them uncertainly and then lowered their arms and turned to disappear into the hills on the far side of the road.

"Let them pass through the line unmolested," Rebecca called. After allowing them a few minutes to make their escape, he brought down his arms.

Everything went smoothly after that. The guns were gathered up by two men who had been directed to the task, and piled beside the road to be removed later. And the gate and the house were destroyed as quickly and efficiently as usual.

Geraint sat and watched. But a sound different from the usual hubbub of voices and tools had him turning his head sharply when the job was almost completed. It was the high-pitched, piping voice of a child calling him. Calling Rebecca. And then the child was beside him, reaching to clutch his boot and gazing urgently into his face.

Idris Parry.

Geraint leaned down. "What is it, child? What are you doing here?" He felt anger well in him.

"You have to leave," Idris called. He was gasping for air and his eyes were wild with excitement and panic. "They know where you are. They are coming for you. They will have you trapped."

Geraint did not doubt the boy for a moment. He knew from experience that children like Idris Parry saw and heard a great deal more than anyone else would ever guess.

"They are coming," the child cried, pointing back in the direction of Tegfan. "I ran on ahead."

Geraint did not waste time asking questions. He did not know quite who *they* were or how many there were. But they would undoubtedly have guns. His men would be in danger. He looked at Aled.

"Fetch this child's father," he said. "Quickly."

But Waldo Parry must have been close by and had heard his son's voice. He was grabbing him by both arms even as Geraint spoke, fury in his face and his whole bearing.

"He has come to save us all," Rebecca said firmly. "Treat him gently. But get him out of here. Fast."

He raised his arms wide and called for attention. It seemed that it would be impossible to achieve when the work of destruction was hardly completed, but such was the power of his presence, it seemed, that silence fell by some miracle almost immediately.

"There are armed men on the way, my children," Rebecca said loudly and distinctly. "Go now quickly and be careful."

Men scrambled away in all directions. Rebecca stayed where she was.

"Go!" he commanded Aled when his friend hesitated and then stayed beside him.

But there was someone else too at the side of the road, not running with everyone else.

"Go quickly," she yelled at him. "It is you they will want more than anyone."

He would have waited until the last of his people were safely out of sight. But he had to get her to safety. He spurred his horse, scooped Marged up when he was already in motion, deposited her on the horse's back in front of him, and galloped up into the hills, Aled close beside him. With any luck none of the fleeing men would run into whoever it was that was coming to catch them red-handed as they destroyed a tollgate. And even if any of them were caught, unless it was himself or Aled or one of the other disguised daughters, it would not be easy to prove that they had participated in the destruction.

The danger was not past, but he drew a deep breath of relief anyway and spared a glance for Marged, who was clinging to him with both arms. But a sudden thought had him reining in hard and turning in his saddle to look back down at the road, bathed in moonlight again. Damnation, but he had forgotten the guns. Perhaps it was just as well, though. He wanted nothing at all to do with firearms.

Aled pulled up beside him.

And in that moment, before they could turn and continue on their way, a lone figure darted out onto the road a short distance from the place where the gate and house had been. A female figure. She stood and looked about her, clearly bewildered, clearly not knowing where to go or what to do.

"Duw," Aled whispered. "Oh, *Duw,* it's Ceris."

And he was galloping back down the slope before Geraint had quite had the chance to comprehend what he had said.

"Ceris?" Marged sat up to peer downward. *"Ceris?"*

"She must have found out too," he said, "and came to

warn us." He could not go back down there with Aled. He had Marged's safety to consider.

But it was all over in a matter of seconds. Aled was back down on the road, Ceris was swept up while his horse was still in full gallop, and they were back on the slope. At the same moment two figures appeared at the far side of the road, one of them bent to pick up one of the guns, and there was a shot. The horse came galloping on, Aled and Ceris still on its back, apparently unhurt.

Marged had a death grip on his robe and on the clothes beneath it, Geraint realized.

"They are safe," she said.

Aled came speeding up the slope. Ceris's face was buried against his chest. "Get out of here," he yelled. "What are you waiting for?"

After a few yards of galloping side by side, they took separate directions.

Chapter
21

Matthew Harley had taken longer than he expected to get back to the constable, Laver. He had been unable to find the Earl of Wyvern and had wasted precious time searching for him. No one seemed to know where he had gone. But luck was with Harley in the form of one of the other constables, who had stayed at Tegfan in case he was needed for some emergency. And of course Laver would make sure that Ceris did not leave her father's house without having her movements shadowed.

Ceris! Harley had to quell a pang of guilt. But if she stayed at home as she ought, then no harm would have been done and she would have won his trust.

But would he have been worthy of hers?

He took the other constable with him, and they found Laver in the village. Ceris was there, going from one house to another, it seemed. She had gone to the house behind the smithy first.

Harley felt that his heart must be somewhere in the area of his boots. And then he saw her for himself, hurrying from the harness maker's house. She went straight down the street, not stopping again. Her pace quickened. She was running by the time she left Glynderi behind.

It was not difficult to follow her. She alternately ran and walked fast. She did not once look back. A few times, when clouds obscured moon and stars, it was difficult to see her, but she made no attempt at evasion. She led them on a straight, if hilly, path to the road and a gate a few miles away.

They were too late. That was obvious as soon as they came over a rise and could see the road below them. The gate and the house were down and men were fleeing in every direction. Some even passed close enough that they might have been apprehended if Harley and the constables had not already decided to pit their meager forces only against Rebecca herself or one of the daughters in their distinctive women's garb.

Either the job had been completed and the men had dispersed in the natural course of things, or they had somehow been warned that someone was coming—someone who might pose a threat. Perhaps there had been spies in the hills. Certainly it could not have been Ceris. She was not far enough ahead. Even as Harley looked he could see her rush onto the road and look wildly about her. She must have seen everyone fleeing, just as he had. It seemed almost as if she was searching for one man in particular.

The blacksmith?

And then he tensed, and he could feel the constables on either side of him tighten their grip on their guns. There was a horseman on his way down, a horseman with flowing dark locks, wearing dark women's robes. There was a moment when perhaps—there was a slim chance—one of the constables might have got off a shot at the rider. But it was gone almost before it was there. He scooped up Ceris and turned back uphill and came within definite range of the guns. But Ceris might be hit.

Harley spread his hands to the sides, fingers wide and rigid. "No!" he said curtly at the same moment as there was a shot. But not from beside him. There were two men on the far side of the road, one with a gun pointing after the fleeing horseman—and Ceris. Harley felt as if the bottom had fallen out of his stomach. But neither she nor Rebecca's daughter appeared to have been hit.

And then he saw what he might have seen before if he had not been so intent on what was happening down on the road. There was another horseman on the slope some distance away, motionless, also looking down. There were actually two riders on the same horse. One of them was clad in white flowing robes and had long blond ringlets.

Rebecca herself. Harley felt the breath hiss into his lungs and was instantly aware of the constable beside him raising his gun to his shoulder and taking aim. But the other rider and Ceris were almost up to her and were going to come abreast of her on the near side.

"No!" he said again with quiet urgency.

A hero's prize was his for the taking moments later when both horsemen came galloping his way before veering off to continue uphill. But again the dark-clad horseman rode between Rebecca and any shot one of the constables might have had at her—him. And Ceris was pressed so close to the daughter's body that there was no getting a shot at him. Yet had they stepped into the open and demanded that the riders stop and surrender, they would as like as not have been ridden down.

And so heroism passed him by and he knew bitter defeat.

It became more bitter when the dark rider turned upward and Harley found that Ceris's head was turned to one side and that her eyes were open. For a fraction of a second that stretched into eternity they looked full into each other's eyes.

Betrayer and betrayed. Though which way around it was, he did not quite know.

Marged clung wordlessly to Rebecca. She had never been on a galloping horse. Seated sideways without the benefit of a saddle beneath her, and with uneven hill country beneath the horse's hooves and darkness all around, she could only sit very still and put her trust in the horsemanship of the man to whom she clung.

Were they being pursued? Or were they riding into an ambush? What on earth had Ceris been doing down on the road? What would have happened if she or Aled had been hit by that one bullet that had been fired? What if Rebecca had been caught? What if he were still caught? Her arms tightened involuntarily.

"Was that Idris Parry?" she asked, speaking for the first time since they had watched Aled rescue Ceris. "What did he say?"

"Is that his name?" Rebecca asked. "The child? He warned that there were people coming—presumably special constables. He pointed in the direction of Tegfan. The woman must have been bringing the same message. Aled Rhoslyn knows her?"

"Ceris Williams," she said. "They were to marry, but Ceris is opposed to violence and destruction. She broke off their engagement."

"But she came out tonight," he said, "to warn him. I believe we are safe, Marged. We must have left any pursuit behind and I have taken a circuitous route."

She looked around her for the first time. She had not realized that he was not taking the direct route home.

"You see how dangerous this all is, Marged?" he said. "Some of us could have been captured or killed tonight. Aled and his woman came very close. And things are not going to get easier. This is just the beginning."

She turned her face in to his shoulder again. "I know," she said fiercely. "I know. But don't continue in the way I know you are planning to continue. Don't. And do stop and take off your disguise. You are far more likely to be seen and caught while you look this way."

Reaction was setting in and the realization of what might have happened tonight and what might yet happen. She could see behind her closed eyes Rebecca riding up against the skyline and calling down to the men hiding inside the tollhouse—men with guns. And she could feel the near panic there had been all around her down on the road when Rebecca had quickly and firmly—and quite calmly—sent them on their way. He had not rushed himself. As usual he had been the last to leave, focusing all the real danger on himself so that the rest of them might get away safely. He might so easily have been caught or shot. As Aled had been shot at. She turned dizzy at the remembered sound of that shot.

The horse had stopped galloping. Rebecca's breath was warm against her ear. "You are shaking," he said. "You are just beginning to understand, aren't you?"

Her teeth chattered when she tried to speak. "Y-yes," she managed to get out at last. "I am b-beginning to understand what my husband must have felt like on that night at T-Tegfan and I am beginning to remember how I felt. I am beginning to realize what might have happened to you tonight and to all the others. But fear and t-trembling are not an indication of cowardice or a sign that like a good girl I will now go home where I belong and stay there."

He chuckled. "No, Marged," he said. "You do not have to go at me so fiercely. Cowardice is the last thing I would accuse you of. And feminine weakness is the second-last thing. I am shaking myself. It is a natural human reaction to danger that is past."

"And perhaps not even that," she said. "We still have to get safely home. I have just recognized where we are. We are up on the moors above Tegfan. I am close to home. Let me down and ride on as fast as you can. Perhaps when I am gone you will take off the disguise and be a great deal safer. It is because of me you will not take it off, isn't it? You still do not trust me. But I don't blame you. Set me down."

And yet she clung to him and breathed in the smell of him. She did not want it to be over so fast. She was only just realizing that he had taken her up with him, that she was this close to him again, that she might never be this close again. But he must go. He must get safely home.

"Not just yet," he said. "There is a shelter up here

somewhere. An old building. Close to here—I have seen it. Come there with me. We both need time to calm down."

Geraint's old hovel. He must be referring to that. Her stomach turned over when she remembered what had happened there just the day before. She had felt such a strange, unwilling tenderness. . . . But she did not want to think of that. She was with Rebecca, the man she passionately loved.

"Besides," he said into her ear, "I don't want to say good night yet, Marged. I want to make love to you."

Her stomach turned over again.

"Will you?" He was whispering.

"Yes." It did not matter that it would happen inside Geraint's old home. Perhaps being there with Rebecca would purge her memory and her emotions of an unwelcome attachment—though it was not quite that, surely.

He found her mouth with his own briefly and rode on a short distance. They had been closer than she had realized. He dismounted, lifted her to the ground, and tethered his horse at the dark, higher side of the house before taking down the blanket rolled behind his saddle, and leading her by the hand to the dark doorway of the old house.

He had not consciously ridden up onto the moors. Or in the direction of the old hovel. But as soon as he knew where he was, he understood the unconscious workings of his mind. He had needed to come back here. With Marged. He needed to go inside the hut as he had not been able to bring himself to do yesterday. With her. It would be pitch-dark inside. He would not be able to see anything. But he needed to go in anyway—to face any ghosts that might be lingering there.

He needed Marged there with him. He needed her as he had needed her yesterday. She had responded to him with sympathy and a little more than sympathy yesterday as Geraint Penderyn. She would respond to him tonight as Rebecca. He put out of his mind the meanness of the deception. He needed her warmth. He needed her love.

He stopped in the doorway and peered inward, his heart

beating uncomfortably. How often he had raced in and out of this door, a surprisingly carefree boy. He could see only a foot or two inside the door. But the dirt floor still seemed hard-packed and covered with no more than the expected rubble of soil and leaves. He could not see farther in, but the darkness would work to his advantage. He led Marged carefully inside, over to the far wall, against the outside of which he had stood the day before. He spread the blanket.

"Lie down," he said to her. "You are not frightened?"

"No," she said. "Not with you."

He pulled off his wig and his mask and was grateful for the cool air he felt against his face and head. He knew that even if the sky cleared and the moon beamed down, the light of it would not penetrate to this corner. He hesitated a moment and stripped away Rebecca's gown and the clothes he wore beneath except his trousers. If anyone came, then he would be the Earl of Wyvern keeping a romantic tryst with one of his tenants.

Not that that would lead to a comfortable situation with Marged, of course.

Her hands came against his bare chest when he joined her on the blanket. Her fingers spread and then moved upward and over his face and hair.

"Ah," she said, and her voice was husky, "you are beautiful. I think you must be beautiful."

He held her palm against his cheek and turned his head to kiss it.

"Strange," she said softly.

"Strange?"

"Do you ever have things blink in your mind, but you cannot grasp them in time to see what they are?" she said. "It happened then. Have I ever met you before?"

"On Wednesday night," he said, trying not to tense. "I made love to you. Remember?" He should not have kissed her hand.

"Yes." She laughed softly. "I remember. I thought you were telling me afterward that this would not happen again.

It would not be a good situation, you said. I thought you did not care."

"Marged," he said against her mouth.

"And then you sent Aled with the money so that I could hire Waldo Parry to help on the farm," she said. There was a catch in her voice, suggesting that she was close to tears. "And I knew that you did care."

"Marged." He set his arms about her and drew her close against him. "How could you ever have doubted it?"

"I gave myself willingly," she said. "There was no compulsion on you to care. There *is* no compulsion."

"But I care." He licked at her lips. "I care very much."

"Oh," she said.

"I believe I said it would not be a good situation *for you*," he said. "I said it would not make *you* happy. You know me only as Rebecca, Marged. Perhaps you would not like the man behind the mask."

"I love you," she whispered.

Ah. Honest, reckless Marged.

I love you. She loved Rebecca. Strangely, the man behind the mask felt almost bereft. She had given comfort to Geraint Penderyn yesterday, had held his hand and listened to him and seemed almost tender in her sympathy for him—for a while. But it was Rebecca she loved, that mythical hero of the people. That man who did not even exist.

"And I love you too," he said, setting his mouth against hers and abandoning himself to the self-indulgence of telling a truth that would horrify her if he told it in his own person.

"Oh." It was as much sob as exclamation. "Make love to me. Let's make love."

It was not a cold night. And the fire of passion lent extra heat. She helped him free her of her jacket and shirt and of her breeches and underclothes. And she helped him unbutton his own trousers and wriggle out of them.

She was beautiful. She was Marged, he told himself in some wonder—warm and shapely and soft and yet firmly muscled too. The calluses on her hands, pressing over his chest and back and buttocks, were surprisingly arousing. Not that he needed much arousing. He was hard and throbbing for her.

"You *are* beautiful," she said before he could say the words first to her. She moved her hands around to hold him and stroke him. He drew breath sharply. "Why am I so bold with you? I have never been so bold."

He had been given the impression that first time that she was in many ways innocent. She jerked when he moved his hand down to touch her as intimately as she touched him. But she relaxed and sighed as his fingers stroked and parted and probed. He could not wait much longer. And he could feel that she was slick with wetness and ready for him.

"The ground is hard," he said when she turned onto her back to receive him. "Come on top of me tonight."

She had clearly never done it this way before. He had to guide her to kneel over him, her knees and thighs hugging his sides, her hands gripping his shoulders. She drew an audible breath when he positioned himself at her entry, and cried out when he spread his hands on her hips and brought her firmly down.

He moved in her with slow, deep strokes, giving her a chance to accustom herself to a new posture for love. He could feel her hair on either side of his face as her head came down close to his, and the tips of her breasts touching his chest occasionally. And then he lost himself as she caught his rhythm and matched it and rode to it. Faster and faster until they came together to a shared and frenzied climax.

She was hot and damp with exhaustion when he brought her down to lie on him and straightened her legs on either side of his own without uncoupling them—and came back to reality.

"I love you, Marged Evans," he said, wrapping his arms and the edges of the blankets over her. When Rebecca dropped permanently out of her life—as he must if he did not first get her with child—he wanted her to be able to look back and believe that he really had loved her. And if she ever discovered the truth, he wanted her to know that Geraint Penderyn had not only betrayed her, but had loved her too.

"Mmm," she said.

He allowed himself the luxury of imagining what it would be like to have Marged in his bed each night, falling asleep after his lovemaking. What further compliment could a man be given for his prowess as a lover?

And he remembered where he was. It was in this corner that his mother had placed his bed, or what had passed for a bed, since it was the warmest and the least drafty. His mother had loved him, he thought. For those twelve years, life had been indescribably hard and lonely for her. But he knew—she had told him often enough—that he had been the light of her life, her reason for living. He would be willing to bet that during the six years before her death she would have exchanged the comfort of her cottage and the security of warm clothes and furniture and regular meals and the friendship of people like Mrs. Williams—she would have exchanged them at any time for this hovel and his return.

No, she would not have. Knowing his mother, he could guess that she was happy for him, that she was glad that at last he would be brought up and treated as his father's son. And she would have understood about the absence of letters. She would have understood that they would not allow him to write to her—just as they must have forbidden her to write to him. She would have known that he loved her, that he never forgot her.

Yes, of course she would have known. How foolish of him ever to have doubted it. How foolish to have dreaded this place, as if he would find here the ghost of an unhappy, disillusioned woman. Her one consolation in her final years would have been the fact that he was being well cared for and that one day he would be the Earl of Wyvern and the owner of Tegfan.

How foolish he had been to be afraid to come back. And

afraid to know anything about Tegfan. Afraid, as if there would be malevolent ghosts here to haunt him.

This sorry hovel had been a place filled with love. And there was love here again. A love that had somehow purged all the old doubts and pain.

His fingers played gently through Marged's hair as she slept.

She was wonderfully comfortable and surprisingly warm. And warm right through to the heart, she thought. He loved her. *He loved her!* And he was still inside her. She could feel him hard again, though he was relaxed. His fingers were gently massaging her scalp.

"I did not want to come here, you know," she said. Perhaps she should not be mentioning this to him, when it involved another man and her disturbing ambivalent feelings for that other man. But she knew that part of loving was being perfectly open and honest with the beloved. "He lived here as a child. The Earl of Wyvern, I mean."

His hand stilled in her hair. "You loved him as a child," he said. "You have memories of this place?"

"One memory is very recent," she said. She hesitated for a moment and then told him about her meeting with Geraint the day before.

He stroked her hair again and said nothing.

"He has had a hard life," she said. "Almost unbearably hard. It is not easy to believe, is it, when he was taken at the age of twelve to a life of wealth and security and privilege and when he is probably one of the wealthiest men in the country now. But happiness does not come from things, does it? I don't believe he has known either love or a home since he was in this place."

"Perhaps," he said, "he felt comforted by your sympathy yesterday, Marged. Perhaps he felt something like love. Was there some love in what you did for him?"

"No," she said quickly. "I love you."

"But there are many kinds of love," he said. "If we love one person, we do not necessarily *not* love everyone else."

"We are talking about the man we both hate," she said. "Of course I feel no love for him."

"I am fighting against a system, Marged," he said, "against an injustice that is larger than one person. I do not hate anyone."

"It shows," she said. "You are so very careful that no one is hurt during the smashing of gates, either on our side or on the other side. And somehow you arrange it that those who suffer material loss are compensated. You are a compassionate man. Is that why you are doing this, then? You are fighting against a system rather than against people?"

"Yes," he said.

"It is better than hatred," she said. "Hatred—hurts."

"Yes." He kissed the top of her head.

And he lifted her off him at last, turned her so that her back was against the blanket, and knelt over her, his thighs on either side of her legs. He began to make love to her again with skilled, sensitive hands and mouth and tongue.

She gave herself up to the physical joys of love. But something had happened, she realized, and she could not seem to do anything about it. She was feeling Geraint's arms about her as he held her and cried, and Geraint's hand holding hers. And she was lying in the darkness of this hovel with Geraint and feeling the tenderness she had experienced yesterday blossom into a different kind of love.

Because she had never seen the man behind Rebecca's mask and could not visualize him as he made love to her, she substituted the face and form of Geraint. She made love with Rebecca and poured out to him all that she had felt for Geraint yesterday. She tried to give him back some of the love he had known here as a child and had never known since.

The rational part of her mind told her that she would be horrified tomorrow when she remembered this, and that she would doubt her love for Rebecca when she recalled that she had made love to Geraint as much as she had made love to him. But the emotional part of her being was far more powerful at the moment than the rational.

"Cariad," she whispered to him when he finally knelt between her thighs and lifted her with his hands to cushion her for his penetration. "I love you. I love you."

It was Rebecca she loved. It was Geraint she visualized behind her closed eyes. She gave her body and her tenderness, trying not to wonder to whom she gave.

He came inside her and she loved—the man who loved her in return.

Chapter

22

Ceris clung to Aled, numb with relief. She had passed large numbers of men fleeing from the road, but the road itself had been in darkness until she was right down on it. She had looked wildly about her. What had happened? Had some of them been caught in the trap? Some of the leaders? *Aled?*

Then the moon had broken free of the clouds and she had been able to see where the tollgate and house had been. There had been just a heap of rubble left. And there had been no one in sight. No one except for two men scrambling down from the opposite side from the one by which she had come, and a horseman galloping down from her side—a horseman looking like a woman in a dark dress, with long dark hair.

He galloped up beside her and swept her up with one powerful arm. Aled. He was Aled and he was safe. He had not been caught. She clung to him, numb with relief. For several moments after the shot was fired, she did not realize what it was. And then she did realize and the numbness deepened. That shot had been fired at them. At Aled.

"Get out of here!" Aled yelled suddenly. "What are you waiting for?"

She turned her head on his chest and opened her eyes. There was another horseman, clad all in white. Even his hair and his face looked white in the moonlight. Rebecca! Ceris's stomach felt as if it turned a complete somersault.

She turned her head the other way as both horses galloped off so that she would not have to see Rebecca. And she clung harder. They had been shot at! The truth of it was only just beginning to hit her. She still had her eyes open as the horses turned to go uphill again. Three men on foot watched them go by. She wondered that they were standing motionless and were still so close to the road. Crowds of men had been fleeing when she had been on her way down.

Several moments passed before the fact registered on her brain that one of the three men—the one whose eyes she had met—was *Matthew*. The truth dawned upon her at the same moment. He had used her to lead him to Rebecca and all her followers. To Aled. If anyone had been caught or hurt, it would have been her foolish fault.

She remembered Marged's concern that inadvertently she might betray some of her knowledge, and her own indignation that her friend should think she could ever do such a thing.

She might have killed Aled tonight. She buried her face against his chest again, moved her hands higher up his back, and tightened her hold.

Two things happened simultaneously. His breath hissed in through his teeth. And her right hand encountered something warm and wet and sticky.

She did not move. She was afraid to move a muscle. "You have been shot," she said against his dark gown.

"It is nothing," he said, though the sound of his voice gave the lie to his words. "I will have you home and safe in no time, Ceris. Just hold tight."

She moaned. "No. Stop, Aled," she said. "You have been shot. You are bleeding."

"I'll get you home," he said. "There is pursuit. Idris brought word. You were bringing the same message?"

"No!" Her voice was agonized. "We have passed them already. They are far behind and on foot. There were three of them. I led them to you."

"You?" His breathing was labored.

"They followed me." She could hear that she was wailing and could not stop herself. "Aled, you have been shot. Because of me."

"Hush," he said. "Hush. I am going to take you home."

"No," she said. She turned her head again to see that they were not far from home. "No, I am coming home with you. You are going to need me. You have been hit."

He did not argue. He rode incautiously into Glynderi and around to the back of the smithy, where his horse was stabled and where the door into his living quarters was situated. Ceris jumped down as soon as the horse came to a halt, and reached up her arms to assist Aled. He looked so strange in his women's clothes and with his face blackened, a part of her mind thought. He slid down awkwardly from the saddle, his left arm curled against his chest, while she tried to steady him and break his fall if his legs did not support him. But he stayed on his feet and even managed to see to his horse, with Ceris's help, before they went into the house.

The bullet had gone through his shoulder. They discovered that after Ceris had somehow got him out of the dark robe and had peeled back his blood-soaked shirt and dabbed away some of the dried blood with a dampened cloth.

"There is a hole at the front," he said faintly. "There must be one at the back too, Ceris. They shot at me from behind."

"Yes, there is," she said. Now that she was doing something she felt calm again, though she knew that reaction would set in later. A few inches lower . . .

"The bullet is out, then," he said. "But do you realize, Ceris, that it must have just about gone through your head?"

Her stomach did a strange flip-flop, but her hand was steady with the cloth. "But it did not," she said.

Before she had finished cleaning the wound and some-how bandaging pads over both bullet holes to stanch any further bleeding, he had his eyes closed and she could see even beneath the blackening on his face that he was as pale as parchment.

Her mind had become even calmer. "There may be a search," she said. "We must get your face cleaned up, Aled, and we must hide or get rid of these clothes. We must get your shoulder covered up. Where will I find a nightshirt?"

He looked at her with pain-heavy eyes.

It took her half an hour to accomplish everything. All the time she listened for any telltale noises from the street. Perhaps they would do a house-to-house search, especially if they suspected that they had wounded one of Rebecca's daughters. But there was nothing. She had made Aled lie down in bed, though he had watched everything she did. She looked around her at last. It looked like a normal bachelor's home.

"What were you doing on that road, Ceris?" he asked.

"Betraying you," she said.

He looked steadily at her and she looked back from across the room.

"And yet," he said, "you have patched me up and hidden all the evidence for me. Tell me the truth now."

And so she told the truth, standing quietly, her arms at her sides. All the truth, including the fact that she had become engaged to Matthew Harley during the afternoon.

"Don't blame yourself," Aled said when she had finished. "It was not your fault, Ceris. You are a gentle woman. It is not fair that you have got caught up in all this violence. I'll get up and take you home."

"You will not," she said, rallying. "You will not move from that bed tonight, Aled Rhoslyn."

"I can't let you walk home alone," he said. "There could be danger out there."

"I am not going home," she said. "I am staying here."

"No," he said. "Your reputation, Ceris. And your parents will be worried."

"I told them I was going up to spend the night with Mrs. Evans and her mother," she said, "since Marged would be going with Rebecca. And I don't care about that other, Aled. I am not leaving you. Not tonight."

He set the back of his good hand over his eyes and was quiet for a few moments. But he did not argue with her. "I'll get up and let you have the bed, then," he said. "I'll sleep on the settle."

"You are going to stay where you are," she said. "I'll sleep beside you. The bed is wide enough."

His hand stayed over his eyes. She was not sure whether the sound she heard was a sigh or a laugh. She unbuttoned her dress and took it off so that it would not get more creased than it already was from the night's activities. She blew out the lamp and climbed carefully over Aled to the inside of the bed. She scrambled beneath the bedclothes.

The worst of the pain had receded. Now it was rather like a persistent and gnawing toothache. He knew he was going to be stiff and sore tomorrow. And yet he would have to be at his anvil and busy at it too if there was anyone snooping around, asking questions, as there was bound to be. He just hoped the bleeding would be under control by then.

She was beside him in bed. He could already feel the warmth of her, though she was not touching him. He slid his arm across and took her hand in his.

"When a man and a woman are in bed together, it is no simple matter to fall asleep," he said.

"I know." Incredibly, he felt her cheek come to rest against his shoulder. He understood then that she had not stayed just to tend to his wounds. She had not climbed into bed with him from any naive assumption that they could sleep peacefully side by side. She was offering herself to him.

It increased his pain to move, but he managed to get his good arm beneath her head, and she came across him of her own volition, careful not to touch his left arm or shoulder, and gave him her mouth, soft and pouted and trembling in the darkness.

"*Cariad,*" he said softly after he had kissed her, "it is my seed I will be putting in your womb if we do not stop right now."

"Yes." There was a sob in her voice.

"Will you take it into you, then?" he asked.

"Yes." He could feel her tears on his face. "But I do not want you to move, Aled. I do not want you to hurt yourself."

"Lie over on your back," he said, "and I will manage."

It was not easy. And certainly not painless. He had to put all his weight on her after she had lifted her shift and removed her underthings for him. And he could not be as careful or as gentle as he would have liked. But they both wanted it, and wanted it badly. Somehow she knew how to lift her legs to twine about his and raise her hips from the bed, and somehow he positioned himself and pushed into the tight, wet little passage.

He heard himself sob when she flinched and made a guttural sound in her throat, but she spread her hands over his buttocks and pulled tightly when he would have withdrawn. He pushed the rest of the way in.

He made it last for several minutes, feeling her first relax and then rock her hips to his thrusts and withdrawals, and then tighten inside. She was hot and wet and indescribably wonderful. He wanted to burst into her at every inward stroke, but it was an act of love and he desperately wanted it to be as wonderful for her.

"Aled!" she cried suddenly in a strange, lost, surprised voice, and he felt her body jerk out of control beneath him. He surged into her over and over again, excited by her climax, until his seed came spilling deep and he released all his energy, all his love into his woman.

His first woman.

His only woman. Ever.

It took him a long while after he was lying on his back again and Ceris was curled up against his good side, his arm beneath her head, to bring the pain under control. But it was a physical thing and would pass off. He focused his mind on what had just happened and on the feel of her, relaxed after love. With his seed in her.

"Aled," she said, "can I bring you anything? I can tell by your breathing that you are in pain."

"Stay where you are," he said. "You are the only medicine I need, *cariad*."

"Aled," she said after a short silence, "I meant it. I will not wake up tomorrow to be horrified at what I have done. I meant it. And I loved it—far more than I ever expected."

He surprised himself by chuckling. "We were not bad for a pair of novices, were we?" he said.

"Have you never—" she began.

"No, never," he said. "It was always you or no one, *cariad*. A pair of virgins we were. Past tense, I am glad to say."

"Aled." She kissed his shoulder. "I love you."

"Yes, *cariad*," he said softly. "Sleep now, is it? Sleep now after the exertions of love."

"Yes, Aled," she said.

Geraint's valet woke him with the announcement that Sir Hector Webb had called and was waiting for him in the visitors' salon downstairs. Geraint turned his head with a frown to look at the clock. It was still early, but it was long past his usual time of rising. He had lain down when he returned home sometime before dawn, not expecting to sleep. Apparently he had.

Sir Hector was pacing the floor of the salon and made no attempt to hide his impatience or his contempt for a nobleman who slept the morning away. There were three other men standing silently side by side inside the door. Two of them—Geraint recognized them as special constables who had been billeted at Pantnewydd—stood motionless. The other was fidgety and ill at ease. Geraint recognized him too.

"Precious time has been wasted this morning, Wyvern," Sir Hector said, frowning in irritation. "This man"—he indicated the one who was not a constable—"called here earlier this morning with important information for you. Harley was forced to tell him that you were abed and had left word that you were not to be disturbed. Of all the nonsense!"

Geraint raised his eyebrows. *Had* he left any such word?

"There were two gates pulled down last night," Sir Hector said. "One not three miles from here. I suppose you have not even heard?"

"One tends not to," Geraint said coldly, "when one is asleep, Hector."

"This man had to come all the way to Pantnewydd with his information," Sir Hector said.

Geraint fixed his eyes on the gatekeeper who had had the company of two constables in his tollhouse the night before. "Well?" he said with haughty impatience. "Out with it, man. What can you tell us beyond the fact that Rebecca and her so-called children wrecked your gate? Is it too much to hope that you recognized someone?"

"That is it exactly, my lord," the man said, bobbing his head nervously. "I did too."

The air Geraint breathed into his nostrils suddenly felt icy. "Well?" He raised his eyebrows, all impatience.

"It was a woman, my lord," the man said. "After all those ruffians had left, I came back down to the road to see what the damages were. And she was down there. She was not disguised like the ones who ran away. And this one was a real woman."

Ceris Williams. "And you had a good look at her?" Geraint asked.

"Oh, yes, my lord," the gatekeeper said. "The moon came out at that very moment, just before one of the riders came galloping down and carried her off. I used to live in Glynderi, you see, and I knew her. She was Ninian Williams's daughter. Ceris Williams."

"I have brought two men with me," Sir Hector said, "just in case the four you have here are about some other business, Wyvern. I would have sent them to arrest her, but it seemed a courtesy to you to come here first."

"Yes, indeed," Geraint said, clasping his hands behind his back. He looked at the two constables. "Off you go, then. Get someone to give you directions. Bring her in. Without force, if you please."

"If she offers any resistance—" Sir Hector began.

"*Without* force," Geraint said, not forgetting that his uncle was a magistrate while he was not. But this was his land. And what the devil had Ceris Williams been doing down on that road? She was not a follower of Rebecca. Had she come on the same errand as Idris? But how had she heard what the child had heard? And who exactly were the pursuers the boy had warned of? What would Ceris say under interrogation? Aled had rescued her. Would she have recognized him? And would she betray him if she had? Marged had said the two of them had almost married. Would Ceris betray anyone else? And if she would not speak, how was he to save her from imprisonment?

The thoughts teemed around in his brain while he strolled to the window and stood looking out, his hands still behind his back, his whole stance discouraging conversation.

"We have them this time," Sir Hector said anyway. "All it takes is one captive. And a woman at that. She will talk if she knows what is good for her."

"Yes," Geraint said. "It would seem that we have the break we have been looking for." Ceris Williams was the sweet little girl who had used to hide behind her mother's skirt and smile at him. She was the equally sweet little lady who had brought him food at Mrs. Howell's birthday party and had stayed to talk with him, though he had recognized the shyness that made it very difficult for her to do so. Ceris Williams had a tender heart. He did not believe she would hold up well under interrogation.

She was at home milking the cows for her mother. She was trying not to think of the tumult of events that had happened the day before. She was trying, for the moment at least, to focus all her thoughts on last night's final event. It was not difficult. There were the physical aftereffects—the tenderness in her breasts, the slight soreness inside between her legs, where he had loved her and given her his seed. And there were the memories of what he had felt like. And the certainty that there had been a rightness about it all.

She wanted to dream. She wanted the milking to last as long as possible so that she could be alone with her thoughts. She knew there were other thoughts awaiting their turn, far less comfortable thoughts. But not yet.

It was at her milking that they found her. One of them pointed a gun at her. The other pulled her arms roughly behind her and bound them so tightly that she soon lost feeling in her hands. The one with a gun turned to point it at Dada when he came running from the field and then at Mam when she came out of the house. Ceris Williams was under arrest for taking part in a Rebecca Riot, the one who had bound her said. They were taking her to Tegfan.

They marched her quickly along, one holding to each of her arms. Deliberately quickly, she thought, so that she would trip and they could haul her up again. If only she could have held up her skirt at the front, it would not have happened at all. But she went down on one knee once and all the way down another time. She kept her head down, though she knew that they passed a few people. She prayed fervently and constantly to the God in whom she believed passionately. She prayed that she would have the strength not to betray Aled. Or Marged or Waldo Parry or any of the others she knew.

She had never been inside Tegfan. It was huge and intimidating. They took her inside one of the rooms that led off the spacious hall. There were three men in there—the Earl of Wyvern, Sir Hector Webb, and the keeper of the gate that had been destroyed by the time she reached it. They all turned to look at her as she came in. It was of the earl she felt most frightened. His face was hard and his eyes were cold. The obvious anger of Sir Hector seemed preferable.

"Well, Miss Williams," the earl said, "we have been hearing some stories about you."

She looked at him mutely. She found herself wondering how Marged would behave in such a situation. Marged was wonderfully courageous. Marged would not look away or tremble—or crack under pressure.

He strolled toward her across the room until he was no more than three feet in front of her. He stood very tall and straight. His hands were at his back. She had the sudden and terrifying impression that he held a whip in them.

"We have been told," he said, glancing briefly to his left at the gatekeeper, "that you were at the scene of a gate breaking last night, Miss Williams. Is this true?"

She stared at him. Very deliberately in her mind she was reciting the Lord's Prayer.

"Perhaps there was an explanation for your being there," he said. "If so, you must say so and you will be allowed to return home. Why were you there?"

Give us this day our daily bread.

"You were taken up by one of the men known as Rebecca's daughters," he said. "Did you know him? Or did he merely kidnap you and set you down somewhere else?"

Aled. Oh, Aled, oh, Aled, oh, Aled. As we forgive those who trespass against us.

He asked her numerous questions. She lost count of the number of times she recited the same prayer. Stupidly, she could not remember any others to recite. And her mind was not lucid enough to pray spontaneously.

And then Sir Hector started on her. He was much louder, much angrier. He shouted at her until he lifted one hand and would have brought the back of it across her face if the earl had not grabbed him by the wrist.

"I don't think violence is going to get anything out of her," he said. "I will try other methods, Hector, but I would prefer to be alone when I try them, if you get my meaning. Leave her with me. She will not escape me and I will get the truth out of her, never fear."

Sir Hector gave a short bark of laughter as Ceris's blood

froze. *What did he mean?* But there was no doubt in her mind what he meant. There was a half smile on his lips, an expression at horrible variance with his cold, cold eyes.

She was on the verge of breaking her silence and begging Sir Hector Webb not to leave her alone with the Earl of Wyvern. But a brisk knock on the door was preceded by its opening. It was behind Ceris. She did not turn her head to look.

"I beg your pardon, sir," Matthew Harley said, his voice breathless. Ceris closed her eyes briefly. "I have just heard. Has she said anything?"

"I believe," the Earl of Wyvern said coldly, "that the cat has got her tongue, Harley, or whatever it is that takes maidens' tongues in Wales."

Ceris heard Matthew exhale through his mouth. She stared woodenly downward at the floor.

"There has been a dreadful mistake," Matthew said. "And I am not surprised she has said nothing. She belongs to the chapel here, you know, and it would be considered sin enough to have her expelled and driven up the mountain."

He knows about Aled, Ceris thought desperately. She looked up fleetingly to see the earl raise haughty eyebrows.

"Ceris and I got engaged yesterday," Matthew said. He sounded almost embarrassed. "We went walking last night. We went quite a distance across the hills. And then we got to kissing and then to other things and"—he laughed— "well, I suppose I tried to go too far and she took fright. She went running off, and before I could catch up to her to apologize, we got all caught up in whatever was going on down on the road. Suddenly there were black-faced men fleeing to all sides of me and Ceris was down on the road. And then a rider in dark women's clothes snatched her up and made off with her. I have been worried silly. That was why I sent this gatekeeper over to you, Sir Hector, instead of dealing with the matter myself. I am sorry. I neglected my duty."

"It is my duty to be up and dealing with such matters," the earl said.

"Ceris?" Matthew came into her line of vision. "Are you all right? Oh, please let them untie her hands, sir. She has been an innocent victim. Did you recognize him, love? Or anyone else? And what did he do with you? If he—"

"I did not recognize him," she said, looking down rather than into his eyes. She did not know quite what was going on. "He dropped me from the horse's back when, I suppose, he thought he was safe from pursuit."

"Thank God." Matthew drew a ragged breath.

They believed him. She did not really listen to all that was said over the next few minutes, but they believed him. Her hands were released and were soon so painful with the pins and needles of returning circulation that she had something to concentrate on.

"I'll take you home, Ceris," Matthew said, setting an arm loosely about her shoulders. "If you can trust me after last night, that is."

Never did words have more of a double meaning, Ceris thought.

Chapter
23

Idris had told her. He had come darting into the farmyard while she was there with his father, talking over with him what his duties were to be. Idris had told both of them.

"They have come for Miss Williams," he had gasped out. "They have dragged her down to Tegfan with her hands tied behind her back."

No longer than five minutes later—she paused only long enough to run into the house to remove her apron and grab her shawl—she was striding from the farmyard and through the gate and down the hill. She did not even listen as she passed Idris trying to persuade his father that it would be all right, that the Earl of Wyvern would not do anything dreadful to Miss Williams.

Ceris had been recognized. Foolish woman. She had gone running out onto the open road without any attempt at disguise. Those two men who had shot at her and Aled must have seen and recognized her. That particular gate-keeper—if he was one of those two men—had used to live in Glynderi. She had been recognized and it had been assumed that she was part of the crowd that had destroyed the gate. And now she had been arrested.

But what had she been doing down on that road? Marged had had no chance to run down to the Williams farm during the morning. She had half expected that Ceris would come up to Tŷ-Gwyn.

Marged quickened her pace so that she was half running by the time she neared the bottom of the hill and turned in the direction of Glynderi and the gates into Tegfan park beyond it. Ceris was the one who had been caught and dragged off to Tegfan with her hands bound. How ironic. Ceris, who was so adamant in her disapproval of the Rebecca Riots that she had broken off her relationship with Aled and almost destroyed her friendship with Marged.

Ceris had been caught.

Marged felt sick over the fact that she had been so very happy this morning. He loved her. Rebecca loved her. They had made love three times in the hovel on the moors before he had brought her home. She had been disappointed that he had donned his whole disguise before doing so, but she had understood. For her own safety as well as his, it was important to him to guard his identity. She refused to be hurt by it. She was too happy. He loved her.

But now this. While she had been wandering about the farm this morning, dreamy-eyed and absentminded, and while she had been talking with Waldo Parry, only half her attention on what they were both saying, disaster had been coming to Ceris.

What would they do to her? What would *he* do to her? Marged had unwilling memories of the nightmare of two years before when Eurwyn had been captured—the trial and conviction, the sentencing, the knowledge that he had been taken away, that he was in the hulks, that . . . She shook her head and hurried on.

She had to stand aside when she was halfway up the driveway to Tegfan for a carriage to pass. She caught a glimpse of Sir Hector Webb of Pantnewydd inside. There were other people with him, but there was no chance to see who they were or even what gender. What if one of them was Ceris being taken off to jail? Marged was already breathless and her legs already felt like jelly, but somehow she stumbled into a run.

She banged the knocker on the front door, not even thinking about going around to the servants' entrance. And she faced the footman who answered the door and the butler who was in the hall with such fierce determination despite the fact that the latter looked at her as if she were a worm, that she was allowed to step into the hall. The butler went to see if his lordship was at home.

It seemed that his lordship was in the library and that he would see Mrs. Evans there immediately. The butler managed to look expressionless and contemptuous all at the same time. Marged hardly noticed. One sweeping glance about the library when she stepped inside revealed to her two walls lined with books, a high coved ceiling, a large desk strewn with papers, a thick carpet underfoot. But they were details her mind did not dwell upon. Geraint was setting down a quill pen and rising from his chair at the far side of the desk.

"Marged?" he said, his eyebrows raised.

He was immaculate and handsome and she hated him. "Where is she?" she demanded. "What have you done with her?"

Geraint, eyebrows still raised, looked pointedly beyond her shoulder until she heard the door close behind her. "She?" he said, bringing his eyes to hers.

"Where is Ceris Williams?" she demanded.

He came around the desk, though he did not come close to her. He stood with feet apart and hands clasped behind his back. The cool, inflexible aristocrat. "News travels fast in a small community," he said. "Doubtless you have heard that she was arrested for involvement in the destruction of a tollgate last night."

Hearing it from his lips suddenly made it all horribly real. Marged feared for a moment that she was going to succumb to panic. She threw back her head and glared at him.

"Ceris?" she said. "A gentler, more timid woman would be impossible to find. Or one more firmly opposed to lawlessness and violence. Someone has made a ghastly mistake."

"Timid?" he said. "I would say it would be impossible to find a braver lady. She said nothing, Marged. Nothing at all. You do not have to fear that she betrayed all your friends and neighbors. She did not."

But if Ceris had refused to say anything, they would be incensed. They would try to make her talk. What would they do to accomplish that? There were instant images of torture and rape. She drew a sharp inward breath.

"There was a mistake," she said. "She was seen on that road, wasn't she? When she went back down to find a lost h-handkerchief that might have been traced back to her. That was it, wasn't it? But that was not Ceris. It was me. I was out with Rebecca last night, smashing gates, not Ceris. It was me."

He looked at her long and hard and she found herself for some absurd reason wondering if Rebecca's eyes were as blue as Geraint's, or if they were gray. Perhaps she would never know. *Probably* she would never know. She was glad suddenly that she did not know Rebecca's identity. She was not sure how well she would stand up against torture or—or that other.

"Marged," he said. "She was positively identified. She was seen from close up. There is no physical resemblance at all between the two of you."

"It was dark," she said.

"She was seen in full moonlight," he said.

It was not going to work. She was not going to be able to free Ceris, and now she had betrayed herself too. But she could not feel fear—yet. Only a deep hopelessness.

"Geraint," she said, using his given name without thought. She took a few steps toward him. "She is innocent. She came to warn us. She must have heard what someone else had heard too, that there were constables coming, and she came to warn us. Because she loves us and cares for us even though she disapproves of what we are doing. She had no part in what happened. Let her go. Please?" She blinked her eyes furiously when her vision blurred.

"Marged—" he said.

"Take me instead," she said, "and let her go. Please, Geraint. I have already confessed to having been there myself last night. I have been at each of the gate breakings. I have helped destroy them with my own hands. If I am being honest about my own guilt, why would I lie about Ceris's innocence? Let her go. What can I do to persuade you to let her go?" She took another step toward him.

He stood very still, an arrested look on his face. "What are you prepared to do, Marged?" he asked her eventually.

What *was* she prepared to do? She realized suddenly what she had insinuated, what she had only half consciously been offering. She thought briefly and with a deep stabbing of pain of Rebecca and the glorious night of love they had shared a mere few hours ago. And she thought too of how she had visualized Geraint during the second and third lovings because she had no mental picture of Rebecca. She thought of Geraint, the boy she had loved for so long and the man who had become a part of her being, however unwilling she was that it be so.

She took the remaining two steps that brought her toe to toe with him. She saw that her hand was trembling as she lifted it to set her palm over his heart. "Let her go." She set the other hand against his chest and let both slide up to his shoulders as she swayed her body against him. She set her forehead just beneath his chin. "I will do whatever you ask of me. Geraint, remember what it is like to be poor and in need and frightened."

He had not moved. His hands were still behind his back. His body was hard and unyielding. He was about the same height and build as Rebecca, she thought unwillingly. She did not want to think about Rebecca. She had to do what must be done to save Ceris, and then she must face whatever must be faced after her rash confession. She must not think of the man she loved.

"It is quite an offer," he said, his voice curiously flat. "Your body in exchange for your friend's freedom, Marged? Your body to be used however I will and as many times as I will?"

Geraint. He was Geraint. He was that vibrant, charming boy she had loved. This cold, hard man.

"Yes," she said.

"Your friend is already free," he said. "It seems there was a mistake. Her fiancé, Matthew Harley, explained that they were out courting, or otherwise amusing themselves in the hills, when a slight, ah, quarrel sent her running down onto the road at quite the wrong place at quite the wrong time. But it was a good enough alibi to satisfy both me and Sir Hector Webb. No one can doubt the honesty or loyalty of my steward, after all. He escorted her home. I wonder that you did not pass them on the road."

He had deliberately held back that information from her. He had allowed her to weave her own rope, fashion her own noose, and tighten it about her own neck. She withdrew her head and her hands and her body from his and stood a couple of inches in front of him, her hands clenched loosely at her sides, her head bowed, her eyes closed.

"Marged," he said, "who is Rebecca?"

"I do not know," she said, her voice low and toneless. "And if I did, I would not tell you. Ever."

"There are ways of extracting information from unwilling witnesses," he said.

"Yes." She kept her eyes closed. "I think I am brave. But I do not know for sure. Perhaps I would break. I am glad he has refused to tell me who he is."

"You have spoken with him, then?" he asked.

"Yes." She felt a sudden surging of anger and of spite. A sudden need to hurt, though she did not know if he would be in any way hurt by the information. "I have loved him too. I have *made* love with him. I love him. I believe his secret would be safe with me even if he had trusted me with it. But he did not."

It seemed to her that the silence lasted a very long time.

And stupidly, inexplicably, insanely she felt suddenly bereft. She wanted to reach out a hand to touch him again, to tell him that she had not quite meant it that way, that she still cared for him, Geraint. That part of her still loved him and always would. And she wondered how she could love Rebecca as deeply and passionately as she did and yet still love Geraint too.

"Marged," he said, "what you have told me in this room must never be told outside it. Do you understand me? You have been typically rash and outspoken and untypically dishonest. You have lied to save a friend who did not need saving. Your motive was admirable. Your method was foolhardy. If you tell this story to someone else, he might believe you."

She lifted her head at last and looked into his eyes. They were so close to her own that she almost took a step backward. But she held her ground.

"I do not have to tell you what jail is like, do I?" he said. "Or what is involved in a sentence of transportation. Your lies would lead you to be transported."

She knew that he knew she had not lied.

"Geraint—" she began.

"Go back home now," he said. "Your mother-in-law and your grandmother-in-law need you."

"Geraint—" She bowed her head again and set her hands loosely over her face. She found herself wanting to tell him that she had lied in what she had said about her feelings for Rebecca. And yet she had not. She did love him—with all her being. And she noticed at the same moment that he was not wearing his usual cologne this morning, that he was wearing no cologne but smelled merely—clean. One of those moments caught at her consciousness again but refused to be grasped.

"Go home, Marged." His voice was suddenly and unexpectedly gentle. "It must be a wonderful thing to have you for a friend. In fact, I know it is. You were my friend once. I remember running home to tell my mother that I had a wonderful friend. My first friend. Go home now. Your lies will go no farther than me and I will remember our friendship."

"Geraint." Her voice was high-pitched and quavering, she heard in some alarm. "Why is life so far beyond our control even when we try to abide by all the rules? Sometimes life frightens me."

She turned, bent on following his advice before she made a greater fool of herself than she had already done this morning. Fortunately he had made no move to reach out to her. If he had done so, she would have gone all to pieces and despised herself for the rest of her life. But the door was flung back before she could take a step toward it.

"What the devil is going on, Ger?" Aled Rhoslyn said, striding inside—the butler hovered helplessly behind him. He stopped dead in his tracks when he saw Marged.

"I take it," Geraint said, "that you have come to bargain for the release of Ceris Williams as Marged has done, Aled?"

Aled was looking deathly pale, Marged noticed. But then the news would have been worse for him than it had been for her. Aled loved Ceris.

"Say nothing, Aled," she said quickly. "Ceris has been released. It was all a mistake."

His eyes met Geraint's over the top of her head.

"Her fiancé vouched for the fact that they were out together, involved in the business of courtship, when they somehow got caught up with a gang of Rebecca rioters about their work," Geraint said. "Miss Williams is a friend of yours, Aled?"

For one moment Marged thought he was going to faint. "You might say so," he said.

"Ah," Geraint said softly from behind her.

It was strange, Marged thought—the three of them together again as they had often used to be as children, Geraint usually leading them into some mischief. And yet now there was the yawning gulf between him on one side and her and Aled on the other. And the terrible tension.

"I am free to go?" she asked.

"Why ever would you not be?" the haughty voice of the Earl of Wyvern said from behind her. "Good day to you, Marged."

She fled, sparing only one hasty look at Aled as she passed. Thank heaven at least that she had been there and had been able to warn him in time against being as foolhardy as she had been.

Why had he pretended not to believe her? she wondered. Why had he let her go? Was he trying somehow to make amends for what he had done—or not done—to Eurwyn? Did he still care?

He took her on the shorter route home, up over the hill at the north end of the park and then across the hills to her father's farm. He took her by that route in order to avoid having to pass through the village. They walked side by side and in silence until they stopped by unspoken but mutual consent close to the top of the park. Close to the place where they had picnicked and become betrothed the day before.

Her eyes were downcast, her face expressionless. He felt heartsick.

"Ceris," he said, "did they hurt you?"

"No." There was almost no sound, but she shook her head.

"You betrayed me," he said.

She looked up at him then. Her eyes were large and calm, though there was pain in them too. He knew that he ought not to have said that. The betrayal had been mutual, but his had perhaps been worse because he had deliberately set out to trap her.

"And I betrayed you," he said.

"Yes." Her gaze was steady and now definitely sad. "Why did you lie for me?"

"Because it was all my fault," he said. "Because you were not guilty of anything except loyalty to your people. Because I love you."

She lowered her eyes again.

"Who was he?" he asked.

She shook her head slightly.

"The blacksmith?" The disguise had been impenetrable in the brief glimpse he had had of the man close to—and even then his eyes had been more on Ceris than on the man with whom she rode—but all night he had been haunted by the conviction that it was the blacksmith.

She stared at the ground between them.

"Did you spend the night with him, Ceris?" He knew that she had. He had had to return on foot from that road whereas she had had a ride. The chances were good that she would have been home long before he reached the end of the lane leading to her father's house. But he had spent the rest of the night watching it, anyway, waiting for her to come home, trying to persuade himself that she was inside, fast asleep all the time. She had returned, walking up from the direction of Glynderi, at dawn.

She said nothing.

"You told me yesterday," he said, "that you were a virgin. Could the same be said today?"

She looked up at him again. "No, Matthew," she said softly. "I am sorry. You will want to withdraw the offer you made me yesterday, and I must change my answer. I am sorry."

"Would you have gone to warn them last night if he had not been with them?" he asked her. He could hear the bitterness in his voice.

"They are my people, Matthew," she said. "I do not like what they are doing, but they do it in the earnest conviction that it is the only way to protest the intolerable conditions of our lives. I went because they are my people."

"And because you love him." He could not leave it alone. "Say it, Ceris. You stayed with him last night. You would not do that for less than love, would you?"

"I am sorry, Matthew." Her eyes filled with tears. "I should never have said yes to you. I was fond of you and I thought that would be enough. You deserve better."

She had been *fond* of him! His hands clenched at his sides.

"You do not need to come farther with me," she said. "It will be better if I go alone from here."

He nodded and watched her turn away. And imagined her small, shapely body spread naked beneath the blacksmith's.

"Ceris," he called after her. She turned to look back at him. "Tell your lover that I am going to catch him and see that he is prosecuted to the full extent of the law. Enjoy him while you may. It will not be for long. He will spend the rest of his life in transportation."

She looked at him for a long time, saying nothing, before turning away again and walking off across the hill. He sat down on the ground and set his elbows on his raised knees and the heels of his hands against his eyes. He should have had her yesterday when he had had the chance. If only he had known how things were going to turn out, he would have enjoyed her to the full. He would have done to her some of the things he liked doing with whores who were willing to earn something in addition to their basic fee. Her blacksmith would have found her slightly worn and bruised when it came his turn last night.

It must have been the blacksmith. Harley raised his head and draped his arms over his knees. He had been a large man, the right build. The blacksmith was one of Rebecca's daughters. And Rebecca herself—or himself, of course—had waited on the hill until the blacksmith came safely back up with Ceris. He had put himself in greater danger by waiting, especially given the distinctive shade of his disguise. Why would he have waited? Because he too knew Ceris and was anxious about her? Because he felt a loyalty to his "daughter"? Because that particular daughter was a close friend of his? Was Rebecca also from Glynderi, then, or close by?

Or was Rebecca closer yet? The idea seemed as preposterous now as it had seemed last night when it had first flashed into his mind. But it might as well at least be pulled out and given some consideration. He ran mentally over some facts, in random order. He was not yet trying to make a coherent whole out of them.

Rebecca had had someone else up on his horse with him. A young man or lad, it had seemed. But he had sat sideways on the horse, his arms about Rebecca's waist. A woman? It seemed very possible. The Earl of Wyvern had been from home last evening when Harley had looked for him, and no one seemed to know where he had gone. His valet had thought he had retired early. The Earl of Wyvern had returned home not long before dawn. He had not seen Harley as he rode across the hill higher up than the Williams farm. He had been wearing neither greatcoat nor cloak nor hat, but there had been a rather fat bundle behind his saddle and he had been running the fingers of one hand through his hair, rather as if he had just removed a hat.

Had he been coming home from a romantic tryst with a whore or mistress? Harley did not know where he was likely to find either in this corner of nonconformist Wales. But he did know one thing. He had learned it in talking to one of the older gardeners after Wyvern's arrival from England. As a boy, before his legitimacy had been established, Wyvern had had two close friends. Aled Rhoslyn, now the blacksmith of Glynderi. And Marged Llwyd, now Marged Evans, who lived—without a man—at the farm of Tŷ-Gwyn, higher up the hill from the Williams farm. Eurwyn Evans had died in transportation after trying to destroy the salmon weir. His widow must be an angry young woman as well as an attractive one—and probably a lusty one.

When he first arrived at Tegfan, Wyvern had disapproved of rising rents, the strict enforcement of tithe collection, and the high and frequent tolls the people had to pay at the tollgates. He had ordered the destruction of the salmon weir and directed the removal of the gamekeepers' mantraps. He had offered employment to the farmer who had lost his farm last year when he was unable to pay the rent. But Wyvern had made no attempt at further changes lately. Not since the Rebecca Riots had flared in this part of the country, in fact. Waldo Parry was now working for Marged Evans, Harley had heard.

Despite a stern, cold manner, Wyvern had been far more

ready to believe his lies this morning and release Ceris than
Sir Hector had been. Sir Hector had not called him a liar, but
he had still believed that Ceris might have seen someone
close enough—her kidnapper, for example—to identify or
might have heard something that could be useful as evidence. He had still wanted to keep her in custody for
questioning. It was Wyvern who had said that they could not
so insult his steward as to interrogate Harley's fiancée.

What did it all mean? Harley asked himself at last. It
made no sense to think what he was thinking. Or did it?
Certainly he knew what he wanted to believe. Wanted quite
desperately to believe. It would be wonderful. It would get
rid of Wyvern and leave Harley free to continue as before
under his new employers, Sir Hector Webb and Lady Stella.
And it might also get rid of the blacksmith. Then Harley
could watch Ceris suffer.

He wanted to see her suffer.

He wanted them all to suffer.

But how could he prove it?

Chapter 24

It was destined to be a wholly turbulent day, Geraint realized soon after Aled had left. His friend had been satisfied that Ceris Williams's name had been cleared and that there was no fear of her being arrested again. He had been less satisfied with the alibi that had been presented to clear her. Geraint had not realized before last night that there was a romantic attachment between the two of them. Neither had he realized that Aled had been shot the night before. It seemed that Ceris had dressed the wound and that there was no sign of inflammation this morning. But Aled had been in pain. That had been obvious from the paleness of his face.

There had been no time for Geraint to mull over in his mind the events of last night. Or the events of the morning. It had been a close-run thing. Ceris Williams's courage had been unexpected, Harley's lies in order to provide an alibi more so. Why had he lied? Because he loved Ceris? There appeared to be a love triangle at work in that situation, something that might yet cause trouble.

And there had been Marged's visit and her rash and

altogether characteristic attempt to save Ceris by taking her place. And her offer of herself to him if that was what it would take to win her friend's freedom—an offer he had found rather unpalatable. And yet he could not help feeling a fierce pride in her and an almost agonized love of her. It had been a real agony this morning to play the part of the Earl of Wyvern, to be cold, to feel her touch and show no reaction to it. And yet his body—and his emotions—were still feeling the effects of several hours of lovemaking with her that had been both tender and passionate.

He wondered if there was going to be any way out of the pit he had dug for himself.

But he was not to have time to think further. His butler arrived with a visitor's card on a tray. After one glance at it, Geraint brightened and directed that Mr. Thomas Campbell Foster of *The Times* be shown in. This was the journalist to whom he had written, a man he knew personally and respected for his work. The man on whom he pinned much hope.

"Thomas." He crossed the library to his visitor, right hand extended, as soon as the latter was shown into the room. "This is a singular surprise, though a very welcome one. What brings you to this forsaken corner of the British Isles?" He must not forget that it was Rebecca who had written to Foster, not the Earl of Wyvern.

"Wyvern." Foster made him a half bow and grinned. "I had been expecting barren wasteland and wild savages, I must confess. It has been a pleasant surprise to find lovely scenery and a language that sounds very musical even if it is unintelligible."

Geraint crossed to a sideboard to pour his friend a drink and motioned him to a leather chair at one side of the fireplace. "Have a seat," he said, "and tell me what brings you here. Is it business or pleasure?"

"Business actually," Foster said after seating himself and accepting the offered glass. "I had an eloquent and impassioned letter from Rebecca inviting me down here to witness at first hand what is happening."

"Ah," Geraint said, sitting down opposite the journalist. "Rebecca."

"I do not know how to contact him," Foster said. "I suppose he will contact me when he hears of my arrival. In the meantime I thought to speak with all the landowners in the area to hear their version of events. I suppose the two versions will conflict. But the challenge of journalism is to try to separate truth from prejudice and hysteria and report accurately what is fair to both sides. I learned to my delight that your Welsh property is in the very center of this new wave of rioting. And so I came to you first, Wyvern. Are you willing to grant me an interview?"

Geraint crossed one leg over the other and pursed his lips. "This new wave of rioting, as you call it, has begun since my arrival here," he said. "It might even be said that I provoked it in a way. I instituted a few reforms and tried to bring about a few more on a larger scale by talking with my neighbors and advocating joint action. I met hostility from all quarters and was forced to abandon my crusading zeal. And then Rebecca appeared. Perhaps I inadvertently stirred something up."

Thomas Foster was looking at him with interest. "This is unexpected," he said. "Are you suggesting that you believe the rioters have some right on their side?"

Geraint thought for a moment. "I suppose it is never right to act against the law and to destroy public property," he said. "But I must confess that I find myself in some sympathy with Rebecca and his followers. They seem to have almost no alternative. They have met with deaf ears for long enough. I am not sure if you are aware, Thomas, that for the first twelve years of my life, before my grandfather discovered that I was his legitimate heir, I lived here among the poorest of the poor. That was a long time ago, but I can remember how it feels to be poor and helpless. If my grandfather had not made his discovery, I am not sure now that I would not be a follower of Rebecca myself." He smiled. "I was always something of a leader. Perhaps I would even have been Rebecca."

Thomas Foster whistled and settled more comfortably in his chair, all sense of formality forgotten. "Tell me more," he said. "This is fascinating and will make wonderful copy in *The Times*. A peer of the realm who is in sympathy with rebels, partly because he grew up as one of them. Tell me everything you know and everything you feel, if you will."

Geraint laughed. "If you have an hour or two to spare," he said. "Shall I replenish your drink first?"

Well over an hour later Geraint was sitting at his desk writing a letter to Mr. Thomas Campbell Foster from Rebecca, inviting the journalist to join her and her daughters and children two nights hence for a meeting.

It was safe to disclose both time and place, Geraint decided. Foster was a man of integrity and a man after a fascinating story. He was not going to turn informer. Indeed, he would protect his sources against all pressure. Geraint could remember a time when Foster had spent a few nights in Newgate for refusing to disclose the confidences of an accused murderer.

There were many places in the hills where a large crowd might gather undetected. If they were far from any road or tollgate, there was not even the chance of a stray constable detecting them. Foster could gather all the information he needed from such a meeting—from Rebecca, from her daughters, from any man in the crowd who cared to speak up and voice his grievances. Geraint half smiled. Or from any *woman*. He could not imagine Marged keeping quiet.

Perhaps after the meeting they would march on a gate and destroy it. Perhaps Foster would come with them so that he could witness and report exactly what happened.

Foster had told him earlier that there was talk of setting up a commission of inquiry to come down to Wales in order to interview as many people as possible to find out the truth behind the complaints and unrest. If Foster was given a good enough story to publish in the foremost London newspaper, then perhaps that possibility would become more of a certainty.

He could only hope, Geraint thought as he signed the letter with a flourish. Hope and keep working toward his goal, though doing so was becoming more dangerous every day.

Ceris and her mother were both working in the kitchen when Aled was admitted to the Williams farmhouse. Both were as pale as ghosts. Ninian Williams came in from outside before any words could be exchanged. He looked thunderous.

"Well, Aled Rhoslyn," he said, "my daughter was betrothed yesterday to Matthew Harley. I will hear today that she is betrothed to you or I will see you outside with your fists at the ready."

"Yes, Ninian," Aled said, his eyes on Ceris. She was stirring a pot of soup that was suspended over the fire, her eyes downcast. "But it takes two to make such an announcement. I will talk privately with Ceris, will I?"

"My daughter lied to us last night," Ninian said. "And then she shamed us and herself and her chapel by fornicating with you while she was betrothed to another man. I am not sure there can be forgiveness for such behavior. We will have to speak with the Reverend Llwyd. But marriage between those who have fornicated together is one step in the right direction. My daughter's consent in the matter is unnecessary."

His dear, gentle Ceris. Obviously after her ordeal of the morning she had made a clean breast of everything to her parents. And Ninian was reacting as any father might be expected to react. He had probably been scared out of his wits when Ceris was dragged off to Tegfan.

"Oh, Ninian." Mrs. Williams lifted her apron over her face. "There is hard you are being on your own daughter. And you a follower of Rebecca yourself if it were not for your legs."

"It is not the following of Rebecca I object to, woman," he said. "It is the lies and the fornicating."

"Ceris," Aled said. "We will step outside together and talk about it, is it?"

Her hand paused in its stirring motion though she did not look up. "Yes," she said. She set down the spoon, wiped her hands on her apron, and turned to the door. Aled followed her out.

"You stay within sight of the house, mind," Ninian said. Aled nodded.

She crossed the yard to the gate leading to the lane. But she did not open the gate. She turned to lean back against it and raised her eyes to his at last.

"Aled," she said, "I told the truth when I said I would not be ashamed today. I should be, but I am not. But you owe me nothing. What I did, I did freely and knowingly."

"Cariad," he said, coming to stand close to her despite her father's eyes, which he could almost feel on the back of his neck. "Geraint told me that you were very brave. I am proud of you."

"Geraint?" She frowned for a moment.

"He was my friend," he said. "He still is my friend."

"And your enemy too," she said sadly. "We live in hard times."

"Did they hurt you?" he asked. "I wish I could have been with you to take the burden from you."

"The constables were a little rough," she said, "though not deliberately hurtful, I think. The earl stopped Sir Hector Webb when he would have struck me. I cannot believe the earl is altogether a bad man, Aled. I think that in some way he is as much a victim of circumstances as we are."

It was something he had to say, though he did not want to know about it. He was afraid to know about it despite the way she had started their conversation. "Harley lied to set you free," he said. It was not a question.

"Yes." Her eyes grew sadder. "We betrayed each other last night, Aled, and of course the betrothal is at an end. But I believe he must still care for me a little to have done what he did this morning. I cannot hate him. But I do not love him and never did. I just—wanted to be married and thought it might work with him. I was foolish."

"We will marry, then, *cariad*?" he asked her. He found his heart beating faster and his breath becoming labored. "Your dada demands it and the Reverend Llwyd will too if he finds out. And indeed it is the only right thing to do when we have been together as we were last night. If I must, if it will make you feel better, I will give up following Rebecca. I will talk to the Reverend Llwyd and set a date for wedding you, will I?"

She was smiling, though her eyes were still sad. "That is the nicest, most loving thing you have ever said to me," she said. "A precious gift. Let me give you one of equal value in return. I will marry you, Aled, and make your home comfortable and bear your little ones and love you dearly for the rest of my life. And if sometimes you do things that your conscience leads you to do, I will respect you even if I cannot agree. As I believe you will respect my values. You must go with Rebecca if you feel you must, and I will sit at home and pray for your safe return."

They smiled warmly at each other before they moved into each other's arms—Aled winced only slightly and she carefully avoided touching his wounded shoulder. They stood, silently embracing, for a few minutes before their attention was caught by loud and persistent coughing from the direction of the house.

Ninian Williams and his wife were standing side by side outside the door. Both looked pleased even though Ninian was trying to maintain his ferocious frown and Mrs. Williams had her apron up over her face again.

They were tramping up over the hills and down through valleys again. They had walked for what must be several miles already. There had been an unusually dry spell of weather. The grass felt dry and almost dusty underfoot.

They were going to a meeting tonight, Aled had said, and then perhaps on to a gate smashing. It was becoming more nerve-racking to leave home and make one's way to the meeting place. The constables were still at Tegfan. One never knew quite where they were or quite whom they were watching. They had followed Ceris the last time even though Ceris had never marched with Rebecca. If they had followed Ceris all the way from her father's house, perhaps they had seen two other people going down the hill too, Marged thought—Waldo Parry and herself.

She had been sorely tempted tonight to stay at home. But not just from fear, it had to be admitted. She was not sure she was ready to see Rebecca again. Part of her longed for him, for his closeness, for his lovemaking. But not just the physical lovemaking, though it was more deliriously wonderful with him than she had ever imagined it could be. There was the feeling of emotional closeness too, the feeling that they belonged together, that they were the best of friends even though she did not know his name and had never seen his face. She felt almost married to Rebecca. Almost but not quite.

She was still feeling dreadfully upset over her encounter with Geraint at Tegfan. And ashamed of what she had offered in exchange for Ceris's freedom. Though she would have done it too, she knew, and would still do it if it were the only way to ensure Ceris's continued freedom. How could she even have dreamed of offering such a thing when she was Rebecca's? Would she be able to go back to Rebecca tonight if she really had given herself to Geraint? It was perhaps a foolish question she posed herself since in fact she had not been called upon to make any such sacrifice. But was not the intention as bad as the deed? She would have slept with him if he had asked it of her.

Marged stumbled against a stone on a hillside and muttered to herself while Dylan Owen steadied her and grinned at her. "One thing about it, Marged," he said. "If you have sprained an ankle, you have only the one way to walk, unlike the rest of us. You will be riding home in style."

They all knew, she thought, that she was Rebecca's woman. Perhaps they even suspected that Rebecca was her lover. No one had said anything openly to her. They were a good sort, her neighbors and friends. But heaven help her if her father ever got wind of the fact.

"If I ride home tonight," she said with an answering grin, "I will spare your corns a thought, Dylan. One single, brief thought."

If she rode home tonight. She half hoped that tonight he would not single her out but would leave her to return home with her friends. She did not know quite how she was to face him. She loved him both tenderly and passionately, but she felt horribly as if she had been unfaithful to him. For not only had she been prepared to lie with Geraint, but also she had wanted to.

There. The thought was full-blown and verbal in her mind. The thought she had been tiptoeing guiltily about for two whole days. When she had touched Geraint and offered herself to him, there had been a stabbing of sexual desire for him in her womb and between her thighs. She had wanted him there, easing her pain and bringing her pleasure. She had wanted to do with him what she had done with Eurwyn and what she did with Rebecca.

There. She had called a spade a spade in her mind and she felt even more wretched than she had before. Not only with guilt but with confusion. How could she love one man and yet want to—to *rut* with another? Did sleeping with a man outside marriage make one suddenly and indiscriminately promiscuous? She knew what answer her father would give to that question. And it seemed he would be right.

But her thoughts were interrupted. They were meeting up with another group in the hollow between two hills, and in the middle of the group, on a slight rise of land, stood Rebecca. He was not on horseback, but he looked as tall and as commanding and as majestic as he always looked.

In one way her first sight of him tonight was reassuring. She felt a rush of love for him that was only partly physical. Looking at him, she was convinced that she loved only him. How could she have doubted even for a moment that her devotion was all his?

There was a stranger standing quite close to him. Most of the men here were strangers to her, of course. But this man was without disguise and he was dressed in clothes that looked both fashionable and expensive. He was looking about him with frank interest.

Aled dismounted and joined the other daughters on the mound with Rebecca. The stranger was there too and another man, disguised like everyone else but not as a daughter. His role became clear when the meeting began. He was an interpreter, translating what Rebecca said into English, though interestingly enough he did not translate what was said in English back into Welsh for Rebecca's comprehension.

Marged did not know why Rebecca chose not to speak in English. Almost everyone she knew spoke the language to a certain extent, and Rebecca was an intelligent man and seemed to be an educated one. And obviously he understood perfectly well what was said to him. But for some reason he chose to speak through an interpreter.

The stranger was an Englishman from London. He wrote for a London newspaper and was gathering information about the Rebecca Riots and the grievances that had led to them. He had spoken with all the landowners in the area and now wished to hear from Rebecca herself and from the people who followed her. If they could convince him that they had good reason to riot and if he could draw the attention of the English to their plight, perhaps he could do them some good. Already the government was talking about sending commissioners to West Wales to do much what he was doing but in a more official way.

It was an exciting idea, that they had already achieved their objective of attracting attention to their cause and that this man had come, willing to listen to their side of the story as well as that of the landowners. Perhaps after all the skeptics would be proved wrong. Perhaps after all good would come out of the necessary evil they had instituted. Perhaps after all Rebecca would become a national hero. It seemed that it was a letter from Rebecca that had brought the reporter from *The Times* to Wales.

Was he capable of writing a letter that could have that powerful an effect, then? Marged fixed her eyes on him. She was becoming so accustomed to the long gown, the wig, and the mask that they were beginning to seem almost normal to her. But for a moment again she felt an intense curiosity about the man behind the mask. What did he look like? What sort of life did he lead? It seemed somehow bizarre that she had no answers to those questions and yet knew him with greater physical intimacy than she had known with Eurwyn even in five years of marriage.

The meeting lasted a whole hour and might have lasted several more if Rebecca had not brought it to an end when the complaints voiced to Mr. Foster of *The Times* began to become repetitive. Many of them had spoken. She had spoken up herself and had told briefly of the injustice Eurwyn had tried to put right and the fate that had befallen him as a result.

Mr. Foster had talked to all the landowners, she remembered. He would have spoken with Geraint. Would Geraint have mentioned the salmon weir to him and the fact that he had had it destroyed soon after his arrival at Tegfan? Would he have convinced Mr. Foster that he was not guilty of the oppression that had existed on his estate for years? She felt angry that his lies might have been believed.

And yet he had destroyed the weir. And he had had all the mantraps removed. Why? She did not want to be reminded of that old question. He certainly had not instituted any reforms since then.

Except that he had prevented Sir Hector Webb from striking Ceris and had opposed taking Ceris away for questioning after Mr. Harley had given her an alibi. And except that he had pretended to believe that the confession she, Marged, had made to him was a lie and had let her go free.

Why had he let her go? She had thought at the time that perhaps he had allowed her that favor so that he could pursue her and make it very difficult for her to order him out of her sight. But she had not set eyes on him for two days.

She hated the fact that Geraint Penderyn, Earl of Wyvern, somehow defied all labels. She wanted so much to be able to dismiss him as an unadulterated villain.

Rebecca was talking to them and Marged's full attention was drawn to him again. He had his arms raised, the sure sign that he was leading them on a new mission. And sure enough, they were to destroy the gate and makeshift house that had been reerected near Penfro—their first mission. Mr. Foster was to accompany them.

Part of her attention was on Mr. Foster throughout the destruction of the gate. Destruction was such a negative thing. She wondered if he was quite repelled or if he was at all impressed by the discipline of their actions, by the courtesy shown the new gatekeeper, though he swore the air blue. As usual, he was given time to remove his personal belongings from the house and to get himself safely away. As usual, they had all been instructed to offer the man no violence, either of word or deed. No one replied to his tirade with even a mild oath. She wondered if Mr. Foster was impressed by the total control Rebecca exercised over his followers without ever having to raise his voice.

Surely Mr. Foster could not fail to be impressed and to realize that they were not a mob with simple destruction on their minds. Surely he could and would help them.

She was tired of the Rebecca Riots, she realized suddenly. She was tired of the destruction and the danger. She was tired of worrying about Rebecca. She wanted peace. But if and when the riots came to an end, would she lose Rebecca? Would she ever see him again? Or if she did, would she know him? She would always know him, she told herself. If ever she passed him on a street or occupied the same building with him, she would know him.

But she might well lose him once these nocturnal adventures were at an end.

But not quite yet. Rebecca dismissed her children and they all went their separate ways, Mr. Foster among them.

And then Rebecca was at her side, leaning down from his horse, hand extended, as usual. She smiled up at him and set her hand in his and her foot on his boot.

She would not think of the end, she thought, snuggling against him and closing her eyes as they rode off in the direction of her home. Not yet.

Chapter
25

Geraint was feeling rather euphoric. Despite the various dangers, everything appeared to be working as he had hoped it would. He believed that as the Earl of Wyvern he had enlightened Foster and aroused his sympathies for the rebels. And he believed that as Rebecca he—and all his followers—had stated their case fully and clearly and rationally. Foster had seen tonight that they were not a violent, hysterical mob bent on mindless violence. He had seen, perhaps, that they were people at war against an unjust and oppressive system.

He trusted Foster to see clearly through to the heart of the matter and to write eloquently enough to arouse the interest and sympathy of a London reading public. If it all happened quickly enough, and if a commission of inquiry really was sent to West Wales and consisted of intelligent and open-minded commissioners, then surely all this would soon be over. The necessity for rebelling in order to draw attention would be past.

He would no longer be Rebecca. She would disappear into thin air and only a very few people would ever know who Rebecca had been. Marged would never know. Unconsciously his arm tightened about her as they rode and she muttered something unintelligible and burrowed deeper into his shoulder. She was actually dozing, he thought with a smile. What an amazing woman she was. And how he loved her. Would he lose her forever when Rebecca disappeared? Was there any way on this earth that Geraint Penderyn could win her love? He did not believe so.

He had taken a route that would bring them onto the upland moors above Tegfan and Tŷ-Gwyn again. He guided his horse toward the ruined hovel that had been home. Yes—home. He had experienced all of a mother's love here, and more lately he had known the love of a woman here. It was ironic that such a bleak and sorry little hut should have housed so much love. He thought of the magnificence—and the coldness and loneliness—of Tegfan.

Marged stirred as soon as his horse stopped. He dismounted and lifted her down, tethered his horse beside the house, where it would be very difficult for anyone else to see, and lifted down the blanket. Marged was standing waiting for him. He backed her against the wall of the house and kissed her. She was warm and relaxed from sleep. It was amazing, he thought, how quickly one could become dependent upon the love of another person. Not just physical love, though he was aroused and ready for her, but emotional love too. He had become dependent upon her affection and respect and friendship. It was rather frightening when he remembered that those gifts were being given to a man who did not exist. And yet he needed the gifts as he needed air to breathe and water to drink.

"Let us go inside," he whispered against her lips, "and make ourselves comfortable."

The warmth and relaxation disappeared. She pushed away from him and turned her back on him, gazing out into the night beyond the corner of the hut.

"There is something I must tell you," she said.

His stomach lurched. She was with child. Oh, God, she

was with child. There was an uncomfortable churning of excitement and despair inside him.

"I love you," she said. "I did not believe it was possible to love as I love you. And yet—and yet I am not sure I have been faithful to you."

He stood very still and waited for her to continue.

"When Ceris Williams was arrested two days ago," she said, "I thought they were going to drag her away to jail and perhaps torture her for information. You heard that she had been arrested, did you? I thought she would be transported even though she was innocent of everything except caring about the safety of the rest of us. So I went to Tegfan and told the Earl of Wyvern that I was the one who had been seen on the road by the smashed gate, not Ceris. I told him I was one of your followers." She paused. "I even told him we were lovers."

Marged! So incurably honest. He knew now what she was going to say to him, though he wondered exactly how she would describe it.

"That was incredibly brave of you, *cariad*," he said.

"Incredibly foolish," she said with a bleak little laugh. "I still do not know quite why he chose to believe that I was lying."

"Who would confess freely to such a thing if it were the truth?" he said. "Why do you think you might have been unfaithful to me?"

He could hear the raggedness of the deep breath she took. "When I still thought Ceris was in custody," she said, "before I learned that she had been set free, I told Ger—the earl that I would do anything to persuade him to release her. No, don't say anything yet," she said hastily as he drew breath to speak. "You understand what I am saying, don't you? I touched him and put myself against him. I was offering my body."

"But he did not accept the offer?" he asked her.

"No," she said.

"Then no harm was done." He set a hand on her shoulder, but she shrugged it off.

"But I would have done it," she said. "I would have given myself to him as many times as he chose to take me. I made the offer. It was he who rejected it, not me."

"You did it to save a friend," he said, touching her shoulder again. This time she let his hand rest there. "We all know the Bible quotation 'Greater love hath no man than this, that he lay down his life for his friends.' Or something like that—I am not sure I have it word perfect. You were prepared to give something of perhaps even greater value than your life, Marged. I can only honor you for it."

Was is such a sacrifice to give herself to Geraint Penderyn that she had suffered this anguish? He could feel the anguish—and the guilt—being passed on to him.

He turned her then and even in the darkness he could see her eyes huge with tears. He drew her against him and kissed her. "Let's go inside," he said.

But she was still not relaxed. She drew back her head and gazed at him. "That is not all," she said. "I have to tell you the rest."

"What, *cariad*?" he asked her.

"I wanted to," she blurted, and she stiffened against his hands. "I don't understand it, but I have to tell you the truth. I love you. I love you with all my heart, though even that seems absurd when I know so little about you. And I hate him with all my heart. And yet I wanted him. It horrifies me, yet it is true. So I was unfaithful, you see, for I was not only willing but even eager. I will walk down to Tŷ-Gwyn now and you can ride safely home. I will—perhaps I will not come out the next time we are called. In fact I definitely will not. Forgive me. I did not mean to—"

"Marged." He pulled her hard against him. He did not believe it was possible to feel so elated and so wretched all at the same time. She had wanted him. And with Marged desire would never be just a physical thing. If she did not hate him so much, and with such good reason, she would love him again. And surely something in her subconscious mind was putting the two of them together—Geraint and Rebecca—and understanding the connection.

And yet there was wretchedness. She had been startlingly honest with him, and yet in his dealings with her as Rebecca he had been nothing but deceitful and dishonest. What he should do, he thought, was tell her the truth right now. He owed her the truth. And no matter what her reaction, he knew her well enough to know that she would not betray him.

"Marged," he said, "there are things in all our lives that we are ashamed of. There are many in my life."

"Don't tell me," she said quickly, looking up into his face again. "Don't say any more. If you feel you must make confessions of your own just to make me feel better, don't. I feel bruised and battered. All I have to believe in at the moment is you and my love for you. Don't say any more tonight. Can you forgive me? If not, let me go home with no more said. If you can, then let us make love. I need you—if you will still have me."

He gazed into her shadowed eyes. It was tempting. So tempting.

"Please," she said. "Say yes or no. Nothing more than that. I could not stand more than that tonight."

"Let us go inside, then," he said. "I love you, Marged."

He could see that she was smiling. "One day you will tell me everything," she said, "all the sordid details of your life. But not tonight. This is the first night when I do not even want to know. I want to love. I want to prove to you and to myself that only you matter to me."

"We will love," he said, guiding her through the doorway and over to the dark corner where they had lain before. "I am on fire for you, *cariad*."

He spread the blanket and lowered them both to it.

She lay relaxed and sated in his arms. He was asleep, something he rarely did during their encounters. She felt happy again. She knew that she was where she wanted to be, where she belonged. Whatever it was that had happened with Geraint two days ago, it was not love. She had confessed all to Rebecca, and he had accepted it. It had made no difference to his feelings. He was a man of incredible generosity, she thought.

She could have known by now who he was. She had sensed earlier that he was about to tell her everything. Why had she not wanted him to do so? Her reluctance had taken her by surprise. Was it that she was enjoying this fantasy? As long as she had never seen his face or heard his name, as long as she knew nothing of his life except what pertained to Rebecca, she could make him into any man she wanted him to be. Had she idealized him? Was he quite as wonderful in real life as she thought him?

Perhaps she did not want to know the reality. A real-life man was a complex person. If one lived closely with a real man, one had to adjust to his ways, learn to accept him as he was, with all his faults and annoying habits. The adjustment with Eurwyn had taken a year or more—perhaps all five years of their marriage. A close love relationship was something that had to be worked on every day of one's life.

Maybe she was enjoying this fairy-tale romance into which real life had not yet intruded.

But she wondered if it must soon face the test of reality whether she wanted it to or not. She had just been doing mental calculations. She had been avoiding the same calculations for a few days. Her suspicions were quite correct. She was four days late. It was not a great deal of time and probably meant nothing at all. She remembered being five days late once fairly early in her marriage, but the sixth day had shattered her hopes with the indisputable evidence that she was not pregnant. This time she was only four days late.

For a moment she felt the dizziness of panic. But she would not give in to it. The chances were that she was only late. And even if it was not that, even if there was a child in her womb, he would not abandon her. He had told her that. And he had told her she could always communicate with him through Aled.

She believed him implicitly. If he had said he would not abandon her, then he would not, even though to do so would

be very easy. How would she ever find him if he did not
want to be found?

But she trusted him. He had withheld truths from her, but
he had never lied to her. He loved her. He had told her so,
and she believed him.

She rubbed her cheek against his bare chest and sighed
with contentment. She allowed herself to relax into sleep.

Matthew Harley was cursing himself for a fool. It was
almost dawn. He had spent most of the night out on the hill
below Marged Evans's farm, chilled to the bone, watching
for something that even at the start he had been far from
sure would happen.

He had just about impoverished himself lately, paying out
bribes—two to the constables who had accompanied him in
his pursuit of Ceris and knew the truth of that night's events,
and one to a footman at the house. The two had been paid
because he had made a fool of himself over a mere tenant
farmer's daughter. The third had been paid because he
desperately wanted to get revenge on someone for all the
troubles that had come into his life lately. And who better to
avenge himself on than the Earl of Wyvern himself?

He was sure that Wyvern was also Rebecca, incredible as
the suspicion seemed.

And so he had a footman spying for him at Tegfan. And
tonight Wyvern had slipped out without a word to anyone.
It was impossible to know where he had gone, though
Harley would bet his last penny that tomorrow would bring
the news of another gate or two having been pulled
down—by Rebecca and her *children*. Harley pinned all his
hopes on witnessing Wyvern's return and somehow seeing
the evidence that Wyvern and Rebecca were one and the
same person.

But where was he to wait? Outside Tegfan itself was not
good enough. By the time he arrived home, doubtless all
disguise and all evidence of Rebecca would have been shed.
From which direction would he be likely to come? There
were as many possibilities as there were directions.

But it was not difficult for Harley to decide which one he would gamble on. The last time he had seen Wyvern coming home in the early morning, he had been riding across the hill, coming from the direction of Tŷ-Gwyn. Harley had concluded at the time that he had been coming from a tryst with Marged Evans. It was very likely that Marged was a Rebeccaite. Her husband had been trouble, and the constable who had been stationed outside the Williams farm had seen her—or a lad Harley suspected had been her—going down the hill at a late hour.

It was very possible that Marged and Rebecca were lovers.

And so Harley stationed himself in such a position on the hill that he could see both Tŷ-Gwyn above and Tegfan below and yet was himself hidden from anyone who did not actually ride or walk right on top of him. And yet for all he knew, he was on a fool's errand. There were hours and hours of chilly boredom to live through and probably would be nothing for his pains at the end of it except a sleepless night and increased anger.

It was time to return home, he decided at last. Probably Wyvern had been tucked up in his bed at Tegfan for hours already. But not so. Before he could move his cramped limbs and show himself to an empty hillside, something caught at the corner of his vision despite the fact that it was still dark. Something light.

There was a horse with two riders outside the gate of Tŷ-Gwyn. One of the riders swung down from the saddle and lifted down the other. For a few moments their images merged, and then the smaller of the two, the one dressed in dark man's clothes, opened the gate and disappeared from sight inside the farmyard. The other stayed where he was and watched and raised a hand in farewell a few moments later. Then he remounted his horse and turned it across the hill, in the direction of Tegfan.

The rider, Harley saw with mounting excitement, was all white. He wore a flowing white robe, a blond wig, and what looked to be a white mask. He was Rebecca, the same figure

Harley had seen last watching the roadway from which the blacksmith was rescuing Ceris.

He must be Wyvern. Unless his path changed, he was riding toward the northern, uphill entrance to Tegfan. Harley wished he could follow him, but he was on foot. There was nowhere he could conveniently have hidden a horse. Besides, he could not have followed on horseback without being seen.

The man on the horse stopped and looked back when he had put some distance between himself and the farm. He must have ridden out of sight of the gate already. Harley watched, wide-eyed, as he pulled off first his wig and then his mask, which appeared to be some sort of cap that he had pulled over his whole head. Then the gown came off and all were bundled up quickly and wrapped in the cloak or blanket or whatever it was bundled behind the saddle. The rider resumed his journey.

Dawn had not yet broken and there was some distance between the rider and Harley. But Harley was left in no doubt at all about the identity of Rebecca. He was the Earl of Wyvern.

He almost laughed aloud in his excitement. He had him. By God, he had him. If only he had a gun or had brought one of the constables with him! He could have taken Sir Hector Webb a far more significant prisoner than Ceris had been. But there was no point in making his presence known since there was no way of effecting a capture tonight. But tomorrow morning early he would ride to Pantnewydd with his news and his eyewitness account of the transformation of Rebecca into the Earl of Wyvern.

He watched from his position on the hill until Wyvern turned into the northern entrance to the park and disappeared from view among the trees. He was tired, Harley thought, but he doubted that he would get any sleep for what remained of the night.

If only he could put the finger on the blacksmith too. He would like to see Ceris Williams suffering through a trial and a conviction and the transportation for life of her lover.

A convicted daughter of Rebecca would surely get life. Yes, he would like to see her suffer through that after what she had done to him.

Harley got to his feet at last, shook out stiff limbs, and started on the walk back home.

Sir Hector Webb was in a bad mood. As he had told his wife numerous times and Maurice Mitchell during a visit the day before, he was being made to feel like a criminal, and he did not like it one little bit.

Here was this upstart reporter from London with his fashionable attire and his cultured English accent when he was very probably not even a gentleman, coming to question them about what was purely a criminal matter. He questioned them about rents and tithes and Poor Law taxes and road trusts and tolls. And all the time Sir Hector would swear that the man was siding with the damned rioters. Were the sharp rises in rents really necessary? What provision was made for a good tenant who could not pay his rent and had to forfeit his land? Why did tolls have to be collected from farmers who were about their business, hauling lime, for example?

The man in his ignorance did not realize that it was the carts with their loads of lime that were mainly responsible for breaking up the roads and necessitating more repairs. But Sir Hector had set him right on the matter fast enough.

It seemed that it was Rebecca who had brought the reporter to West Wales. He had had the gall to write and invite *The Times* to send someone to investigate. Crimes did not need investigation. They needed solving. The criminal needed to be caught and punished harshly enough to discourage anyone else from trying to follow in his footsteps. And yet this reporter would give no information at all about Rebecca. He would not even show the letter.

Sir Hector would wager that the man would arrange somehow to talk with Rebecca. Then he would be fed a parcel of lies and no doubt would believe them. Well, if Sir Hector got wind of it and if the reporter would still give no information, he would have the man arrested for something—for aiding and abetting a criminal, perhaps.

And if the reporter was to be believed, the government was seriously considering sending commissioners to West Wales to investigate the unrest and its causes. What was there to investigate? These were *crimes* that were being committed.

Sir Hector was in such a bad mood that he merely growled a greeting to Matthew Harley when the latter called quite early one morning and asked for a private word with him. He was shown into the study.

"Harley," he said with a curt nod. "I suppose you have heard that the Penfro gate went again last night. Damned scoundrels with the gall to attack a gate they had already destroyed once. I'll catch the pack of them if it is the last thing I do."

"Sir." Matthew Harley observed his usual respectful manner, yet even Sir Hector could see his eyes gleaming with suppressed emotion. "I know who Rebecca is."

Sir Hector went very still.

"Rebecca and the Earl of Wyvern are one and the same person," Harley said, triumph in his voice.

Sir Hector gaped for a moment, and then his jaws snapped shut. "Oh, nonsense, Harley," he said. "Pure wishful thinking. You had me hopeful for a moment."

"I saw it for myself, sir," Harley said.

Sir Hector looked closely at him and then frowned. He stood before the fireplace, his hands clasped at his back, his feet braced apart. "Suppose you tell me exactly what you did see, Harley," he said.

"I suspected it before," the steward said. "When I looked for him one night to give me permission to take constables and pursue the rioters, he was not at home, yet none of the servants knew he had gone. And I saw him return alone on horseback very late the same night. But that was only suspicion and not even worth reporting. I waited for more definite evidence, sir."

"And?" Sir Hector made impatient circling gestures with

one hand. "Come, man, this is not a theatrical performance, though I can see you are relishing every word."

"Last night," Harley said, "I heard that Wyvern had left the house again and I lay in wait for his return up in the hills, from which direction he had come the other time. But this time I saw more. It was just before dawn, sir, and I had all but given up hope. And then I saw Rebecca."

Sir Hector hissed in a breath.

"He was in full disguise," Harley said. "He was escorting a woman home—that would account for the late hour. But after he had left her and ridden even closer to me, he peeled off the disguise, hid it away in a bundle behind his saddle, and continued on his way down to Tegfan."

"Wyvern," Sir Hector said in little more than a whisper. "I'll be damned. He was Wyvern?"

"None other," Harley said, the triumph back in his voice. "We have him, sir. With your permission, I will return to Tegfan now and have the constables there arrest him and bring him before you."

But Sir Hector did not immediately respond. He was looking at Matthew Harley, and yet his gaze passed right through him. "No," he said. "Unless we could find the disguise—and it is doubtless well hidden—the only proof we would have is your evidence. It would be your word against his. The word of the Earl of Wyvern against that of his steward. It might well not stick."

Matthew Harley flushed. "I do not believe my integrity has ever been called into question, sir," he said.

"This would be different," Sir Hector said. "We cannot risk it. No, we need to catch him red-handed."

"It should not be difficult now that we know the truth," Harley said. "It will be merely a matter of watching and following him, sir. Perhaps we can net some of the other leaders too. I have reason to believe that the main one besides Wyvern—Charlotte he is known as—is the black-smith at Glynderi."

But Sir Hector was not really listening. He was frowning even more deeply. "If only we could manipulate things in such a way that he is discredited even with the people," he said. "You realize that he is very popular with them, Harley? He is damned polite to all the gatekeepers he displaces, as if he were asking them to dance at a court ball. He allows them to leave and to take their personal possessions with them. And as if that were not bad enough, he pays them compensation out of what he calls the coffers of Rebecca. I wondered where the money was coming from. Now I know. We have to discredit him."

"But how, sir?" Harley ventured to ask. "Perhaps the people do not even realize who he is. He wore his disguise even with his woman last night. Perhaps just exposing his secret would be enough."

"Perhaps." Sir Hector wandered to his desk and sat down heavily in the oak chair behind it. "I need time to think this out. Give me a day or two. What we need is a gate that is smashed in a less gentlemanly manner than usual."

"If there were constables—" Harley began.

"No, no, no, no." Sir Hector drummed his fingers on the desktop. "We have to make *him* behave badly."

"There is a gatekeeper at the Cilcoed gate quite close to Tegfan, a Mrs. Phillips," Harley said. "She told me a while ago that she is not afraid of Rebecca because the Earl of Wyvern himself had promised her his personal protection. I don't know how that fact will help us, sir. It just entered my head now."

"Did he indeed?" Sir Hector's fingers drummed harder. "A day or two at the longest, Harley. I will come to Tegfan and have a word with you. I will think of something. In the meantime you can be thinking too. And keeping your eyes and ears open."

"Yes, sir." Matthew Harley bowed respectfully and turned to leave.

"Harley," Sir Hector said. "Well done. I will not forget this. Neither will Lady Stella."

"It is a pleasure to be of service to you, sir," Harley said.

Chapter 26

"Well, Wyvern." Sir Hector Webb spoke heartily and rubbed his hands together as he paced to the library window at Tegfan and gazed out at lawns and trees. "It seems we are close to the end of this madness of rioting and gate smashing."

"You think so?" Geraint sat back in the chair behind the desk, his elbows on the wooden arms, his fingers steepled together. "One hopes you are right, Hector."

"This reporter from *The Times*," Sir Hector said. "I daresay he will print the truth and enough soldiers will be sent here at last. The rebellion will be crushed and the ruffian who calls himself Rebecca will be caught and suitably punished."

"It is an outcome we must hope for," Geraint said. "But I have heard that Foster has interviewed Rebecca and some of the people. Perhaps he believes what they have said."

Sir Hector turned his head to look over his shoulder at Geraint. "But who are the people who read the newspapers, Wyvern?" he asked. "And who among their readers would advocate granting rebels what they demand? Pretty soon every commoner in the country would be demanding something and destroying property and harassing law-abiding citizens. There would be anarchy. No, the reporter's articles will only help our cause, mark my words."

"It seems likely," Geraint said, "that a commission of inquiry is about to be sent down here, Hector. Thomas Foster says so, and letters I have received from London confirm it. They will talk to everyone, rich and poor. I suppose it will be for them to decide if the Rebecca Riots are justified or not and if anything should be done to redress the people's grievances."

"It sounds," Sir Hector said, his eyes narrowing, "as if you may still be in sympathy with the rabble, Wyvern."

Geraint looked directly back at him, eyebrows raised. "I am merely saying," he said, "that if and when the commissioners arrive, the matter will be out of our hands, Hector. And out of Rebecca's too. The issues will be judged by impartial observers—we must hope. We must hope too that some just settlement will be made. We do not, after all, wish to oppress the people who are to a certain extent in our care, do we? Just as we do not want to be terrorized by a mob. Though they have behaved with remarkable restraint so far."

Sir Hector was watching him with pursed lips. "Well," he said, "you have always spelled trouble for my wife's family, Wyvern. I don't know why I would expect anything to change now. I shall take myself off to have a talk with Harley. About sheep. I assume he is still in charge of the business of your farms?"

Geraint inclined his head and watched his uncle stride from the room. Perhaps he had been unwise. Perhaps until this whole matter was settled it would be better to pretend to think in harmony with the other landowners and not to breathe a word about fairness or justice.

But he was tired of pretending. And that was all he seemed to have done for several weeks. With Sir Hector and the other landowners and with his own people when he was not wearing disguise, he pretended to be the mindless aristocrat, guarding his wealth and his property and his consequence at all cost. With the followers of Rebecca he pretended to be the people's champion, one of them but with the strength and the courage to lead them. With Marged . . .

Geraint sighed and locked his hands behind his head. He was tired of pretending. And pretense was not even a recent thing with him. For years he had pretended that Geraint Penderyn had not existed before the age of twelve. He had pretended that Tegfan did not exist or Glynderi or the rudely thatched hovel on the moors. Or Marged . . .

He was tired of pretending. Geraint Penderyn was a real person with a real lifelong history. His roots were in Tegfan and the vast estate surrounding the house and park. The Earl of Wyvern was also a real person and had grown through hardship and adversity and stubborn will into the man he now was. And even Rebecca was real. Rebecca was not the mask, but the man behind the mask. And the man behind the mask had been shaped by all the experiences of Geraint Penderyn and the Earl of Wyvern and had come to confront the peculiar set of circumstances that had met him on his return to Tegfan. Rebecca, one might say, was the culmination of everything that had shaped him throughout life.

Rebecca was his destiny.

Three persons—Geraint Penderyn, the Earl of Wyvern, Rebecca. And yet they were one, all inextricably woven together. And he wanted to be that one person. He wanted to be done with pretending and be himself—his final, complete self—with everyone he encountered. He wanted to be done with masks, both real and figurative.

He was going to ask Aled to arrange a meeting with the committee, Geraint decided. He was going to suggest that the Rebecca Riots in this particular part of West Wales be suspended until they saw how Thomas Foster and the commission of inquiry could help them. Perhaps they could make a public declaration through Foster that they were doing so as a gesture of goodwill.

And Marged. Perhaps he could bring himself to go to her and tell her the truth. She was both his lover and his love. He owed her the truth perhaps more than anything else. She had loved Geraint Penderyn until she was sixteen and he was eighteen. She loved Rebecca. She hated the Earl of Wyvern. It was impossible to predict how she would react to hearing the truth. Would her fond memories of Geraint and her love for Rebecca outweigh her hatred for the earl? At one moment he thought that they must. She loved so totally and so passionately—his loins ached at the very memory of her passion. But at the next moment he was less sure. She blamed the Earl of Wyvern for her husband's death and there was no doubt of the fact that she had loved her husband dearly.

But fear of her reaction must no longer stop the truth from being spoken, he thought with a sinking of the heart. He was going to have to tell her. It was very possible, even probable, that he would lose her as a result, and the thought of losing her—again—was frankly terrifying. But it was a risk that must be taken. He owed her the truth. Besides, he was sick of pretending.

Always pretending.

They talked about sheep for a while and about horses and about crops, all in the hearing of other people. And then they strolled out across a lawn and in among the trees, where they could safely discuss other matters. It was almost dark among the trees. The clouds above were heavy with the promise of rain.

"Any further developments?" Sir Hector asked.

"Yes, sir." Matthew Harley's tone had changed from businesslike to excited and conspiratorial. "I spent a long time scouting around after returning from Pantnewydd yesterday. I found the bundle—and inside it a white gown, a white wool hood and mask, and a blond wig. The bundle was in an old gamekeeper's hut on the northern boundary, one that is no longer used. I was on the brink of having him arrested after all, but I waited for your visit and your instructions."

"Good man," Sir Hector said, pausing to shake the steward by the hand. "But it still cannot be done. Anyone could have hidden the things there, Harley. Even their discovery in Tegfan park and your eyewitness account may not be sufficient to convict Wyvern. And we certainly do not want him to slip through our fingers when we are so close. No, we need a little more patience and a little more planning. And there is still the difficulty that he is fast becoming something of a folk hero."

"You have a plan, sir?" Harley asked respectfully.

Sir Hector looked carefully all about him, but there were no gamekeepers in sight. They were safely alone among the trees.

"This is it," he said. "Tomorrow night the Cilcoed tollgate, the one kept by Mrs. Dilys Phillips, is going to be destroyed—by a Rebecca and a group of followers of my choosing. They will carry guns and they will be brutal and unruly. Mrs. Phillips will be roughed up and beaten— perhaps worse. She is old and frail, I have heard, and may not survive the shock and the manhandling. All the better. And the whole thing will be witnessed by Mr. Thomas Campbell Foster of *The Times*. He will be invited by Rebecca."

Harley frowned. Guns in the hands of a mob sounded dangerous. And the beating and perhaps killing of an innocent and defenseless old woman disturbed his conscience. But he was an angry and bitter young man, and he wanted to see other people suffer as he was suffering, most notably the Earl of Wyvern and Ceris Williams and the blacksmith. And this plan just might do it. Besides, he was not being asked to be personally involved.

"Foster will be convinced if the leader is dressed right," he said. "But what about the people, sir? Will they believe that their precious Rebecca would go out without the bulk of them and would behave with uncharacteristic violence?"

"They will have no choice," Sir Hector said. "Rebecca and perhaps Charlotte will be caught the same night. Rebecca will be unmasked and will turn out to be the Earl of Wyvern. And the people will realize that they have been duped, that their Rebecca has been leading them by the nose only to betray them and discredit them before the English reading public and the government, which is about to send a commission here. He will not have a friend left in the world, Harley. Not a single one—for as long as he has left in this world. I shall press for the death penalty. If Mrs. Phillips should happen to die, I will not even have to press hard, will I?"

"How are they to be caught?" Harley asked.

"It will be tricky," Sir Hector admitted. "Rebecca must receive a message from Foster, and I am not sure that Foster knows how to contact Rebecca. Perhaps it can come through the blacksmith. You are sure of the blacksmith?"

"Absolutely sure," Harley said.

"Foster will send the message that he wishes to meet the two of them in some secluded spot in the hills," Sir Hector said, "in order to obtain a little more information for his articles. They will, of course, go in disguise since they will not wish Foster to know their identities. Constables will be waiting to grab them. We will set the meeting for half past ten, a half hour before the gate goes down."

"It sounds perfect," Harley said. He laughed. "Almost too perfect."

"It had better work," Sir Hector said grimly. "If it does not, Harley, they will know we are on their tail. I want you to watch tomorrow night. Watch Wyvern leave. If for any reason he does not do so, send a messenger in all haste and I will postpone the attack on the gate. But I do not anticipate any problem."

"No, sir," Harley said. "It all sounds masterly. If only you can get the message to Rebecca."

"Leave that to me," Sir Hector said. "It will be done, Harley. Now, we had better return. We do not want to arouse suspicion by spending longer than usual in company together."

They turned back in the direction of the house and the stables.

* * *

Idris Parry stayed where he was for a full minute, his back flattened against the broad trunk of a tree. But it seemed they really had gone. Gone where, though? To the stables, probably, to fetch Sir Hector Webb's horse. Or perhaps up to the house. Either way, it was not safe to go dashing up to the front door. Not that he would get anything for his pains by doing that except a clipped ear and a kicked backside.

Idris sped off through the trees in order to make a wide detour around to the back of the house and the kitchen entrance. He would ask for Glenys Owen, he decided. He would say he had an urgent message for her from her dada or one of her brothers.

That part was easy enough. The boy who answered his knock on the door reluctantly agreed to fetch Glenys and meanwhile shut the door again. Glenys appeared, wide-eyed and fearful that all her family had dropped dead in a heap. But she was indignant and discouraging when she knew Idris's true errand. How could she take him to the earl? she asked him rhetorically. She never went out of the kitchen herself and never set eyes on him.

But she did—much against her better judgment, she explained—point out to Idris the window of the library, where she had heard the earl spent much of his time. At least, she *thought* it was the library. Actually, she admitted, she was almost as ignorant of the layout of the house as Idris himself.

Idris peeped through the window and was relieved to see the Earl of Wyvern seated behind a large desk, his chin resting on his steepled fingers, apparently staring into space. There was no one else in the room as far as Idris could see. He tapped on the window and made urgent beckoning signals when the earl looked up, startled.

"Do step inside, Idris, won't you?" his lordship asked, all formal politeness after he had slid open the sash window and Idris was stepping over the sill. He sounded faintly amused, Idris thought.

"Rebecca is in trouble for sure tomorrow night," Idris said, gazing about him in awe. Had all the books in the world been gathered in this one room? The carpet under his feet was softer than his bed, he would swear. "And so are you. Sir."

"You like what you see?" the earl asked, his voice definitely amused now. He had switched to speaking Welsh, Idris noticed. "If my sources are correct, Rebecca is not going to be anywhere around tomorrow night, lad. Perhaps never again. And as for me, I can look after myself. Is your dada enjoying his new job?"

"They know who Rebecca is," Idris said, gawking at the inkstand and letter opener on the desk and wondering if they were really silver or just polished tin. "And they are going to trap him and make him look bad and catch him tomorrow night. They know where he hides his stuff too." He looked at the earl and knew that he finally had the man's full attention. Humor was all right in its place, Idris thought, but people ought not to laugh merely because one was nine years old and not a grown man.

"They?" his lordship asked, lifting his eyebrows in a gesture that made him look wonderfully haughty—Idris had practiced imitating the expression but could succeed only in looking surprised.

"Sir Hector Webb," Idris said, "and Mr. Harley."

"Indeed?" The earl clasped his hands behind his back, another gesture that Idris had tried to imitate until his mother had asked what he was hiding and his father had threatened to come and look if he did not answer smartly. "Suppose you tell me everything you came here to tell me, Idris. *If* you feel it right to give the owner of Tegfan information about the enemy, Rebecca, that is."

Idris giggled. But he was feeling too full of importance to give in to childish hilarity. He told his lordship everything he had heard and wished as he spoke that his hair would curl like the earl's and that his eyes were blue.

The earl was looking at him intently by the time he finished speaking. "I believe, Idris," he said at last, "I am going to have to give you employment at Tegfan. You might as well have a legitimate reason for being here since you are always here anyway."

At first Idris was indignant. His dreams would all come true if the earl was serious. But this was not the time to talk about such matters. Idris wanted to know what he could do to help thwart the dastardly plans of the true enemy. He wanted to be taken seriously. He wanted to sit down with his lordship so that they could plan out a scheme together.

"It could well be," his lordship continued, setting a hand on the boy's shoulder and squeezing it, "that you have done more for the cause of Rebecca this morning, Idris, than anyone else has done before you. Well done, lad."

Idris felt that his chest might burst. He would gladly at that moment have died for his hero. "What can I do to help?" he asked.

The earl looked gravely at him. "You have done enough, lad," he said. "You must go directly home and not let Mr. Harley suspect that you overheard any part of that conversation."

"But there are things to be done, sir," Idris said impatiently. "You will not be able to ignore the invitation to meet the man from the newspaper in London. Rebecca will have to go out, because if she doesn't, Mrs. Phillips might be hurt anyway."

"We will leave that matter in the hands of Rebecca," the earl said. "I want you to go home now, Idris. With my heartfelt thanks."

They were not quite enough. "Rebecca will collect her bundle from the usual place tomorrow night," Idris said, "and they will be lying in wait. She will not even get one foot out of the park. And then she will be dragged over to the Cilcoed gate so that it will seem to be her who destroyed it and hurt Mrs. Phillips."

"I believe Rebecca will realize that and plan accordingly," the earl said. "I would send for cakes and lemonade, Idris, but I do not want anyone to know you have been here. The day after tomorrow I will bring a barrel of cakes up to your house."

Duw, but he hated being treated like a child who could be fobbed off with the prospect of good things for his stomach. "I will take the bundle with me now, sir," Idris said. "I will keep it safe at the house and Rebecca can get it from there tomorrow."

His lordship drew a deep breath and expelled it from puffed cheeks. "Idris," he said, "do you not realize that there may even now be a watch on the place where the bundle is hidden?"

"If I couldn't spot watchers a mile off," Idris said scornfully, "I would be dead by now, sir, or in one of those big ships on my way to the other side of the world."

"And so you would," his lordship had the grace to admit. "Do you know the old ruined hovel almost a mile from your own house, Idris? The one built against a rock face?"

"Where you used to live?" Idris said.

The earl smiled at him. His eyes crinkled in the corners. Idris was going to practice that expression too. "That is the one," his lordship said. "Will you take the bundle there, Idris? And leave it there and not go anywhere near it for the rest of today and tomorrow? I am going to regret this. What am I doing deliberately involving a boy in dangerous matters?"

But Idris was not going to lose his chance now. "Remember when you were a boy, sir," he said, "and how much you would have wanted to do something to help. Something really important."

"Heaven help us," the earl said, "you are right. In those days I would have been willing to give a right arm for something as exciting as this."

"I'll be on my way," Idris said, crossing the room back to the window. "I'll not fail you, sir. If there is anything else I can do . . ."

And then be damned if the earl did not stoop down and grab him as he had done once before on the road below Tŷ-Gwyn and hug him hard enough to get all the breath whooshing out of him.

"Be careful," he said. "I must be mad to allow this. If by

any chance you are caught, Idris, you must say you found the bundle and thought your mother would be pleased to have it. If that explanation does not work, you will be brought here to me and I will vouch for you. Go now."

Idris went. One thing about the earl he was never going to imitate. He was never going to hug children just as if they were helpless infants. When he was grown up, he was going to treat children as if they were adults. But it was the only flaw he could detect in his hero. And even heroes, he supposed, could not realistically be expected to be quite perfect.

Aled was alone in his forge, his apprentice having already been sent home for his dinner.

"Good day, my lord," he said with a curt nod when Geraint walked in. "What may I do for you?"

"We have an audience?" Geraint asked, raising his eyebrows.

"Not to my knowledge," Aled said.

"But there may well be certain people set to keeping an eye on me and all with whom I associate," Geraint said. "I'll be brief, Aled, and then I'll be on my way."

"Trouble?" Aled frowned.

"One might say so." Geraint gave a brief summary of the story Idris had told him an hour before. "Rebecca and Charlotte and perhaps some of the children from hereabouts are going to have to go early to the Cilcoed gate, Aled, to destroy it and to rescue Mrs. Phillips. Hector will doubtless burst a blood vessel when he arrives later."

"It will be dangerous, Ger," Aled said.

Geraint grinned. "When was this game not dangerous?" he asked.

"And you are loving every moment." Aled's frown deepened.

"Regrettably," Geraint said, "this is going to have to be our swan song, Aled. Rebecca and Charlotte are going to have to disappear without trace after tomorrow night. We will have to hope that we have accomplished what we set out to do, which was to attract enough attention that something will be done to change the system here and make it more fair to the ordinary man and woman—and child."

"Our swan song," Aled said, shaking his head. "And then the swan dies. But you are right. Tomorrow night's scheme has to be thwarted. Foster is to be there, then, to observe the chagrin of the second Rebecca?"

"I thought he might enjoy observing both," Geraint said. "Rebecca will send to invite him to come a few hours earlier than originally planned. All will be over tomorrow night, Aled. I cannot say I am sorry. You will pass the word around here as usual? But not quite as usual. I think this is too dangerous for women. You will neglect to let Marged know?"

Aled nodded and Geraint turned to leave, anxious not to stay too long and perhaps arouse the suspicion of anyone who was set to keep watch in the village. Though he did not believe there were any spies at the moment. He would have sensed their presence.

There was someone else walking along the street, though. Marged had just stepped out of Miss Jenkins's shop and they met outside the chapel. As luck would have it, the heavy clouds that had threatened all morning had just decided to drop their load in a miserable drizzle. And he had an umbrella—a large black affair—while she did not.

"Marged?" He acknowledged her with a nod as he put the umbrella up. "You are going home?"

"Yes," she said, that tight, angry expression she reserved exclusively for him descending on her face. "*Alone*, thank you."

He turned, nevertheless, and offered his arm and raised the umbrella over her head. "I could not allow it," he said. "Take my arm and I shall escort you."

But he knew that today was not the day to tell her the truth, after all. The truth must wait another two days.

Chapter
27

Marged clamped her teeth together. It was almost impossible to get the man to take no for an answer. She always felt helpless before the power of his will—and she hated to feel helpless.

There was nothing formidable about a two-mile walk home even though most of the journey was uphill. And there was nothing so very uncomfortable about walking through rain. Rain was the norm in Wales. They had had an unusually dry spring so far. And it was not even a downpour, just a steady drizzle.

And yet here she was being escorted home beneath a large black umbrella. Her arm was linked through his and she was compelled to walk close to his side. The umbrella was almost like a tent, creating an illusion of intimacy. She could smell his cologne. As usual, she was very aware of him physically, and as usual she resented the fact.

This morning, before walking to the village, she had finally admitted to herself that there was a strong possibility she was pregnant. After five years of barrenness as Eurwyn's wife it was hard to believe, but it must be so. And she had also made the decision that if nothing happened within one week from today, she was going to tell Rebecca. Not that she would try to force him to marry her—though her mind shied away in panic from the alternative. But he had a right to know, to plan their child's future with her if he wished.

She had walked to the village on a very slim pretext and despite the fact that her mother-in-law had warned her of the impending rain. She had needed to be alone, to have time to adjust her mind to what seemed to be inevitable. She had not even called on her father, though she felt guilty about the omission.

And now this. She was going to have to walk all the way home at Geraint's side—very much at his side—beneath his umbrella. And she was going to have to feel the pull of her unwilling attraction to him while in all probability she was with child by another man—the man she loved.

"There is no need to walk all the way home with me," she said hopefully when they were at the end of the village street. "You will get wet."

"Marged," he said. "Soon you and I are going to have to have a serious talk."

He was not going to let it drop, then, what she had told him the morning Ceris had been arrested. He was going to exact a price. "What about?" she asked him. "We have nothing to say to each other."

"I believe we do," he said. "We were fond of each other as children, Marged. More than fond. We fell in love when we were older. I believe it happened to both of us. Perhaps it would have deepened into something else if you had not been so very innocent and I had not been correspondingly gauche. And now? There is still something between us. I know I am not the only one to feel it. One can sense such things."

She closed her eyes tightly for a moment, wishing she could shut out this whole absurd, impossible situation. How dare he! *But he is right,* an unwelcome voice said inside her head. She wished that he was not approximately the same height and build as Rebecca. Perhaps that was what so confused her. With her eyes closed she might almost imagine . . .

She opened her eyes resolutely. They had reached the turnoff from the river path to the hill track.

"Listen carefully, *my lord,*" she said. "There is nothing between us. Perhaps you think you have some power over me because of what I told you at Tegfan a few mornings ago. But I will not allow you such power. If it is blackmail you think to attempt, then I shall go to Sir Hector Webb with my confession. And if you think I bluff, try me. I will not be your mistress. I believe that is what you were leading up to?"

"If you say so," he said. "*I* did not say so, Marged." Her foot skidded a little on wet grass and he clamped her arm more firmly to his side.

"Let me repeat what I told you on that occasion," she said. "I have a lover. I love him. I am probably going to marry him." Sometimes she wished her tongue would not run away with her, but she was not sorry she had said it. Let him know the truth. Let him know that there was no point at all in continuing to harass her.

"Ah," he said quietly. "Has he asked you, then, Marged?"

"No," she was forced to admit, though she was tempted for a moment to lie. "But he will. He loves me and he is an honorable man."

"And will you accept?" he asked.

"That is between him and me," she said.

He stopped walking and turned her toward him, his free arm coming about her waist. He held the umbrella over them both, tilted slightly her way. She could hear the rain drumming more heavily on its surface. She had nowhere to put her own hands except against his chest. Awareness suffocated her and—and the horrifying similarity.

"Rebecca," he said quietly. "His mission must be almost at an end, Marged. It seems that he has accomplished his goal and that it is now the government's move. Are you sure he will not abandon you when this is all over?"

How dare he! What did he know of Rebecca or the love they shared?

"He will not abandon me," she said. "He promised not to abandon me." *If she was with child.* He had promised that he would stand by her if that happened. He had told her she could always get a message to him through Aled. But even apart from that, she knew he would not abandon her. That promise had been made after the first time they lay together. Their love had deepened since then. He had told her that he loved her.

She seemed to have silenced him. He did not speak for a while but searched her eyes with his own. It was difficult not to look away. And it was difficult not to want to move closer.

"I wish," he said, "I had been a little wiser at the age of eighteen or that you had at sixteen. That was where we went wrong, Marged. Had I been wiser I would have courted you more slowly and far more chastely. I would have taken two or three years over it. We would have been married for several years now. We would have had little ones together."

She did not understand for a moment why she could no longer see him clearly or why there was a sharp ache in her throat or why she had to bite down hard on her lower lip. She did not understand the deep welling of grief she felt.

"Don't cry," he whispered. "It's not too late, love."

"But it is," she wailed. "It is too late."

And then she realized what she had said and the tone in which she had said it. *As if she regretted that it was too late.*

"It is not too late for us to marry," he said. "Or to have babies. Or to love. Marry me, Marged. Please?"

She hated herself. *Hated* herself. For she found herself wanting desperately to say yes. She found herself convinced that she loved him and that she wanted what he was offering—marriage with him, children with him.

She must be mad! Or she must be living in some horrible nightmare.

She could not marry Geraint. She was Rebecca's lover and she loved him. She was going to marry him if he asked.

And she could not have babies with Geraint. She was already having one with Rebecca.

"I think you must be insane," she said. "Do you seriously think I would marry Eurwyn's murderer?"

"That is a little unfair," he said. "Through ignorance and irresponsibility I was unavailable to help him when I might have done so. But I am not solely or even mainly to blame, Marged. Even he must bear part of the blame. He knew the law and he knew the risks he took. He knew the consequences of being caught."

"Ah, yes." The old familiar hatred and contempt were coming to her rescue. She embraced them eagerly. "Of course it was all his fault for being greedy enough to want the salmon for the people when the owner of Tegfan—the *single, absentee* owner—needed them all for himself."

"You did not listen to me, Marged," he said. "But no matter. If you are determined to see me as the blackhearted villain of your life, I suppose there is nothing I can say. Except that I love you and always have. Except that I will continue to want to marry you and will ask you again. Come, take my arm. We had better get you home out of the rain. It is getting heavier."

"Don't ask me again," she said as they resumed the uphill climb. "If you keep on doing so and I keep on saying no, I may put a dent in your insufferable arrogance. That would be dreadful."

"Yes." She looked up to find that his whole face was lit up with laughter. He looked so startlingly handsome and attractive that all her insides seemed to be performing somersaults and cartwheels. "I cannot think of a worse fate, Marged."

They walked the rest of the way in silence. He escorted her right to the door of Tŷ-Gwyn but would not come inside. She stepped into the passageway and closed the door before leaning back against it. He had asked her to marry him. The reality of it was only just beginning to hit her. Geraint Penderyn, Earl of Wyvern, had offered her marriage. She might have been a countess. She might have been Geraint's wife.

Ah, Geraint. The sharp pain was back.

Idris had watched the Earl of Wyvern go inside the old hovel quite early in the evening and Rebecca came out several minutes later. The boy was well hidden and he had not moved a muscle since he had seen the earl riding up the hill. But even so, as Rebecca mounted the earl's horse and turned its head to the slope on the opposite side from Tegfan, he spoke quietly and conversationally.

"You may go home now, Idris," he said. "Is it too much to ask that for once you stay there all night, where it is safe?"

He did not wait for an answer, but Idris grinned to himself. Yes, it was too much to ask. There was going to be too much to be observed tonight for him to waste the time sitting with his mam and his sisters or sleeping. He rose out of his hiding place and bounded down the hill in the direction of Tegfan.

It was amazing how inefficient and inept they were, he thought scornfully an hour later. It had obviously not entered any of their heads to check the gamekeeper's hut to see that the bundle was still inside. Or to think that perhaps the earl would leave earlier than he needed for the supposed meeting with the man from London. Idris had been in hiding for some time before three constables took up their positions, ready to pounce on Rebecca when he emerged from the hut.

It was almost enough to make a person laugh, Idris thought. They all thought themselves so well hidden, and yet a herd of oxen could hardly have made more noise. Even without Idris's warning the earl would have been perfectly safe. He would have detected their presence a mile off.

And then finally, along came Mr. Harley in a fine state of excitement, not even trying to keep quiet.

"He has gone already," he announced when he was close to the hut, and all the constables came shuffling out of hiding. "That fool of a servant failed to inform me that he left early. Perhaps he planned another gate smashing before his appointment with Foster. But no matter. Vanity will take him there eventually—how could he resist having his name in the London papers? And there are four constables awaiting him and his right-hand man when they get there. But we are going to have to be doubly sure of bagging him now that the simple way of doing it has slipped through our fingers."

Idris concentrated on not moving an eyelash.

"I have been sent a dozen more constables," Harley said. "They are at the house now. Come back there with me and I will give you all your orders. I am going to station you all at various points around the park and a few of you about the smithy in Glynderi. If they escape capture elsewhere, they will be caught before they can reach home. This is the last night for Rebecca and her daughters, you may rest assured."

The constables moved off behind the steward as he strode back downhill in the direction of the house. Some of them murmured complaints, though Idris did not listen to their exact words. His heart was beating up into his throat and almost deafening his ears. The earl was for it. And Mr. Rhoslyn. Even if they left their disguises up on the hill, somehow Mr. Harley and Sir Hector and the constables would not be thwarted this time. Somehow they would trump up damning evidence.

The trouble was, Idris thought, he could not decide what to do. There was no one to run to. The earl was gone and so was Mr. Rhoslyn. So were his dada and most of the other men. Probably Mrs. Evans too. Suddenly and unwillingly Idris realized how helpless he was as a child. He could run to the Cilcoed gate, he supposed, as he had done to that other gate, to warn everyone. But what were they to do if they could not return home? There was no one to turn to. Only women—and Idris never expected too much of women. And Mr. Williams, but he was so very far away and in the opposite direction from the Cilcoed gate.

There was only one person left that he could think of.

And he disapproved of the rioting. And what could he do anyway? But at least he was adult and male and close by.

Idris wormed out of his hiding place and took to his heels as if he was being pursued by fleet-footed hounds.

The Reverend Meirion Llwyd was sitting at his desk in the small box of a room at the manse that passed for his study, writing his Sunday sermon. He was frowning in concentration over the exact wording, though the whole task was unnecessary, he knew. Once he started speaking from the pulpit and got launched into his text, the emotion of the moment always took him and provided him with both the ideas he was to expound upon and the words with which to do so.

His frown deepened when someone started hammering at his front door—with the sides of both fists, by the sound of it. One of these weeks he was going to be able to get his whole sermon prepared without interruption. He sighed and got to his feet, pushing his chair clear of the desk with the backs of his knees.

"Idris Parry," he said when he had opened the door. The boy all but fell inside. "And what are you doing so far from home at this time of night?" It struck him that the child might have been poaching and was being pursued. And the Reverend Llwyd would hide him or provide him with an alibi, though he would be supplying the devil with one more coal for his fire by doing so.

The boy's eyes were wild. "They have lured Rebecca and all the others out," he said, gasping between words. "And they have set a trap for them when they return. They will never get home."

The Reverend Llwyd had tried not even to think about Rebecca or the fact that almost every man from his congregation—and Marged, he suspected—followed the man, whoever he was. The Reverend Llwyd believed that vengeance was the Lord's prerogative. But they were his people, the sheep of his flock—and one of them was his daughter, his own flesh and blood.

"Tell me quickly, boy," he said. "Everything you know."

Idris told—everything, even down to the identity of Rebecca. It seemed that the Earl of Wyvern was in grave danger even though he knew about the one trap that had been set for him and would probably get close to home safely. And Aled Rhoslyn was in equal danger. And perhaps all the men who lived in the village. Lurking constables would see them return home and would draw their own conclusions—especially if the men had blackened faces.

The Reverend Llwyd thought for a moment while Idris Parry hopped from foot to foot. But no longer than a moment—he would have wished his sermons came so easily if he had spared a thought to the matter.

"We must have a little while before the constables arrive in the village," he said. "Quick, Idris. But listen carefully first. Go and find Gwilym Dirion and any other lad you can think of. Take them with you and fan them out so that between you you don't miss one single man returning to Glynderi. Divert them. Send them up into the hills and around to Ninian Williams's farm. That is where they are to come, all of them. Get them to clean up on the way."

"Yes, sir." Idris was at the door already.

"We are going to have a party," the Reverend Llwyd announced. "I am going to hurry around to all the women and send them up with all the food they can gather together. Ninian Williams and his good wife are giving a party to celebrate the engagement of Ceris to Aled Rhoslyn. Now, on your way, is it?"

Idris exited the house so fast that the door was left swinging on its hinges.

The Reverend Llwyd grabbed his hat and his cloak and followed the boy outside, though he did take the time to close his door behind him. The shadows of little boys slunk past him as he hurried along the street, knocking on doors, issuing hurried commands. Most of the women, eyes wide with anxiety for men out with Rebecca, agreed to call at various farms on their way out to Ninian Williams's so that there could be a proper community celebration when the men came home.

Before setting off for the party himself, the Reverend Llwyd returned home for his Bible. He set off on his way with it tucked under his arm. He paused twice in his walk along the village street to bid two strangers a good evening and to wish them God's blessing.

Word had somehow been kept from Marged. The crowd was smaller than usual since only the men from the vicinity of Tegfan had been called out. It was easy to see that Marged was not of their number. It was a relief. Geraint did not know quite what danger they were facing. Perhaps they were being foolhardy. But no, they were not that. There was Mrs. Phillips to rescue. And a human life was worth any risk.

His spies could see no one lurking in the vicinity of the Cilcoed gate except Thomas Campbell Foster, who had been invited to come early and to stay late. But it was a great deal earlier than usual—not even quite dark. One felt strangely exposed to view when not enclosed by total darkness.

He led the way down onto the road as usual and proceeded along the road to the gate as usual, riding upright at the head of his men, in full view of whoever might be inside the tollhouse. His spies had said only Mrs. Phillips was there. But his flesh crawled as he neared the gate.

And then a little whirlwind came rushing out through the door brandishing a large club and swearing eloquently enough to put a navvy to the blush—in Welsh.

"Get away from here," she said when she ran out of swear words. "Cowards and bullies. The Earl of Wyvern will give you what for, he will. And I will smash the knees of every one of you. Come and get it if you dare."

Geraint smiled behind his mask despite himself. He rode as close as he dared, bent from the saddle, and spoke with quiet courtesy. "We wish you no harm, Mrs. Phillips," he said. "We have come to rescue you. There are those coming after us who plan to hurt you simply because Wyvern promised you his protection and they wish to teach him a lesson."

"Oi." Mrs. Phillips peered suspiciously up at him. "I know you. I know that voice. What are you doing here dressed like that for, then, my——"

He bent lower toward her. "Let it be our secret, my dear," he said for her ears only. "I promised that you would be safe from harm, did I not? Let me keep my promise, then. You will ride up with me and I shall take you to a place of safety."

"This is my gate," she said. "It is my job to defend it. I have to charge you all—all except you—for passing through it. *Duw,* you look like a corpse with that mask on."

"I believe you have served the road trust well, Mrs. Phillips," he said, trying not to think of the urgency of the moment. "I am pleased with the service you have given. I am going to see to it that you retire honorably and comfortably on a pension from Tegfan in a cottage somewhere on the estate. Will you come with me? I am afraid my men are going to destroy the gate and the house—after your possessions have been removed. This will be a lesson to those who will be coming in an hour or so's time."

"The real Rebecca?" she said. "Shouldn't we stay to catch them?"

"They have guns; we do not," he said. "Sometimes discretion is the better part of valor, my dear. Charlotte, my daughter," he called over his shoulder, "ask one of the men on foot to oblige me by lifting Mrs. Phillips before my saddle, if you please. And then have a few more remove her possessions from the house."

Mrs. Phillips looked at him severely when she was before him on his horse's back, in the place Marged usually occupied. "I think *you* are the real Rebecca after all," she said. "They all say that you are courteous to the gatekeepers and never do them harm or carry guns. And they say you pay them from the coffers of Rebecca."

"Sometimes," he said, "extreme measures are needed in

extreme times, Mrs. Phillips." He raised the arm that was
not about her waist to hold her steady and gave the order for
the destruction of the gate. But out of deference to the
gatekeeper, he did not stay directly in front of it as he
usually did, but began to ride up the hill.

"You can stop," she told him when they were only
partway up the slope. "It is not a place I exactly love, you
know. But when Mr. Phillips died, it was here or the
workhouse. We never did have any children to look after us
in our old age. But now I will have a cottage of my own and
a pension? There is kind you are, my lord. I will say so even
though it is very naughty of you to dress up like this and put
the fear of God into innocent people."

Although there were fewer men than usual, both the gate
and the house were gone within a few minutes. There was
still no sign of the impostor Rebecca and the ruffian gang
hired by Hector. Geraint raised his arm again and all his men
turned to him for further instructions.

"The deed is well done, my children," Rebecca told them.
"Go home now quickly."

He watched them scramble up the hill and make off
together in the direction of Glynderi—perhaps for the last
time as followers of Rebecca. Certainly it was the last time
for him. He would never get away with this again. He must
take Mrs. Phillips to a place of safety and then return to
Tegfan with all speed—and brazen out all accusations that
might come his way either later tonight or tomorrow.

There was nothing they could prove. And his job was
completed. Aled came up beside them and together they
rode after the walking men.

He missed Marged dreadfully, Geraint thought. He wondered what she would say tomorrow when he called at
Tŷ-Gwyn to tell her the full truth. He had tried to pave the
way yesterday by getting her to admit her attraction to him
in his own person. And it had almost succeeded. But
perhaps he had only made matters worse.

And what the devil had she meant by saying that Rebecca
had promised not to abandon her? He had made her that

promise the first night he made love to her, when he was
promising to stand by her if she was with child. Was she?
He had tortured himself with the question for longer than
twenty-four hours.

Was Marged pregnant?

And then infant shouts were audible above the sounds of
the horses' hooves and labored breathing. Idris! The lad
needed to be chained to his mother's apron. And he had
other lads with him! They were darting among the men,
yelling and gesticulating. Idris himself made straight for the
horses.

"They have the park surrounded," he cried, "and the
smithy too. Everyone is to go around behind the hill and up
over it to Mr. Williams's farm."

Damn! He might have guessed they would have the final
trap set. And obviously they knew about Aled too.

"Why there, lad?" he asked, leaning down while holding
Mrs. Phillips steady.

"There is to be an engagement party for Mr. Rhoslyn and
Ceris Williams," Idris said. "The Reverend Llwyd has
arranged it all. You are to get there as fast as possible."

"Well, I'll be damned," Geraint said.

"It is a good thing I proposed to Ceris first," Aled said
dryly. "Come on, lad, ride with me." He reached down a
hand.

All the men were changing direction and increasing their
pace.

Chapter
28

Marged had relinquished the spinning wheel to her mother-in-law and was playing her harp and singing at the request of Eurwyn's grandmother. She was feeling a certain melancholy enjoyment of the quiet evening. Change was imminent. She was not quite sure what was going to happen, but something was going to. If Rebecca married her—*when* Rebecca married her, would he be willing to take on two other women too? Two women who were related to her only through her first husband? Would he be able to afford to take them on even if he was willing? Perhaps Waldo Parry would continue to work for them so that they could live independently.

"There is busy the lane is tonight," her mother-in-law said, pausing in her spinning as Marged came to the end of a song. She sat in a listening attitude.

And then Marged heard it too—the sound of footsteps and voices. She crossed to the small window and peered out into the darkness. Actually it was not so dark. The moon and stars were beaming down from a clear sky. There were definitely men going past. And then she both heard and saw horses—two of them. Her face jerked closer to the glass. One of the riders was Rebecca. The other—Aled—was bending to open the gate, and the two of them were riding into the farmyard.

"What is happening, Marged, *fach*?" her grandmother asked from the inglenook beside the fire.

"Visitors," she said, and darted for the passage and the outer door.

"Marged!" Rebecca was calling for her even before she had the door open. There was a note of urgency in his voice.

Had they been out without her? she wondered. Or were they on their way and had come for her? But there was someone on the horse with Rebecca, she saw as she hurried across the farmyard toward him.

"This is Mrs. Phillips from the Cilcoed tollgate on the other side of the village," he said. "They are after us, Marged. We have to get to Ninian Williams's farm. May Mrs. Phillips take shelter here for the night? I'll make other arrangements for her tomorrow."

"Of course." Marged looked in some bewilderment at the little old lady who had used to live in Glynderi until the death of her husband. Rebecca was swinging down from the saddle and lifting Mrs. Phillips down even as she spoke. "Ninian Williams's?"

"He is giving an engagement party for Ceris and me," Aled said with a grin. He was scrubbing at the blacking on his face with the sleeve of his robe. "Your father has arranged it."

"Oh, *Duw*, it feels good to have my feet on firm earth again," Mrs. Phillips said. "I do remember your Eurwyn's gran well, Marged Evans."

Rebecca was escorting her to the door. Marged went after them to open it. She was feeling rather as if she had stepped into some bizarre and senseless dream. "They are after you?" she said.

"Take Mrs. Phillips in, if you please, Marged," Rebecca said. "Your in-laws would not appreciate the sight of me. I must be going."

But her mother-in-law had come to the door, drawn by curiosity. Her mouth gaped when she saw Rebecca.

"You are not to worry, Mrs. Evans, *fach*," Mrs. Phillips said. "It is only Rebecca. And a more courteous gentleman I could not hope to meet this side of the grave. He has rescued me from ruffians who would have harmed me—if they could have got past my big stick." She cackled with amusement.

Marged caught at Rebecca's sleeve. "You are going?" she said. "To Ninian Williams's?"

"There is not a moment to lose," he said. "They may be at our heels even now."

"I am going with you," she said. "Mam, look after Mrs. Phillips, will you? Give her my bed. I will sleep on the settle when I get back." She stepped inside the door, grabbed her cloak from a hook inside, and strode over to the horse, which Rebecca had already mounted.

He reached down a hand and helped her up. "I have the feeling this is going to be the denouement," he said. "I suppose it is fitting you be there, Marged."

They followed Aled through the gate and turned downward toward the Williams farm. He had sounded reluctant, Marged thought, turning her head to look into his masked face. They had been out tonight—to Mrs. Phillips's gate— and had not let her know. Had that been Aled's oversight or had it been done on Rebecca's instructions? *I suppose it is fitting you be there.* They were grudging words. Did he not really want her there?

"Don't look at me like that," he said. "There was a trap set for us tonight, Marged, and I knew about part of it. I could not stay at home, though. I had heard that they were to set up their own Rebecca to harm Mrs. Phillips and discredit me with my own people. There was more danger than usual tonight and still is. I instructed Aled that you were not to be told."

"Because I am a woman," she said.

"Yes, because you are a woman," he said, his voice

exasperated. "Not because I did not want you with me, Marged."

But there was no time for more conversation. They turned into the laneway leading to Ninian Williams's farm and were there a minute later. The door was wide-open and there was light and noise coming from inside. There were a few men in the yard, scrubbing their faces at the pump, and two women bearing towels.

"Down you get, men." Ninian himself was greeting them in the yard. "I will have your horses put with ours and no one will know the difference. Into the house with you. We have an engagement to celebrate and now we will have both halves of the couple in attendance. Hello, Marged. I am glad you could come at such short notice."

They were inside the house a few moments later, blinking in the lamplight. Rebecca had a hand against the small of her back. The room was full of men and women and even a few children. The kitchen table was laden with food, as though the party had been planned a week ago. And then silence fell.

"Rebecca," Mrs. Williams said, her hands clasped to her bosom. She sounded frightened.

"Aled, you are safe." Ceris flew toward him, her hands outstretched as he peeled off his dark wig. "Take off the gown quickly and we will hide it with the wig. Wash your face."

Marged continued on her way across the room to hug her father, who was standing with his back to the fire. "Thank you, Dada," she said into his ear. She was just beginning to understand what was happening. The trap must have been set in the village and this had been her father's idea to give all the men an excuse to be away from home. But Rebecca need not have shared the danger. He might have ridden safely home.

The Reverend Llwyd patted her waist. "Get rid of that disguise quick," he said, looking across the room at Rebecca. "There is no hiding the truth from everyone any longer. Get it off and we will have Ceris push it under the manure pile with Aled's."

Marged caught her breath in a gasp and whirled about to gaze across the room. Of course! But she did not want it this way. She had wanted it to happen when they were alone together. She did not want it to happen now. She was not ready for it. She was not sure she wanted it to happen at all. She would be staring at the face of a stranger—her lover.

The wig came off first. Mrs. Williams took it from his hand. The mask, as Marged had suspected, was a cap that fitted right over his head and face. It was peeled away next and handed to Mrs. Williams.

The silence became almost a tangible thing.

"Duw," someone said softly.

"We have been betrayed. We are done for after all." It was Dewi Owen's voice spoken into the silence though no one responded to it.

"Off with the gown!" the Reverend Llwyd said. "Ceris, take those things out with Aled's now. The Lord be praised that everyone is safe. And everyone *is* safe, Dewi Owen. His lordship, the Earl of Wyvern, has been your Rebecca from the start."

Geraint Penderyn dragged the white gown of Rebecca off over his head and Ceris whisked it away with the rest of his disguise and Aled's.

Then he looked across the room and met Marged's eyes.

There was no shock in her eyes, no accusation, no anger, no bewilderment. Nothing. She stared at him blankly.

And then someone came darting through the door and broke the tension like a knife slicing through butter.

"They are coming," Idris Parry called in his piping child's voice. "A whole crowd of them on their way up the hill. All of them on horseback."

"Thank you, Idris." The Reverend Meirion Llwyd, from his position of command before the fire, raised both arms, his Bible clutched in one hand. "Let us show these men, my people, how the Welsh celebrate an engagement, the solemn promise of a man and a woman to enter into matrimony together in the sight of the Lord. Not with noisy frivolity but with the singing of the praises of our Lord."

Incredibly, Geraint saw, everyone gave the minister his or her full attention and all put on their Sunday faces. And yet there was no sense of false piety. Ceris had come back from the manure pile and had joined Aled in the middle of the room. They smiled at each other with warm love and joined hands.

"Let us give them Sanctus in full harmony," the Reverend Llwyd said. "And think about the words we are singing, if you please. You will start us, Marged."

Marged hummed a note and without further ado the house was filled with the glorious music in four-part harmony. *"Glan geriwbiaid a seraffiaid,"* they sang. Geraint joined his tenor voice to the next line. *"Fyrdd o gylch yr orsedd fry."*

The room was crowded. Nevertheless there was a space all around him, as if he had some sort of contagious disease that no one wanted to come in contact with. He was going to look suspiciously unlike a partygoer. But someone must have had the same thought—two people actually. Idris moved to his side and gazed worshipfully up at him. Geraint smiled and set a hand lightly on the boy's head. And then Marged was at his other side, her shoulder almost brushing his arm. He turned his head to look at her, but she was singing and resolutely watching her father, who was rather ostentatiously conducting. If she felt his eyes on her, she did not show it.

The door, which Idris had closed behind him, crashed inward.

Sir Hector Webb, Matthew Harley, and a dozen special constables filled the doorway and the space beyond it until the third and final verse of the hymn came to its glorious conclusion.

"Sanctaidd, sanctaidd, sanctaidd Ior!" everyone sang, clinging to the words and the melody with all the passion of

a deep faith and an equally deep love of music. *Holy, holy, holy Lord.*

Sir Hector and Harley looked about the room with sharp eyes. Harley's lingered on Ceris and Aled and lowered to their joined hands.

The Reverend Llwyd kept his arms raised to hold the people silent and looked politely at the new arrivals. "Good evening," he said in heavily accented English. "Ninian, here are more guests for your party."

"What is going on here?" Sir Hector asked, his frown ferocious.

"We are celebrating as a community the engagement and impending marriage of two members of my congregation," the minister said. "Ceris Williams and Aled Rhoslyn."

Harley's head snapped back, rather as if he had been punched on the chin. He drew back among the constables.

"Aled Rhoslyn!" Sir Hector exclaimed. "Aled Rhoslyn was out with Rebecca tonight, smashing tollgates. He is Rebecca's chief daughter, the one called Charlotte."

"I am flattered," Aled said. "Second only to Rebecca? It sounds like a great honor, sir."

"And you." Sir Hector's arm came up and he pointed accusingly at Geraint. "Rebecca! Traitor! I'll see you hanged, Wyvern. There will be nothing as soft as transportation for you."

"Hector." Geraint clasped his hands behind him and strolled toward the door. "You are making an ass of yourself. Do I understand that Rebecca has been out again tonight and has slipped through the fingers of these constables—again? And that somehow you think Aled and I were involved? Ceris would not have been amused if her betrothed had decided to go gallivanting with a white ghost instead of attending their engagement party. And I had the honor of being invited—Aled and I have been friends since boyhood, you know. You had better go and search elsewhere—unless Ninian would care to invite you to join the party?" He turned his head and raised his eyebrows.

"You would be very welcome, sir," Ninian Williams said.

"And all your men too. There is plenty of food for everyone."

"Harley," Sir Hector called over his shoulder, "take the men and search every inch of this farm. And what did you do with Mrs. Phillips, Wyvern? Kill her and hide her body with all the rest of your things?"

"Mrs. Phillips?" Marged sounded startled. "From the Cilcoed tollgate down the road, do you mean? She is spending the evening and night with my gran at Tŷ-Gwyn. She is lonely out there at the gate and sometimes slips away for a night. She says that no one ever wants to pass through at night anyway. Is she in trouble?"

"No," Geraint said. "She is elderly. I will have a word with the lessee of the trust on her behalf." He turned back to Sir Hector suddenly. "It was not her gate that went down tonight, was it?"

"You know it was, Wyvern," Sir Hector said between his teeth. His face was deeply flushed. He was realizing, perhaps, that he had come too late, that he had lost the game, and that there would be no other chance.

"Well, then," Geraint said, "it is a blessing that she chose this night of all nights to absent herself from her post."

Sir Hector stood glaring about him, his eyes taking in the women gathered there with the men, the feast spread out on the table, the Bible tucked beneath the minister's arm, the newly betrothed couple, flushed and hand in hand in the middle of the room.

A cough drew his attention behind him. "Nothing, sir," Matthew Harley's subdued voice said. "Except that his lordship's horse is in with Ninian Williams's."

"Well?" Sir Hector impaled Geraint with a glance.

Geraint raised his eyebrows. "I beg your pardon?" he said haughtily. "Is my horse incriminating evidence, Hector? Is the Earl of Wyvern expected to *walk* to a tenant's party?"

It was evident from the slumping of Sir Hector's shoulders and the dying light in his eyes that he was giving in to defeat. But he rallied briefly. "We will leave you to your *party*, then," he said. "But just remember, the whole lot of you, that the next time you decide to go out smashing tollgates, we will be waiting for you."

"Gracious, Hector," Geraint said, "you have us all shaking in our boots. I shall have to give up being Rebecca. And Aled will have to give up being—Charlotte, was it? And all these men will have to give up being my children. Whatever are we expected to do for amusement now?" Scorn and sarcasm dripped from every word.

Sir Hector turned and strode out the door.

Matthew Harley stood there for a moment, looking at Ceris before transferring his gaze to Geraint.

"You will have my resignation tomorrow," he said.

"And you will have a letter of warm recommendation to take to your next employer," Geraint said quietly.

Harley turned to follow Sir Hector and the constables. A minute or so later horses could be heard leaving the farmyard and cantering along the lane to the main path back to Glynderi.

"My lord?" Eli Harris spoke hesitantly. "It has been you all the time, then?"

"It was me all the time," Geraint said. "Do none of you remember how I had to be in the thick of every piece of mischief when I was a child?"

They all gawked at him.

He grinned about at them. "I am merely that child grown to manhood," he said. "Did you think that wealth and a title and an English education would change me into a different person? I was getting nowhere fast as the Earl of Wyvern when I returned here. Come, you must all admit that. I met suspicion or coldness or open hostility wherever I turned. All my suggestions for change and reform were spurned— either by you or by my fellow landowners. And so I had to become Geraint Penderyn again. And once I was Geraint, then I had to become Rebecca. There was no one else to take the job, was there? And I was ever a leader, especially when it was mischief that I must lead others into."

"He convinced me and the rest of the members of the

committee," Aled said, "that he was the man for the job. And I believe his actions have proved that we were right."

"Well, I for one," Ifor Davies said boldly, "will thank you, my lord, and will shake your hand too if you will shake mine." He walked toward Geraint, hand outstretched.

"Me too," Glyn Bevan said.

The ice was broken and the men formed a rough line to move forward for the privilege of shaking their Rebecca by the hand.

"I think it is not being too optimistic to say that our goal has been reached," Geraint said. "Mr. Foster of *The Times* has assured me that his editor and the paper's readers are avid for more details of the Rebecca Riots, and that they appear to be sympathetic to our cause. And a commission of inquiry is almost certain to be set up here—I have heard that one of the commissioners is to be Thomas Frankland Lewis, himself a Welshman and familiar with life on a Welsh farm. And I have heard too that the commissioners will allow everyone who cares to testify to have his say—or hers—rich and poor alike. We will all have a chance to give our side of the story."

"*Duw* be praised," Morfydd Richards said, and her words were greeted by a flurry of fervent amens.

"It is more than praise we must give to our God tonight, Morfydd Richards," the Reverend Llwyd said sternly. He waited until everyone's attention was on him before continuing. "We must pray for forgiveness for all the lies we have spoken here tonight and for our Lord's pardon so that our souls do not spend eternity writhing in hellfire."

Everyone gazed mutely at him as he raised his arms.

"Let us pray," he said.

All heads bent and all eyes closed.

Except Geraint's. He looked all about him as unobtrusively as possible. But he was not mistaken.

Marged was gone.

Chapter
29

She should have gone home. But her mother-in-law and probably Gran too would be sitting up with Mrs. Phillips, and they would all be bursting with curiosity to know what had happened at the Williamses'.

She could not have gone home.

She should have gone somewhere else, then. Anywhere else. But she had not been thinking. She had been acting purely from instinct. And she did not have the will or the energy to go somewhere else now. She leaned her arms along the roof, as he had done on another occasion, and rested her face on her hands as he had done then.

Except that then she had known him only as Geraint Penderyn, Earl of Wyvern. She had not known . . .

But her mind shied away from what she had not known.

She knew he would find her there. Perhaps that was why she had come, though she wished herself a thousand miles away. She had never been one to shirk reality or to avoid confrontations.

A confrontation was inevitable.

She did not hear him coming, but she was not surprised to hear his voice close behind her.

"Marged," he said.

"Go away," she said without raising her head. The confrontation might be inevitable, but there was no reason why she should not fight the inevitable.

"No," he said. "I am not going anywhere."

He was speaking Welsh, she realized. In Rebecca's voice. She shuddered. "Then I will go away," she said.

"No." His voice was soft, but she knew he meant it. He was behind her. A quite solid building was in front of her. He was not going to allow her past. Well, she had known it was inevitable. But she was not going to lift her head or turn to him.

"It was rape," she said.

"No, Marged," he said.

"I did not consent to lie with the Earl of Wyvern," she said.

"I was Rebecca," he said—and oh God, he *was* Rebecca. Why had she never realized it was the same voice, speaking a different language? "You consented to lie with Rebecca, Marged."

"Rebecca was a mask," she said. "There is no such person."

"You always knew there was a man behind the mask," he said.

"But I did not know it was *you*. I hate you. You know I hate you."

"No," he said. "When I asked you yesterday to marry me, Marged, you almost said yes. I saw the tears in your eyes and the agony behind the tears. You want to hate me, but you cannot."

"I hate you," she said.

"Why?" he asked. "Give me the reasons."

There were too many to number. "You killed Eurwyn," she said.

"No, Marged," he said. "There was a whole tragic set of circumstances there and they took the life of a courageous man who fought for his people. I was only one link in that chain. I accept responsibility for my ignorance and neglect, but I did not murder him. Does your hatred rest solely on that?"

It did. She did not want to think of the rest. It was too painful.

"Marged?"

"I thought you had come to *apologize* to me," she cried, surprising even herself by the passion in her voice. "I thought you had come to reassure me, to tell me that you loved me. But all you could do was talk with Dada and looked me up and down as if I had forgotten to put my clothes on."

He had nothing to say for a moment. "Ah, Marged," he said, "I was such an insecure, guilty, embarrassed young puppy. You looked so proud and so scornful and I was so terribly ashamed."

"And then you went *away*!" All the pain of it was back again, as if she was still sixteen and wore all her emotions on the outside. "You just went away without a word. You never wrote. You stayed away for ten whole years. And when I wrote to you—*twice!*—about Eurwyn, you did not even reply. You will never know what it cost me to write those letters, to write to *you* when I had married Eurwyn. You did not even acknowledge receiving them."

"Because I did not, Marged." There was pain in his voice too now. "I went away with raw emotions. I did not know who I was. The only anchor of my existence—my mother— was dead and I had made a total disaster of my first love affair. I felt unwanted here and yet did not know where else I was to belong. I only knew it was not here, though my heart ached for this place and these people. And for you. I was too young to deal with the pain. I thought I could end it by cutting it off instead of suffering through it. So I put it all behind me. When I inherited, I appointed Harley to run the estate for me. He had strict instructions to keep every-thing concerning the estate from me, and my secretary in England had similar instructions to deal with any correspon-

dence from Wales without showing it to me. I thought it had
worked. I thought I had forgotten Wales. And you. I was
wrong on both counts."

It was Geraint, she thought, her eyes closed against her
hands, who had been her lover. It was his body that had
loved her own, penetrated her own. It was Geraint. Her
mind could not yet quite grasp the reality.

"Marry me, Marged," he said.

"No!"

"Why not?" he asked her.

"You deceived me."

"Yes," he said. "I did."

She hated him anew for not trying to justify himself, for
simply admitting his guilt. He gave her nothing to fight
against.

"Marry me," he said.

"No."

"Marged," he asked, "why did you tell me yesterday that
Rebecca had promised not to abandon you?"

She froze. Oh God, oh dear God, yes, she had said that to
him. Her wretched tongue!

And then he touched her for the first time. One of his hands
slid around her and spread itself lightly over her abdomen.

"Do we have a child growing here, *cariad*?" he asked her
softly.

She felt that somersaulting and cartwheeling again.

"I think so." She wished she found it easy to lie.

"You must marry me, then," he said.

"No." She considered trying to push his hand away, but
she did not think he would remove it and she did not want
to wrestle with him.

"Marged," he said, "I know what it is like for a woman
shunned by her family and her community and living alone
up here. And I know what it is like to be the child of such
a woman. To love her to distraction because there is no one
but her to love and to sense her unhappiness and her
loneliness without fully understanding them or being able to

do anything about them. Is that what you want for yourself? And our child?"

She heard herself moan before she clamped her teeth together.

"I will not allow it," he said.

He ought not to have said that. She bristled.

"I love you," he said. "Marged, I love you. I always have. I always will."

And he ought not to have said that either. She was not made of stone.

"Marged." His hand began stroking over her abdomen. "Remember how this child got here. On whichever occasion it happened, it was good. It has always been good. It was always done with love, from the first time to the last. Love on both sides. Our child was begotten and conceived in the right way and for the right reason. It is a child of our love."

Again the moan. This time she did not cut it short.

"Marry me," he said.

He knew she was close to saying yes. But she did not say it. And suddenly he did not want her to say it. Not like this. Not with her face hidden on her arms. Hidden from him. From the truth.

His hand rested, splayed, against her. Against the place where their child grew. Their child—his and Marged's. He leaned forward and rested his forehead against her neck.

"Marged," he said softly, "forgive me. Forgive me."

She turned then, after shrugging her shoulders sharply and batting away his hand. Her face was angry.

"As easily as that?" she cried. "I forgive you and shed a few tears over you? I marry you because I am with child by you? We live happily ever after?"

This was better, he thought, though he could think of nothing to say.

"I told the *Earl of Wyvern* that I followed Rebecca," she said. She was yelling at him, her hands balled into fists at her sides. "I told him that I loved Rebecca, that I was his lover. And I told *Rebecca* that I had offered myself to the Earl of Wyvern. I admitted that I had *wanted* him."

"Yes," he said.

"I *abased* myself," she said. "I was *honest*. I felt that a relationship with Rebecca could not possibly work if I was not honest."

"Yes," he said.

"Can you say nothing but *yes*?" She was almost screaming at him.

"You have been nothing but honest with me," he said. "I have been nothing but deceitful with you. Except in one thing, Marged. I have always loved you. I love you now. I can only beg for your forgiveness."

There were tears in her eyes suddenly and she was biting her lower lip. "It was *you*," she said. All the passion had gone from her voice. "It was all you. You who kissed me that first night. You in chapel the next morning when I was still tingling with the memory. You in the wood. You inside the hut. You who tricked me into offering my body in exchange for Ceris's freedom. You who tried to persuade me to inform against the followers of Rebecca. You who . . ." She threw up her hands in a gesture of frustration.

"Yes," he said. "Yes, Marged. And I who started the child inside you."

She moaned again as she had done earlier. "You are *Rebecca*," she said, looking at him with incredulity once more. "And you are Geraint. You are both."

"Yes," he said. "And the Earl of Wyvern, Marged. I am all three. None of them is a mask. I am all three. I cannot offer you one without the other two. I cannot offer you Rebecca, whom you admire, without Geraint, to whom you feel an unwilling attachment, or without the Earl of Wyvern, whom you hate and despise. I am all three. I offer you myself as I am, unforgiven if it must be so."

Somehow he possessed himself of her right hand. He drew a deep breath. It must be done. And something in him rather fancied doing it—he was the Earl of Wyvern, after all. He went down on one knee before her.

"Marry me," he said. "Not because you must, Marged. Not because there is to be a little one we have created together. But because you love me, *cariad*. Because I love you. Because we have found paradise together. Because there is the rest of a lifetime ahead and neither of us would wish to live it without the other. Because you are mad enough to accept me with all my flaws. Because you are brave enough to be my countess. I love you, Marged Evans. Marry me."

Her eyes had widened. But when she spoke, it was to utter an absurdity.

"I have Mam and Gran to look after," she said.

He got back to his feet and took her other hand. He was sure of her suddenly. "They are as much my responsibility as yours," he said. "We will have to see if they wish to stay on at the farm with Waldo Parry to work for them, or whether they would like to move into a cottage with a pension while I rent the farm to the Parrys."

"It was you who sent Waldo to help me," she said. "The coffers of Rebecca are really the coffers of the Earl of Wyvern."

He said nothing.

"You were wonderful as Rebecca," she said. "You were kind and compassionate."

"I am also Wyvern," he said.

"You helped the Parrys," she said. "You destroyed the salmon weir." She smiled fleetingly. "You helped me pick stones."

"Marry me," he said.

She sighed then and leaned forward to set her forehead against his chest. After a few moments she set her arms about his waist.

"Yes," she said finally against his shirt. She sighed again. "Geraint, I thought I was *promiscuous* because I loved you both and wanted you both."

His arms closed about her and he lowered his cheek to the top of her head. "You will marry us both," he said, "and be doubly loved."

"Geraint." She raised her head and gazed into his eyes. "Do you know what I did once inside this house and felt ashamed of the whole time and afterward?"

"You made love to Rebecca," he said.

"I was never ashamed of that," she said. "But I could never put a face on Rebecca except the grotesque woolen one. I gave him your face in my imagination and your identity. I made love to Geraint Penderyn and then wondered how I could have done so when I loved Rebecca."

Ah, Marged. Incurably honest to the last.

"You knew," he said. "Beneath the level of conscious thought you knew. And talking about this house, this *mansion* . . ." He grinned at her.

"It is better than a mansion." She set one hand gently against his cheek. "It is where your mam loved you and raised the little boy I adored. It is your home, your heritage, your roots. And it is where we loved, *cariad*."

He realized that his eyes had filled with tears only when she wiped one away with her thumb.

"Mrs. Phillips will be sleeping in my bed tonight," she whispered. "Take me into your home, Geraint. This home. Make love to me."

He lowered his head and kissed her.

"And to Glynderi to call on your father tomorrow morning," he said some time later, "to make a confession and to arrange a wedding, love."

"Yes." She smiled at him. "But tomorrow, Geraint. Not tonight."

"Tomorrow," he agreed. "Let us go home, then, *cariad*."

Home. She set an arm about his waist and her head on his shoulder as he led her there. It would never again be his place of residence as it had been when he was a child. But it would always be home—the place in which he had known all the significant love of his life. First his mother, now Marged.

She kissed his cheek, sighed with contentment—and perhaps with anticipation, too—and preceded him through the doorway.

Historical Note

In reality the Rebecca Riots lasted far longer than they appear to in this book—from November 1842 to October 1843. The special commission sent to investigate the causes of the unrest published its report in March 1844. Most of the commission's suggestions were adopted eventually, beginning with a law passed in August 1844, improving the system of road tolls for the ordinary Welsh farmer. "Rebecca" and her "daughters" did not ride out into danger in vain!

For the sake of pacing in my novel I have made it appear that everything happened within the course of a few weeks. My apologies to historical purists.

Some of the men who played the part of Rebecca were ruthless and cruel men, forcing their neighbors to participate and terrorizing their enemies. Others gained a reputation for gentleness and courtesy despite the basic destructiveness of their mission. It is this latter image of Rebecca that has passed into Welsh legend—and into the pages of my book.